ALSO BY RICHARD HAWKE
AVAILABLE FROM
RANDOM HOUSE LARGE PRINT

Speak of the Devil

COLD DAY
IN HELL

COLD DAY
IN HELL

A NOVEL

Richard Hawke

RANDOM HOUSE
LARGE PRINT

Cold Day in Hell is a work of fiction. Names, characters, places, and incidents are the products of the author's imagination or are used fictitiously. Any resemblance to actual events, locales, or persons, living or dead, is entirely coincidental.

Published in the United States of America
by Random House Large Print in association
with Random House, New York.
Distributed by Random House, Inc., New York.

Library of Congress Cataloging-in-Publication Data
Hawke, Richard, 1955-
Cold day in Hell : a novel /
by Richard Hawke.—1st large print ed.
p. cm.
ISBN 978-0-7393-2583-4
1. Private investigators—New York (State)—New York—
Fiction. 2. New York (N.Y.)—Fiction. 3. Television
personalities—Fiction. 4. Large type books. I. Title.
PS3608.A886C65 2007
813'.6—dc22
2007002654

www.randomhouse.com/largeprint

FIRST LARGE PRINT EDITION

10 9 8 7 6 5 4 3 2 1

This Large Print edition published in accord
with the standards of the N.A.V.H.

For Powell Harrison . . . usual suspect

PART 1

1

ON THE LAST DAY of her life, she took a yoga class. She wore what she always wore, a full-body black leotard and a too-tight faded gray T-shirt with a red crab on it, a no-particular-reason gift from her younger brother many years before. Normally, she wore a burgundy headband to keep her hair out of her face, but just the day before, she had instructed her hairstylist to "change everything," and he had responded by giving her a short feathery cut, something she could hand-dry and hand-comb, something that would look good even when, technically, it was messy. Her yoga instructor had commented on it as she was rolling out her mat. He was a pole-thin Iranian with dark deep eyes. A slight man. As lithe and limber as a wet noodle, he was the fantasy at one level or another of at least three quarters of the female students in the class. Probably one or two of the males as well. He spoke with a rich British purr.

"I wouldn't have thought you could be even more beautiful. This is so nice. Very nice."

Her short bangs slipped away from the instructor's flirting fingers, and a slight blush no larger than the size of a nickel dotted each cheek. As the instructor moved over to the wall and slid a CD into the boom box, she smoothed a corner of her mat with her toe, then raised her foot and tucked it against the inside of the opposite thigh, folding her palms together as she balanced perfectly on one leg, like a flamingo. She gave a little shake of her head, her new hair falling quicker than usual, then gently closed her eyes. The floodgates of serenity opened.

She had three hours to live.

THE BEST I FIGURE IT, I was on the witness stand at about that exact moment. Actually, I can be more specific. I was on the witness stand, yawning. I'd just checked my watch as the big yawn was building—quarter to four—then turned my attention from the watch face to the slender pale face of the defense attorney who was fidgeting in front of me. The yawn wasn't entirely intended as commentary, although the sentiment was shared by any of the dozen or so people sitting in the stuffy windowless courtroom. The pale defense attorney shot a wounded look at the judge, who in turn did an admirable job of keeping a straight face as she doled out her reprimand.

"Mr. Malone, the court is aware that outside this room you lead a most fascinating life. But perhaps you'll make a concerted effort to at least pretend that you have the same interest in the seriousness of these proceedings as the rest of us?"

Her rounding out the statement with the question mark was, I recognized, shortcut for, **Can you cut me a freaking break here, Fritz?**

I nodded. "Of course, Your Honor. My apologies to the court. I assure you, my yawning has nothing to do with these proceedings. I've been having some trouble with my sleep lately."

The judge addressed the defense lawyer. "I've been having some trouble with my sleep as well, counselor. Perhaps we can start trimming the sails here?"

"But Your Honor—"

"Proceed, counselor. The oxygen in this room is finite. We're wasting it."

He proceeded. I sent my next yawn down to my feet. You can do that; it's a trick you can perform so long as you're ready. I turned my glassy eyes on the defense lawyer as he continued his attempts to take bites out of my testimony. It wasn't going to work. My testimony was solid. I'd been hired back in the fall to set up a sting on an outfit that had been taking the notion of trademark infringement to a whole new level. The scammers had devised a method of sidelining as much as a quarter of legitimate orders earmarked for certain retail stores and replacing the merchandise—at bloated markups—with their own identical knockoffs. They then arranged for the return of the originals while hiding the return on the retailer's end through timely hacking in to the retailer's electronic bookkeeping. Legitimate stores all over the city had been unwittingly moving the knockoffs right alongside the real deals. It was only when rumors of the scam reached a certain level of management that I'd been contacted and asked to bring along my magnifying glass. It took me about a month to locate a coward among the scammers, but once I did, it was a fairly easy matter of putting the fear into him. His legs went jelly, I got from him what I needed, and I proceeded to set up the sting. My end of things was airtight, which was why the pasty-faced defense lawyer's attempts to puncture my story were boring me to tears.

"Mr. Malone . . ." He grasped his hands behind his back and took a few stiff-legged steps, as if his knees were no longer working. "As you well know, my client has a completely different recollection of the events you have laid out for us this afternoon. . . ."

I glanced up at the bench. The judge was sending a yawn down to her feet, I'm convinced.

THE WOMAN'S NAME WAS Robin Burrell. She was twenty-seven years old. Five-eight, 128 pounds. Chestnut-brown eyes, chestnut-brown hair. There was a farm-girl freshness to the face, a few pale freckles on the bridge of her nose. She had been raised a Quaker just outside of New Hope, Pennsylvania, and she still attended meetings every Sunday morning at the Quaker meetinghouse on East Fifteenth Street. I would be told that the Sunday before she died, Robin stood up to address the circle at her meeting, made a halting start as she fought to make eye contact with her fellow worshippers, then dropped back into her chair as sobbing tears overtook her. Support from the Friends had been unstinting. Everyone knew that things had been brutally rough for Robin, especially the past several months. And not just the Friends. Everyone in the damn country knew it.

By all reports, Robin was graceful and limber on her final day, though she was apparently suffering a small cold. The class was advanced vinyasa, which Margo tells me is for fairly committed practitioners. Margo herself sticks with hatha yoga, which isn't all that slouchy, either, as far as I'm the judge. I've let myself into her apartment more than once and been confronted with a Margoesque pretzel in the middle of the floor.

Robin Burrell had set up her mat next to the large plate-glass window that serves as an entire wall of this particular yoga studio. The studio is above a hardware store on upper Broadway. The day after Robin died, I spent some time sitting on a bench outside a Ben & Jerry's across the street from the hardware store and got a sense of how visible the yoga students were near the large window. A tall, striking woman like Robin Burrell, balancing sideways on a yoga block while moving her long legs like a nutcracker . . . it's a show that could have given a curious passerby reason to pause.

"She was one of my most devoted students," the Iranian instructor would tell me. "When I tell the class to hold a pose, Robin would become like a sculpture. She made exquisite lines. Quite extraordinary."

Robin made her exquisite lines in the large window for an hour, then left class thirty minutes early, rolling her mat into a tight tube and mouthing, "Gotta go. Sorry," to her instructor, who at the time was heels over head against the front wall, looking like a frozen salamander.

The fellow at the front desk reported that Robin didn't slip into the small changing room but instead simply pulled on a pair of UGGs and shrugged into a large navy coat that came all the way down to her boot tops. Her ten-class membership had expired with that class, but she told the guy at the desk that she was in a hurry and she'd reup on her next visit. She pulled a copper-colored wool cap from her pocket and tugged it down over her new haircut.

I'd say I was just outside the courtroom talking to a cop friend of mine around the time Robin took off from the yoga place. He was telling me that there had been some sort of ruckus with the Marshall Fox jury and that Judge Deveraux was calling in several armies of lawyers. That explained the tsunami of reporters and cameras hurtling toward Courtroom 512.

A FINE POWDERY SNOWFALL had begun by the time Robin left the yoga studio and started for her home. Her apartment was seven blocks away, on Seventy-first, half a block from Central Park. She stopped at an ATM on Seventy-seventh, then at Fairway, where she picked up a half-dozen oranges, a half-dozen kiwis, two green apples, a wedge of Manchego cheese and a box of Throat Coat tea.

A few blocks later, on Amsterdam, she stopped at a Korean market and scored a package of tissues, some throat lozenges and a dozen packets of a product called Emergen-C. The clerk was watching a tiny black-and-white television on the counter next to the cash register. The fluffy five o'clock news was being overridden with live courthouse coverage of the latest development in the months-long drama of the Marshall Fox trial. The clerk took the twenty that Robin offered and made change. As he counted the bills into her hand, he looked up at her face.

"You her." His eyes lit up, and he indicated the television excitedly with his chin. "You **her**!"

Several other people in the shop turned their heads. Robin Burrell took the change and hurriedly left the shop. She reached her building—a five-story brownstone—several minutes later and let herself in. Hers was a floor-through on the first floor. She'd lived there for six years, the lucky legal holder of a rent-controlled lease. The entire east wall of the apartment was exposed brick. The kitchen was in the rear, overlooking a small patch of backyard that Robin shared with the gay couple in the basement apartment. Her bedroom was a narrow windowless room just off the kitchen, accessible by a heavy sliding wooden door that rumbled noisily on its rollers. She often referred to it jokingly as "the crypt." Some joke. The front room was the largest room in the apartment, with high ceilings, a large marble nonworking fireplace, and a curved front wall featuring nine-foot-high bay windows. Normally, Robin kept her curtains pulled when she was home, especially the past several months. However, the week before Christmas, she had purchased a monstrously large Douglas fir and, with the help of one of her downstairs neighbors, set it up in front of the bay windows. It filled the entire space. She told her friend Michelle that decorating the oversize tree was therapeutic. For two generations, Robin's family had owned and operated a Christmas-tree farm just outside New Hope, until her father's unexpected death the previous summer had forced them to sell the property. This had been Robin's first ever Christmas without a homegrown tree. According to Michelle, Robin had felt particularly close to the street-bought tree, saying that she'd bonded with it, orphan to orphan. The tree was nearly as wide as it was tall, and because of this, it blocked from view anything and everything that took place in Robin's front room.

Robin came home from yoga class and plugged in the tree's all-white lights. In the kitchen, she sliced one of the oranges into quarters and ate them standing at the counter. She set the cheese on a wooden tray, along with a small knife and one of the apples. She brought this into the living room.

In the bathroom she stripped off her yoga clothes, tossing them into a corner, then got into the shower. As she stood under the hot jets, she would have seen her own body reflected in the mirror mounted on the wall opposite the showerhead. This was one of the details that the Gentleman Jew (as Robin had dubbed the lead prosecutor) had skillfully managed to prod from her on the witness stand: at her lover's request, she had purchased the mirror and mounted it on the shower wall.

He liked to watch.

After her shower, Robin probably hand-dried her hair, then pulled on a pair of jeans and a green V-neck sweater. She put on some music. Ravel's **Bolero.** I have a friend who can't listen to **Bolero** without climbing the walls. He describes his problem as "aural claustrophobia." The slow relentless build drives him nuts. I sort of know what he means. After Robin put on the **Bolero,** she lit two new tapers (she dug out the old nubs and tossed them in the trash), three block candles, and four tea candles in holiday holders. There's no telling precisely when she turned on her television or when she checked her answering machine. What is known is that the **Bolero** went on around ten past six. The basement neighbor recalled hearing it beginning its build as he left to meet his boyfriend and some friends for drinks on Columbus.

THE CORONER PUT Robin Burrell's death at anywhere from six-thirty to eight, eight being roughly when the stringer for the **Post** leaned precariously over the railing from the top steps of Robin's stoop and saw her mutilated half-naked body lying in its grotesque twist beneath her Christmas tree. No fool this guy. He snapped the picture, called his contact at the **Post,** the columnist Jimmy Puck, and waited until Puck had roared uptown to the scene before heading with his camera down to the diner next to the **Post**'s offices and phoning the police from there.

It was around that same time, across the park, that Rosemary Fox's maid accidentally dropped a garlic press on her boss's phone machine and heard the same gravelly-voiced message—word for word—that the police would soon be retrieving from Robin Burrell's machine.

"I'm coming, you whore. Can you taste the blood yet?"

THERE HAD BEEN an all-out fistfight in the jury room. My cop friend—his name was Eddie Harris, like the jazz guy—had gotten me into Courtroom 512 to witness the fallout. Harris was a member of the arrest team that had taken Marshall Fox into custody the previous spring. He'd gotten his fifteen minutes of fame on the stand in late November, describing for the jury—as well as for the gazillion viewers tuning in—the cooperative demeanor Fox had displayed when the police arrived at his East Side penthouse with their warrant. Fox had known they were coming. At that point, half of America had known they were coming. Harris described how Fox had invited the officers in for coffee and donuts.

"**Donuts?**" the assistant prosecuting attorney had asked, practically contorting his eyebrow into a calculated question mark. "Sergeant, did you think the defendant was mocking you and your fellow officers? Did you feel that Mr. Fox was making light of what was a very serious situation?"

The officer shrugged. "It's what he does. He's a comedian."

"But did you think that his crack about the donuts was particularly funny? I mean, under the circumstances?"

Harris's response had been the leading sound bite of the day.

"You mean the cops-and-donuts thing? I'm no expert, but that's pretty old material, isn't it? I'd have expected something a little better, a big-deal guy like that."

Harris cut me loose once we'd gotten inside the courtroom. The place was packed. First and foremost were the ladies and gentlemen of the media, doing the usual spot-on parody of themselves. A high-profile murder trial is, for lack of a better analogy, like an irresistible gigantic piñata, and for the two and a half months of this one, the reporters, columnists, on-air legal specialists, and news-talk hyenas had been giddily landing blows pretty much around the clock, each angling to be the one in the public eye when something colorful and provocative spilled out. Members of the media far outnumbered those attending the trial for more personal reasons—friends and families of the two victims, for example.

The courtroom was buzzing.

Peter Elliott, the assistant prosecuting attorney, was standing at the prosecution table, stretching his back. I managed to catch his eye, and he acknowledged me with a head bob. I'd done some work for Peter in the summer, before the trial got officially under way. Background checks on some of the potential jurors; no real heavy lifting. Kicking over trash cans and looking for rats. Nobody is ever a hundred percent happy with all twelve members of a jury, but Peter had been philosophical about the seven women and five men who had eventually landed on the Fox jury, allowing that he could have imagined much worse. Over the course of the lengthy trial, he had cause to reconsider that opinion. The warning signals had sounded softly at first—grumbles, evident bad chemistry between some of the jurors, notes of complaint and irritation passed along to the judge—the real problems beginning once the defense rested and the case had been handed over to the jury. There were plenty of obvious factors to account for frazzled nerves in the twelve people whose lives had been yanked away from them for nearly two months already. But Peter blamed the Christmas break for the most serious unraveling. When the trial started, nobody had anticipated the proceedings moving past November and certainly not continuing into the holiday season. The jury had been sequestered since the beginning of the trial, but of course the judge made arrangements for time with family in the days surrounding Christmas. It was Peter's feeling that the days of freedom had done real damage to the fabric of the jury's exhaustive deliberations rather than releasing some of the pressure. He surmised that the break had only served to sharpen the anger of the more impatient members of the panel. Judging from the rumors that were swirling around Courtroom 512, it seemed that maybe Peter's fears were correct.

I gave myself up to the natural tides and, after a few jostling minutes, was gently bumped up against the real live version of a woman I was more accustomed to seeing in a plastic box with a square hole cut into the front. Her name was Kelly Cole. A palomino blonde with large chocolate eyes, she was tapping the nonbusiness end of a pen against her slender lips and frowning down at her reporter's notebook. The little squiggle between her eyebrows was the sole blemish on her milk-smooth face. I pointed it out to her.

"Baby's first frown line," I said. "So cute."

The tapping pen halted. The line evaporated. "Well. Fritz Malone. Can it really be? What brings you here? I wouldn't have thought celebrity trials were your kind of thing."

"They're not. I was down the hall putting the screws to some pirates. The riptide brought me in." I indicated her notebook. "Looking for your lead?"

"As a matter of fact, yes. Though I don't know why I think it makes any damn difference. Do you think the viewers pay one iota of attention to my syntax?"

I rejected a lame joke about the alluring reporter's syntax and instead asked, "So what do Ms. Cole's sources tell her about what's going on here?"

She gave me a "nice try, buster" look. "Who says Ms. Cole has those kind of sources?"

"The kind of sources that leak good dirt on our airtight jury? I don't know, I guess I just consider you more wily than the average bear."

"Well, the defense is itching for a mistrial here, but everyone knows that. That's hardly a secret. A contentious jury is their best chance, and this one seems to be a powder keg these days."

"Eddie Harris told me there'd been a fight."

"That's the word on the street."

"You really don't have the details?"

She shrugged. "We can speculate. Either the truck driver is finally fed up with the schoolteacher or the actress-waitress is tired of being hit on by the guy who owns the bar. That's how my scorecard looks."

"What about the foreperson?" I asked.

"Foreperson. Honestly. A person could choke on PC shit like that."

I pressed. "I've heard some rumors."

"That Madame Foreperson tried to get herself removed? Could be. According to the people who're keeping score, she's seemed the most fragile of the bunch." The reporter pulled something from her blazer pocket and flipped it open. For a second I thought it was a cell phone, but it turned out to be a compact mirror. She checked out the goods, taking a scrape with her fingernail at the edge of her lipstick.

I asked, "So what's the office pool saying?"

"On Fox?"

"Yes."

"Oh, the cowboy's going down for it, no question about it."

"No question? Mr. Simpson managed to squirm off the hook."

She slipped the mirror back into her pocket. "Mr. Simpson was an anomaly. There's no race card here. Besides, that's Hollywood. We do things differently in New York. We tear down the mighty for breakfast."

She sounded more than a little eager for a verdict of guilty, and I told her so. "You're drooling, Ms. Cole."

Something deep in her eyes pulsed. "I'm entitled to my opinion. So long as I don't broadcast it."

"And your opinion is that he did it."

"**Them.** The bastard killed both of them. Any idiot can see that."

The door to the jury room had just opened, and twelve of Marshall Fox's alleged peers began the shuffle-march into the jury box.

I noted, "All it takes is one idiot."

"Would you like to put up a wager?"

"Not with you, sweetheart. Not with your inside information."

If eyes were bricks, I'd have had my head staved in. Her milky skin went red. "Screw you! That is so **fucking** yesterday, I can't believe you're even saying that."

I raised my hands. "Whoa. You're right. I'm sorry. That was stupid."

"You're damn right it's stupid! Give me a break already." She gave her head a toss. How she knew it would make her hair fall perfectly into place was beyond me. "You'll excuse me. I've got to go earn my measly nickel."

With that, another of Marshall Fox's former girlfriends moved off, bumping and grinding her way through the crowd to get to the media corral.

· · ·

THE CORONER DETERMINED that the blows to Robin Burrell's head, powerful though they were, weren't what killed her. For certain they stunned her, but chances were—unfortunately—that they didn't even make her lose consciousness. Her attacker handcuffed her ankles together and, with a second pair of handcuffs, bent one of Robin's arms behind her back and cuffed her wrist to the chain of the first pair of cuffs. Robin was extremely limber—freshly so—and she probably bent backward easier than most.

It was shards from the broken shower mirror that he used to cut her. He also used them to cut the jeans partway off. The largest shard was the one that killed her. It was surmised that the killer must have seen to it when he smashed the mirror that he came away with at least one large, jagged piece. This was the one found protruding from Robin Burrell's neck. The reflecting side was facing her.

Just in case she had wanted to watch.

JUDGE DEVERAUX SUMMONED the two lead attorneys to the bench. Each attorney was trailed by several lackeys, but the judge made a backhanded motion dismissing them. This talk was for the big boys only. Peter Elliott made a play to remain included, but his boss, Lewis Gottlieb—the Gentleman Jew—placed a hand on his shoulder and dismissed him.

Generally speaking, Sam Deveraux had been receiving high marks for his handling of the Fox trial. Physically, he was an imposing figure: a six-foot-three, 240-some-odd-pound, fifty-seven-year-old African American with a large expressive face and a voice whose rich resonant rumble seemed capable at times of causing the walls around him to tremble. It was definitely capable of causing the people around him to tremble, as had been evident throughout the trial whenever the judge employed his mountainous energy to bring the histrionic or the shrill or the incendiary back into line. In a trial featuring no shortage of bona fide celebrities, both on the witness stand and in the audience, Sam Deveraux had emerged as the freshest and most impressive personality of the lot.

The two attorneys bounced slightly on their toes as they conferred with the judge. At the defendant's table, Marshall Fox's mood seemed inappropriately spry, considering the circumstances. He was bantering with his various attorneys, at least one of whom, it was generally acknowledged, had been included on the team for the sole purpose of providing the defendant with a fawning sycophant, a ready-made audience for the entertainer's fabled need for attention. His name was Zachary Riddick, and he was known in courthouse circles—and beyond, for that matter—as a headline grabber, one of those self-satisfied bottom-feeders in the profession who've determined that being provocative and noisy can go a long way toward covering over a basic lack of legal expertise or skill. He had boyish good looks—a trifle too boyish, in Margo's view—and had learned how to get his name on some of the various A-lists around town, popping up at celebrity bashes or high-profile fund-raisers, usually with a fresh piece of arm candy. Riddick and Fox had been acquainted even before Fox's arrest, and when rumors began growing of Marshall Fox's imminent arrest in the two Central Park murders, Riddick had bobbed immediately to the surface, offering vigorous denouncements of the district attorney, the New York City Police Department, Marshall Fox's competition in the late-night wars, you name it. Professionally speaking, his presence on Fox's defense team was considered a joke. But as I say, it seemed to amuse Marshall Fox to have him around.

A burst of laughter erupted from the defendant's table. Marshall Fox was pantomiming trussing up Zachary Riddick like a rodeo steer. Judge Deveraux's molten gaze cleared the heads

of the two attorneys in front of him as he took
in the defendant's table, and the little party
broke up.

"Jesus Christ."

A man seated near me in the rear pew gave an
exasperated sigh and pushed himself to his feet.
Fiftyish. Thinning brown hair. A pleasant face except for its currently being creased in irritation.
He was wearing an eight-hundred-dollar suit and
looked like a million bucks. I recognized the face.
Alan Ross, director of programming at KBS Television. Ross was the man responsible for plucking
Marshall Fox from a dude ranch in South Dakota
and bringing him east to make him a star. Margo
had interviewed Ross for an article in **New York**
magazine soon after Fox's fuse had hit the powder.
Intelligent man. Very candid about his ambiva-
lence concerning his role in "creating" Marshall
Fox. **New York** had titled the article "My Fair
Fox," cuing off Ross's comments comparing his
machinations to the egomaniacal meddlings of
Professor Henry Higgins in the musical redo of
the Pygmalion story. I'd met him—I'd swung by
the restaurant where Margo was conducting the
interview. He'd been polite, almost courtly, and
extremely complimentary of Margo. Since Fox's
arrest on multiple murder charges, Ross had been
a frequent presence in the media, soberly but
firmly defending his protégé and somewhat fa-

mously conducting public hand-wringing for having brought the former ranch hand into the limelight in the first place.

Ross grunted an acknowledgment as he moved past me out of the pew. He made his way to the banister separating the courtroom seating from the defendant's table. The executive was too far away for me to hear his exchange with Riddick and Fox, but from the expressions on both men's faces, it appeared that Ross's message was a duplicate of Judge Deveraux's. **Shut your stupid traps!**

The conference at the bench broke up, and the two attorneys returned to their corners. The judge waved a clerk over. Lewis Gottlieb huddled with Peter Elliott, and from where I was sitting, I wasn't seeing a terribly pleased expression on either face. Alan Ross returned to the pew. As I scooted back to let him pass, he gave me a game smile.

"Welcome to the tawdry follies." He sat down heavily next to me. "Franklin, isn't it?"

"Fritz," I corrected him. "Fritz Malone."

"Right, right. Alan Ross." He offered his hand, and we shook. Ross leaned back and crossed his arms over his chest. "I used to be legendary for my low blood pressure. Amazing what a little celebrity murder trial can do to you, isn't it?"

"I try to steer clear of them as often as I can," I said.

"Oh? Did you take a wrong turn on your way to traffic court?"

"I was down the hall on business."

"Private investigation. Do I recall correctly?"

"You do."

"Just couldn't pass on the train wreck, eh?"

I shrugged. "Guilty."

Judge Deveraux dismissed the clerk. He looked out over the packed courtroom, taking his time, sweeping his head slowly, like a lighthouse beam throttled down to a slow crawl. Taking hold of his mallet, he lifted it with both a solemnity and a certain degree of weariness, as if its weight over the course of the trial had been increasing daily and it had now, at this moment, reached the absolute maximum poundage that the judge would be capable of lifting.

"Give my best to Ms. Burke, will you?" Ross said.

I nodded. "Will do."

The judge's mallet fell, making, as it always did, a sound like that of a large bone being snapped in two.

"Order!"

THE SLICING TOOK PLACE in Robin Burrell's bedroom. The crimson of her pillows alone was testament to that much. Her radio alarm clock was among the numerous items found strewn on the floor next to the upturned bedside table. The clock had come unplugged from the wall: 6:48 was frozen on its face.

Was she dead already or still dying when her body was dragged along the short hallway into the front room? I have to hope she was already dead, that's all I'll say about it. She was placed under the huge Christmas tree, cuffed and bent backward, the large wedge of mirror glass protruding from her throat. And then, just as in the case of the two murders for which the star of **Midnight with Marshall Fox** was currently on trial, Robin Burrell's right hand had been placed palm down against her breast, inches above the newly stilled heart, and, as with the second of the Central Park victim's, affixed there with a simple four-inch nail driven all the way in to its head.

THE JUDGE ASKED that the courtroom be cleared of members of the press as well as any onlookers who did not have a direct role in the trial. A collective grumble rose from the ranks of the reporters as they made their way out of the room. Ross excused himself and squeezed past me. I was starting out of the pew when I heard my name being called above the low din.

"Fritz!"

It was Peter Elliott. He waved me over. "Can you stick around?"

"You heard the judge."

Peter swatted the air. "Forget that. We had you on payroll. You can stay. I'm not sure how this is all going to go. If this jury disintegrates, you might have to keep me from killing myself."

I took a seat in the now empty front row. Across the aisle from me sat Rosemary Fox. Her extraordinary beauty was as placid and hard-edged in person as it appeared in photographs. As I watched, her husband turned from the defense table and mouthed something to her. Then he gave his trademark gesture, the one with which he had been signing off after his hour and a half on the air for three years, five nights a week, right up until the day of his arrest. He brought the fingers of his right hand to his lips for a kiss, then placed the hand softly over his heart.

Rosemary Fox remained as still as a steel statue. I can't even characterize the look that was likewise frozen on her face. Molten? All I can say is that it wiped Marshall Fox's famous smirk right off his face. You'd have thought he'd just rounded the corner into the path of an oncoming train.

Judge Deveraux had turned to the jury. His voice came on like a low rumble of thunder. "One thing I want to make clear to all of you right now, before I go any further. You **will** be going back into that jury room first thing tomorrow morning. You **will** continue to deliberate. And you **will** be delivering a verdict to this court, even if I have to sit in there with you and hold your hand and slap you silly and referee all the **crap** that's been going on for too damn long now. Do you hear what I'm saying?"

He placed his hands down flat and leaned forward. He looked like he was ready to bound right out of his chair. "I want to see twelve heads nodding. **Now.**"

3

THE SNOW HAD NEITHER let up nor intensified but was still coming down like finely sifted sugar. Nearly a dozen police cars, along with two ambulances, were clogging the narrow street, their lights flashing blue and red tattoos on and off the snow-powdered trees, the parked cars and the gawkers. The latter were growing in numbers and animation by the minute. Yellow crime-scene tape embraced the front of five attached brownstones. But it was the middle one that was receiving most of the attention, the one with the oversize Christmas tree all atwinkle in white in the high front windows.

I followed the scores of footprints to the edge of the onlookers. A bank of spotlights had been set up and directed at the brownstones. The illuminated area looked not so much like daylight as like the light of a flashbulb stilled at the moment of going off. Inside the apartment with the Christmas tree, real flashbulbs were going off.

Not a good sign.

Having gotten as far as I could, I pulled out my cell phone and hit the code for Margo. She answered immediately.

"Fritz! Where are you? You're never going to guess what's happened."

"One of your neighbors has been murdered."

"Oh. You know." She sounded disappointed.

"Poke your head out the window."

I looked up at the top floor of a brownstone across the street from where all the activity was taking place. Several seconds passed, then I saw a form pass in front of a window. The window went up. Margo Burke leaned out into the abyss, holding the phone to her ear. In my ear, her voice said, "I don't see you."

"Down here. Not too tall, not too short, just right." I waved my free hand.

"There you are!" She waved back. "I've been watching out the window for about an hour. It's a murder, right?"

"I believe it is."

"Oh, Jesus. And you see who it **is**?"

"I see whose apartment it is," I said.

"Oh, Fritz, come on. It has to be her."

"You're jumping to conclusions."

I saw her switch the phone to her other ear. "I'm not jumping to conclusions. Come on, this was Marshall Fox's **lover,** for Christ's sake."

I reminded her, "Former. And what of it? Since when do you have to be involved with a celebrity to get whacked in this town?"

"Whacked. Well, aren't you Mr. Mob tonight?"

"Besides," I said, "we don't know yet if it's her."

The line crackled. Even though we were separated by only a few hundred feet, I guess our signals first had to travel untold miles up into space before bouncing back down to us. "You know the policeman's secret handshake. Why don't you go find out?"

Which is what I did. And, of course, she was correct. The first official homicide victim of the New Year in the borough of Manhattan was Robin Jane Burrell. Age twenty-seven. Originally from New Hope, Pennsylvania. Or, as one of the tabloids would put it the following day in a caption beneath the grim photo of the woman lying trussed beneath the Christmas tree: NO HOPE.

KELLY COLE WAS REPORTING from the dark snowy steps of the courthouse. Even though there was no logical reason for it, the news department still felt that the courthouse steps were the appropriate backdrop for the story about the

fracturing Marshall Fox jury and Judge Deveraux's refusal to accept a deadlock. The other
breaking story, the discovery of the body of
Robin Burrell in her uptown apartment, was tag-
teaming with the jury story. Margo and I were
watching the news on TV.

"Kelly Cole told me no one pays attention to
her syntax."

Margo's hand froze halfway to her open
mouth. The popcorn remained poised for the
toss. "Her what?"

"Her syntax."

"When did she tell you this?"

"At the courthouse. We were shooting the
breeze before Deveraux cleared the room. May I
add, it was a very light breeze."

Margo's wrist snapped. As she chewed the
popcorn, her eyes traveled several times between
me and the television. "She's pretty."

I shrugged. "If you like them blond and curvy."

"Well . . ." **Munch-munch.** "She has lovely
syntax."

We were in Margo's living room, keeping the
couch company. I was also keeping a short glass
of whiskey company, dipping into it like a crow
at a birdbath, making it last. The bowl of popcorn was on Margo's lap, and she had her arms
wrapped around it like she might sing it a lul-
laby later. The spines of Margo's several thou-

sand books stared back at us from the solid wall of bookshelves, along with the television set, which Margo had rolled over from its usual resting place in the corner of the room. The dimmer was on low. The snow outside the window was still sifting down like an ever-falling veil. But the reportage of murders and contentious jurors pretty much killed the mood.

"It looks like they're not going to mention it," Margo said.

The coverage had switched from the courthouse steps back to the scene outside Robin Burrell's building. The reporter on the scene wasn't saying anything different from what he had said at the top of the newscast. An anonymous call to 911 at around 8:40 had led police to the scene, where they had discovered the murdered body of Robin Burrell lying on the floor in her front room. All that police were saying was that the woman's death "did not appear to be accidental." No mention was made of the cuffing of the victim's feet, or the trail of blood stretching from the blood-soaked bedroom to the front room, or the mirror shard that had been jammed into her throat. But what Margo was referring to specifically was the fact that no one was reporting that the body of Robin Burrell had been arranged in the same fashion as the bodies of the two women for whose murders Marshall Fox, America's favorite television bedtime companion for the past three years, was being tried. Not so much the handcuffs, which had appeared on only one of Fox's alleged victims. And not the mirrored glass, which was unique to the Burrell killing. But the hand placed over the heart. Fox's signature sign-off. In the case of the first victim, a ballpoint pen had been used, a crude but effective enough means to hold the hand in place. Ten days later, the killer had upgraded to the hammer and nail.

"They're not telling because the police haven't let it out," I said.

"Except they told you."

"That's because I know the secret handshake."

"Besides which, you're not likely to stand up in front of a television camera and start blabbing."

"Only if they tickle me in the right spots."

"Hey. How long have I known you, and I still don't know the right spots."

"But I applaud the tenacity of your efforts."

Before coming upstairs to Margo's, I'd gotten the lowdown from homicide detective Joseph Gallo, of Manhattan's Twentieth Precinct. Gallo was normally a cool customer, a regular Mr. Ice. But this one had rattled him. His face had been pale and grim as he briefly sketched out the scene for me. He was especially grim when he told me about the hand being nailed over the heart. He'd fixed me with a look I'm not used to seeing on Joe Gallo's face. Little bit of dread, little bit of fear.

"We might not have him. I'd have bet my father's farm it was Fox. I swear I could see those two dead women in his eyes. But Jesus, Fritz. It might actually not be him. After all this. This thing here is a pure carbon copy. The freak who did those women might still be out there. I don't even want to think about it."

I declined Margo's gesture to refresh my drink. She fixed me with her frankest look. "You **are** staying the night." If there was a question mark attached to her words, it was completely silent. I confirmed that I was staying. "That's good," she said. "You won't think less of me if I confess that I'm a bit spooked?"

"Not at all."

"Good. I'll go put on my bedroom eyes."

Which she did, though I didn't get to see them much. It's not that there wasn't sufficient ambient light in the bedroom; it was that the ambient light was still pulsing blue and red from across the street, and Margo's eyes remained clenched shut the entire time. An hour later, as she lay curled asleep under her quilt, I was out of the bed and leaning on the windowsill, looking across the street through the snow into the apartment on the first floor. The huge Christmas tree remained lit. A peculiar sensation was going through me as—I couldn't help myself—I imagined Robin Burrell's destroyed body lying lifeless in her front room. It was a sensation I've experienced numerous times. An occupational hazard. It's a chill that runs through me. A sensation of cold dread, as if the temperature of my blood has suddenly dropped by a good thirty degrees or more and is going to remain there. The feeling is one of my blood being replaced by a maliciously cold silk, threatening to freeze me up. I know what does it. It's broken bodies. It's the rupture of violence and then a heart gone abruptly as still as a stone. Dead still. It jolts me more than I think I sometimes know. It's life made inconsequential. And I hate it.

As I stood at Margo's window, I had a particularly unsettling feeling. A similar dread had visited me just a week previous, after I spent an hour talking with Robin Burrell in her apartment. The apartment had been uncommonly warm, and Robin had asked me if I could reach around her as-yet-undecorated Christmas tree and shove open the large windows for her. Which I did. That wasn't when the chill took me. It happened afterward, when I was standing at Margo's bedroom window—just like this, elbows on the windowsill, frown on the face—watching as Robin perched precariously on a footstool, mindfully stringing the small white lights on her gigantic tree. The chill had come when she glanced up from the tree and caught me watching her.

4

ROBIN BURRELL WAS an extremely organized person. She had divided the letters and the printed-out e-mails into three categories and set them in separate piles on her dining table.

"These are the general ones," she had told me, indicating the largest of the piles. "They're pretty much 'you go, girl' letters. A lot of them are very sweet. 'Keep your chin up. Don't let them get you down. We're behind you.' That kind of thing."

I picked up a letter from the pile. It was from Karen from Texas. That's how the author of the letter had signed it. It was written on holiday stationery, a sheet of cream-colored paper bordered with red silhouettes of reindeer. Karen's handwriting was round and precise. She made her O's large and, in words with two of them in a row, strung them together so they looked like the eyes of an owl. Karen might have been eleven or eighty, it was impossible to tell.

Dear Robin,
    On TV you look very brave. I'm sorry the lawyers are being so mean to you but I guess that is their job. I thought I should tell you that when you look right into the camera you look like you regret everything that happened from the bottom of your heart. I am including you in my prayers. God bless you.
Karen from Texas

"Most of the ones in that pile are from women," Robin said. "Though with some of the e-mails, if they don't sign their names, it's sometimes hard to tell from the e-mail address."

The other two piles had interested me more. There were fewer letters in these piles. Mostly, they were e-mails that Robin had printed out. One of the piles contained messages from men who wanted to either meet Robin, date her, introduce her to their family, marry her, or take her far, far away from New York. This last category included a proposed thirty-day hike in New Zealand.

"That one actually made me think twice,"

Robin said. "Thirty days in New Zealand sounds like a paradise to me right about now."

"What do you think of Gary?" I held up a photograph of a thirtyish man wearing a red baseball cap and posing alongside a six-foot-tall Minnie Mouse. Gary's was a marriage proposal. He wrote that he lived in the Finger Lakes district of central New York State, owned a house and a small boat, and had a contact at one of the local wineries, so he could get "the good stuff" at below cost.

"It says here he's single and never been married. What's a grown man with no kids doing down in Disney World getting his picture taken with Minnie Mouse?"

"Please don't make fun of him," Robin said. "I'm guessing he's a very lonely person. That's what a lot of these seem to be from."

"Which piles are the kinky ones in?"

"I put those in with the hate mail." She tapped a finger on the remaining pile. "Listen, I can't thank you enough for doing this. Are you sure you don't want any tea or something? A drink?"

"I'm fine."

"I feel bad imposing myself on you this way."

"You're not imposing. Don't mention it."

She picked the top sheet off the third pile. "A lot of these are just stupid horny stuff. Still, it's creepy, being on the receiving end. But some of the others get really nasty. I just figured either way, nasty or stupid, they've come from people I wouldn't want to run into in a dark alley, so I bunched them all in as hate mail."

She scanned the paper in her hand, and tears came to her eyes. She handed it to me. Her voice was choked. "Why is this happening?"

～ 5 ～

THE POST HIT THE STREETS before dawn
with its lurid photograph on the front page,
showing Robin lying dead beneath the Christmas
tree. It wasn't evident from the angle of the photo
that her body had been arranged to resemble the
two murder victims in the Fox case, but it didn't
really make any difference. The leaks had begun.
Leaks and rumors. A tabloid can run marathons
on leaks and rumors alone. The **Post** suggested,
and the talking heads parroted the suggestion,
that Robin Burrell had not been murdered by a
copycat killer but that Marshall Fox was innocent
after all of the two murders for which he had just
been tried and that the original killer was again
on the march. **Women, lock your doors.**

The morning talk shows couldn't get enough
of the murder of Marshall Fox's former lover. The

same faces that had been choking the studios of **Court TV** and **Larry King Live** for the months leading up to and during the trial were all risen and shined to weigh in on this latest development. I caught a few minutes of Alan Ross expressing his deep regret for Robin Burrell and her loved ones while at the same time clearly thrilled to be making the case for Fox's innocence in the earlier murders. I mentioned to Margo that I'd run into Ross in the courtroom and that he'd passed along his greetings.

" 'ow is old 'enry 'iggins anyway?" she asked, butchering her own pretty face with god-awful contortions. She was less than thrilled when I suggested she retire her cockney.

As I clicked robotically from station to station, I knew that Joseph Gallo could not be enjoying his morning coffee. I felt a little bad—but only a little—that I had lied to Gallo the night before. When I'd told one of the cops on the scene outside Robin Burrell's building that I needed to speak with the detective in charge, it was primarily a preemptive move. I wanted to explain why it was that a competent check of the various fingerprints that were no doubt being lifted inside Robin's apartment at that very moment was going to include the name of Fritz Malone in the results. I'd explained to Gallo that Robin Burrell had asked me into her home a few weeks before to take a look at the mail she'd been receiving as a result of her televised participation in the Fox trial. I told him that I had taken some of the letters and the printed-out e-mails out of the apartment, to give them some additional study. The e-mails weren't so important—the police would be able to retrieve those from Robin's computer—but I had the only copies of the letters.

My lie had been in telling Gallo that the letters were in Queens, at Charlie Burke's house. Charlie is my friend, my former boss, my former partner, Margo's father, all of the above. I told Gallo that I'd taken the letters and e-mails out to Charlie's so that he could go over them with me. If the homicide chief had known that they were actually right across the street at Margo's, he'd have had me fetch them right away. Gallo made me promise to bring the letters into precinct headquarters first thing in the morning.

I showered and broke a bagel with Miss Margo. She was still glued to the tube. I was feeling heavy and sluggish, and I guess it showed.

"Do you want to go back to bed?" Margo asked. "That **is** one of the advantages of being self-employed, you know."

"It can also be one of the downfalls." The TV was driving me nuts. It usually does. A photograph of Robin Burrell came on. I aimed the remote and clicked the set off, tossing the remote on the coffee table.

Margo frowned. "Hey."

"Sorry, sweetheart, were they saying something new?" I hadn't intended the note of sarcasm that leached in.

Margo smirked. "If it's going to be another scintillating lecture about the media, please hold on while I get my notebook. I wouldn't want to miss something."

"Sorry."

"I'll say. You're dragging around here like you've got a hairball you can't cough up. Maybe you should go back to bed and get up on the right side. What's going on?"

"I should have told her to get out of town for a while."

Margo's eyes narrowed. She lifted her coffee cup with both hands, floating it under her chin. "Oh. I see."

"What do you see?"

"I see a little blame-gaming, that's what."

"She was concerned."

"Of course she was concerned. There is a world of wackos out there, and she was exposed to God only knows how many of them. That doesn't mean if one of them got to her it was **your** fault."

"I know that."

"You don't look like you know that."

"I could have told her to be more careful."

"Stop it right there." Her cup rattled to the table. "Look at me. Robin Burrell did **not** hire you. Okay? She was not one of your clients. She was not your responsibility. **Capisce?** She was a neighbor to whom you were nice enough to lend an ear and take a look at some of her screwy fan mail."

"One of her screwy fans, as you put it, might have slit her throat and trussed her like a calf and run a nail through her heart."

"Maybe so. And thanks for the graphic reminder while we're at it. But maybe not. There may be a hundred other answers to who did it, you don't know. You **do** know what my dad says about jumping to conclusions."

I did know. Charlie Burke was a walking, talking rule book of investigation techniques and pointers. Back when he was whipping me into shape, I wanted to strangle him sometimes, the way he peppered me with his aphorisms.

"The Sayings of Chairman Daddy," I grumbled.

Margo's voice lowered. "We can turn this thing nasty if you'd like."

"Now who's getting up on the wrong side of the bed?"

"Hey, I'm trying to help you here." She gestured toward the window. "You spent an hour in the woman's apartment. You came over here with a pile of the woman's mail. Maybe you even went and talked to her a second time, I don't know. And now she's dead. You have no connection with that whatsoever. You were the good guy. I don't happen to think you have a single thing to regret."

"I regret that she's dead."

I regretted something else, too. Immediately. I regretted saying what I'd just said in the particular heavy tone I'd said it in. I **was** sluggish. I wasn't picking up on Margo's cues quickly enough. **Maybe you even went and talked to her a second time.** Margo crossed her arms then instantly uncrossed them. Suddenly, they were awkward appendages.

"You'd better get that stuff off to your cop."

I shook my head slowly. "Not on this note."

She leveled her look at me. "I saw you standing at the window last night. You thought I was asleep."

"I wasn't thinking about whether you were asleep or not."

"Oh. Well. Thank you."

I took a deep breath and let it out slowly. "I'm going to apologize. But I'm not sure for what."

"Then don't."

"Look, a woman who asked me for some help was murdered right across the damn street. I know it's not my responsibility, but sue me, I feel bad about it. I woke up and I couldn't get back to sleep. I went to the window and took turns feeling sorry for the dead woman and feeling sorry for myself. I can't justify the pity party, but there it is. I think that's pretty much the whole picture."

She let my words hang in the air. "I accept your apology."

"You forced my apology."

"I know I did. I accept it anyway."

I looked at my watch. "This is pretty early for daytime drama, don't you think? It's been swell fighting with you, lady, but I've got to be going."

Margo's voice was without inflection. "You're going to get involved with this thing, aren't you?"

"I'm taking the letters to Joe Gallo. I have to do that."

"But you said you were going to copy them first."

"That's right."

"If you need something to read, I've got a zillion books right here."

I went into the bedroom and grabbed my coat off the chair. I fetched a PBS tote bag from the closet and went into the living room and collected Robin Burrell's letters and e-mails and put them in the tote. When I popped into the kitchen to say goodbye, Margo was still at the table, holding her coffee cup up near her chin once more.

"**Did** you see her a second time, Fritz?"

I took a beat. "Would it actually matter if I had?"

Even though she was already stock-still, I got the impression that she froze just a tad more. Maybe it was her eyes.

"Not the answer I wanted to hear."

I hoisted the tote bag onto my shoulder. "Yes," I said. "I did. She needed to talk again. We got together a second time."

Margo took a sip of her coffee. Her eyes narrowed like a cat's. "I know."

HOMICIDE DETECTIVE JOSEPH GALLO had never met a mirror he didn't like. I know that's an old saw, but its cut is nonetheless true. If Gallo ran his hand down his silk tie once in the twenty minutes we spoke together in his office, he did it a hundred times. Gallo's face was handsome the way Dracula's face is handsome. Good bones, seductive black eyes set in deep sockets. There are no fewer than three dapper television detectives Gallo has been overheard claiming to be the model for. The thing is, he

might be right. Central casting could do a hell of
a lot worse than Joseph Gallo.

The detective was on the phone. As he signaled me to take a seat, he rolled his eyes at
whomever it was he had on the line. The sleeves
of his pale blue shirt were folded back to his fore-
arms in perfect rectangles. His top button was
loose, and his tie was artfully askew. A copy of the
Post was on his desk. Facedown.

"Of course I'm looking into it. What do you
think? I want to know that just as much . . .
Right. Exactly . . . No, I've got a man on it . . .
Yes, he's a good man." A minute later, he hung up.
His hard jaw was askew. "Ask me what I think of
the First Amendment. No, don't bother. I'll tell
you. I think it's not worth the toilet paper it's
printed on."

"Don't let yourself get quoted on that."

"If I weren't sworn to uphold the law, I'd kill
somebody over at the **Post**."

"The photo?"

"The frippin' photo, you'd better believe it.
There's nothing I can do to stop them from
printing what amounts to pornography, as far
as I'm concerned. They've got their lovely First
Amendment. But do you know something? That
picture was taken nearly forty minutes before the
911 was called in. We had the call traced, natu-

rally. It was a pay phone at that diner next to the **Post.** We got the waitress to ID the photographer. The whole time this jerk is en route from the murder scene, Jimmy Puck is mucking around outside Burrell's building, getting the lay of the land. I don't know why people even read that weasel. The woman could have been in there bleeding to death."

I placed the tote bag on top of the **Post.** "She did bleed to death."

"You know what I mean. Look, I know she must've died within minutes. Her throat opened up like that. But those schmucks didn't know that. All they're thinking about is beating the other guy. Getting to press lickety-split with their goddamn photo. Their almighty scoop. That's what your First Amendment does. It lets you screw up your priorities."

"A cop with a beef about the press," I said. "I'm shocked, shocked."

Gallo looked ready to take a bite out of me then relaxed. A hand drifted to his hair and gave it a pat. "Right. Sure. What's new on the planet three? Sometimes a guy's just got to bitch."

"It's a free country," I said. "Amendments and all."

He eyed the tote bag. "Okay, now, run it by me again how it was you got your nose into this.

I have to say I wasn't paying a lot of attention last night."

"Sure. You know Cafe La Fortuna? It's down near the end of Robin Burrell's block."

"Sure. They've got that photo in the window of John Lennon and Yoko Ono hanging out in their back garden."

"Right. Well, I go there pretty often."

"I don't recall seeing any pictures of you in the window."

"I'm not the guy who wrote 'Sexy Sadie.' "

"Hey. John Lennon didn't become John Lennon by writing 'Sexy Sadie.' "

"What I'm saying is that I pop into the place fairly often. I was there a couple weeks ago, and Mrs. Carella came over to me. Mrs. Carella is the owner. She came over to me and pointed out a woman who was sitting in the back."

"Let me guess."

"You guess Yoko and I'm leaving."

"Robin Burrell."

"Correct. I recognized her from TV. You'd have to live in a darker cave than mine not to know that face. It wasn't so surprising to see her. I knew she lived right across the street from Margo."

"Ever talk to her before?"

"Before La Fortuna? No. But Mrs. Carella

said that's exactly what I should do. I should go talk to her. She said Robin had come in earlier and taken the table in the back and started to cry. I'll tell you something, you don't cry around Mrs. Carella without her swooping in. She got Robin to tell her what the problem was. It was all this mail and e-mails from these creeps all over the place. She was spooked. Mrs. Carella knows what I do for a living, she thought maybe I could help. She's like an Italian yenta. Except with the Sicilian accent. 'Fritz, meet Robin. Robin, meet Fritz. You two sit here and share some biscotti and get to know each other.' "

"Sounds lovely. So is that what happened? Did you get to know her?"

I shrugged. "I heard her story. You know what they say about private eyes."

" 'It's not the eyes, it's the ears.' "

"Exactly. I listened. Robin was scared. She was depressed. She was blaming herself for the entire mess. You know how it is. If she hadn't gotten involved with Fox in the first place. Blah blah. All the usual stuff."

"So you placed a manly hand on hers and told her not to blame the victim."

"I kept my manly hands to myself."

"Ms. Burrell was a pretty woman."

"You noticed that, eh? They sure do hire the best around here."

Gallo indicated the tote bag. "What's your gut tell you, Fritz? Is the killer in there?"

"Could be. None of them scream, 'Lock your door, little girl, I'm on my way!' She told me there had been some calls, too. As soon as her name and picture started getting bounced around in the press. Eventually, she got an unlisted number."

Gallo perked up at the mention of nasty phone calls. "Were any of the phone calls explicitly threatening?"

"She said mostly they were just jerks being jerks."

"But no death threats."

"None she shared with me."

"Any repeats? Same guy over and over?"

"She didn't say. She got the unlisted number pretty quickly, and that ended it."

"Not quite," the detective said. "Here. Let me play something for you."

There was a miniature cassette player on the desk. I hadn't noticed it. Gallo centered it, pushed the rewind button then hit play. There were several static-filled seconds, and then came a gravelly male voice.

"I'm coming, you whore. Can you taste the blood yet?"

Gallo hit the stop button. "How would you like to come home to that? This was left on Robin

Burrell's answering machine last night. Apparently the unlisted thing didn't faze this guy."

"It's not so hard to get a number if you really want it."

"Definitely not. Now, here's your scoop of the day—and you heard it **here** first. That message? What you just heard? An identical message was left last night on the machine of one Rosemary Fox."

"Mrs. Marshall Fox herself?"

Gallo nodded expansively. "I'm not saying this is necessarily the creep who got to Robin Burrell last night, but it does give you that funny feeling."

"What kind of feeling does it give Rosemary Fox?"

"I'm trying to throw a dozen men around her, but she's balking. The Foxes aren't what you call benevolent friends of the New York City police at this particular point in time. They've got that loudmouth lawyer of theirs saying Fox will hire his own people to protect his family, thank you very much."

"Riddick?"

"Right. Zack the hack. We'd like to keep all this quiet. I mean, these phone threats. But you know how Riddick operates. He's called a press conference for noon today. How much do you want to bet he's going to have a cassette player of his own with him?"

"It doesn't help his client to advertise death threats made to his wife," I said.

"You think he cares about that? It helps **him**. Who the hell do you think is Zachary Riddick's biggest client?"

"Can't you stop him? Tampering with evidence? Something like that?"

"We can bust his chops. But believe me, if he wants this tape out there, he'll get it out there."

"So what do you think you're dealing with here?"

Gallo aimed his palms at the ceiling. "You know what? You'll have to get back to me on that."

I asked to hear the message again. Gallo hit the rewind button then replayed the message. The voice was clearly being disguised. It was menacing, but in what sounded to me like a calculating way. I asked, "What time was this left? Does Robin's machine have a time stamp on it?"

"It was left at six-forty-one."

"That's just around the time Deveraux was biting the heads off the jury."

Gallo picked up a stack of black-and-white photographs from the desk and started leafing through them. "We found no signs of a forced entry."

"So Robin either knew her attacker," I said, "or, more to the point, knew him and trusted him enough to let him in. Or else she got this message and showed unfathomably stupid judgment in opening the door to the first stranger who came along."

"Exactly. We're working on both scenarios."

"Robin Burrell was not an unfathomably stupid person," I said.

"I'm sure she wasn't."

He tossed one of the photographs on the desk. I picked it up. It was a close-up of a tray holding a piece of cheese still in its cellophane along with a knife and an apple. Gallo went on, "We've traced Ms. Burrell from a yoga class she took over on Broadway. On the way home, she buys cheese and fruit. She also buys throat lozenges and Kleenex and other stuff for a cold. Her yoga instructor confirmed that she was sneezing and sniffling in class."

"It's cold season," I said.

"If you're popping lozenges and drinking Throat Coat tea, I don't see that you're eating cheese. Especially set out all nice on a tray like that. She was expecting someone."

"In that case, why does stupid scenario number two have legs? You're saying it wasn't a stranger."

"Because I don't want to rule out something that might still hold up. You don't toss out a scenario just because it might be a little stupid. Think about it. What's one way to get inside someone's apartment without forcing your way in?"

I got it. "Be there when they're opening the door."

"Right. Leave a message that will scare the hell out of them. A woman in her apartment alone? You get a message like that on your phone, especially on an unlisted number? That's got to spook her. She's not going to feel too good just sitting there. So you leave the message and be there waiting when she comes running out the door."

"Right into your arms."

Gallo nodded. "Or merge the two stories, if you want. It's someone she knew who made the call, disguising his voice, and he stood there waiting. Either way, he flushed her out. He got her to open the door."

"If it'll make you feel any better, I can sort out the cheese mystery for you."

"Sure, Fritz. Sort away."

"The person she was expecting was me."

Gallo blinked. "You. What are you telling me? You had a date with Robin Burrell the night she was killed?"

"Don't go smearing me with that brush, Joe. I didn't have a date. She wanted to talk some more about all the nutsy stuff that had been going on lately. I was testifying on that pirating case, and we'd arranged that I'd swing by when I got out."

Gallo rested his chin on his fingertips and studied me. "Margo know about this date?"

"I just told you, it wasn't a date."

"This little cheese party, then?"

"Is that question relevant to your investigation?"

"So the answer is, she didn't. What's going on here, Fritz?"

"Nothing's going on. I make a living out of other people's problems. Robin Burrell had some problems."

"Was she your client?"

"Now you're sounding like Margo."

"Oh. So you've had this conversation with Ms. Burke?"

"A similar one."

"And she's okay with your breaking cheese with the pretty lady across the street?"

"Joe, if I didn't know any better, I'd say you're prying."

"You don't know any better."

"Okay. Margo's nose is out of joint. I'm doing what I can to put it back in place."

"We've established that Robin Burrell was a pretty woman."

"From where I sit, Margo's no side of burnt toast. Robin Burrell was upset. If I was able to calm her down some, that's not a crime. Check your codes. Have you got one for 'unlawful assisting of damsel in distress'?"

"Okay. None of my business. But I wish you'd told me about this last night."

"Cops scare me," I said.

Gallo picked up one of the crime-scene photos and shook his head sadly at it. He dropped the photograph back on his desk, leaned back in his chair and laced his fingers carefully against the back of his head.

"The guy did a real chop job on your cheese friend. We're looking at one sick, angry bastard here. And when word gets out that Ms. Burrell was found with her hand mutilated against her chest like those other two . . ." Gallo let the sentence hang.

"Any more thoughts on whether it's a copycat or if this guy actually did the Central Parkers?"

"The answer to both those questions is maybe. But I sure as hell hope it's the first one." He indicated the tote bag. "I wish you could tell me he's in there."

"Sorry, Joe."

Gallo came forward in his chair and plucked one of the e-mails from the bag. As he read it, I took a few of the other photographs and flipped through them. It was a reckless thing to do. I knew there was likely to be at least one of them that could get under my skin. There was. The wiseass crime-scene photographer had fashioned what he'd probably thought was an art shot. The photograph was taken looking down from the crown of Robin's head as she lay on the floor. Her hairline, her eyebrows and her nose were in the foreground, slightly blurred. The focus of the shot was on the mirror fragment protruding from Robin's neck, just above her collarbone. The photographer had angled the shot to capture the reflection of a portion of Robin's face. This wasn't exactly the last memory of the woman's deep hazel eyes that I'd have preferred to hold.

Joe Gallo finished reading the e-mail. He set it faceup on his desk, squaring it perfectly. "Suspect number one." He made a rueful face. "So begins the glamorous side of law enforcement."

～ 6 ～

I'VE NEVER BEEN SITTING on top of the world myself, so I don't honestly know what that's like. For that matter, who can say that having the number-one-rated late-night show in the midnight slot and getting mountains of money thrown at you truly qualifies as "sitting on top of the world," but that was the tag that **Time** magazine had given Marshall Fox when they'd put his grinning mug on their cover just three months before the murdered bodies of Cynthia Blair and Nikki Rossman surfaced in Central Park a little over a week apart. Fox's emergence on the entertainment scene three years earlier, almost literally from nowhere ("South Dakota isn't nowhere," Fox joked during the first week of his show, "we prefer to think of ourselves as just south of nowhere"), and his blurringly fast trajectory to stardom had made the high school dropout and former ranch hand a household name almost overnight. Fox's particular combination of easy charm, faint naughtiness and at times downright reproachful wit struck an immediate chord with viewers. The **Time** story called it "a near-fluke-ish alchemy."

One has to conjure the incongruous image of a cowboy Lenny Bruce wandering in from the heartland. Like Bruce, Mr. Fox is not one to mince his words, a trait that also lands him in the grand American populist tradition of Will Rogers or Mark Twain. But ask any female fan of Marshall Fox if she thinks either of those two venerable sagebrush sages had even a fraction of the edge or especially the sex appeal of this new kid on the block, and you're likely as not to hear a resounding "As if!"

Within months of its debut, **Midnight with Marshall Fox** was a ratings gold mine for the network. The diamond-blue eyes and the slightly damaged nose peered out from newsstands all over the country. The guy was hot goods. Even Margo, who is not one to be easily starstruck, contracted a case of Fox fever and stayed up past pumpkin time to get her dose of the man. When

Fox took up with socialite beauty and celebrity heartbreaker Rosemary Boggs within a year of landing in New York and the two tied the knot a mere three months later, they were given the sort of ink once reserved for royal couples. The media could not get enough of them. **Vanity Fair** reportedly paid the Foxes over a million dollars to pose as scantily clad modern-day Antony and Cleopatra (**Cowboy & Cleopatra**) for the cover of their magazine, snakes and all. Rosemary was rumored to have balked at the idea and made the photo shoot a living hell. Regardless, the results pumped sales to the top of the publication's all-time figures, and when Fox convinced his wife to come on the show the week after the magazine hit the stands—complete with snakes and the peekaboo gold toga—the show's already boffo ratings likewise flew right off the charts. The Foxes were a force, the new bionic couple. About as "it" as "it" gets.

Not quite two years into the marriage, the cracks began to appear. Rumors of fights. Whispers of drugs. Suggestions of a serious wandering-eye problem on the part of Fox. During an extended European vacation for the lady of the house, speculation grew that Fox was ready to pull up stakes and make his way back to the heartland. Finally, the trial separation, accompanied by the almost immediate parade of women looping their arm through that of the late-night entertainer. High-profile carousing. High jinks. The unexplained police presence at three A.M. outside Fox's rented bungalow at Chateau Marmont. An unlicensed handgun setting off alarms at JFK. The incident with the shattered glass table and the bleeding Peruvian supermodel—reportedly seven stitches across the nineteen-year-old's shoulder blade.

And then April.

The murders.

Blood in Central Park.

The week of Fox's indictment and jailing for the slayings of Cynthia Blair and Nikki Rossman, **Time** splashed the single word TUMBLED across their cover photograph of the late-night celebrity dressed in an orange jumpsuit and shackled like Houdini, wrists to waist, ankle to ankle. An ill-timed programming decision the night of the arrest had resulted in the re-airing of Rosemary Fox's appearance on her husband's show. Two minutes into the segment, just as one of the snakes was coiling its way down her arm and onto Marshall Fox's desk, television sets across the country abruptly went black. Some accounts—surely apocryphal but too delicious not to report—had the sound of Rosemary Fox's furious shriek traveling the full distance from the couple's Park Avenue penthouse all the way across Central Park to the West Side. Not likely. Even so, an actual witness to the scene of Rosemary's incensed phone call to Alan Ross at the network did report the base of her telephone cracking as she slammed the receiver down over and over again.

THE WORD ON CYNTHIA BLAIR was that the ambitious thirty-two-year-old was strung about as tight as a person can be strung while managing to function. Some of it was simply Cynthia—she'd always been the classic type A— but a lot of it was her job. Cynthia had been fast-tracking her way up the KBS ladder from the word go, impressing her bosses with her ability to transform her entry-level "shut up and fetch coffee" position into one where she could and did make a real contribution. She had the hunger. More importantly, she had the talent. The network knew it had a comer. When the plan was devised to bring in the charming cowboy and give him his own show, Cynthia had lobbied successfully to be the risky show's producer and had launched into the enterprise with the full force of her tigerlike energy. It was hair-pulling work. In order to siphon off some of the stress from her work, Cynthia would steal away from the office whenever possible and put herself through various tortures at a nearby health club. The cords on either side of her slender neck stood out like hard cables as she strained against machines set to resistances that were patently inappropriate for the woman's trim 112-pound body. But Cynthia Blair liked to push limits. She attacked the StairMaster as if she were charging to the top of a burning building to rescue a stranded child. She performed military-style sit-ups until she was on the verge of puking. She put serious fear into some of her kickboxing partners. It was her style, what she needed in order to contend with her natural tendency to engage with life at a highly pitched intensity.

When she couldn't make it to the health club, she sometimes emptied the contents of her stomach into the toilet across the hall from her office.

Over the course of the Marshall Fox trial, the nature of Fox's working relationship with Cynthia was dissected in great detail, the consensus being that the contrary bullheadedness of the two personalities had contributed to an atmosphere in the offices that could range anywhere from slightly ginger to all-out war zone; at the same time, some damned good television was born of the star and his tenacious producer squaring off. For a show that was essentially about laughter, the success of **Midnight with Marshall Fox** was revealed to followers of the trial to be in many ways dependent on the good stuff extracted from blow and counterblow.

"This is how Marshall works," Alan Ross had testified. He had explained that, contrary to the impression of most television personalities, Marshall Fox was not at all interested in surrounding himself with yes-men. That wasn't the world he'd grown up in. "With Marshall, it's not something so basic as being friendly. He likes to spar. It's all about provoking and being provoked. That's just how he is. Those jokes and quips you hear every night? Trust me, some poor soul on the staff has to suffer deeply before Marshall signs off on them. His best work comes from knocking heads with someone. He's a digger. He likes to rattle around in places people would just as soon keep private. That's where the really good stuff is. Marshall has an instinct for that. It's why the show has been such a success. You laugh your brains out while you're watching, but you're also nervous. He's brilliant, the way he goes about it."

Ross went on to say that Cynthia Blair had been the perfect producer for someone like Fox. He described her "solid backbone" and her unwillingness to cave in gracefully to her boss's bullying. Instinctively, she knew that Marshall thrived on "the fight."

"Personally, I thought that Cynthia moving on from the show was inevitable. Working with someone like Marshall is exhausting. Believe me, I know. I've been there. No question the dynamic between the two was creating some great television, but ultimately there's going to be a burnout factor. Even with someone as driven as Cynthia was. At least that's my view. Marshall was a definite challenge to Cynthia, but she'd mastered it. Marshall and I even had some discussions about it. He agreed with me that Cynthia was ready for something new to sink her teeth into. She was definitely going places."

Most of Fox's associates who testified took pains to stress that the "combat" between Cynthia and her boss had always been strictly professional, just the way the two of them chose to do business. Lawyers for the prosecution hammered away hard at this point but were unable to solicit a statement from anyone that, in fact, Fox and Cynthia Blair had not liked each other. Even so, nobody who testified attempted to pretend that the termination of the professional relationship hadn't been particularly nasty. Or sudden. Around two o'clock on the afternoon of March 22, shouting and yelling—much more than usual—had been heard coming from behind Marshall Fox's closed office door. Two voices. Marshall Fox and Cynthia Blair.

No one who heard the muffled battle was able to identify the precise point of the argument, although the single most agreed-upon quote heard distinctly by those testifying was: "Liar! You fucking, **fucking,** two-faced liar!" It was Cynthia Blair, not Fox, who hurled that one, and she had said it over and over again. Eventually, Cynthia emerged from Fox's office and stormed into hers, which adjoined her boss's. There was a loud crash and the sound of broken glass, followed by a steady pounding sound that went on for about a minute. This was followed by several tense minutes of silence, after which the producer's door flew open and Cynthia stomped to the elevator clutching a cardboard box under one arm. She stood at the elevator, glaring up at the ceiling, slamming her hand against the down button over and over and over until the elevator arrived and the door slid open. Cynthia swore harshly under her breath as she got on the elevator, though no one's testimony squared on the specifics of what she said.

The pounding that was heard coming from Cynthia's office had resulted in a large hole that was found in the Sheetrock wall—the wall she shared with Fox—that looked as if she had attempted to launch a cannonball through the wall and catch her boss at his desk. The cannonball turned out to be Cynthia Blair's Emmy Award (the crashing sound had been the glass of the small display case across from Cynthia's desk), which was fished out from the hollow area within the wall, along with the framed photograph of a smiling Marshall Fox embracing Cynthia (who was embracing her Emmy) that had previously held the place of honor in the display case, next to the award. The glass of the frame was broken, spiderwebbing out from a point directly in the center of Marshall Fox's face. As one of the secretaries testified, "It looked like she'd punched him out."

Three weeks later, an early-morning dog walker in Central Park came across the clothed body of a young woman lying at the base of Cleopatra's Needle, the stone Egyptian obelisk rising from a small hill behind the Metropolitan Museum of Art. A red scarf that was later identified as belonging to the victim was knotted around her throat, and her face was covered with tiny puncture wounds from what proved to be a ballpoint pen, the very pen that had been used to fix the victim's hand in place over her heart.

The body of Cynthia Blair was discovered on April 16. What with the grisly nature of the murder and the location of the body, the story led the local newscasts. Once the woman's identity was released a day later, the story strapped on rockets. Overnight, Cynthia Blair achieved star status. Her angular visage saturated the airwaves. The attractive, hardworking, go-get-'em "woman behind the man" story got immediate traction. From the offices of **Midnight with Marshall Fox,** a statement was released offering condolences to Cynthia Blair's family, along with the announcement of a $500,000 award for the capture and conviction of Cynthia's murderer, half of which was being put up personally by Marshall Fox. The show went on immediate hiatus. It resumed a week later—several days after Cynthia Blair's celebrity-heavy funeral—with a program that felt like the **Titanic** the day after. Fox had wept openly several times. The plug was pulled on a video tribute to the show's former producer partway through, it was so distressing. Midway through the program, the band performed a dirge that seemed interminable, during which Marshall Fox wandered between his desk and various parts of the stage like a man in a haunted dream.

Margo had insisted on watching. I'd lobbied for whiskey and a couple of games of pool at Dive 75, but Margo won the toss. She's a freelance writer, and her beat requires her to keep an ear to the ground concerning all things cultural, fluffy and otherwise. So I watched the show with her, both fascinated and disgusted by the chutzpah of Marshall Fox and his people for dragging America through such a moribund hour of television.

High marks to Margo for prescience. At one point during the grim proceedings, she turned to me on the couch and said, "So what do you think? Did Fox do it?"

"Do what? Kill his producer?"

"Yes."

"You're not serious, are you?"

She did a head-bob thing that she does, her eyes going up to a corner of the ceiling. "I don't know. Not really, I guess. Maybe."

At that point, a week after Cynthia Blair's murder, the police had not released the detail of the dead woman's hand having been affixed to her breast with the ballpoint pen. That all changed three days later—a Sunday—when a second body turned up in the park. Unlike Cynthia Blair, this one showed signs of rape, or at any rate sexual activity, in the hours prior to death. And whereas the cause of death in the case of Cynthia Blair had been strangulation, the second victim had received several severe blows to the head and then had her neck opened up. Blood everywhere. In addition, a pair of handcuffs dangled from the left wrist. As with Blair, this new body had been deposited at the base of Cleopatra's Needle. Most telling to the police, its right hand had also been affixed over the heart, this time with a four-inch nail. Only this time, that last detail leaked out.

Slowly at first, but gathering momentum soon enough, the eyes of the country began to take a second look at the devastated Marshall Fox.

I LEFT GALLO'S OFFICE and walked to the copy shop on Broadway where the photocopies I'd had made of Robin Burrell's notes and e-mails were waiting for me in a paper bag behind the counter. I picked up a copy of the **Times** and took the subway to Forty-second Street and hoofed it over to the Keppler Building, where I keep my office.

Miss Dashpebble was out. That's my nonexistent secretary / receptionist. Being nonexistent, she's always out, but that never seems to stop me from noting her absence. When Margo and I want to take a break from behaving intelligently, we'll sometimes amuse ourselves with whimsies concerning the latest Dashpebble escapade. Quite the life this gal leads—no wonder she can't find the time to lick my stamps and answer my phones.

I went into my office and set my feet up on the desk. There was nothing in the **Times** about Robin's murder that I didn't already know. Marshall Fox's lawyers—particularly Zachary Riddick—were saying to anyone who would listen that the Robin Burrell killing proved their client was innocent of the murders of Cynthia Blair and Nikki Rossman. They claimed that Robin's murder proved the original killer was still at large. Riddick was calling for Fox's immediate release from prison. He was caterwauling for Sam Deveraux to declare a mistrial. In addition, he wanted a televised apology from the United States district attorney's office. God knows what else the grandstander wanted. Maybe a key to the city for the poor persecuted Mr. Fox?

I threw the paper on the floor. Newspapers don't throw well. I was dissatisfied. Some people actually enjoy being grumpy and out of sorts, but I'm not one of them. Being out of sorts only makes me more out of sorts.

I picked up the phone to call Margo, then set it back down. A quick replay of our morning's tiff didn't suggest any new tack. I could understand Margo's jumpiness about a gruesome murder taking place directly across the street from her building. No question about it. I think the problem we'd had was that Robin Burrell's mur-

der had also unnerved me—though in a different fashion—and it didn't seem that Margo was
willing to grant me the latitude to be spooked by
it. Charlie Burke and I have chewed this fat numerous times, and we concede that there are
times when you just don't bring your work home
with you. Or maybe the better way to put it is
that you **do** bring it home (how the hell are you
going to leave it behind?), but what you don't do
is share it. "You have to suck it up," Charlie says.
"You keep your problems to yourself. My wife is
my wife, she's not my shrink." Half of me thinks
he's right about it. And honestly? The other half
of me doesn't have a clue.

I swung my chair about to look out the window. The sky above the calliope of tall buildings
was steel gray. Twenty-three floors below, the
snowy rectangle of Bryant Park looked like a large
white slab, like a behemoth gravestone fallen on
its face. As I watched, two bundled figures entered the park on the west side and began making
their way east, hand in hand, cutting through the
precise middle of the park. Halfway across, the
figures dropped onto the snow, on their backs,
and began flapping their arms and legs.

I turned back to my desk and sorted through
the photocopies of Robin's "fan mail." I skimmed
through and divided them into two piles as I
went: Passive and Aggressive. Basic psychology

suggested that more likely than not, most of the writers in the "aggressive" pile were essentially cowards, mean-spirited worms who got off on sending crude, nasty notes to an attractive woman who had been dragged through the mud on national television. The tone of many suggested Marshall Fox fans who were enraged over Robin's testimony and by the seamier side of their hero that had been extracted from her on the stand. There was the standard string of **Fuck you, bitch, cunt** that one would expect, as well as aggressively colorful suggestions concerning anatomical actions that Robin might want to consider performing on herself or have conducted on her person by second and even third parties. What can I say? It's a human subset that has always existed, and although it was certainly possible that the writer of one of these notes could have decided to act on his or her misogynist hostility by viciously butchering Robin Burrell in her home, my sensors weren't alerting me to any clear candidates.

I took longer with the second pile. Where I could distinguish between male and female, I did, and I set the female ones to the side. This left me with a collection of men who had admired Robin Burrell sufficiently to take the time to grab pen or keyboard and reach out to her. No doubt there were some authentic souls of compassion represented in this group. I'm not so cynical that

I won't allow for the existence of the truly good-hearted. Maybe even the majority of the various marriage proposals and offers of companionship had been put forth with the purest of intentions. We can only hope that the world still holds more angels than devils. But if there was a true freak lurking in the e-mails and letters, my sense was that he wouldn't be in the overtly hostile missives, the aggressives. He was going to be here, lurking among the sweethearts.

From this second pile, I extracted the letters that included names and return addresses as well as the e-mails that readily identified their sender. This reduced the number of so-called passive correspondents to twenty-seven. Now all I had to do was bring in a medium who could let her hands hover over the two piles then pick out the killer. Hell, I've got the easiest job in the world.

I abandoned the piles and unlocked my lower desk drawer and took out my Beretta 92. I broke down the gun and gave it a cleaning on a piece of cloth that I keep for that purpose. The smell of copper solvent is a poor man's intoxicant, but I'm not making any excuses. I think clearly when my hands are occupied with small habitual tasks. I could have as easily taken apart and put back together one of those wooden cube puzzles you can still pick up for a buck in Chinatown (I had one in my desk drawer as well, though not under lock and key), but in the end I'd have the same wooden cube I started with. At least this way, when I was done, my "personal assistant" was newly cleaned and shiny.

I put the gun back into the drawer and locked it. I draped the oily chamois I'd used to clean the gun over Nipper, which is the name of the RCA Victor fox terrier that sits cock-headed in front of the large gold gramophone horn. I've got a life-size antique of the dog and record player in the corner of my office. A client gave it to me once in lieu of making good on his bill, telling me it was worth considerably more than he owed me. Like a considerable fool, I'd let him get away with it.

I locked up the office and headed over to Grand Central, to the food circus downstairs, where I grabbed a couple of slices from Two Boots, after which I spent a few minutes holding up a wall in Vanderbilt Hall, taking in the dim cavernous room and eyeballing the people moving every which way across the marble floor. It doesn't take much to entertain me. On the news just a few days earlier, I had learned that there was a stretch of now-unused train tracks well below the level where I was standing that had been used in the thirties and early forties to bring Franklin Roosevelt into the city from his home up in Hyde Park. And not just Roosevelt but his car and driver as well. The tracks led right to a specially built freight elevator so the car could be loaded in and brought up to street level; that way the president could make a discreet exit onto Park Avenue, all a part of keeping the public unaware of his inability to move freely without the aid of crutches or a solid elbow nearby. I thought of Charlie. Ten years earlier, a bullet half the size of a thumbnail had nullified his ability to ever walk again. End of story. No secret train tracks and fancy arrangements. Charlie was parked in his wheelchair out in Queens, restless and resigned.

More snow was threatening as I headed back up Forty-second Street. The gunmetal sky had darkened considerably. I popped into the coffee shop at Coliseum Books and picked up what I still call a medium-size cup of coffee. I have no clue what they call it. The baristas were talking about the Robin Burrell murder. The one serving me—a tall skinny kid with buckshots of acne scars on his cheeks—cracked a joke about it. The kind of crap you hear from people these days, especially kids. His coworker took him on.

"You better not be saying that. Someone come cut up your throat, how you gonna like it?"

The kid handed me my change. He was still chuckling at his own joke. "That be all?"

I felt the lecture rising in my throat, but I swallowed it. What was I going to do, grab this kid by the collar and slap him around like the original Mr. Heavy? For Christ's sake, I was only here to buy a cup of joe.

I took my mysterious-size coffee over to Bryant Park, and even though the temperature was hovering near the freezing mark, I fished a newspaper from a trash bin to clear the snow from one of the slatted park chairs and sat down at a metal table. I had the snow-glazed park to myself, no one else in the immediate vicinity being quite so idiotic as yours truly. I recognized that the kid joking behind the counter had affected my heart rate. I could feel the hinges of my jaw holding tight. I looked out over the empty park, trying to spot the snow angels I knew were out there somewhere.

No luck. No angels.

I hugged the cardboard cup with both hands and watched the mist of my breath mingling with the steam coming off the brew. They formed their own sifting cloud, and with the peculiar mood I was in, I went easily into the blur.

~ 8 ~

ROBIN BURRELL HAD FELT that she needed
to justify to me her former involvement with the
likes of Marshall Fox. She didn't need to do anything of the kind, not from my side, anyway, but
I guess she'd needed to do it for herself. It was on
my second visit to her apartment that she told me
the story. A little wine, a little cheese, a little cau-
tionary tale.

Robin met Marshall Fox the night that Kelly
Cole threw the contents of her martini into his
face and instructed him to get the hell out of her
life. The incident took place on a warm summer
evening on a large tiled patio overlooking the
yachts of Long Island's South Fork. The party
was being thrown by Alan Ross and his wife, Gloria, the end-of-summer bacchanalia that the couple threw every September at their sumptuous

estate in East Hampton. The Rosses' annual bash regularly featured among its guests the cream of the entertainment industry's A-list. Actors. Actresses. Movie and television directors. Supermodels. Writers. Studio heads. The hot bodies. A collection of the shakers and movers and so-called beautiful people kibitzing under the Chinese lanterns, toasting one another in the cool marble salons and occasionally fornicating in the comfortably refurbished boathouse at the edge of the property. Gloria Ross's talent agency, Argosy, represented nearly half of the party's attendees, while most who were not on the Argosy client list yearned for inclusion. The affair was unofficially referred to as "the audition," it being well known in the industry that key calls went out from the Argosy offices both in New York and Los Angeles in the days following the Rosses' annual party. Other agencies braced for the inevitable raids on their client list. Simply knowing that one of their hot actors or actresses or directors had attended the infamous East Hampton affair was enough to rattle the bladder of the related agent. Gloria Ross's industry nickname was "the Comanche," for the ruthlessness of her raiding parties. It was a nickname that brought the head of Argosy no end of delight. She often referred to her new acquisitions as her scalps.

Marshall Fox was an Argosy client, though

Gloria Ross had hardly needed to steal him away from anyone. When Alan and Gloria Ross first came across the brash young wrangler and tour guide during a vacation in the Black Hills, the only organization with any claim on Marshall Fox was Moose River Guest Ranch, where Fox was employed. The story became showbiz legend. Captivated by the wit and easy sex appeal of their talkative guide, the Rosses had devised a plan midway through their weeklong trail ride and proposed it to the cowboy at week's end. Beaming like a brand-new father, Alan Ross had clapped a hand on Fox's shoulder. "I've been angling all my life to say something this corny. Kid, how'd you like to be a fucking star?"

ROBIN HADN'T ATTENDED the Rosses' party as a guest. She was part of the hired help. An acquaintance who ran a catering business had called her at the last minute in a panic: "How would you like to spend the weekend in the Hamptons?" Two of the caterer's helpers had gone AWOL, and the woman was scrambling to fill their places.

Robin had been forced to make a real effort not to gape. Celebrities seemed to pour out of the woodwork. Brad. Nicole. Justin. She thought she might weep at the sight of Meryl Streep—a personal favorite—whose simple elegance and wicked little laugh were beyond captivating. Robin trolled the party with a drinks tray, dispensing champagne and martinis. She spotted Marshall Fox soon after he arrived at the party. The popular talk-show host was accompanied by a striking blonde, Kelly Cole, the reporter from Channel 7 News. In her plunging silk blouse and capri pants, Kelly Cole looked anything but the earnest reporter clutching the microphone in front of City Hall. As for Fox, he was sporting a radiant tan fresh from a week in Maui and was—no surprise—the life of the party, charming all comers, passing his celebrated banter around for all to sample. Robin admitted that she had always considered the entertainer deadly handsome. "Disturbingly appealing," as she would later say on the witness stand. The infectious and exceedingly mischievous smile. The slightly damaged nose. The alert blue eyes. Fox's lean, muscular frame moved easily in bone-white slacks and a simple gray V-neck sweater. Under a vigorous cross-examination, Robin would confess to having difficulty taking her eyes off the entertainer as he moved about the party.

At the time, Marshall Fox had been several months into his well-publicized estrangement from his wife, Rosemary, an estrangement that had already seen a number of high-octane if short-lived affairs with women of notorious beauty. The

word on Fox was that he was a decidedly passion-
ate and skilled lover. "**Voracious**," came the grinning report from a particular Hollywood actress
who was not known for suffering klutzes in her
bed. Interviewed on one of the entertainment
tabloid shows, the actress had looked directly into
the camera and pronounced, "Let's just say this is
one hungry cowboy and leave it at that, okay?"

Robin's first direct encounter with Fox came
midway through the party, when she found herself cornered on the large patio by a large
drunken British film director who had snared
the last drink from her tray then locked a grip
on her free arm as he looked her up and down
with red bleary eyes.

"By **fuck,** if I couldn't bend you over this rail
right now and give that lovely USDA a proper
nailing."

In the process of attempting to free herself,
Robin lost control of the empty tray, which clattered loudly to the patio floor. The director tightened his grip on her arm. As he moved closer,
Robin was treated to a putrid exhaust of Scotch
fumes.

"Let's have us a fuckin' kiss. Come here now."

"**Jeremy!**"

Robin whipped her head around. It was Marshall Fox. As Fox made his way across the patio,

he tossed his drink glass into the shrubbery. My God, Robin thought. Cowboy saves the day.

The Englishman gave Fox a sloppy smile. "Hallo, Marshall. Stinkin' little bash, in't it? I take it you've seen these lovely appetizers?"

"Let her go, Jeremy," Fox said evenly. His voice held a low, liquid menace.

The director scoffed, "Fuck all, Marshall. Don't be a prig."

Fox glanced at Robin, then addressed the director. "Jeremy . . . **old chap.** How about for just one moment you pretend you're not an asshole. Hmm? I know it's hard, **old chap.** None of the rest of us have ever been able to do it. But why don't you give it a try?"

Without warning, Fox's left arm shot out, his open hand catching the Englishman square in the chest. As the director went tumbling into a deck chair, Fox grabbed Robin's other arm and yanked her free. She stumbled up against him. Fox grinned and took a chivalrous step backward.

"I apologize for Jeremy. We don't know who it was that let him off his leash."

Still muttering, the director attempted to rise from the deck chair, but Fox placed a foot on the arm of the chair and succeeded in toppling it. The Englishman tumbled onto the tiles and went silent. Fox bent down and retrieved the tray that

Robin had dropped and handed it to her. "It's so hard to get good guests these days."

He squeezed off another smile and left the patio by a nearby set of winding stairs, rejoining Kelly Cole, who was standing barefoot down on the grass, tolerating the stories of two overexcited young screenwriters. Robin had a sense that the entertainer knew full well she was watching him.

It wasn't long after midnight that Kelly Cole lifted a martini from Robin's tray, instructed Marshall Fox to get the hell out of her life **immediately** and then proceeded to launch the contents of her martini glass at him. The reporter's aim was perfect, and the drink landed squarely in Fox's face, the olive bouncing off his cheek. Robin had never seen a face as red with fury as Kelly Cole's. The reporter's expression was volcanic. For his part, Fox took a beat, then reached down to pick up the olive off the ground and blithely handed it over to his infuriated date. "I'm sorry, sweetheart, but I think this fell out of your ass."

Cole's slap seemed to echo back all the way from the boathouse. She stormed into the mansion. Fox produced a handkerchief and dabbed at his face and the front of his shirt. Conversation in the immediate vicinity had stopped, and Fox shared a bemused expression with astonished faces.

"Favor? The next time Ms. Cole orders herself a martini, could someone please ask the bartender if he can't make it really, really, **really** dry?"

Soon afterward, Robin was down on the lawn, taking a moment to look out at the moon-blue water and the several boats that were anchored just offshore, when she became aware of a couple tangled together in a nearby hammock. Just as Robin realized that the couple were doing exactly what it sounded like they were doing, someone tapped her on the shoulder from behind.

"Hello there."

Robin wheeled around. It was Marshall Fox. He offered his hand.

"The name's Fox."

Robin realized she was blushing mightily. She hoped it didn't show in the moonlight. Fox made a show of guiding her hand into his and giving it a small squeeze.

"This is where you tell me **your** name. My name, your name. Then we've had what is called a communication."

Robin withdrew her hand. "I'm . . . My name's Robin Burrell."

"It's good to meet you, Miss Burrell. Though I feel like we're old friends at this point, don't you?"

"I meant to thank you before." She indicated the patio.

"Jeremy? Hell, don't mention it. By tomorrow that gin sponge won't even remember it happened. He won't remember a damn thing about the entire party. Which, now that I think of it, might not actually be such a bad thing. Tell me the truth, hasn't this party been boring the pants off you? I'm dead serious, I can think of three thousand places I'd rather be. I love Gloria and Alan and all that, but this just ain't really my kind of orgy."

"I've never been to one of these parties," Robin stammered.

"Well, you don't want to make a habit of it, trust me."

"People seem to be enjoying themselves."

As if on cue, low moans rose from the couple in the hammock. Fox's eyebrows rose. "I suppose they are. It's a regular bunny farm around here, isn't it? How about you? Are you enjoying yourself?"

Robin felt the color rising again to her cheeks. "I'm not supposed to enjoy myself," she said. "I'm the hired help."

Fox asked, "So where do you hail from, Miss Burrell?"

"I'm from Pennsylvania originally. New Hope. But I've lived in Manhattan the last six years."

"Do tell. What part?"

"Upper West Side."

"Jews and Commies, I know it well. Which are you? Are you a Commie?"

"Me?" She laughed. "No."

"Jew?"

"I'm a Quaker."

"Quaker? Good Lord woman. I love thou people's oatmeal. Upper West Side, huh? Ever since I hit town I've been an Upper East Sider myself, though the fact is I ran away from home a few months ago. Maybe you heard. You probably have. My so-called private life seems to have taken up residence on Page Six these days. Now I guess I'm a Jew **and** a Commie."

"Excuse me?"

"Upper West Side. I'm holing up on Central Park West."

"I'm on Seventy-first," Robin said. "About halfway down from the park."

"You don't say." Fox touched her lightly on the arm. Robin could have sworn she felt a tiny electric shock. "How sweet is this? You're practically the girl next door. You and I should meet up in the park sometime and walk our dogs together."

"I don't have a dog."

Fox made a face. "I thought all of Manhattan's

beautiful women had dogs. We'll have to do something about that. I'll tell you what, New Hope. May I call you New Hope?"

Robin laughed. "If you want."

"I want. Listen, New Hope. Maybe I can come by your place sometime and you can take **me** out for a walk. How does that sound? Forget the dog. Walk the Fox. What do you say?"

"I don't know. I don't think you—"

Fox clapped his hands together. "Good. Excellent. I like this. This is good. You know, I've been hanging out with the wrong sort of people long enough. This will be good. So when are you free?"

"I'm not sure if—"

"Tuesday?" He put a hand to his ear. "Is that what you said? Good Lord, I'm free Tuesday, too! What are the chances? Now, please don't go getting yourself another dog between now and then, dear New Hope. I happen to be well trained, but I do still bite. Sometimes. Maybe you can do something about that for me. We'll have to see."

Up on the patio, one of the guests let out a peal of laughter that sounded exactly like that of the Wicked Witch of the West. Fox glanced over his shoulder then turned back to Robin. His voice lowered, as did his manic energy. He leaned closer. "Whatever you've heard about me, New

Hope, I want you to know that only half of it's true. Swear to God."

In the wee hours of the morning, as Robin bunched her pillow under her chin and opened herself to the oncoming sleep, a voice in the deep recesses of her mind thought to ask the right question.

Which half?

9

THE COFFEE WAS COLD long before it was gone. I poured the final inch onto the snow. A squirrel that had been clinging stock-still to a nearby tree scampered down to investigate. He sniffed at the mocha snow then looked up sharply at me. With attitude. That's your New York squirrel.

A light snow had started to fall. I was halfway across the park when my cell phone rang. I fished it out of my pocket.

"Where are you?" It was Charlie Burke.

"You'll never guess. You caught me on a beach in Tahiti. I wish the girls back home would take up this whole grass-skirt thing. It's a winner."

"You wish. Come on, where are you?" He sounded urgent.

"I'm in Bryant Park."

"Well, you want to get up to Central Park right away. To the Boathouse."

"And why do I want to do this, Charlie?"

"I spoke with Margo earlier today. She told me you've been helping that girl that got killed last night." He paused, and I expected him to say that Margo had also told him we'd had an argument about it, but he didn't go there. "She says you're nosing around in the girl's murder."

"I never said that."

"Right. Margo mentioned that, too. But she can tell. My kid's got good instincts, Fritz. Besides, you don't always hide things too good."

"There are people who might consider that a virtue," I said. "So what's happening at the park?"

"I've been monitoring." Ever since losing the use of his legs, Charlie had transformed the office in his house into what his wife called the House of Wires. Charlie was more up to speed on computers and the Internet than I'd ever be. He also had two television sets; he kept one tuned to NY1 and used the other for channel surfing. Plus, he monitored the police and fire department frequencies religiously. He went on, "Your girl with the cut throat? Looks like she's got company."

I stopped in my tracks. Literally. "There's been another murder?"

"Somebody out there is a very busy boy," he

said dryly. "Not to mention a very angry one. This doesn't look good, Fritz."

"Who says it's related to Robin Burrell?"

"First officer on the scene got a little too excited just now. Called in a thirty-c then started blabbing, 'Same as last night, same as last night.' "

Thirty-c is police code for homicide by cutting. I switched directions and angled toward Sixth Avenue. "You said the Boathouse?"

"That's what I'm hearing."

"And you got this when?"

"It's fresh, buddy. Not two minutes ago. You hurry, you'll beat the mobs."

I pocketed the phone and took off running.

THEY WERE STILL STRETCHING the tape when I arrived. A crime-scene photographer was leaning against a police van, fiddling with his camera. The snow was coming down a bit harder, and he was shading the camera from getting wet. The body was just off the trail leading up from the small parking area of the Boathouse Café into what's called the Ramble. If you want to take a curvy path through the woods of Central Park, or if you want to go see rats the size of small dogs, or if having sex with a fellow anonymous adventurer of the same sex is your bag, then the Ramble is your place. The person who had happened upon the body and phoned it in was a pasty-faced blond man with a walrus mustache, a faded Greek fisherman's cap and leather chaps. I don't know, maybe he was looking at the rats.

Joseph Gallo was conferring with one of his officers. His long camel coat hung on him beautifully. Of course. He and his fellow officers were standing next to a large boulder, the trail twisting out of sight behind it. Atop the boulder, a pair of crows were pecking angrily at the snow. I waited next to a small tree until Gallo looked up and saw me. He said something to the uniformed cop then stepped over to me.

"Let me guess. You were just cutting through the park on your way to the ice rink."

"Those aren't the kind of guesses you can build a career on."

"You seem to be my brand-new shadow, Malone. What gives?"

"Charlie Burke plucked the thirty-c out of the air. He says it smells like Robin's killer."

"Yeah, I was just giving Officer Loudmouth over there a talk about that. I told him next time why don't you just call the media directly." He shot his cuffs to tap a finger against his watch. "I give them five minutes tops."

"You could seal off the park."

"Haven't you ever heard of the precious First

Amendment? What do you take me for, a stinking Commie?"

"Sorry, Joe. Must've confused you with someone else."

Gallo grunted a laugh. "Believe me, after today I'm going to wish I **was** someone else. Goddamn back-to-backs not more than eighteen hours apart. This is most definitely not the way we're supposed to start the New Year."

"And we're talking the same killer?" I asked. "You've already determined that?"

"We haven't determined a thing. I only beat you by five minutes. I haven't even introduced myself to the corpse."

The lieutenant brushed at the snowflakes settling on his shoulder. "If you want to make yourself invisible, feel free. You've got to keep out of the perimeter. I like a clean crime scene."

I pointed at the boulder. "How about that rock?"

"If you feel like mountaineering."

Another cop was using a tree next to the boulder as one of his corners for the crime-scene tape. I ducked under the tape and scrambled up to the top of the boulder. With the leaves gone, I had a nice view of Central Park Lake below me, the row of overturned rowboats running along the south shore, the cast-iron Bow Bridge arching over the lake. The intensity of the snow was already increasing, and in just a matter of minutes, the overturned rowboats had already started fading to white. The lake itself was partially covered with a thin film of ice in a shape reminding me of a piece from a jigsaw puzzle. Directly below was the large flat rock where people like to go sunning in warm weather. It was abandoned now, of course, except for a trio of uninterested mallards.

The body was lying about twenty feet from the base of the boulder. I couldn't see much at first, as a pair of forensics experts and someone in a long black coat were squatting on either side of it. I could see pants legs and a pair of men's brown dress shoes. Through the legs of the forensics cops, I could make out a large area of blood-stained snow and leaves. As Gallo approached the scene, he looked up to where I was standing. "How's the view?"

"It's a man," I said.

Gallo tapped the side of his head. "We could use a natural like you on the force. What else can you see from up there?"

"Nothing. Your men have the better seats."

The figure in the long black coat turned and looked up at me. "Some detective." She rose and gave her lower back a solid stretch. Like the two forensics cops, she was wearing a wool NYPD cap, her short hair tucked in so that none of it would become part of Gallo's crime scene. Her smirk arrived as if on wings.

"Hello, Detective Lamb," I said.

She squinted up at me. "Fritz Malone. Long time no see." Maybe not the strongest Long Island accent I've ever heard, but strong enough to defend itself.

"I guess we've just been haunting different corners of the city."

"Yeah, well. No shortage of corners."

Megan Lamb was a junior detective in Joe Gallo's homicide squad out of the Twentieth. I'd known her for several years. We first met when she invited me to a diner in the Village one afternoon to chew me out for what she considered my interference with an investigation she was involved in. I was guilty as charged, and we'd had a spirited fight over it. Generally speaking, I found her somewhat guarded, but it's not uncommon for women cops to keep their armor at the ready just as a matter of course. Still, I liked her. She had a passion for her job. She'd wade in plenty deep in the interest of the victim. The previous winter Megan had landed herself in the headlines by fatally shooting a serial killer and rapist in the line of duty. The Swede. Both Megan's partner and her closest friend had been slaughtered by the Swede minutes before Megan's arrival on the scene. Though she'd been hailed in the press as a hero and eventually been given the all clear by the department's investigatory panel (standard procedure when a police officer fatally dislodges their weapon), a degree of murkiness had lingered around the circumstances of the shooting, and only a few weeks after her return to active duty, Megan had put in for extended leave. Some weeks after, rumors reached me that Megan was having a rough time of things and that she wasn't exactly conducting herself in the healthiest of fashions, and I'd made a point to cross my path with hers one night, trying to pass it off as a coincidence. She'd sniffed me out and told me exactly what she thought of my "charity mission." Nobody likes a hovering angel. I know I don't. She'd remained off my radar screen until this past May. She was back on active duty, and her next fifteen minutes of fame came for being the cop who had slapped the cuffs on Marshall Fox when he was taken into custody for the murders of Cynthia Blair and Nikki Rossman.

Now Megan went into a pocket of her coat and pulled out a stick of gum, unwrapped it, and popped it into her mouth. She's a fairly small-framed woman; the long coat threatened to swallow her. After methodically folding the wrapper and sticking it back in her pocket, she squinted up at me again. "Don't go falling on my crime scene, Malone, okay? It's deteriorating fast enough as it is. You just make like a statue and stay put up there."

"You're the boss."

Megan indicated Gallo. "He's the boss. I'm just the working stiff."

I could see more of the victim now. A tie. An overcoat. The head was twisted to its left and partially submerged in a clump of red snow and dead leaves. Even from up on the boulder, I could tell the location of the source of the blood.

Megan turned to Gallo. "Fresh as a daisy."

Gallo grunted. "Dead daisy."

One of the forensics specialists spoke up. "She's right. This guy isn't an hour cold."

From my perch, I was able to see one of the local television news vans pulling into the Boathouse Café parking area.

"Your favorite vultures have arrived," I announced to Gallo.

Gallo turned to the cop whose radio call Charlie Burke had picked up and directed him to go head off the press. "Read my lips, Carr. **No comment.** Think you can handle that?"

Megan Lamb had pulled a small notebook from her coat pocket, and she scribbled down a note. "We need to get a tarp up here, Joe. This guy's going to be a snowman in another five minutes." The wind had kicked up and the snow was driving sideways. Megan brushed some of it from her sleeves and stepped gingerly around to where one of the forensics teams was carefully removing a clump of leaves and old snow from the victim's face. She looked like a kid in that large coat. She bent down to take a look. "Jesus Christ."

All I could see from my vantage point was the look on Megan's face when she straightened again. She looked as if she'd taken a brisk slap.

Gallo asked, "What've you got?"

Megan indicated me. "Okay if he hears?"

"Yeah, sure. What is it?"

She puckered her lips. It looked almost like she was giving a smooch to the falling snow. Her breath frosted around her face as she exhaled. "It's the lawyer, that's what it is. The loudmouth."

Gallo stepped closer to the body and bent over for a look. "Son of a bitch. That's exactly who it is."

I edged closer to the edge of the boulder, careful not to tumble off the slippery edge as I got a better look at the uncharacteristically silent, cold body of Zachary Riddick.

~ 10 ~

EXCEPT FOR THE CABBIE who drove Zachary Riddick to Central Park, the lawyer had last been seen alive at 12:20 on the day he was murdered. This was at the news conference, where Riddick had bellyached for a mistrial to be declared and for the immediate release of Marshall Fox from custody. He had been pure Riddick, decrying "the abysmal miscarriage of justice" and working up the sort of lather that Joan of Arc could have only dreamed of from one of her defenders. He also managed to slip in the phrase "my good friend Marshall Fox" or "my personal friend Marshall Fox" fourteen times, according to Jimmy Puck's column in the **Post**. And as Joseph Gallo predicted, Riddick had produced a tape player and played the phone threat that had been recorded on Rosemary Fox's answering machine.

I'm coming, you whore. Can you taste the blood yet?

The police did what they could to track Riddick's whereabouts in the several hours between the end of the news conference and the discovery of his body in Central Park. Rosemary Fox reported speaking with him briefly on the phone some minutes after the conclusion of the news conference. Riddick had told her he would come by her apartment later in the afternoon to discuss where things stood. He did not disclose his plans for the intervening hours. One would presume lunch. But the contents of Riddick's stomach, once his body was turned over to the medical examiner for the up-close-and-personal, showed nothing since the twin stack he had shoveled down at his local diner—where he was a regular—at approximately 7:45 that morning. One of the local stations went ahead and dug up the waitress who had served him, a moon-faced Ukrainian who informed the viewing audience, "He luks fine when he leaves here. You think, He vull be back tomorrow like always. Who can know he vull be kilt like that? I hud no idea."

The police had questioned everyone they could round up in Central Park in the immediate minutes after arriving on the scene. They showed photographs of Riddick. A few people said that they might have seen him, but the information provided no real insights into the murder. Riddick had entered the park from the southeast corner, dropped off by a taxi. The cabbie was tracked down. He had picked Riddick up at Church Street, a few blocks from the courthouse. On the ride uptown, the two shared an animated conversation on the subject of Marshall Fox's guilt or innocence (the cabbie saw the new murder the same way Riddick did, proof that the real killer of Cynthia Blair and Nikki Rossman was still out there); however, Riddick failed to reveal what his purpose was for heading into the park. The cabbie reported a good tip. He last saw his fare heading into the park via the walkway that runs by the zoo at approximately a quarter to one.

Speculation centered on the possibility that Riddick was on his way to meet someone for lunch at the Boathouse Café—he'd been known to eat there on more than one occasion—but no one surfaced claiming to have been stood up by the lawyer for a lunch date.

Essentially, Zachary Riddick took a cab to the park, briskly walked the quarter mile to the area of the Boathouse and saw his life end amid blood and snow and dead leaves on a nub of a hill overlooking Central Park Lake.

The police weren't saying much. I'd had to poke and prod just to pick up what little I knew.

. . .

IT WAS DIFFICULT to go anywhere in Manhattan the next several days without getting caught up in a conversation about Marshall Fox and this new set of murders. In point of fact, it was difficult to get anywhere in Manhattan in general, unless you were going by subway. Eight additional inches of snow had fallen on the city in the space of twenty-four hours, slowing street traffic to a skidding crawl and leaving the curbs lined with large cloudlike mounds. After the snow stopped, the temperature had tumbled to record lows, locking the city in an arctic freeze. An elderly woman in Fort Apache froze to death in her unheated apartment. A visitor from Columbus, Ohio, lost a leg to a skidding taxi. In Sunset Park, two sisters aged six and nine died when snow leaching from the roof into their bedroom ceiling melted and dripped onto their space heater, igniting a fire that gutted the entire second floor of the house. The mayor put out a call for all nonessential businesses to remain closed. Stores were shuttered. School classes were canceled. Trash collection was suspended. In general terms, as much as a city of nine million restless inhabitants can ever truly grind to a halt, that's what happened.

Two nights after Zachary Riddick's murder,

Margo and I attended a talk on Wicca given at the American Museum of Natural History. The museum is only several blocks from Margo's place, but getting there was half the fun. Margo went down on her lovely can as we approached Columbus Avenue but then got the last laugh a minute later as my lunge for a lamppost failed to keep my feet beneath me and I slid to the ground like a cartoon drunk.

Margo had done a recent piece for **The Village Voice** on the woman giving the talk, so she was curious to hear the presentation. The woman was a Wiccan herself, though in civilian life, she ran a small advertising agency out of her apartment in Chelsea. You know what they say, scratch an ad exec, find a Wiccan. It turned out to be a good talk, much more engaging than I had expected, but even so, the buzz in the auditorium during the reception afterward barely included the word "Wicca." The murders of Riddick and Robin Burrell had taken place a mere quarter mile from the museum, and their grip on the crowd was palpable. Even the Wiccan, when Margo introduced us and told her what I did for a living, shrugged off my compliment on her presentation and asked my opinion on Marshall Fox in light of these recent killings. The woman was in her sixties, overweight in a hippie-gone-willingly-to-seed way. She was wearing wire-rimmed glasses and a gold breastplate necklace that shot off reflected light every time she moved. A thick graying braid nearly as stout as one of her arms snaked down her broad back.

"Innocent until proven guilty," I said colorlessly.

"But your opinion. I'll share mine. Mr. Fox is serving as a touchstone, if you will."

"Touchstone."

"I see these as ritual killings. Maybe not so much sacrifices. But more a ritualized and symbolic cleansing. Purifying."

"You'll excuse me, but I fail to see what is purifying about slitting innocent people's throats."

The Wiccan brought her fingers together as if in prayer. Her tiny smile was astonishingly smug. "Innocence is in the eye . . . or, should I say, the heart of the beholder. From the sphere the killer or killers are operating on, these subjects were clearly anything but innocent. In fact, they were probably considered a poison, or represented a poison, and so it was necessary to remove them from the world."

I glanced at Margo again to see how she was taking this. She had slipped on her inscrutable mask. "So where does Marshall Fox fit into all this?"

"He's the touchstone. Or maybe it's more accurate to say the godhead."

"I'm sure he'd be flattered to hear that."

"Mr. Fox held a position of great significance for millions of people. Don't forget your Simon and Garfunkel: 'And the people bowed and prayed to the neon god they made.' The television is our society's alternative altar. A person such as Mr. Fox takes on the symbolic role of the deity."

I said, "And religion makes some people go cuckoo."

She nodded. "There is a history of excess and frenzy, yes."

Excess and frenzy. I liked that. You could slap that headline on the morning paper each day of the year, and you'd never be wrong. I asked, "So you don't think that Fox murdered those two women last year?"

The Wiccan pushed her glasses back up on her nose. "I don't. I believe each killing was performed by a unique participant."

Margo's mask dropped. "You mean a different person for **each** killing? That's four separate murderers."

"That is correct."

"My God. That's crazy."

"From the perspective of our sphere, absolutely. But you recall Charles Manson and the so-called Manson family? This was a group of people completely at peace with their actions. Ritualized killings. Purgings. Cleansings. Symbolic. Iconic. However you wish to term it."

I blurted, "What was so iconic about Robin Burrell? Or any of them?"

"I could hardly say with any certainty. All were intimates of Mr. Fox. We know that much. Perhaps the killer or killers perceived that the victims had betrayed Mr. Fox or were a source of danger to him. Or that they were in some way corrupting him."

"That's a joke."

Margo asked, "Do you really think it's some kind of a cult? Four different killers? The idea makes my skin crawl."

"It's merely a theory, dear."

I said, "I can tell you the police wouldn't be too happy with your theory."

She gave her tiny smile again. "People do not kill in order to make the police happy."

The morning after the Wicca talk, Margo and I had another tussle. It started while I was shaving, though the seeds had been planted ten minutes earlier, right as Margo was stepping into the shower, when I had told her that I was planning to go to Robin Burrell's memorial service that morning. I'd fudged somewhat. I was actually planning to attend Robin's weekly Quaker meeting, not precisely her memorial service. A phone call to one of the Quaker elders in charge of the meeting had informed me that Robin's death would be the unofficial agenda that Sunday morning. Margo had taken the information in deafening silence, pulling the shower curtain closed with a little extra something.

I was running a razor down my cheek when Margo, in her robe and with a twisted towel piled high on her head, passed behind me on her way out of the bathroom.

"Got to look good for your big date?"

She moved into the apartment, tightening the sash on her robe. The bathroom was warm from her shower, but her exit left behind a chill nonetheless. I took a deep breath and squared off with my reflection. "Let it go."

Margo barked from the next room, "I heard that."

I should have counted to ten. Instead I barked back, "If you did, then you were eavesdropping. I wasn't talking to you."

The face in the mirror shook its head sadly. Not good. Margo gave a response that I didn't hear. But I caught its drift. She went on to the kitchen. I quickly finished up the shaving, rinsed off my face and followed her. She was running water into the kettle, staring a hole deep into the sink.

"This isn't like you," I said. "What's wrong?"

She cranked off the water. "Let me check. You **are** talking to me this time?"

I made certain of an even tone. "I'm talking to you."

"Nice." She set the kettle on the stove and kicked up the flame. It's one of those stoves that makes a **click-click-click** when you're activating the pilot light. Maybe it was just me, but I thought she let it click a few seconds longer than necessary. "This isn't like you, either," she said.

"What isn't? Attending funerals and memorial services for the victim is straight out of the handbook. You know that. If you don't believe me, ask your old man."

"I'm aware of that." She turned to face me. "But a victim is not necessarily a client. Do they say anything about that in the handbook? Or is your pretty little client writing you checks from beyond the grave?"

I didn't say anything. Margo knows a cheap shot when she hears one. She pulled the towel from her head and coiled it tightly in her arms. **She** might have been counting to ten.

"Okay, let's back up a second," she said. "I know you feel bad about what happened to that woman. Of course you do. So do I. For Christ's sake, so does anyone in America who is paying attention, which, as best I can tell, seems to be pretty much the whole damn country. But I'm sorry, Fritz, whether you spoke with her a few times or not, it's none of your **business.** I'm sure you have this fantasy that you could have protected the beautiful maiden across the street, but that's not how it played out. Some crazy psychopath got in there and slit her throat. But we have a police force in this city, as I'm sure you've noticed. **They're** looking into it. That's their job. Robin Burrell is their client. She's their responsibility."

She unwrapped her arms and set the towel down on the counter. One of the edges was too near the stove flame, but I didn't say anything.

"What is it exactly that you don't like about this?" I asked. "It's not as if this is the first time I've taken up a case on my own. You know that."

"I do know that. Daddy used to do it, too, and it drove Mom nuts."

"I'm not your daddy. And you're not—"

I stopped myself. One of our relationship's more tender spots was Margo's fear that in being with me, she was on track to replicate her mother's life. On its face, the concern was absurd. But it was an argument we had agreed not to enter into. Many times.

I went on, "You know what I'm saying. There's someone running around this city slicing people's throats. And too damn close to home to suit my tastes. I know the police are investigating. They're doing their thing. And Joe Gallo's a good cop. He'll probably nail the guy. But another set of eyes never hurt. For Christ's sake, Margo, this is what I do. What do you want, for me to take up bridge?"

The kettle began to whimper. Margo shut off the flame and picked it up. "I don't like being jealous," she said flatly. "It's one of the most pathetic emotions."

"There's nothing to be jealous of. What do you—"

The kettle went down with a rattle. Her eyes were hard black pebbles. "You were **quiet** about her! You didn't tell me that you went over there more than once. You tried to hide that from me."

"That's not true."

"Oh, bullshit, Fritz. It is true, and you know it. You never really said to me what it was you two talked about."

"Not true. She showed me her letters and the e-mails she'd gotten. I told you that."

"That takes **two** visits? You brought that stuff up here after the first time you saw her."

"Perhaps you can remind me of the last time you came home from one of your interviews and recited everything back to me word for word."

"This is different."

"Why is it different?"

"Because she lived right across the street. Because she was a beautiful woman."

"This city is lousy with beautiful women. Present company very much included."

Margo fingered the ends of her wet hair. "Right. My name is Medusa, it's nice to meet you." She fetched her favorite teacup from the drying rack and set it on the counter. "Listen, Fritz, I'm not going to let you charm your way free of this. I've already said I'm jealous, and that's embarrassing enough. We both know I'm not normally the jealous type. So I'm asking myself, what is it? Maybe it's just that she was on TV all those weeks and she was all that people were talking about. The woman had an affair with **Marshall Fox,** for Christ's sake. A very vivid affair, I might add. Thanks to that stupid trial, I practically know more about that woman's sex life than I know about my own."

"I'm here to remind you whenever—"

"Shut up. All I'm saying is that every horny hound in America must've had that woman in their dreams, and the next thing I know, you're dropping by to lend her a shoulder to cry on and being just a bit too blasé about it."

"What was I supposed to do, run up here and—"

"Let me finish." She very nearly stomped her

foot. It had been a long time since I'd seen her this upset. She took a sharp breath. "I watched you sitting at that window the other night. What can I tell you, Fritz, girls don't like that. I can't know what you're feeling when you go to that place. You go very far away. No Margos allowed. Nobody allowed, as best I can tell. I hate it. And now it's Sunday morning, and you're going off to the dead girl's funeral or whatever you want to call it. And I know you. You're going to get into her head. That's how you do what you do. I know you. You're going to get into her head and you're going to get into her life and you're going to get into her ugly, stupid death. And I just wish this one time that you wouldn't."

She snatched up the kettle again and began pouring water into her cup.

"You forgot the teabag," I said gently.

With lightning speed, she rattled the kettle to the stove, snatched up the teacup, and smashed it against the side of the sink. She was left holding the broken cup handle, attached to nothing. She threw that into the sink as well.

"You should just go. Really. Go. This is all now officially very stupid. Just go to your stupid funeral. Do whatever it is you need to do. Just do me a fucking favor, will you, and don't come home dead."

~ 11 ~

THE FRIENDS MEETING that Robin had attended was at the old Quaker meetinghouse on the edge of Stuyvesant Park, off East Fifteenth Street. Technically, the park wasn't named for Peter Stuyvesant, early Manhattan's first director general, but for his wife, Judith. It would have rankled old Pete to see anything other than a Dutch Reformed church built on land that was originally part of the Stuyvesant homestead, but the Quakers had wisely waited until 189 years after the Dutchman's death before building their house of worship, so they were spared the pugnacious peg leg's fabled wrath.

The meeting room was a large rectangle capable of holding several hundred people. It was arranged with rows of pews facing the center of the room. A photograph of Robin Burrell was taped in the middle of one of the front pews. The photograph was black and white, a solemn posed shot dominated by Robin's dark eyes. Painful to look at, difficult to turn away from. I took a seat in the pew opposite. As others came into the meetinghouse and took their seats, they folded their hands on their laps and closed their eyes for several minutes. At some point I attempted to follow suit—when in Rome—but an afterimage of Robin's face from the photograph sizzled in the darkness, and I opened my eyes.

Quaker meetings are as much about silence as they are about talk. Maybe more about silence. At no signal that I could discern, the gentle shuffling and settling in were dispensed with and a stillness settled over the room. The meeting had commenced. There were close to a hundred people attending. Some remained with their eyes closed, but just as many sat with eyes open, gazing down at the floor or off into the middle distance.

After maybe ten minutes of the silence, a man rose to his feet. I placed him in his mid-thirties, with tortoiseshell glasses, a clipped brown mustache and a plaid sweater vest. His hands were clasped in front of him, and he rotated his head slowly as he spoke, taking in the room. The voice was soothing, smooth as butter.

"I'm struck by the affection for Robin that I

am feeling here this morning. The enormous . . . affection." Here he paused to make eye contact. Slowly. Methodically. Person by person. He continued, "I'm struck with the thought that under different circumstances, if another of us had passed on, Robin would have been here this morning, participating. Robin's affection, her sense of concern, her caring, they would all be here in the air, just as our thoughts and concerns for her are now passing among us. I'm struck by that thought. What I'm struck by is not so much Robin's absence but her presence. It's in this way that I feel Robin is still very much with us. We think of her, as we are all doing this morning, and she is alive to us. The affection and the concern that Robin showed for all of us while she was still among us—that's what I still feel. That Robin hasn't died. And I suppose I'm hoping that in some way, maybe in this way, through us, Robin can continue to live on."

He scanned the room again then sat back down and bowed his head. Seated next to him was a young Asian American woman with tears flowing freely down her cheeks. A minute later, a large, fleshy, red-haired woman got to her feet and cleared her throat. "Robin used to always ask me how Pepper was doing. Some of you know Pepper got hit by a taxi in August. You can still tell when I take him out for his walks. His hips aren't right anymore. He walks funny. It was the best they could do at the hospital. I mean the animal hospital. Anyway, um, Robin, she always asked about him. It was real . . . It was nice of her."

She began to blush, and she sat back down. Only a few seconds passed before another person stood up and muttered a few sentences about God knowing more than we do. Others followed. Most of the messages were brief. A thought. An aphorism. A prayer. One middle-aged man stood up and started to tell a story about him and Robin rushing around the neighborhood getting donuts before one of the meetings. There didn't seem any real point to the story, and midway through it, the man's voice cracked and he sat back down.

A long silence followed, and I found myself— as I'm sure others were doing—staring once more at the photograph taped onto the pew. I didn't want it to happen, but as I sat looking at the picture, the crime-scene photographs I'd seen in Joe Gallo's office—the cruel, garish, mindless damage—shimmered into focus in my head, interfering with the simple solemn face in front of me. Sometimes I hate my job.

At the conclusion of the meeting, a coffee-

and-pastries reception was held in a small gym-
nasium in the adjoining building. The red-haired
woman who had spoken about her dog was
standing behind one of the folding tables, feeding pastries onto several plastic trays. As I took
one of the Styrofoam cups of coffee, she gave me
a sugary smile.

"Hello. I don't know you. Are you new to
meeting?"

"I'm . . . Yes. This is my first time."

"First time at all or first time here?"

"First time at all."

She asked, "Were you a friend of Robin's? We
expected some of her friends might show up this
morning."

"I knew her, yes," I said.

She shook her head sadly. "Isn't it awful? I just
can't believe she's gone."

An elderly couple angled in for some pastries,
and I moved over to give them room.

"What about you?" I asked. "Did you know
Robin well?"

"Me? Not really. I mean, not outside of meeting or anything. There was one time Robin and I
did end up at the same brunch afterward. But,
you know. By coincidence."

I indicated the people milling about. "What
about some of the other people? She must have
had some close friends here?"

The woman smiled again. "We're all close Friends."

I got her meaning. "Right. Of course. I don't mean strictly in the Quaker sense."

Other people were coming in for the sweets and coffee. I was still blocking access, so I slipped around behind the table. The red-haired woman handed me a box of pastries. "You just volunteered. I'm Martha, by the way."

"Fritz."

I laid out the pastries on one of the plastic trays just as a large lumpish man came by. He moved like a lava flow, nabbing three pastries at once and continuing on without a word. "Lots of people here were very fond of Robin," Martha continued. "I guess you could tell that. The community really rallied around her when all that horrible trial stuff began happening. Except we didn't see a lot of Robin during most of that. She wasn't going out much, it was too big a hassle for her. The way she was being hounded. But we'd get word how she was doing from Edward."

"Edward?"

"He's the elder who spoke about Robin in meeting."

"The guy with the mustache?"

"Yes."

I scanned the crowd and found the man in question standing in conversation with the Asian

American woman who'd been crying off and on during the meeting. Another man was standing just behind them, leaning against the wall with his thumbs hooked into the belt loops of his faded jeans, as if hoping to be mistaken for James Dean. He was about my height and build, with longish stringy blond hair, a narrow nose and a noticeably small mouth. There was a slightly rodentlike quality to his face, and he appeared to be following the conversation closely, though I couldn't tell if he was part of it or merely eavesdropping. The man named Edward was impassioned, punctuating his words by slapping the back of one hand down into the other, over and over.

"You say he's an elder?" I asked Martha. "Obviously you're not talking about his age. Does that mean he's a muckety-muck in the Quaker hierarchy?"

She laughed. "I guess you could put it that way. Edward is one of our leaders. We call them elders."

"And you're saying that he stayed in touch with Robin while she was going through her difficulties?"

"We're a community. We're a family. That's part of the role of the elders, to be available to members of the family who are in distress."

"Does Edward have a last name?"

"Well, of course he does. It's Anger." I gave her a look. "No, I'm serious. That's his name."

"Ed **Anger**?"

"Edward Anger. You say it enough times, it sounds completely normal."

I looked over again at Edward Anger. He'd taken the young woman's hands between his. "Who's the woman?"

"Oh, that's Michelle," Martha said. "Michelle Poole. She's a friend of Robin's."

Edward Anger released the woman's hands and steered himself into the crowd. I turned to Martha. "Permission to unvolunteer."

She gave me a peculiar look, then laughed. "Oh. Sure. Thank you for helping. It was nice meeting you, Fritz."

"Same." I swung around from behind the table and made my way across the room. The rat-faced James Dean was on his way to the food table. Our shoulders bumped by accident, but only one of us murmured, "Sorry." Not him.

I stepped over to Robin's friend. "Michelle?"

"Yes?"

"Hi. My name is Fritz," I said. "I understand you were a friend of Robin's."

Her face could have been a piece of porcelain. Not a blemish to be found. Her jet-black hair was cut in one of those forever-mussed styles—in Michelle's case, an "I might look like I just rolled out of bed but don't I look great" look. Her eyes were quite large, particularly for a person of Asian extraction, her mouth was small, her cheeks liable to cause riots among women of weaker bones. She was wearing a stylishly ripped T-shirt, one side way down off the shoulder, over a black leotard and a pair of faded blue jeans that might as well have been wrapped around two pipes as a pair of human legs.

She eyed me with caution. "Yes."

"I was wondering if we could talk."

The caution melded into clear suspicion. "About Robin?"

"I'm a private investigator. I'm looking into what happened to Robin. It would be wonderful if—"

She interrupted me. "I know who you are."

"You do?"

"You're the detective. You live across the street from Robin's."

"I don't actually live there."

"But it's you. Robin talked about you a lot. She said you were a real calming influence. That's a quote."

I asked, "Could we sit somewhere?"

"Sure."

I followed her over to a bench near the door, and we took a seat. She crossed one pipe over the other and shifted around to face me.

"Yeah. She liked you. I mean, this whole past year it's like everyone was always trying to get a piece of her. First that asshole Fox, then all the magazine and TV people. Those creeps who were calling her up and writing to her. Who could blame her for getting all paranoid about people? All Robin wanted to do was crawl into her bed and put her head under the pillow. She said you seemed different. Like you really cared. It's really cool to get the chance to meet you. But, I mean, well, not under the circumstances."

"I'm sorry about what happened."

"It still creeps me out. I mean, I still can't believe it. You couldn't meet anyone sweeter than Robin, I swear. Her hooking up with Fox in the first place was the craziest thing, I'm telling you. It was like some kind of weird fantasy. When he got arrested for killing those two women, Robin literally threw up. Literally. She'd slept with this guy for something like three months. I mean, I'm not pretending she was some kind of saint or anything. I'm not saying that. She had her thing."

"Her thing?"

"Sex. Robin had a healthy sex life. Normally healthy. Not a freaky sex life, like they tried to say during the trial. She was a healthy American girl living in New York City in the twenty-first century, hello? You don't go out and slaughter a person just because she wasn't a virgin."

"Is that your theory? That someone killed Robin because they were disgusted with what they considered an immoral lifestyle?"

"God, I don't know. I'm just thinking out loud. Who can get into the mind of a freak? She was a good person. She was a good Quaker. It's Robin who got me into the whole Quaker thing. She brought me along one day, and I really enjoyed it. You don't have to sign up or anything like that. That's part of what's so cool about it. They accept you however you are."

I spotted Edward Anger over by the sweets table. "What about him?" I said.

She followed my gaze. "Edward? What about him?"

"I understand he kept in touch with Robin while she was holing up."

"Sure. He called her now and then. I think he went over to see her a few times. Checked up on her."

"Any Quaker queasiness on his part about Robin being caught up in this whole Fox thing?"

Michelle laughed. "Oh, you mean like a scandal? No way. I just told you, the Quakers are very cool people. They've got that whole thee and thou rap, but come on, have you ever been to a Catholic church? I'll take thee and thou over smite and hellfire any day."

"Mr. Anger was quite eloquent," I said.

"Oh, sure. Edward can't say 'good morning' without turning it into a beautiful speech. That's just the way he is."

I let it drop. "Did Robin ever talk to you about Zachary Riddick? I remember seeing some of her testimony. Riddick did a real sleaze number on her."

Michelle rolled her eyes. "No kidding. I was right there in the courtroom when he started up with that crap. Robin asked if I could be there for moral support on the days she was testifying. Were you watching the day he actually hit on her right there on the stand? Unbelievable. This is a defense attorney? The man is cross-examining the witness and he's practically reaching a hand up her dress. I don't mean literally. But really, he might as well have been. Robin told me afterward that was exactly how she felt up there. It was disgusting. Explain to me what is the relevance of a witness's personal life, anyway. That whole thing was so disgusting, what they did to her. Fox is the one who seduced **her,** not vice versa. He's the one with the reputation. But Riddick was trying to make Robin out as the aggressor. Like she was some sort of slut. Which couldn't be farther from the truth."

"I know he was," I said. "He was wrapping his whole defense around the fact that Fox and his wife got back together once he'd managed to free himself of all these wanton women who'd been taking pieces of him just because he was a celebrity down in the dumps. Riddick was just trying to find the angle to make the guy look wholesome."

Michelle exploded. "He murdered **two women!** What the hell kind of wholesome is that?"

Heads turned our way. Tears had leaped to Michelle's eyes, and she wiped at them angrily with the back of her hand. "I'm sorry, but he was a real freakazoid. I mean, Riddick. Fox, too. But Riddick. Do you want to know what he did?" She dabbed at her eyes with the back of her wrist. "When he was getting ready to put Robin on the stand, he called me into his office. I don't know why I went. It was a stupid thing to do. But I don't know how these things work. I thought, Anything I can do to help Robin. I got there, and he tried to get me to give him dirt on her. On Robin. I couldn't believe it. But here's the thing. He'd actually investigated **me.** He started telling me about stuff **I'd** done, he had a list with some of the men I'd dated, stuff like that. Like **I** was relevant to any of this? There was this one guy I'd gone out with just a couple of times, but there really weren't any sparks. Riddick had dug this up. We hooked up with Robin one night, and there was actually some chemistry between them. Things were already fizzling with us, and he called up Robin and asked her out. Robin checked with me first. There's no way she would have gone out with him if it had bothered me, but I could've cared less. I told her to go for it. They dated a bit. I think they slept together a few times. And it ended. Nothing to it. Life in the city."

"But Riddick was trying to pump it up?"

"You bet. He kept trying to get me to say that I was secretly pissed off at her, that she was sexually aggressive and was a man-eater and all this crap. I told him to go to hell."

"It's an old ploy," I said. "Lawyers try that move all the time."

"Well, here's the thing. While I was in his office? He came on to **me.** Big-time. It was just like he did with Robin when she was on the stand. The guy's digging into my sexual history, and I don't know, I guess it gets him all turned on. For some reason, he thinks he's God's gift to women. But I can tell you, he was no gift to me. I probably should have contacted some lawyers' association or something. That couldn't have been ethical, what he was pulling. You know what his basic move was? He started telling me what I looked like. I mean, like, describing me in detail. To me. As if I don't know what I look like? Maybe he thought he was coming off as complimentary and sexy, but no way. I couldn't wait to get out of that place. Then two days later, I was at a café near where I live. A place I always go. And there he was, just sitting there. Like he was waiting for me. With this big smile on his face."

"Are you saying he was stalking you?"

"I don't know. But it happened another time, too. I saw him on the subway platform. I mean, I guess it could have been a coincidence. But it was so soon after seeing him in the café. And there was that smug look on his face again. He started to come down the platform, but the subway pulled in right then, and I got on it. I hopped off at the next stop and waited for the next train."

"Did you tell anyone about this?"

"About Riddick stalking me? Not really. I mean, I told a few friends. But I made a point not to mention it to Robin. Things were tough enough for her already. Still, it spooked me. I've been looking over my shoulder ever since."

"I guess there's no need for that now."

"You mean with Riddick being dead? Yeah, well, you'd think so. But can I tell you something?" Her eyes traveled around the room again before returning to me. Her voice lowered, and she scooted closer to me. A scent of vanilla scooted over with her.

"Even though he's dead and everything? I've still been having this really creepy feeling that someone is still watching me. Or, you know. Following me. I'm probably nuts, but I really feel it. It's like . . . I don't know. It's like somebody's eyes are literally on my skin. I can't describe it, but it's kind of freaking me out."

"Have you actually seen anybody?"

"**Seen** seen? No. But someone's there. I just know it. Right after I heard about Riddick being found dead in the park, I was heading back to my apartment, and I could have sworn there was someone following me. And it's happened once or twice since. I don't like it. First Robin's killed, and then Riddick. And the phone message that was on Robin's machine? I don't know what to say. This town is beginning to freak me out. I'm getting really scared."

I gave her my card. "If it happens again, call me. Chances are you're just being paranoid, which is perfectly understandable. But call me anyway. Just get yourself somewhere very public and call."

Michelle shuddered. Tears had come again to her eyes, but they didn't fall. "I just can't believe what happened to Robin. I mean, one day she's alive and then . . . I can't even begin to think how scary that must have been for her. Jesus. What kind of monster would do something like that?"

I tapped the card. "You'll call me."

"Oh yeah." Her moist eyes blinked at the card. "You'd better believe it. I'll cry bloody murder. Top of my lungs."

I prayed it wouldn't come to that.

~ 12 ~

TWO BLOCKS WEST of the Quaker meeting-house, I ran into Megan Lamb. She was behind the wheel of a departmental Crown Vic, which was angled against the curb. A man was behind the car, leaning his full weight against it, while Megan called out to him through the open driver's-side door.

"Get to the middle! The grid's going to take out your leg!" She glanced up as I approached, showing no sign of surprise. "Malone. Do you want to make yourself useful?"

I continued past her and positioned myself next to the guy who was leaning against the trunk. Young guy. Fresh-faced. "Watch out for the grid," he muttered. "It'll take out your leg."

The Vic had fudged the turn onto Fifteenth

Street, and the left rear tire had found an icy groove of snow. No traction. A thin rectangular metal mesh grid had been wedged under the tire. The two of us leaned against the trunk.

The guy grimaced. "She's going to race it."

He was right. Megan laid on the accelerator as if kicking out of the gate at Daytona. The tire let out a giddy squeal as it spun in place. The rear of the car trembled but otherwise didn't budge. Megan's voice sounded above the squeal.

"Push!"

The guy and I shared a look. "You tell her," he said. "I'm less than zero."

I stepped over to the open door as Megan let off the gas. "All you're doing is polishing the ice," I told her. "We've got to get you rocking forward and back. On the forward, just tap it."

She gave a noise that seemed to be an assent, and I returned to the rear of the car. We managed to get it rocking slightly, and after a few back-and-forths, Megan began tapping the gas. Third time was a charm. The fresh-faced guy and I leaned hard in to the car. The acid burn went through my arms, and the car swerved slightly to the right then stuttered back onto the street. A blur sailed past my knee. The metal grid. It impaled itself in a snowdrift.

As Megan eased the car over and double-parked, the fresh-faced guy turned to me. "Ryan Pope. You're Fritz Malone."

Nice of him to handle both sides of the introduction. I asked, "You're Megan's partner?"

"That's right."

"Maybe she should be letting you drive."

"Do you know what the sane man said to the control freak?"

"What?"

"Nothing."

Megan got out of the car. Her hands were bright pink and she cupped them, blowing into them. "He telling you about the flat?"

"You had a flat, too?"

"Uptown. On Lexington," Pope said. He indicated the knees of his pants, which I now saw were soaked and soiled.

"And then you got down here and skidded into the curb."

"I guess there's no point in my buying a lotto ticket today," Megan said.

"I don't know. I came along. Maybe your luck has changed."

"Are you coming from the Quaker place?"

"I am."

"I guess it's all over?"

"Yes."

Megan frowned. "Then my luck hasn't

changed." She looked up into the blank sky for a few seconds, then back at me. Her cheeks were two fierce pink spots. "Joe warned me you'd probably be poking around on the Burrell murder."

"Keen instincts your boss has got."

"I don't suppose there's any point in my even going over there."

"To the meetinghouse? There are probably still some people hanging around. They do the coffee-and-pastries thing afterward."

Megan addressed her partner. "Ryan, why don't you get over there and see who's left to talk to. If you find any live ones, hold on to them. I'll be right there. I want to debrief Mr. Malone here first. I have the sense that he got all the goodies."

Pope nodded wordlessly and started off down the street.

I turned to Megan. "Newbie?"

"Pope? Not any longer. He's growing up fast. Joe paired me with him when I came back in April. The kid didn't exactly have the clout to say no."

"Why would he want to say no? Not because you're a woman?"

"Please. The woman thing was the least of it. You know perfectly well why."

"Madden."

She nodded. "Cops get spooked about cops who lose their partners. It was easier for Joe to assign me a greenie."

She was referring to Detective Christopher Madden, Megan's partner the night she unloaded her entire service weapon into Albert Stenborg, the Swede. Having just nailed the identity of the monster who had been brutalizing young women in the city for over two months, Megan had radioed Madden from Chinatown that she was headed to Stenborg's houseboat in Sheepshead Bay and to meet her there. She'd arrived to find her closest friend mutilated and dead at Stenborg's feet, and after taking the monster out, she'd also discovered Chris Madden's body on the galley floor, surrounded by a pool of blood. His heart had been carved out of his chest and stuffed into his mouth.

"Let's go someplace," Megan said. "I'm not built for this cold."

We found a Joe Jr. on Third Avenue and took a booth by the window. Megan pulled out her cell phone and punched in a number. "Who am I looking for? At this Quaker place."

I was shrugging out of my coat. "You're not going to believe me."

"Try me."

"Edward Anger."

She cocked an eyebrow at me then spoke into the phone. "Ry? Megan. See if someone named Edward Anger is still there. If you find him, call me." She disconnected the call.

The waitress came by, and we ordered a pair of coffees. Megan asked, "What gives? Did you speak with this Anger guy?"

"No, but you'll want to. He's big cheese at the meetinghouse. They call them elders. It seems he was checking on Robin's mental health from time to time."

"Interesting. In person?"

"I believe so. I got this from a friend of Robin's. Michelle Poole." Megan was jotting the names down in her notebook. "Edward Anger gave a nice speech about how Robin's spirit was still with us."

"Lovely. It's what happened to her body that's my concern."

"I assume you saw it," I said. "I mean the body."

"Oh, I saw it all right. What kind of sick bastard does that thing with the mirror glass? Do you know about that? He shoved a piece of her bathroom mirror right here." She placed her fingers on the upper part of her throat. "Like he wanted her to watch herself die. Real cute."

"I saw the photos."

"Try it in living color."

"No, thanks."

She flipped her notebook closed. "All I keep thinking about is her up on the stand testifying. You could see she knew she'd made a mistake, ever mixing herself up with Fox. She regretted the whole thing. Do you remember what she said? When she broke down on the stand?"

"I missed that part."

" 'I just want my life back.' That's what she said. 'I just want my life back.' I don't know where you happen to stand on the great hereafter, but if there is one out there, what do you think that poor girl is cooing now? Same thing. 'I just want my fucking life back.' "

Our coffees arrived. Megan ignored hers. Her gaze went out the window to where a snowball battle was taking place on the sidewalk. One of the snowballs hit the glass just below Megan's face. She showed no reaction.

She turned from the window. "Joe says you knew her? Robin Burrell."

"Not really. I talked with her a few times."

"A few times. I guess she made an impression. I've got to figure there are better places you could spend your Sunday mornings than a Quaker meeting."

I felt as if I was slipping into a version of the conversation I'd had with Margo. The difference was, Megan Lamb sounded genuinely interested. She placed her elbows on the table and rested her chin in her hands. "What gives?"

I shrugged. "Sometimes things get under your skin. You must know about that. Robin Burrell was ninety-nine percent a total stranger to me. A few short meetings, nothing more. But it doesn't matter. I don't like that someone thinks they can burst in on someone else's life and take it away like that. It pisses me off."

"You take it personally."

"I don't take it personally. Don't try to put that on me. It's one of the things I do. I root out the creeps who do this kind of thing to people. I get a better night's sleep when I can drag them through your door and hand them over to you. If I'd been the priest my mother wanted me to be, I'd have a different take on it."

"Good night's sleep. I think I read about that once." Megan released her chin and poured some milk in her coffee, stirring it slowly with her spoon, in miniature figure eights. "I've got a brother. Josh. A couple of years younger than me. Do you know what he makes me do? My little brother? Whenever I catch a body, Josh makes me describe the victims to him. He sits me down and draws out the details."

"Is our Josh a moribund little fellow?"

Something flashed in her eyes. Just as quickly, it vanished. It looked like anger. She set down the spoon. "Not at all. Just the opposite, in fact. I'd be dead without Josh."

"What's with the curiosity?"

"It's not curiosity. It's for my own good. He

doesn't want it festering inside me. I'm sure it sounds silly, but Josh is a very intuitive person. It's ugly. A murdered person is ugly. You've seen it, you know what I'm talking about. It's ugly. I'm trained to overlook the ugliness and get on with my job. Josh thinks what I do is poison. His making me describe it to him in detail is sort of a detox, for lack of a better word. He thinks it helps me to get it out of my system."

"Does it?"

"I don't know."

"Do you feel better after you've done it?"

"Better?" She weighed the empty space above her hands. "It's nice that there's someone who cares. I'd feel a lot worse without that."

She looked out the window again. It wasn't difficult to see that something troubling was rolling around in her head. When she turned back to me, her energy had shifted.

"You're a cowboy on this case, Fritz. You're just galloping in for reasons of your own. Whatever they are, that's your business. I don't really care. What I want is to catch the person who killed Robin and Zachary Riddick. And it's not a pride thing with me. I don't give a damn how I catch him. I'm not going to waste my breath telling you to steer clear. You know the drill. We've had this conversation before. You know the difference between inquiries and interference.

Don't interfere. That's the message. The end. Pope and I are the leads on these killings, and don't think Joe Gallo's not right on my back. We can't let this get out of hand. The city doesn't need a mad slasher running around, turning our beautiful new snow red. Thank you for Mr. Anger. I'll follow up. I'll talk to the Poole woman, too. If it hadn't been for my damn flat tire, I'd be reading you the riot act for interfering, but like I said, all I want is to nail this bastard. Whatever it takes. I really don't like sitting in a chair describing dead people to my baby brother. It makes me feel like a cripple."

"A cripple."

"Yeah. I don't like it."

"Have you described Robin to him yet?"

"No, I haven't."

"So then the ugliness is still in your system."

She didn't respond. She didn't have to.

~ 13 ~

I GRABBED A CAB uptown. My phone had vibrated while I was talking to Megan, but I hadn't answered it. It was Margo. She'd left a message.

"Do you remember that time you came with me when I was meeting a bunch of other writers for drinks? We talked shop and about pitching ideas for articles and who's the biggest **ass** on the **ass**-ignment desks? Do you remember what you said to me later? How you couldn't find a way in? That it just wasn't a language you spoke? Maybe . . . maybe you want to think about that when it comes to us sometimes. I'm sorry, Fritz. We've gone over this before. I don't know these murdered people of yours, and I don't want to. They're dead. But you go and slip into their lives and get this whole thing going that I just can't relate to. And I don't want to relate to. It's not a language I speak, you know? I . . . I don't know exactly what I'm saying. Nothing. I'm saying nothing. Forget it. I hate leaving messages. Look . . . I'm having dinner with some friends tonight in the Village. How about you stay at your place tonight? Make it easier. I know you'll be bereft without me, but you can handle it, tough guy like you. We can talk about all this when . . . God. Never mind. This is nuts. Margo Motormouth, signing off."

I pocketed the phone and stared down the cabdriver, who was eyeing me in the rearview mirror. Tough guy like me. This wasn't a new dance, this thing with Margo, though it had been a nice long stretch since the last time we'd gotten out of synch like this. I try not to be knee-jerk defensive, so I didn't put the blame on her. Not all of it, anyway. The problem with what I do for a living is that it doesn't stay at the office. Hell, I **am** the office. It's mobile work, but as much of it gets done with the head as with the feet. Margo was right—I **do** slip into the lives of dead people. Usually, they're already cold when I meet them, but sometimes not. Sometimes they're like Robin Burrell, and I get a taste of the live item before he or she meets the abrupt fate. Margo wasn't like Megan Lamb's brother, Josh. That's what she was reminding me in her phone message. Three's a crowd, and when the third one is, to put a blunt point on it, fresh kill, Margo wants no part of it. Or, to be fair, a limited part. She'd been disingenuous during our argument earlier. She does get jealous. My focus turns to other people when I'm working. Sometimes too much of my focus. Tough guy like me. I hate the sight of broken bodies. It disgusts and disturbs me every bit as much as it drives me to seek out who the hell is responsible. I don't blame Margo for not wanting to hear about it. I don't want to share. "You just suck it up," Charlie used to tell me. "A butcher'll wash his hands before he heads home. You do the same. If you can't do it, think about maybe not going home for a while."

The cab dropped me off at the Church of the Sacred Heart just as the second service was letting out. Shirley Malone was standing at the door at the top of the steps, testing the staying power of Father Manekin's ear. As the priest spotted me coming up the steps, I could have sworn he breathed a silent prayer.

"Fritz. How good to see you."

"Father."

"I'm afraid you're too late. I've already issued the congregation its marching orders for the week."

"Shame. What was your topic?"

My mother answered for him. "Equanimity. That means you're no more important than anybody else." She gave me her version of the evil eye, something to which I long ago developed a Kevlar-like resistance. Father Manekin saw his opportunity to make a break for it.

"Don't remain a stranger, Fritz." He gave my mother's hand a squeeze. "I'll remember what you said, Shirley."

"What did you say?" I asked after the priest had slid off to another of his flock. Shirley presented me with her elbow so that I could walk her down the steps in regal fashion.

"That's between Theo, myself and the Lord."

I felt blessed for the exclusion.

We picked up an armful of lilies at a shop on Ninth then made our way to the subway and caught the number 7 to Queens. It's been said that my mother looks like Maria Callas by way of Audrey Hepburn, which might also stand for a description of the quicksilver blend of her personality, though what is generally meant is that she is a skinny thing with a swan's neck, a strong flirtatious face, and a jet-black hairdo. She's hovering near sixty, but if you mention that to her, you might get a black eye from her tough little fist. Stuff a force of nature into a size-four dress and there you have her. Shirley grew up in Hell's Kitchen—as did I—and remains there still with only her memories of the place as it once was, before developers and gentrification-level rents steamrolled not only the color out of the area but the very name itself. It's now tagged Clinton, which is a designation that'll put you to sleep before you've even finished saying it. Shirley is a bona fide ghost of the old neighborhood. Far fewer haunts, but those that remain she clings to with her notorious tenacity.

We got off at Fortieth Street in Sunnyside and walked the several blocks to Calvary Cemetery. Shirley crossed herself before entering, shooting me a look.

The recent snowfall had left the cemetery with a smooth white covering, broken by the thousands of chalky stones poking out of the ground like uneven teeth. We walked several hundred feet along the road before making our way over the snow to the simple stone that read: PATRICK MALONE. Shirley let out a gasp. "There it is."

"It" was not the stone itself. She was referring to the small bouquet of daisies sitting atop the stone. I started forward, but Shirley put her hand on my chest. "Don't walk." She scoured the site. "Damn it all. There should be footprints."

She was right. Assuming that the flowers had been left off earlier in the day—which was the anniversary of my uncle Patrick's remains being identified, and the date agreed upon for the official registration of his death—there should have been footprints in the fresh snow. But there were none.

"He's too clever," Shirley hissed. "He knew the forecast and he got here early, damn his eyes." She stepped forward and planted her lilies in the snow. Then she plucked the daisies from the tombstone, crossed herself and buried her face in the flowers.

A year before I was born, an undercover cop in the NYPD's Organized Crime Task Force working to infiltrate the gangs in Hell's Kitchen lost one of his informants, nineteen-year-old Patrick Malone. My mother's twin brother. The undercover cop had worked diligently for months to flip Patrick, recognizing in the young tough a muted streak of humanity and tending it diligently, the way a good gardener tends his plants. What the cop failed to tend with equal care were safeguards to protect Patrick from his ruthless cronies should the facts behind the relationship ever come to light. Which is exactly what happened. The cop was found out, and ten days after Patrick's disappearance, an extra-strength black trash bag washed up on the sand at Rockaway Beach in Brooklyn. Five days after that, Shirley Malone stood with her head bowed as the scant contents of the bag—no other bags were ever recovered—were lowered into a grave at Calvary Cemetery. My mother allegedly uncorked her first bottle of whiskey that same afternoon and managed to work her way halfway down the label before the cop came by to check on her and put a stop to it. It was a week after the funeral that the cop and Shirley began their affair. It would last all of four months. The cop was married. One child and another on the way. He wouldn't find out until several months after breaking things off with Shirley that she was pregnant with me and planning to see it through. Her relationship with the bottle was moving along nicely by that point as well. After I was born, the cop made a point of keeping tabs on me and my mother when he could, dropping in on us now and again. Sometimes I was invited to leave the apartment for an hour while the two hashed things out. To some extent, despite his spotty presence in my life, my old man managed to mold me, if not directly as often as I'd have preferred then at least by dint of his considerable persona and the name he made for himself as he rose steadily up the ranks of the police department. I steered in the direction of the NYPD myself for a while—managed one year at John Jay—though I fell with a pronounced bounce from that particular path. Eventually, my father was named police commissioner for the city of New York. Commissioner Harlan Scott. But one summer afternoon four years into his post, he stepped down without notice or explanation and, five days after that, disappeared forever from the face of the earth. One would have had to be watching closely—which I was—to see that my mother's relationship with the bottle moved to a deeper level after the old man's disappearance. Even fifteen years later—eight years after Harlan Scott was officially declared dead—she never tires of reminding me how the important men in her life have a habit of disappearing.

The freaky thing about the daisies on my uncle's grave was this: Harlan Scott had made it a point every year on the anniversary of Patrick Malone's declared death to join my mother at her brother's gravesite and leave off a clutch of daisies. In the fifteen years since his disappearance, every year without fail, the daisies had continued to appear. I knew it wasn't my father. The lead weight in my stomach told me that he was every bit as dead as the uncle I'd never met. But my mother has another way of viewing matters. It's not stretching the truth to say that she looks forward to the annual anguish of discovering the mysterious daisies on her brother's tombstone. Even though she married (and, later, divorced), no other man on earth was going to take my father's place in her emotions. The inexplicable daisies gave my mother the kind of false hope that fuels constant low-level heartache, a pain with which the small tough woman was, unfortunately, all too comfortable.

After several silent minutes, we left the grave-site. As she always did, my mother paused just outside the cemetery. She slowly scanned the buildings running both ways in front of us. One year she'd brought binoculars. But generally, the tactic was to remain visible for a minute or two, in case someone was watching. The windows of the buildings stared back blankly. Hundreds of opaque empty eyes.

Shirley wanted a drink. I'm not my mother's keeper, so we ducked into a place called the Lounge. Dark. Stale. I could swear the same elbows were on the bar as the year before, and the year before that. We took a table next to a silent pinball machine, and I fetched an old-fashioned for the lady and for myself an Irish coffee, heavy on the Irish.

Several months after Commissioner Harlan Scott disappeared, I'd gotten a referral to Charlie Burke, private investigator out of Queens, and procured his services to snoop around and see what he could find. I'd never trusted the official investigation. It's easy to make enemies when you're a cop on the rise, especially once you've reached the top. Easy target. Fair game. Charlie managed to shine his light on any number of characters who might have been happy to assist in the obliteration of Harlan Scott, but ultimately nothing rock-solid. Along the way, I picked up my PI license and put myself under Charlie's tutelage. It was a better fit for me. Attempting to follow in the old man's footsteps had been downright quaint of me, or just plain stupid. I'm better suited for contract work or just being nosy on my own. Charlie declared that I had the raw material already in place, it was just a matter of fine-tuning, picking up some of the tricks and the bumps and bruises of experience. He also did a smart thing. Or, if not smart, extremely shrewd; the equivalent of attaching an endless belt of ammunition to a weapon. He sat me down one evening at his local, a bar not that far from the Lounge. I remember his every word.

"Your old man. What do we know? I'll tell you. We know one of two things. He either disappeared because he wanted to, and he's got no intention of being found except on his own terms, or he was taken out. Forget the first one, it's the less likely. That second one? Listen. Somebody bad killed your father. Someone with the poison in their blood. My advice to you is that when you take on a case, it doesn't matter what kind it is, you keep in mind that what you're looking to do is nail someone with the poison in their blood. Doesn't matter if it's only a little poison. Embezzler, guy cheating on his wife, insurance scammers, doesn't matter. It

comes from the same source as the creep who
took your old man away from you. They're
cousins, all these schmucks. **That's** what you go
after. Every time. It's their blood you're sniffing
for, Fritz. Poison blood. Get it off the street.
Every time. You want to do right by your old
man? There's your ticket."

When I reminded Shirley that she wasn't allowed to smoke in the bar, she quietly cursed the
mayor. She dropped the celery-green pack back
into her purse.

"I noticed where the girl lived who got her
throat slashed the other night," Shirley said.
"That's little missy's front yard, isn't it?"

"She goes by the name of Margo."

"I figured you knew who I was talking about."

"The murder happened right across the
street."

"Did she know her?"

"Did Margo know her?"

"I know it's not fashionable to know your
neighbors in this city, but stranger things have
happened."

"She didn't know her," I said.

"If I were an associate of this Marshall Fox
character, I'd be leaving on the next train. You
know who did this, don't you?"

"**You** do?"

"Of course I do. Not the specifics, but it was a

fan. A demented fan. An obsessed fan. Someone's trying to make it look like the original killer is still out there, like Marshall Fox is completely innocent of those two murders last year. He wants to sow the seeds of doubt in the jury's mind so that they don't come in with a guilty verdict. Everyone knows this is the world's stupidest jury and they can't make up their minds even when it's as clear as a bell. You wait, you'll see. Some nutcase with pictures of Marshall Fox plastered all over his walls. That's your killer."

"And the reason for these particular victims?"

"Friends of Fox. Like those first two. They're just trying to go with the pattern."

"The pattern was women with whom Fox had been involved," I pointed out. "Zachary Riddick is a square peg."

"Did I say the killer was brilliant? The lawyer probably just got under his skin and he decided to do Riddick in while he was at it. I'm not the police. I don't have all the answers."

Her drink was finished, and she wanted another one. I'd cut her off after two and then hope we'd have to wait in the cold air awhile for the elevated subway. I replenished my mug while I was at it. Cold gray Sunday would have been perfect in front of a toasty fire with little missy. My day was feeling like the booby prize.

"Except for roses and black-eyed Susans,

daisies were about the only flower your father could identify. You knew that, right?"

Of course I knew that. She pointed it out to me every year. She picked up her glass and took a noisy sip.

"He was devastated about what happened to Patrick. He took the blame. Thing is, your uncle had too big a soft spot. He ran with all those crazies, but his heart wasn't in it. Not really. He was a good boy. Harlan spotted that. You've never seen a man so miserable with remorse. I should have hated him. I should have ripped his eyes out. He killed my brother. Sweet Patrick." She picked up her glass again and held it near her chin.

"I've been trying to be furious with your father from the day they found Patrick. What happened between us made no sense. I should be furious. And you know . . . I might be. I don't care what you think, Fritz. He's out there. Your father is alive and he's out there and he's letting you and me know it. He's either stark raving mad or he's scared half to death or he just has his reasons. Or all of the above. But one day I'm going to catch that bastard laying his little daisies on my brother's grave. You've never really seen me furious. You think you have, but you haven't. You'd better be there when it happens. Your father's going to need you there to protect him."

She sniffed back a tear and raised her glass. "Patrick Malone."

I tapped her glass with my mug. "Patrick Malone."

She stared at me as she downed her drink. Never took her eyes off me. "You look just like him, you know," she said.

Of course I knew. She told me so every year. And she didn't mean my uncle Patrick, either.

～ 14 ～

THE TUESDAY AFTER the Hamptons week-
end, Robin swore to herself that she was not remaining home after work simply because she had
told Marshall Fox that she had the night free.
Michelle had called up suggesting that the two
meet up in the Union Square area for drinks, but
Robin had begged off, claiming she was tired and
looking for an early night.

"It's not Fox, is it?" Michelle said. "He hasn't
actually called you, has he?"

Michelle didn't believe for a minute that Marshall Fox had been serious. Robin agreed with her.
He'd been drinking, she reminded herself, plus
God knows what else. Robin couldn't claim to be
up on all the drugs of the moment, but she had
seen enough bizarre behavior during the Hamptons party to know that there had been more con-

sumed than just the cocktails she'd spent all night circulating. She had already played over and over in her mind her encounters with Fox and determined that she'd been taken in—almost taken in—by the celebrity's prodigious charm and his serial flirting. It's absurd, she told herself. The man goes out with supermodels and Hollywood actresses. I was the **hired help.** Get a grip.

In fact, Fox hadn't called. Not the Sunday after the party, not Monday, and not Tuesday. Of course he hadn't. It was absurd. For all Robin knew, Fox had patched things up with Kelly Cole, and the two of them had shared a good laugh about the crazy martini-throwing incident, and that was that. Robin had stayed up and watched his show Monday night just to see—she told herself—if Fox made any mention of the event in the Hamptons. He didn't, though he had made a joke that sounded to Robin like it might have been an oblique reference to the striking blond newswoman and the drink-throwing incident. But maybe not. Robin had caught sight of herself in the mirror on the wall next to the television set and told herself to snap out of it already.

To her regret, Robin had talked about the party at work, letting slip the fact that Marshall Fox had flirted with her and had sort of asked her out. Denise from Graphics was a huge Marshall Fox fan.

"Has he called yet?" The question came on what seemed to be a half-hourly basis. On Tuesday Denise was nearly beside herself. "Has he called? You **are** checking your machine, aren't you?" Denise had even offered to check Robin's home answering machine for her. "Look. When he does call, you do **not** erase that message. I'm serious. I swear, I'll pay you to let me record it. You have to promise me. Oh my God. Marshall **Fox**."

But he hadn't called. By two o'clock, Robin had made a particular point about not calling home anymore to check her machine. At the end of the day, Denise had demanded that Robin call one more time.

"He starts taping the show at five. He might've called right before."

There'd been no messages. Good, Robin told herself. That's that.

LATER THAT NIGHT, her chin pressed hard against her pillow, Robin had panicked. What was she doing? This was insane. As she twisted her head to look over her shoulder, what her eye fell on first was the television set atop her dresser across the room. The set was muted, and Marshall Fox was signing off. He placed his hand over his heart.

Robin shifted on her elbows and tried to bring her hands together to form a T, for "timeout." She sputtered, "I . . . please . . . stop . . . **please.**"

Marshall Fox took a grip on her shoulder and squeezed. "Shhhh. Come on, New Hope. Just relax, baby. Go with it."

And he didn't stop. Quite the opposite. Robin closed her eyes against the flickering light on her bedroom wall and did as she was told. No need to panic, she told herself. He's right, just go with it. It's not really so bad. In fact . . .

As her cheek moved along the pillow, she had a fleeting thought of Denise. Oh my God, if she could see me now. This was followed by another thought, and it made her laugh out loud. He's the fox; I'm the chicken house.

Behind her, Fox continued to croon. "That's right, New Hope. Thatta girl. You're getting it . . ."

～ 15 ～

PETER ELLIOTT CALLED ME at home around ten. I was sitting in my perfectly ratty armchair, eating wasabi peas and thumbing through a copy of **The Horse's Mouth,** trying to get into it. A Margo recommendation. It seemed like it might be good if I could actually focus on it. But the going was tough. The ringing phone got me off the hook. Which is a pun, if you think about it.

"There's been another phone threat."

I set down the book and sat up in the chair. "You're kidding."

"Word for word, exactly like the other ones. I just got a call from Joe Gallo."

I asked, "Who got it?"

"That's the thing, Fritz. This one doesn't make any sense. At least not yet. It's a total blank. The person has no connection with Marshall Fox whatsoever. I mean zero. She doesn't even watch the show."

My radiator began clanging. It does that when it's pressed into action for too long. It sounds like someone is swinging at it with a ball peen hammer. I switched ears. "So what're the details?"

"There aren't many. It's a woman who lives on East Eighteenth Street. Thirty-four. Single, with a boyfriend. She and the boyfriend were off on a ski trip this past week, but they didn't miss any of the news. Woman says her boyfriend is a real news junkie, so they had CNN on all the time when they weren't out skiing."

"Sounds romantic," I said.

"The point is, they caught a couple of the replays of Riddick playing that damn tape at his press conference. CNN must think it's the audio holy grail, they've been playing it so often. You just wait, it's going to find its way into a music mix of some sort. That's the world we live in these days."

Music mix. I vaguely knew what he was talking about.

Peter continued, "Anyway, this woman heard it a couple of times when they were out in Colorado Springs or wherever it was. She told Gallo that Robin's murder already had her sort of freaked out. She and Burrell are the same age, and according to Gallo, the two look a little bit alike. Not that it makes any difference. My eighty-three-year-old grandmother is freaked out by what's going on, and she's long past her girlish beauty. But it's out there. I'm sure you can feel it, right? People are on edge. It wasn't helped by the **Post** publishing that damn photo."

"Jesus. Don't get Joe Gallo started on the **Post**."

"Started?" Peter laughed. "That would mean he actually stopped."

"So let's hear what happened."

"What happened was that they got back to the city this afternoon, and the boyfriend dropped her off. She lives in Chelsea. The woman told Gallo that when she takes a vacation, she doesn't call in and check her machine. Cell phones these days, I wouldn't want to be in the answering machine business. So she gets home and checks her messages, and there it was. **'Can you taste the blood yet? Whore.'** The whole thing. It could practically be a prerecorded message. The woman lets out a scream that you could probably hear halfway down the block."

I thought a minute, biting down on a few wasabi peas to help stimulate things. "You said it was so much like the other messages that it could have been a recording. Maybe it **was** a recording. Maybe it was a prank from some not-so-funny friend."

"Right. Gallo thought of that, too. But it was

recorded on her machine the same day that Robin Burrell was killed, and Riddick didn't broadcast Rosemary Fox's tape until the day after Burrell was killed. Gallo's people are running tests on the answering machine just to triple-check everything, but Joe has already told me he can tell it's not a recording being played back. It was live. The same loony who left the message for Robin Burrell and Rosemary Fox left one for this woman on the same day."

"What's her name?"

"Allison Jennings."

I took another pause to think it all over. "Why are you calling me, Peter?"

"I was wondering when you were going to ask that."

"You can stop wondering."

"How's your plate looking, Fritz?"

"My plate is full of wasabi peas. For that matter, my plate isn't even a plate. My plate is a bowl. Why do you ask?"

"The Jennings woman is freaked out."

"So you said. I can imagine she is. But she has a boyfriend, Peter. I know you think I'm swell and all, but you're not calling me up so that I can go comfort her."

"Margo would have my head on a platter," he said.

I muttered, "If there's room."

"What? Trouble in paradise?"

"It's nothing. Like you said. A lot of people are freaking out."

Peter asked, "Can you go see Allison Jennings tomorrow?"

"Why should I do that?"

"It makes no sense that someone completely unrelated to Marshall Fox would get one of these same phone threats that the others got. The police are missing something. I thought you could talk to her, maybe nose around in her life and see if you can come up with the connection. It could be important."

"I'm assuming the police are already doing that," I said.

"They are. But that doesn't mean adding you to the mix might not be helpful."

"Who'd be paying my freight on this? It can't be Mr. Gallo and the good people of New York."

"I'm hiring you. Actually, just call it an extension of the work you did for us vetting the jury in the spring."

"Did you tell Joe that you were putting me on the trail? I've already crossed paths with his lead investigator." I had the sudden image of Megan Lamb seated across the room, wringing her hands and describing gory details for me. Or rather, for her.

"Gallo knows," Peter said. "He said what you

said. You're already his shadow on this thing. I got the rap. Anything you uncover, you take to him immediately, blah, blah, blah."

I sniffed. "A law lecture. At our age."

"Gallo wants this thing nailed and finished. I mean, who doesn't? I told you about my granny. Shelly's got it, too. The heebie-jeebies. To be honest, I can't shake the 'waiting for the other shoe to drop' feeling, either. Riddick and Burrell within twenty-four hours. I know there's been nothing for three days. But maybe it's the weather and all this snow that has him socked in like it has the rest of the city. That's the feeling I have. This guy's holed up, but there's still unfinished business out there."

"You're thinking Rosemary Fox?"

"I was. And now I'm thinking Allison Jennings. I just don't know. Gallo told me he recommended she get back out of town if at all possible, but she says after just taking the week off for skiing, she's way too swamped at her job."

I could hear noise in the background. A child's screaming laughter and a woman responding. Peter's wife, Shelly, I presumed.

The attorney lowered his voice. "You know what, Fritz? I don't want to spook Shelly any more than she already is, but I've actually been thinking of getting her and the kids out of the city until this whole thing blows over. I'm sure it's nerves about the trial. My damn jury is ready to explode, and I'm getting this awful feeling that even if they don't, Fox is going to walk. Either way, I'm looking at my wife here and I'm thinking, Don't be an idiot. Some nut is out there. Who knows what he's thinking? Get her the hell away from here."

"I'll talk to Jennings," I said. "We need to establish her link with these phone threats. That's something we could actually run with."

"Excellent. Let me give you her cell number. She's not staying at her place tonight. At Gallo's suggestion, she won't be at her boyfriend's, either. She'd be just as easy to track down there. She gave Gallo the address of where she'd be staying tonight, and he said he'd post a car outside. He didn't tell me where it was. You call her cell in the morning, and the two of you can set up a place to meet. If you can, could you swing by my office after you've talked to her? There's something else I need to go over with you."

I agreed to stop by, and we hung up. I returned the rest of the wasabi peas to the bag and stowed it in the cabinet. The radiator had ceased its banging while I was talking to Peter, but now it started up again. The room was stuffy, so I cracked a window. I poked my head outside for some air and spent a minute looking down the block at the green and red holiday garlands straddling the street farther down Mulberry. The lights of the Italian restaurants were popping and blinking, but the street itself was nearly abandoned. It seemed like the entire city had gone to ground.

Before I got into bed, I jotted down some notes, circled a few of them, drew an arrow here and there, and layered in a number of question marks. I considered calling Margo to let her know that I was now officially on the case. I had a client. A paying client. Maybe that would mollify her. The radiator in the front room clanged and banged again as I picked up the phone. In the distance, I heard the urgent blaring horn of a fire truck. The sound grew louder as the truck passed a block or so away, and then it faded again into the night.

I set the phone back down and turned off the light.

~ 16 ~

ALLISON JENNINGS WANTED me to meet her in Brooklyn Heights. First thing in the morning, I took the subway under the river to the Clark Street stop. My low-level claustrophobia kicked in when we were under the East River, but I've got some tricks I use to deal with it. On the crowded cattle elevator up to the street level, there was a rabbit-fur hat in my face, and I wanted to snatch it with my teeth and spit it out onto the floor. But I maintained a civil composure and got through the short ride.

Allison's boyfriend came along. His name was Jeffrey. I met them at a pastry shop on Piermont Avenue. As I came in, Jeffrey rose from his chair and met me at the door. The first thing he did was ask to see my PI license. He took it with a trembling hand and stared at it as if it needed deciphering.

He asked, "Do you carry a gun?"

"Sometimes."

"Are you carrying one now?"

I tapped the area of my heart. "I'd introduce you, but he's shy."

Jeffrey handed me back the license. "She's really freaked out. Anything you can do to make her feel safer, I'd appreciate it."

Allison was sitting at a small table about fifteen feet from the door. Jeffrey's security check completed, the two of us joined her. She was a brunette. She looked hopeful and scared all at once. Jeffrey sat down and took her hand. I considered taking the other one, but we weren't here for a prayer meeting. I introduced myself and asked Allison to tell me the story. I knew it already, but details get dropped and added as tales move down the line. In this case, the details were few, and Allison's rendering essentially matched the version I'd gotten on the phone from Peter Elliott.

"What's going on?" Allison asked, a tremor in her voice. "I'm really confused. Why does this man want to hurt me?"

"We're going to figure that out," I said. "Let me ask you some questions. From what I understand and what you just told me, you have zero connection with Marshall Fox."

"None. I don't even watch his show."

"Okay. Put Fox out of your head for the moment. We can look for the Fox link later. I want to focus on who might have some sort of problem with you directly. Why don't you tell me what you do for a living?"

She told me that she worked for Reuters news service. I knew the building—it's in midtown, not far from my office. Allison worked as the manager of human resources.

"That's hiring and firing?"

"Basically, yes. Though most of my time is spent in recruitment."

"You check qualifications, references, do interviews? That sort of thing?"

"Correct."

"Have you fired anyone recently?"

She paused. "We announced a large layoff right before Christmas." She managed a small laugh. "Nice and Dickensian, isn't it? Some people went immediately. Others received notice that their positions were being phased out over a matter of a couple of months. We give good severance packages. But yes, I guess I've fired a lot of people recently."

"How does that work, a mass layoff like that?"

"It's a grueling couple of days. I see everybody one at a time, and I give them the news."

"That must be fun."

"Most people are surprisingly okay about it. Layoffs are part of the culture these days. That's not to say they're happy. I get the word that we have to make so-and-so many cuts in such-and-such department. I talk with the department heads, we go over their staffs. Except in rare cases, it's almost always a matter of seniority. I mean, sometimes there's a bad job report that can move someone up on the list, but usually it's last one in, first one out. Either way, it's painful. It's like I'm the village executioner."

"You say people are pretty good about it. But do some people get angry? Have you ever had anyone threaten you personally?"

She and Jeffrey shared a look. "Go on," Jeffrey said. "Tell him."

Allison turned back to me. "It's nothing. Yes. Some people do get upset. Of course they do. Who wouldn't? Like I said, these last cuts came right around Christmas. Which I argued against, by the way. Plus, the job market really stinks right now."

"You're reluctant to give me a name, is that it?"

She looked like she was ready to cry. Jeffrey squeezed her hand tighter and answered for her. "There's an implied confidentiality in the work Ally does."

I ignored him. "Ms. Jennings, were you also reluctant to give this name to the police last night?"

"I could lose **my** job if one of our former employees brings a lawsuit. I'm sure this guy isn't the one who left that message. It makes no sense. The last thing I need is him finding out I sicced the police on him."

"Okay. Let's put him aside for a minute. I assume you also interview people for new positions. Have there been any job candidates in the past six months or so who struck you as peculiar?"

"Peculiar?"

"Excessive in some fashion. Too eager. Too friendly. Too boastful. Too secure or too insecure. Someone who behaved like he had the job in the bag when in fact he didn't."

"Yes."

"Yes to which?"

"Yes to everything you just said. That's what you get in my position, all the types you just listed."

"Let's concentrate on the ones who didn't get the job."

"That's the majority. One position, scores of candidates."

"I'm looking for a man, someone who stands out. Maybe he wasn't necessarily aggressive. Something off in the body language. Or he had an odd way of putting things. Did any of the candidates come on to you? Even subtly?"

"I'm not sure what you're getting at."

"I'm just fishing. If someone unhinged thought he'd made a personal connection with you and then he didn't get the job. In his eyes, you rejected him not only for the job but also personally. Does anyone like that come to mind?"

She shook her head. "No. I'm sorry."

I was getting nowhere. But most times that's how you have to play the game. You rack up the miles on fruitless roads. I tried a new tack. "Back to the people you had to let go. Did any of them ever say to you that losing their job was going to make things difficult for them or their family?"

"I guess so. It really depends. The ones who are single, they have a little less to worry about, and most—"

I had a thought. "Hold on. Clear your mind for a second. Stop looking for a man. Think of the women. Specifically the married women. I'm not expecting you to know the circumstances of everyone's private life, but I'm sure sometimes you get a sense. Does any woman stand out who seemed upset over how her husband was going to take the news? Maybe someone who mentioned that her husband was recently laid off himself or was out looking for work or maybe just made a large investment? A house. Or the kids' tuition. Someone who worried that she was really going to be strapped by losing her job? Did anyone seem uncommonly scared?"

Jeffrey spoke up. "You mean like a woman who was afraid her husband was going to yell at her or even beat her up for losing her job?"

"Exactly. That's one example. The violent spouse. Does anything like that come to mind, Allison?"

"Possibly." She nibbled lightly on her lower lip before continuing. "There **was** a woman during the pre-Christmas layoffs who said exactly what you just said. But people say stuff all the time. I mean, it's a figure of speech."

"What's a figure of speech?"

" 'My husband is going to kill me.' "

I took out my notebook and slid it across the table. I handed her a pen. "It's time for names, Allison. I want this one, and I want the man you mentioned who got angry when you fired him. This is no time for you to be protecting anyone. Do you remember the names?" She nodded. I reached across the table and tapped my finger on the notebook. "Write them."

She scribbled down a pair of names. "I'm not going in to work today. I'm just too freaked out. But if you'd like, I can call my assistant and have her pull the files on these two."

"That'll be good. I know where your building

is. Tell her I'll stop by later this afternoon." Allison produced a business card and handed it to me. I tucked it into my notebook and thanked her for her time.

Jeffrey accompanied me to the front door. He looked like he could use some air.

"I don't get it. Why would somebody want to kill Allison? Do you really think it's got something to do with her job?"

"I plan to find that out."

"I'm afraid to leave her side."

I looked back at Allison. She was staring a hole into her hands. I turned back to Jeffrey. "If I were you, that's exactly what I'd do. I'd be on her like glue."

~ 17 ~

PETER ELLIOTT STUCK his thumbs in his maroon suspenders and put his feet up on his desk. I settled into a brown leather chair that smelled faintly like a new shoe. "All you need is a stogie in your mouth, counselor."

Peter laughed. "Shelly hates it when I smoke cigars."

"Shelly is a civilized woman."

"No argument there. So you met with Ms. Jennings?"

I gave him a rundown. He listened without interrupting, consulting the ceiling as I spoke. When I was finished, he brought his feet back down to terra firma and drummed his fingers on the desk.

"Okay. Those sound like lukewarm leads."

"That's how I see it, too. But they should be tracked down."

"Give them to the police. It's the Fox connection we want."

"That's a zero," I said.

"Anything to the Jennings woman looking like Robin Burrell?"

"I didn't see it," I said. "I mean, she looks more like her than you or I do. Though maybe you've got dishy legs. I've never had the privilege."

"Ms. Burrell did have a nice set of sticks, didn't she?"

"She was not an unattractive woman."

Peter scoffed, "Come on, Fritz. The woman was gorgeous."

"But no sexual predator."

The attorney held up a hand. "Please. If I never hear that term again, I'll be grateful. You've got to give Riddick credit for that one. He really pounded it into the jury. Basic brainwashing 101. What was I supposed to do, go up there and ask the witness to explain to the jury that she **wasn't** a sexual predator? That just keeps the damn term floating out there longer."

"You weren't exactly painting Robin Burrell as a nun."

"It's an ugly business. We had to bring out the extent of Fox's sexual deviance. That was key. The man liked it rough. He liked his toys. Especially his handcuffs. Burrell was our best witness to Fox's fun and games. I'm not saying I enjoyed dragging her through the mud."

"America enjoyed it."

"Yeah, well. America enjoys all sorts of things."

Nikki Rossman, the second victim, had been found with one end of a pair of handcuffs fastened around her left wrist. Under Peter Elliott's questioning, Robin had revealed that early in her five-month affair with Fox, she had relented to his urgings that the two indulge in various bondage games, particularly the ones including the use of handcuffs. The testimony had been damning to Fox. What Peter hadn't anticipated was that Fox's defense team would take up the challenge and attempt to portray Robin as the aggressor, the one who had encouraged country boy Fox to loosen up and try some new things. Unfortunately, their cause was bolstered when they invited to the stand a man who testified about "some pretty inventive sex" with Robin Burrell back when the two were undergraduates at the University of Pennsylvania. The man described several episodes that had involved his binding Robin's ankles and wrists with knotted socks and securing them so she was essentially immobile during the ensuing sex. Worse for the prosecution, he had insisted on the stand that the idea of the bondage had not generated from him but from Robin. Peter Elliott objected to the testimony and tried to get it struck from the record, but the judge had allowed it. From that point on, Fox's defense team never missed an opportunity to portray Robin as not only a willing and eager partner to the colorful sex she and Fox had indulged in, but as the initiator. The notion took hold, and soon enough, Robin's image in the media rarely appeared without at least a passing allusion to her spirited sexual history. Riddick had also managed to dredge up the fact that while she was an undergraduate, Robin had become pregnant not once but twice, each time terminating the pregnancy. Judge Deveraux did order this irrelevant factoid stricken from the record, but even so, Robin's stability as a witness for the prosecution had taken its hits.

The buzzer on Peter's phone buzzed. The call was short.

"That was Lewis," Peter said, hanging up. "He'd like us to come into his office."

If I thought the fragrance of Peter's office chair suggested a new shoe, state's attorney Lewis Gottlieb's entire office positively reeked of a tannery. Gottlieb was acting as lead prosecutor in the Marshall Fox trial. For a man nearing his seventy-fifth birthday, he was still in impressively good physical condition, tall and unstooped, rumored to jog three miles every morning before

taking the train down to the city from Westchester. It had been widely rumored that Gottlieb
was on the cusp of announcing his plans for re-
tirement just before the indictment of Marshall
Fox on multiple counts of murder and that Peter
had been instrumental in convincing his mentor
to stay on and crown his career with what would
no doubt be recorded as one of the more notorious prosecutions of the Manhattan criminal
court system. Word along the grapevine was that
Gottlieb was apoplectic at the possibility of
losing such a white-hot spectacle of a case as
the Marshall Fox prosecution. The notion was
unimaginable, the sort of wrong note that a person like Lewis Gottlieb quite simply would not
tolerate.

Peter had admitted to me on our way down
the plushly carpeted corridor to Gottlieb's office
that the esteemed attorney was especially nervous
about the jury's increasing fractiousness.

"A hung jury is the least of his worries. Lewis
has Deveraux's promise—off the record—that
he'll do everything humanly possible to get everything through to a conclusion on this go-around.
It's not the mistrial that's got Lewis worked up,
it's the prospect that the jury will actually let Fox
go free. If things were to go that way . . . I don't
even want to think about it."

Lewis Gottlieb was cordial with me but cool.

The lawyer rose from behind his imperial desk and gave me his large freckled hand to shake. "Mr. Malone. I understand you are back on board."

"So I'm told."

As I took a seat, Gottlieb addressed his younger colleague. "What does he know?"

"Fritz knows nothing," Peter said. I thought I detected a slight smirk, but I might have been mistaken. Gottlieb stared at me for several seconds.

"The foreperson," he said at last.

"Nancy Spicer. What about her?"

Gottlieb steepled his large hands and lowered his chin onto them. "You vetted her for us."

"I vetted all of them. What about her?"

Gottlieb raised a frosty eyebrow. The watery brown eyes moved to Peter, who cleared his throat. "Mrs. Spicer had a nervous breakdown. I don't mean since she's been on the jury, though she's cruising in that direction. This was six years ago. She lost it completely, Fritz. Took a real dive. She spent thirty days in an institution."

I let out a low whistle. "We don't like that."

Lewis Gottlieb agreed, "We don't, Mr. Malone. We don't like it in the slightest."

I asked, "Does the defense know?"

Peter answered, "Not yet."

"How did you find out?"

"It's complicated," Gottlieb said. "And not relevant. We can go into that later."

"I'm sorry. I'm not sure what else to say. I ran everyone down as best I could. Something like that should have been flapping in the wind. It should have hit me in the face."

"Spicer's husband had it suppressed," Peter said. "You would have had to dig for it."

"That's what you were paying me—"

Gottlieb interrupted, "That's not important right now. You're not in here for a scolding." He looked again at Peter and nodded.

"Lewis doesn't like the husband," Peter said. "Bruce Spicer."

I remembered Spicer. Vaguely. He worked as a clerk in a hardware store on Third Avenue. I remembered swinging by and talking to him in his cherry-red vest. The vest had made more of an impression on me than the man. "What don't you like about him?"

Gottlieb answered, "He's born-again. A Bible thumper."

"A born-again Christian," I said. "Is that really a basis to not like someone? I mean, in a professional sense?"

"I'm not anti-Christian," Gottlieb said flatly, lowering his hands to his desk. "What I'm saying is that the man is unstable."

"I thought it was the wife who was unstable."

"Both of them, Mr. Malone. Our jury fore-person has been institutionalized and treated with depression medications, and her husband has thrown a handful of chicken livers at a doctor who was on his way into the office." He sat back in his chair and folded his arms on his chest. In case I had fallen asleep during any part of the last ten seconds, he repeated, "Chicken livers."

Peter spoke up. "Bruce Spicer was arrested six years ago as part of a group of anti-abortion pro-testers outside a clinic that performs abortions. In Livingston, New Jersey. Same year as his wife's breakdown. Big year for the Spicers. Spicer's ar-rest has been expunged from the record. It was part of a plea arrangement."

Gottlieb said, "Mr. Malone doesn't need to know the details. The point is, Bruce Spicer is a lunatic. And his wife wants off the jury."

Peter added, "In a big way."

"Along with eleven of her peers, from what I understand," I said.

Gottlieb waved his hand dismissively. "Our twelve peers good and true can go hang them-selves from the Brooklyn Bridge when this is all over, as far as I'm concerned. I don't give a damn about them. The point is, I want this to **be** over before they do it. Now, Mrs. Spicer wants out, but Sam Deveraux isn't having it. The lemmings would all try to follow. I'm letting Sam take care of that. What we have here, Mr. Malone, is a related but separate issue that concerns us all on a more profound level." He paused. "Peter? I will let you do the honors."

Peter took a breath. "Lewis wants us to consider that Bruce Spicer is responsible for the murders of Robin Burrell and Zack Riddick."

"Spicer?"

"It's just a theory. But you remember that whole big fuss when Zack brought up Robin Burrell's abortions. It sounds far-fetched, I know. But think of it for a minute. Nancy Spicer's been in there bawling her eyes out to get off the jury. Bruce Spicer is no big fan of people who get abortions; he's got a history of being very much an in-your-face person when it comes to that issue. Hard to call this a motive for murder, but hang in there. We've also got Zachary. Riddick's playboy reputation isn't exactly the kind of thing that endears the born-agains. What Lewis is saying is you've got a situation here where a person like Bruce Spicer could have been looking for some creative ways to get this trial tanked, free his wife, and rid the earth of at least two infidels."

"Infidels?"

"I'm just saying Lewis wants us to take a strong look at this. Face it, **someone** is killing these people. Someone is royally pissed off. Where the hell do we start?"

I pulled out my notebook. Gottlieb demanded, "What have you got there?"

"A list of people I want to talk to in connection with Robin Burrell and Riddick."

Gottlieb aimed a fat finger in my direction. "Put Bruce Spicer at the top of that list. Do you hear me? Chicken-liver-tossing son of a bitch. Go after him first. Born-again bastards like that should choke on their own intestines, as far as I'm concerned. I've got no goddamn time for those people. Him. You go get him."

PETER ACCOMPANIED ME downstairs. There were several other people in the elevator with us, so we didn't say anything. The moment we were outside, Peter spoke urgently.

"This is tricky territory, Fritz. Very tricky. I'm sure you understand that. We've got a real balancing act to figure out here. Lewis has said categorically that we are not taking his theory to the police. It's not the most ethical call, but that can't be helped. It's a matter of containment. We don't want word getting out about Nancy Spicer's mental health problem or about her husband having been arrested. Nancy shouldn't be on the jury—that alone would provide the defense with some serious artillery to push for a mistrial—so we don't want them to know. But here's the other thing. If Bruce Spicer gets approached by the police or, for that matter, by you, he could blow the whistle himself. If he simply lets the papers know that he is under suspicion of any kind for these murders, it all explodes in our face. Husband of the foreperson? There's nothing even Sam Deveraux would be able to do at that point. The trial would be officially out of hand. Everything would collapse."

"But if Spicer actually is the killer, he's not going to go blabbing to the press."

"We have no idea what he would do. Maybe it's a catch-22 and maybe it isn't. The point is, there's nothing but risk involved no matter which way you look at it. It's certainly possible that Spicer isn't the killer. I admit, it's a wild hunch. Then again, Lewis Gottlieb didn't become Lewis Gottlieb with bad hunches. That old man's got an awesome track record." Peter glanced around, as if afraid that someone might be listening in. "Look, I know Lewis tried to whip you into action just now. And I'm not necessarily countermanding his orders. But if you've developed any leads on these murders that you really like, it wouldn't bother me if you run after them first. I'm not officially chasing you off Spicer. Like I said, Lewis has a phenomenal instinct."

"He's also got a phenomenal hatred of born-again Christians."

"It's not even that. Do you remember that abortion doctor in Albany who got gunned down a few years ago? He got all sorts of threats and there was all this vilification on different right-to-life websites? You remember that?"

I did. The doctor had been shot at point-blank range as he was leaving his clinic. The shooter didn't even try to escape. Some passersby grabbed him, but he offered no resistance. He just stood there holding a damn placard and waited for the police to come.

Peter held up two fingers. "Two things. The guy who did the shooting? He was a member of the group that Bruce Spicer is mixed up with. He was one of the people who got hauled in along with Spicer during the chicken-liver incident. Lewis did a little investigating on his own and discovered that."

"I did crap work for you, Peter. I'm sorry."

"Forget it. Number two. Big number two. The doctor who was killed was a close personal friend of Lewis. They went back over thirty years."

I allowed the information to seep in. "Then we might not be talking 'awesome instincts' here, Peter. We might be talking someone who's leading with his anger. What you're telling me is that your boss wouldn't mind revenge."

Peter let his breath out slowly. "I don't know what I'm telling you. That's the whole damn problem. I know I don't have to remind you how important this case is."

"I know it's important, counselor. I just hope you're ready to let it go if things start to fall in other directions. Look, I know you and Gottlieb have spent the better part of the past ten months trying to nail Marshall Fox to the wall for Blair and Rossman."

"But?"

"But Robin Burrell and Zachary Riddick were killed in the same fashion as those two women. If you're cutting me loose to find out who did these recent murders, you just have to understand that I'm not going to be operating with a closed mind about Marshall Fox's guilt or innocence. If I—"

Peter exploded. "Fox's **innocence**? Jesus, Fritz, cut me a big fat fucking break right here, you have **got** to be kidding!" He implored the heavens. "That son of a bitch slaughtered his . . . uh-uh. Forget it. Don't even go there. We've got him. I don't care if that jury does fall apart and blow away, we got the bastard who killed those two women! Our case is solid. Someone is trying to blow smoke all over the whole damn thing. **That's** what's happening. If it isn't Bruce Spicer, it's someone else."

"All I'm saying—"

He wasn't finished. "These are copycat killings.

Come on, don't get yourself all turned around. That's exactly what the killer wants. I need you thinking straight here." He pointed a finger at me. "We got the right killer. We got Fox. There's nothing to investigate there. Zero. You do what we've hired you to do. Is that understood?"

He didn't wait for an answer but turned abruptly and pushed back through the revolving door. It was one of those ultra-smooth revolving doors. It took the power of Peter's force, swallowed him up instantly, and continued revolving after he was well out of it and back inside the building. I stood a moment watching my own reflection flashing in the door panels.

I SWUNG BY THE Reuters Building. A folder was waiting for me. It contained two résumés. Back at my office, I gave the résumés a look. I was just reaching for the phone to call Megan Lamb when it rang.

"Mr. Malone? This . . ." The wavering signal gobbled up the rest of the sentence. It was a woman's voice.

"I didn't catch that," I said.

"It's Michelle Poole. From the Quaker meeting. He's **here**!"

"Who? Who's where?" I bolted upright in my chair. "Where are you?"

"I'm in my apartment. Remember I told you I've been feeling like someone's following me all the time? I felt it again when I was coming down the block just now. He's really there. I saw him. He was definitely following me. I . . . I peeked out my window a minute ago, and he's still . . . oh my God."

"Give me your address!" I grabbed a pen and scribbled down the address. "Give me your phone numbers. Home and cell." I scribbled those down as well. "I'm on my way. Listen to me. Call my number every five minutes. You got that?"

"But what—"

"Call! If you get voice mail, just say hi and hang up. Whatever you do, stay away from the window. Just hang tight."

"I'm scared. Hurry. Please. I don't—"

I nearly took out the tax accountant who works two doors down from me. He was shuffling toward the men's room, holding a key attached to a clipboard. I missed him by an inch.

~ 18 ~

I HIT THE STREET in five minutes. Four of
them were spent on the elevator going down
from my office to the street. It was lunchtime.
The elevator eased to a stop over and over again.

Twelfth floor . . .
Eleventh floor . . .
Ninth floor . . .
Eighth floor . . .
Fourth floor . . .
Third floor . . .

Outside, I hailed a cab. I tossed a handful of
bills on the front seat and told the driver to go
reckless. Eight minutes later, I had him pull over
a block from Michelle Poole's building.

Michelle lived on Twenty-seventh Street, near
Third Avenue. Close enough to where Zachary
Riddick had lived, I realized, to account easily for

Michelle's several sightings of the lawyer. As I got out of the car, I registered this factoid and tucked it away in a deep file. Riddick hadn't necessarily been stalking Robin's friend. The woman was just jumpy. In that case, maybe—

I spotted him.

He was standing outside of a stone church in the middle of the block. The church had large red doors, and he was leaning up against one of them, smoking a cigarette. My heart slammed against my rib cage.

It was Ratface. The guy I had noticed at the Quaker meeting. He was wearing a baseball cap, but otherwise he was dressed the same as before. As I watched, he pulled a fresh cigarette from a pack in his coat pocket, lit it off the first one and flicked the old one to the sidewalk, just missing a man walking by. The man must have said something to him. Ratface gave the man the finger, took a drag on his new cigarette and refixed his gaze on the building across the street. As I rounded the corner, he looked up and saw me. The red door behind him opened, and as an elderly woman exited the church, Ratface flicked his cigarette to the sidewalk and ran inside the church. I picked up my pace. Full speed.

The church was dark except for the altar area. In the rows of shadowy pews, I could make out a dozen or so people sitting quietly in the dark.

There was a center aisle as well as aisles running down either side of the church. They appeared to be empty. There was no way Ratface could have already raced down the length of any aisle and disappeared into another part of the church. He was here. In the dark. I started to pull out my gun then hesitated. Not here. Not yet, anyway.

I started slowly down the center aisle, checking the faces of the people in the pews. I couldn't imagine that he would have had the wherewithal to slip into a pew and try to blend in. My mind gave me an image. A man shrinking with tremendous quickness, his clothes dropping to the floor as if he has vanished altogether, and a black hairy rat scurrying out from under the clothes and darting into the shadows.

I was nearly right.

"Hey!" Partway down the pew I was approaching, a man leaped to his feet. "What in the world . . . ?"

Ratface bobbed to his feet at the far end of the pew. As soon as he'd entered the church, he must have hit the floor and scurried beneath the pews, making his way forward on knees and elbows. He took off running. He was through the door at the end of the aisle before I was halfway down the narrow pew. I leaped onto the pew, where I could run faster.

"Move!"

The man sitting in the pew lurched forward. I cleared him, pounding my way to the end of the pew. I hit the aisle and raced to the door. Behind it, a set of winding stairs led to the basement level. I heard a sound from below—a clanging—and took off down the stairs. They wound down to a basement hallway that ran under the altar. A small kitchenette. Two restrooms. A large open room with a piano and folding chairs. And a door directly to my left. I paused. I tried the door. Locked. Or perhaps the doorknob was being held. I squeezed the knob and tried to twist it. It seemed like it was giving a little.

Wrong.

I heard a sound behind me and turned in time to see the women's room door swinging open. The door caught me directly on the jaw. Sparks pierced my vision. At the same time, I felt something happening in my left side. Ratface shoved me to the floor, leaped over me and started running down the hallway. I looked down to see a long black piece of plastic sticking from my side. I tugged on it. It was a kitchen knife. The blade felt cold as I pulled it out. As soon as the blade cleared my jacket, blood began pumping onto my fingers.

Immediately, my mouth went dry. In the darkened hallway, the blood looked like oil. I staggered to my feet. I guessed that the other end of the hallway could only lead to a similar set of stairs and back up into the church. I made the calculation and, clutching my side, plunged through the sparks and back up the winding stairs. I swung myself around the railing at the top and emerged at the altar area, right next to the choir stalls. Off in the pews, shadowy figures were moving about swiftly. Someone cried out, "There he is!" But they might have meant me.

I moved across the front of the altar just as Ratface appeared, running up the far side aisle in the direction of the front door. I veered and aimed for the center aisle but lost my footing as I hit the marble steps leading down from the altar. I went down. Ratface was yanking the door open as I got back to my feet. I looked down and saw a swirl of blood on the marble. Somewhere in the darkness of the church, a woman screamed.

I lurched forward.

Outside.

He was a good block ahead of me, heading east. I took off after him. He dodged the cars on Third Avenue more deftly than I was able to, though at one point he surfed precariously on a patch of ice and allowed me to gain on him. I was grunting like a gimp racehorse, the vapor of my breath coming out in husky bursts. The wound in my side felt like it was packed with nails.

He was opening distance between us. As I dodged a woman pushing a baby stroller, I felt my cell phone vibrating. No time for that. I bore down. There were only two more blocks before we'd hit the FDR Drive, and beyond that, the East River. If he attempted to cross the FDR, my job was done. There was no way he could negotiate all those lanes of speeding traffic. As he neared Second Avenue, he barreled past an Asian woman, and she fell to the sidewalk. An instant later, I grunted, "Sorry," and hurdled cleanly over her, my lungs warning me they were ready to explode.

At First Avenue, he veered to his right. Son of a bitch. There's a residential complex called Waterside Plaza at Twenty-fifth Street and the FDR. An angled walkway crossing over the highway leads to the complex. Ratface hit the walkway at full speed. I was losing him. Fear is a mighty fuel, and he was burning it well. I pounded up the cement walkway, which spilled onto a large plaza. I saw my quarry leaping down a short set of steps to a narrow walkway that fronted the river. It also led to one of the complex's apartment towers.

I pulled my gun and stormed forward, nearly tumbling down the short flight of stairs to the lower plaza. My vision was starting to play games with me. There was a large glass entranceway to the apartment tower. It seemed the only place he could have gone, and I headed for it.

I never made it.

The son of a bitch had ducked behind a stone

support pillar opposite the entrance. I saw his reflection in the glass just as he lunged from his hiding spot and hit me full force, his lowered shoulder connecting with my ribs. He drove me sideways all the way to the low cement wall overlooking the river. I hit the wall hard, my gun rattling to the pavement. What little oxygen I had in my lungs left me. Ratface was still with me, still down low. The sparks returned to my vision, and my arms came down on the man's head and neck as uselessly as if they belonged to a rag doll. When I felt a grip tighten around my ankles, I knew exactly what he had in mind.

As he rose, he brought my legs up with him. I saw his face for just an instant. His cheeks were hot red. Frothy saliva was overflowing his mouth. Then my arms were pinwheeling, and my head whipped backward. I spotted the Huxley Envelope sign upside down across the river, then looked down at the bruise-colored films of ice along the shoreline below me. Ratface let out a powerful grunt.

I saw my feet. They were above me. Then they were below me. In the air. I was falling. The burning in my lungs this time was my own voice crying out into the cold air as the river ice rushed forward. The last thing I remember—funny—was my cell phone vibrating again. My world went black even before I hit.

PART 2

~ 19 ~

NIKKI ROSSMAN SLID down farther in the tub, to the point where the water was just touching her chin. She lifted her right foot and gently eased her big toe into the faucet so that it was snug and secure. She took a shallow breath and held it. She wanted to still the water completely. Her body appeared rubbery beneath the water, like something manufactured in a factory. Nikki recalled a movie she had seen a few years back, a high-tech Pinocchio-like story that had included a large workroom featuring thousands of white rubber torsos hooked on a seemingly endless hanging conveyor belt. The marble-white torsos had produced an inexplicably erotic feeling in Nikki. They were genderless. Breasts would later be added to some; to others, subtle six-pack stomachs and a solid rubber package where the legs came together. Nikki had won-

206 • RICHARD HAWKE

dered at the time why it was she found the torsos
so disturbing and compelling. She had imagined
lifting one of them off its hook and pressing it
against her own body, embracing it with all her
strength. In her imagination, the artificial torso had
proved malleable, a pliant rubber that, in response
to her own body's warmth, would begin to con-
form to her contours, molding itself around her as
she squeezed and squeezed and squeezed.

Nikki looked at her pale body rippling under
the water. She was still amazed at the marvels
of modern science. Or was it modern medicine?
Both. Under the water, her slender legs zigzagged
like some sort of cubist rendering. Her tiny waist
appeared magnified and liquid. Her flat tummy
undulated. Calories burned, calories avoided, a
love affair with her gym, plus the lucky draw of
petite genes. Now, still feeling so new after nearly
six months, the beautiful, perfect swell of these
fantastic marble-white breasts.

She touched one of them. Pliant. Just as
promised. She pinched it, and then she stroked it
and cupped it. Then again. Pinch, stroke, cup. Her
lustrous hair floated on the surface of the water
like an island of golden sand. With her other hand,
she reached lower. The toe was snug in the faucet
hole. It felt almost stuck there; she could imagine
that it was. She lifted her free foot and set it against
the tiled wall, as far up as she could manage. She

flexed her toes as forcefully as she dared, backing off when she sensed the low flinch of her calf muscle wanting to cramp. The toe in the faucet really did feel stuck now.

He likes it when I can't move. He likes it a lot.

Arching her back, she tilted her head to the point where the water lapped at the V of her hairline. Her torso rose while her hand stirred and wandered. Bathwater slapped rhythmically against the sides of the tub.

Half an hour later, Nikki got out of the tub. Rain was splattering against her window. She dried herself off and smoothed lotion over her arms, her thighs, her breasts. She removed the tags from the new plaid skirt and fastened it with the oversize safety pin around her waist. She modeled the purchase in the mirror, folding her arms over her breasts and swiveling this way and that, making the thin wool pleats swish. Do schoolgirls still wear these? she wondered. When he had asked her to buy it—giving specific details and insisting on giving her the money—he had told her precisely what he had in mind for the next time they got together.

And he had told her not to forget a change of clothes.

Nikki folded a loose cotton skirt into her bag. She chose the black V-neck pullover that she had decided not to throw out after the augmentation. It had been one of her favorites. The nurse at the clinic had clued her in: "Don't throw away the old stuff just yet, honey. It might find an all-new life."

The nurse had been right. The black V-neck pullover was nice and tight. Even more of a favorite than before.

"Wicked," she said to the mirror. Then she expertly applied her makeup, ruffled her damp hair—she was going to let it dry on its own into a tangled mane—and fastened the chain with the special pendant around her neck.

"Wicked," she said again.

And off she went to die.

MEGAN LAMB SLAPPED a two-pound cut of flank steak onto her cutting board and went at it with her large knife. She recalled the old anti-drug campaign: This is your brain. This is your brain on drugs.

As she hacked at the meat with her too-dull knife, she reworked the slogan: This is your brain. This is Brian McKinney's brain . . . on my cutting board!

A cord of bluish gristle required some sawing before Megan was able to sever the beef into two pieces. With a modified **Psycho** swing, she planted the knife into one of the pieces and let it remain there. She placed the other piece in a metal bowl of mustard and teriyaki marinade. The simple move triggered an image from several months before, not one that Megan welcomed. The image was that of Albert Stenborg's brain being lifted from its skull casing and settled onto a metal pan to be weighed. Joe Gallo, among others (Josh, to be sure), had urged Megan not to attend the Swede's autopsy, but she had ignored the pleas. She'd needed—or so she'd felt—to see the monster disassembled. She had hoped for some catharsis in hearing firsthand the medical examiner's dispassionate litany of damages wrought by the hail of bullets from Megan's service weapon. When the time came to extract the brain, Megan had inched closer to the table, determined to take a hard look. Only several hours later, seated in the dark corner of Klube's, had she realized that the answers to why Albert Stenborg had been the man he'd been and done the things he'd done weren't located in the spongy grayish pulp weighing three pounds, five ounces. For answers to those questions, the issue was more a matter of the monster's heart and what it was about his life that had damaged that tender organ so horrifically. These were answers that would never come.

Megan glanced out her small kitchen window at the wedge of a river view her place afforded. The call was for heavy evening rain—a classic April dousing—but nothing had started yet. The low clouds gathered over the river were gray and milky, belly-lit from Manhattan's excessive wattage. Across the Hudson, a series of silent lightning flashes was illuminating the scant skyline of Hoboken. Staccato blasts making it look as if the small city were suffering through a bombardment.

MEGAN OPENED a bottle of pinot grigio and poured half a glass. As early as a month ago, she would have poured a second glass and set it on the coffee table in front of where Helen usually sat. Megan had had no clue she was in possession of such a maudlin streak, but life is about discovery, isn't it? Sweet Helen. Megan went into the living room and looked at the framed photo on the bookshelf. It was the last photo that had been taken. Helen holding forth in this same room on New Year's Eve, waving her champagne glass as she presented her laundry list of resolutions, angling for "the perfect year." After Helen's murder at the hands of Albert Stenborg, Megan had put the picture in the frame and tried out dozens of different locations around the apartment. None had satisfied her, and she had seriously considered taking it to the photo shop on Greenwich and having them make multiple copies so she could display Helen's infectious laugh throughout the apartment. The shrink the department was sending her to didn't think that was such a good idea. Megan had made the mistake—she thought of it as a mistake—of telling the shrink about her practice of pouring the extra glass of wine and placing it where Helen usually sat. The shrink hadn't thought that was a good idea, either.

Today would have been Helen's birthday. Tonight. Now. Josh had promised to come directly from the airport, even though Megan had insisted she'd be fine. But he'd called several hours ago from the tarmac in Memphis. His phone breaking up. **Heavy rains. Delays. Not sure. Will call back.**

The rain began during Megan's second glass of wine. This time a full glass. The book on Cynthia Blair's murder was on the coffee table. Woefully thin for a ten-day-old murder. Cynthia Blair had last been seen alive at approximately four-thirty on the afternoon of April 15 by the Korean woman where Cynthia took her laundry to be done. Cynthia had returned to her apartment with two bundles of folded laundry in a Crate & Barrel shopping bag; she'd opened one of the bundles, rifling through it while leaving the other untouched. Details. Megan had ordered a chemical check on the clothes that Cynthia Blair was wearing when she was murdered, to determine which piece of newly laundered clothing she had opted to don before heading out later in the evening. Was it the pants? The blouse? The underwear? Socks? Or—least likely—was it the scarf that had been used to tie off her windpipe for the several minutes required to guarantee her death? It had proved to be the blue-and-white-striped underwear. Conclusion to be drawn? Nothing. Zero. Or at least nothing that Megan could come up with. She felt dulled, as though her instincts were numb. Her mind felt clumsy, and she wished Joe Gallo had never assigned her this homicide. Cynthia Blair was now a week in her grave, and her murder book was still thin.

And Brian McKinney was an asshole.

"I hear your vic put on fresh panties before she died," McKinney had needled that morning, pressing his hands on her desk as if keeping it from floating off. "Good work, Meg. Have you tracked down where she bought said panties? Might crack this whole case open in no time."

They say that everybody has somebody who loves them, but to Megan this merely meant that in McKinney's case, somebody was loving an asshole. She knew at least some of the reasons he was such a jerk to her. But he was **such** a jerk, she figured there had to be even more reasons than just the obvious ones. This time he had gone too far. Megan had been tipped off. Tomorrow's **Post** was going to have a scoop under Jimmy Puck's byline. **Unnamed sources confirm that Ms. Blair was in her third month of pregnancy at the time of her murder.**

Great. Just fine. One more cat out of the bag. Rusty bucket. Leaky bag. Oh, what the hell. Megan finished her wine and poured another glass. She supposed she should be grateful for getting a full ten days into her investigation with the information of Cynthia Blair's pregnancy remaining under wraps. Cynthia Blair wasn't McKinney's case, he didn't have anything to lose in handing a goodie like Cynthia's hitherto unreported pregnancy over to Jimmy Stupid Name Fat Butt Puck. Megan knew that the smirk would be firmly in place on McKinney's face when she walked into the station the next morning. And she knew what Joe Gallo would tell her: **Don't take it personally.**

But she wasn't taking it personally. Not this time. It was Cynthia Blair's parents Megan was thinking about. They'd be the ones taking it personally. Megan had been in Joe's office when the Blairs had arrived directly from the airport, the two nearly drained of the ability to speak, imploring Joseph Gallo with tear-reddened eyes to end the bad dream right now and present their daughter to them, alive and vibrant. The Blairs took the news of their daughter's pregnancy as if they had just been told she was composed entirely of green jelly beans. They couldn't take it in, and they had made Gallo repeat the information three times. Four times, actually, though at that point Joe had turned the chore over to Megan. Maybe it would be better coming from a woman. Megan had felt her skin begin to crawl as she detected the Blairs latching on to her. She was only a year older than Cynthia, and at least to the naked eye, she was a competent, capable young woman in a high-stress environment in the overwhelming city of New York. Just like Cynthia. Only she was still alive. Megan thought that Mrs. Blair in particular was more than ready to go quietly unhinged, take Megan by the hand and tell her, "Pack your things, honey, we're going home now." Megan had led the questioning—pro forma, she knew it from the get-go—about Cynthia's personal life, and did the Blairs have any indication from their daughter that she was seeing anyone in particular? Both Megan and Gallo knew that the questioning was a hollow exercise. People who knew Cynthia much better than the pale couple from Tucson and Cynthia's close friends and recent work colleagues had all responded to similar questions and offered up nothing except that they'd all thought Cynthia Blair had been too ambitious to have a personal life. That was the general rap. Her life had been her career. Or vice versa. The Blairs offered nothing beyond their full-scale wonder, consternation, and inability to process how the both of them had entered into this surreal dream together and how in the world they would find a way out of it. Joe Gallo had promised them that the information about Cynthia's pregnancy would remain private. "It's part of the investigation. But beyond that, it's nobody's business but yours."

The Blairs had shared a look. It was Cynthia's mother who voiced the thought. "I don't guess it's any of our business, either. Cindy didn't seem to think so."

THE MEAT IN THE MARINADE remained on the kitchen counter. An intrepid cockroach, having traveled from its favored nesting area within the electrical outlet behind the refrigerator, up the side of the cabinet and across the large open plain of the countertop, lay on its back in the marinade, its infinitesimal feet kicking uselessly, the armor of its skin no protection against the saturating juices. It would be dead by midnight.

The rain was falling steadily, a dim roar, a soft, ceaseless **shoosh.** Droplets bounced off the sill of Megan's open window, hitting the side of the toaster oven in a fanlike splatter. Crumbs moved erratically in the growing puddle. A rumble of thunder, and the lights in the apartment flickered, then went off altogether, then flickered back on under a minute later. The clocks in the apartment—the clock radio in the kitchen and the bedside clock radio—kicked to their default, blinking 12:00 . . . 12:00 . . . 12:00 . . .

OUT AT THE HUDSON PIER, Megan was sitting on one of the stone benches, hugging her knees to her chest. Rain dripped off the brim of her NYPD baseball cap onto the backs of her small hands. She was drenched, wearing only a windbreaker and her thick gray sweats, her feet bone-cold in a pair of saturated Converse low-tops. Her head was bent forward, and she was singing softly into the dry space. She hated the song. Insipid, stupid, ridiculous song. Devoid of all meaning, infantile, banal. Vaguely insulting, even. But the tune had her. She was helpless. It sucked the words out of her as if it were a parasite.

Happy birthday to you. Happy birthday to you . . .

~ 20 ~

IT HAD BEEN one of those rumors that go around. In the age of instant communication, it spread like a galloping virus.

Marshall Fox trolls the Internet.

The buzz was that, like millions of his fellow citizens, Marshall Fox liked to cloak his identity and go out there and talk dirty. **Very** dirty. Entire sites had cropped up devoted to alleged "sightings," lists of anonymous e-mail addresses that may or may not have been those of the popular late-night celebrity. Exchanges between the "willing" and the "alleged" were posted. Some of the postings had the ring of, if not truth, at least possibility. They **sounded** like Marshall Fox. They employed his jokes, his manner of speaking, key phrases that were associated with him. Of course, anyone with the ability to type and talent for mimicry could handle that. Most people knew well enough that it was largely considered a game. A celebrity impersonation. Cyberchat with a cyber wax figure. Cybersex with a personable fraud.

For a while it had been all the rage. The term "Fox-Trotter" had been coined to refer to the Fox pretenders. Fox himself encouraged the fad. Several nights a week, he would fashion a comic bit around some of the more outrageous postings attributed to him. As he sifted through handfuls of e-mail messages, his eyebrows would rise in mock amazement, the mischievous grin stretching across his face.

"So, apparently, I was in touch last night with an Ingrid and an Olga. Seems they were determined to tell me everything I wanted to know but was afraid to ask about Swedish meatballs." He milked the laugh and brandished another of the messages. "Look. Here's one from some fellow named Sven." Then, in a falsetto voice and a butchered Swedish accent, "De-yer Mr. Fox. Whatever yew dew? Stey awey from Innnngrid and Oooolga?"

NIKKI ROSSMAN LOVED the Internet. She had once heard it referred to as the portal to instant depravity, and she agreed completely. The Internet had opened up for Nikki an entirely new section of the day. Not really day but morning, though for Nikki, it was just an extension of the night before. Nikki lived in Tribeca, lower Manhattan, an area with no shortage of clubs and bars, and she loved to dance. She especially loved to get stoned and dance. She was an excellent dancer; her bones disappeared and she was all fluid movements, either fast and furious in all directions at once or slow, dreamy, undulating. She loved the glow of perspiration. She loved noise, the more deafening the music, the better. In a jam-packed club with the music pounding, a person can let loose with the sort of full-throttle screams and shrieks that at any other place in the city would give someone cause to snatch up the phone and punch 911. Nikki loved to shriek on the dance floor. It was a self-prescribed turn-on. She'd read something somewhere once about chakras; it hadn't made sense to her except the part that said loosening one could clear the way for loosening the others. Nikki took to the dance floor with a hopped-up vengeance, whooping and shrieking at the top of her tiny lungs, and in time she could **feel** the release taking place deep below. It made her hungry for sex—not ever much of a problem in most of the clubs. There were places. Dark corners. Bathrooms. If the night was nearly played out anyway and the guy was cute, there was her place, his place, someplace to go for it. The only risk was that the sex might not hit the spot she wanted it to hit; after the music and the dancing and the chakra-shaking shrieking, the guy had better close the fucking deal, that's all she could say. She even had a name for the kind of sex she wanted it to be. Cataclysmic. It could be hit-or-miss, she knew that. But baby, when it hit—when it was cataclysmic . . .

A man she once met at the Cat Club had referred to her as "a tight little package." Nikki loved that description. She thought of it every night as she readied herself to go out, worming her way into her panties, zipping up her baby-doll skirt. Tight little package. Open me first. She'd touch her wrists, the sides of her neck and her cleavage with any of the dozens of scents she lifted regularly from her job at Bloomie's, imagining that the heat generated on the dance floor would activate the scent and send it out in all directions. Warm blood for the wolves.

Great fun.

Then along came the Internet. It was nothing cataclysmic; it couldn't be. Hit the mute button and it was quiet as death. No pounding rhythms. No strobing lights. No pulsing sweat machines moving together around a cramped dance floor. It was a whole different thing. Tamer, no question about it. And a lot of the time, pathetically puerile.

Still, it was there, and it was constant. A portal to instant depravity. Four A.M. Ears buzzing. Chakras only partially satisfied. Turning the key and coming into her apartment alone. Nikki found it uncanny, all these freaks sitting out there God knows where, ready at the click of a mouse to climb into her virtual pants. What a riot! Thousands of them. Unseen by the human eye, cyberspace literally crawling with spunk—that was the only way she could put it. What a **freak** show. She loved it. Yes, you had to wade your way through the lamebrains—or, as her friend Tina called them, "numb nuts"—but like with anything else, a little practice, a little savvy, you could find what worked for you. They were there, the dudes with the moves. Or maybe some of them were chicks in disguise, but what did she really care? You weren't going to get any safer sex than this. It was a lark, a harmless way to spend some tawdry minutes before climbing into bed alone and kissing the world good night. And some of these guys were good. Nikki liked to think that she was good, too, that she could give as good as she got. Like in the so-called real world. Lord only knows if 90 percent of the people she chatted up would have registered as big fat zeros on her radar if she'd run across them in person. But in her apartment, lit only by the white glow of her computer screen, what difference did it make? None. Nikki's prompt was always the same: **I'm typing with one finger. Tell me what to do with the other nine.**

Very silly. Very immature. But get a clever respondent on the line, someone who had the touch, so to speak, and it wasn't a bad way to top off the evening before brushing the teeth and giving a quick run of the cold cream.

And sometimes, of course, she took it offline.

NIKKI HAD CHECKED OUT some of the so-called Marshall Fox sites. She never for a minute felt that she was actually in touch with the **real** Marshall Fox, but still, it was fun. Some of the pretenders were exceedingly creative and funny, and not a few showed an impressive flair for the erotic, which Nikki enjoyed.

One morning she had been online with two of the fakers. One of the fakers was far superior to the other. He had the stuff. He wasn't quite as clever as the real Marshall Fox, but come on, that guy had a whole bank of writers feeding him lines. But this guy was doing all right. He was pretty funny.

The other one? She wished he'd go away. She wondered if he might not be a twelve-year-old kid just getting his rocks off. Her friend Tina actually enjoyed fooling around with young boys online, but Nikki thought it was creepy. She wasn't into that kind of thing. This guy had just sent her a typo-ridden posting including a long-winded joke that Nikki had already read online the week before. It was about a talking dog and a beauty pageant contestant and . . . it was stupid. She wished the other fake Marshall Fox would send something. It had been ten minutes since he had sent her anything. He'd probably gotten offline. That's where I should be, Nikki told herself. Her elbow hit the mouse as she twisted in her chair to see if dawn's early light was beginning to show. Not yet. Thank God.

Nikki scanned the talking-dog joke. Her orange fingernails clattered on her keyboard.

Dogs know when I have just had sex.

What the hell. She hit send. A minute later, a message appeared on her screen. It wasn't from the kid, or whatever he was. It was from the other fake Marshall Fox. The good one. Nikki realized what she must have done. When her elbow hit the mouse, she must have clicked back to the other guy's last message.

Lucky dogs.

She typed, **I'm glad you think so.**

The screen was still for nearly a minute. Nikki thought maybe she had lost him. Then:

I want to be a lucky dog.

Nikki giggled out loud as she typed back: **The lucky dog who knows I have just had sex or the lucky dog who just had it with me?** Oh God. I've got to stop this and get some sleep. She hit send.

The answer came back immediately.

Both.

THE CYBER-FLIRTATION HAD gone on for close to two months. He adopted a new identity, just for her. Lucky Dog. For him, Nikki dropped Love Bar and countered with Bitch. He wrote back that she was clever.

Why, I bet you can even do tricks.

He also preferred four in the morning for his online dalliances. He wrote that he was always awake at that hour and enjoyed corresponding with her while the rest of the world slept. Nikki deduced from the comment that he must be located somewhere on the East Coast. When she put the question to him, he responded: **I'm Marshall Fox, remember? Where else would I be writing from?**

Right. Of course.

They got into a rhythm. At four on the nose, Nikki would shoot out a one-word command.

Speak.

Within seconds came the response.

Woof.

And off they went. Lucky Dog was a riot. So long as they were just bantering back and forth, he kept his postings short. He knew how to make her laugh. He was quick. He picked up on little things she'd mentioned and shot them back to her with his particular skew. They could have been talking in a bar. More than once she found herself wishing that they were.

He was good. It was almost creepy how good he was, almost as if he were crouched behind her as she sat at her computer, whispering into her ear, deftly guiding her hands, guiding her thoughts. Sometimes that was precisely what he wrote:

I'm there with you. I'm in the kitchen at the moment, fetching a glass of warm water. Hang tight, I'll be right back in. I want to hold it up against your neck.

And a few seconds later:

Okay, I'm back. You can feel it, can't you? It's not too hot, just a little warm, right? Good. Why don't you take my other hand and give that lovely breast of yours a soft touch. You know where. That place we both like.

And damned if she couldn't **feel** it. The slight warmth on the back of her neck, almost like a breath. And somebody's fingers running very lightly over her . . .

SHE WANTED TO meet him. Yes, it was probably a stupid idea. It would probably ruin everything, but what the hell? She wanted it. Maybe it could be fun. God forbid, maybe it could be cataclysmic.

She broached the subject.

Does Lucky Dog want to come out and play?

It had been a frustrating evening. Nikki and Tina had gone clubbing and ended up in an argument. Over a boy, no less. A hard-bodied Honduran named Victor. They met him at the Vault. Correction. Nikki met him at the Vault. The two were already on the dance floor when Tina came back into the club. She'd gone outside to make a phone call. Victor was hot. Awesome moves, he had Nikki spinning like a top. He lifted her clear off the floor, a rock-solid arm around her small waist. He had dark lashes, cocoa skin, an almost feminine mouth. He'd been into Nikki, she could tell. But something screwed up somewhere. Nikki skipped off to the bathroom to sharpen her makeup, and when she came back, Tina and Victor were practically screwing right on the dance floor. Twenty minutes later, they were practically screwing in the dark hallway on the way to the bathrooms. Nikki purposefully hip-checked Tina as she passed by the two of them, and Tina followed her into the bathroom and nearly tore her eyes out. Nikki had left the club and ended up at Sugar. The cute bartender was there. So was his girlfriend. It looked to Nikki like the breakup wasn't a whole lot in evidence. The bartender set a Cosmo in front of her. "Six dollars." She left the drink on the bar.

Lucky Dog didn't respond for nearly five minutes. Great, Nikki thought. Three strikes and I'm out, now I've chased **him** away. She was just about to send a follow-up telling him she hadn't meant it, when up popped his response:

Do I have this right? You want to take me out for a walk?

Her heart skipped its next beat. She typed: **Only if you promise to heel.**

A minute later: **Pull hard enough on the leash, baby, I'll do whatever you want.**

Nikki stared at the screen for a long minute. The cursor blinked urgently. He was waiting. She tried to imagine him, but no image came to mind. She had never put even a fantasy face on Lucky Dog. He was a cipher, something strictly in the ether. If she shut down her computer right now, she could keep it that way. They could still play online. They could keep doing their silly things to each other. His hands could still get to her only via her hands. She could remain in complete control. In her darkened apartment. Alone.

She thought of Tina and Victor. The cute bartender and his girlfriend. She ran a hand across her flat, firm tummy.

Well, screw **this**.

She typed: **Your town or mine?**

Lucky Dog responded: **I'm already here, sweetheart.**

In New York?

That's a fact.

Get out. I don't believe you.

Would you like me to prove it?

Yes. Prove it.

A minute passed, and then he wrote back, asking what part of the city she lived in.

Tribeca.

What time do you leave for work in the morning?

Around ten.

Perfect. E-mail me right before you leave. I'll tell you what to do.

Getting bossy, aren't we?

Pause: **You ain't seen nothing yet.**

In the morning, she did as he had requested. He instructed her to go to the drama section of Ruby's Books on Chambers Street and look through the copies of Shakespeare's **As You Like It.** She followed the instructions. Ruby's was only a couple of blocks past her subway stop. Nikki felt considerably self-conscious the entire time, trying not to be too obvious about looking over her shoulder as she approached the store and made her way to the drama section. He must be watching. But where is he? There were only three other customers in the store, an old lady and two gay guys, and none of them was paying any attention to her. There were four copies of the play on the shelf. The first copy of the play she leafed through had nothing in it that she could see. When she pulled the second copy off the shelf, a small envelope fell from it. Inside was a note and something small wrapped in tissue paper. The note read: **And how exactly do you like it?**

The tissue contained a slender chain to which was attached an aluminum dog tag. The word BITCH was inscribed on it. Nikki clutched it to her breast and burst into laughter.

She kept the dog tag in the pocket of the white coat she had to wear on the job. Her fingers ran over it so much she was afraid she might wear down the word. At four the following morning, Nikki hopped online.

Okay. Where?

He wrote back: **Tribeca Animal Hospital on Lispenard Street.**

What???!!!

Ten o'clock tonight.

Are you nuts?

Wait and see.

She gave it one more thought, then typed her response. She lifted her index finger, gave it a kiss and hit send.

MARSHALL FUCKING FOX.

At five minutes past ten, a tan Lincoln Town Car pulled to the curb in front of the Tribeca Soho Animal Hospital. The back door opened, and for Christ's sake, **Marshall Fox**—the real Marshall Fox—was sitting there, prairie-wide grin and all. Nikki was speechless. What were the chances? Who in the world was ever going to believe a coincidence like this? Tina would freak. Or wait. Was someone putting her on? Was this all an elaborate hoax? She looked closer. Maybe it wasn't really Marshall Fox at all. Maybe it was just someone who looked a ton like him.

"Come here," he said, and he waved her over.

She finally found her voice. "You're Marshall Fox."

"Do you know what else I am? I am one lucky

little dog." He reached his hand out. "Now come on over here. I'm not going to bite."

Three hours later, he'd be proving himself a liar on that count.

Fox and Nikki rode aimlessly around Manhattan, drinking champagne and snorting lines of what Fox promised was the highest-quality pure cocaine. He was, if this was possible, even more charming and funny and sexy in person than he was on television. Nikki was amazed. He **sounded** like Lucky Dog. He really did sound the way he had in his e-mails. **His** e-mails. Marshall Fox. The real Marshall Fox.

"I'm going to spend the entire night pinching myself," she declared as he filled her glass with more bubbly. "Marshall fucking goddamn Lucky Dog Fox!" For the tenth time that night, she placed her fingers against his cheek. "You're still real. I am blown away."

At midnight, he had her between his legs. He watched Columbus Circle go by outside the tinted car windows as he hummed to himself, one hand lazily stirring the woman's blond hair. Yessir. Lucky, lucky dog.

She had to know. She insisted on knowing. What in the world was going on here?

He explained. No, it had never crossed his mind to go dipping into the anonymous world of cyber-flirting and cybersex, not until the purported Marshall Fox Internet exchanges had erupted to become all the rage. He had found it amusing; witness his use of the craze on his show for a while there.

"Did you notice about when I stopped doing those bits?" he asked.

Nikki told him that the show was usually over by the time she got home. "I mean, I love it and all. I just don't get to see it all the time."

"We phased out a couple of months ago. I'd finally gotten curious and gone online. I knew most of the sites. My staff had been monitoring them all. I pulled the plug on the bits soon after you and I started going back and forth. I told my producer it was time to let it drop."

The Town Car was cruising slowly up Central Park West. Nikki knew that the celebrity was separated from his wife and that he was living in one of these buildings here somewhere. She eyed him with suspicion. "You've done this before, haven't you? Hooked up with someone like this."

He raised his right hand. "I swear. Never. This is the very first time."

She smoothed her skirt. "What if I really had been a dog? I mean, you know."

"I knew you weren't, sugar. I checked you out."

She thought a moment. "Ruby's."

"I was parked outside. I got me a nice long

look as you came up the block. Did you feel the binoculars on you?"

She giggled. "You're a freak."

"I liked."

"Well, still, I could be a certified psycho. You know how this town is."

Fox proceeded to tell her her full name, where she was born, her current address, where she worked, where she went to college, her Social Security number, even the date of her breast implant surgery and the name of the clinic that had performed the procedure.

Nikki's jaw dropped. "Explain."

Fox pressed a button on his armrest. "Danny? Miss Rossman thinks you are a shit for snooping into her life the way you did. I think she's right. Though she does have to admit, you did great work on such short notice."

The driver twisted around and gave a thumbs-up through the thick glass pane. Nikki saw his eyes drop down to her legs before they returned to the road.

Fox explained, "Danny followed you after you left the bookstore. I couldn't exactly do it." He laughed. "Jesus. We're really talking cloak-and-dagger here, aren't we? Anyway, he got hold of your name at Bloomingdale's and then hustled to get all the rest of it. The man is good. No better assistant in the world. I'm sorry about the invasion of privacy. But hey, all's well that ends well, as Billy Shakes likes to say."

Fox's apartment was in the San Remo on Central Park West. He directed Danny to take the two of them there, and Nikki stayed the night.

"We can do this straight or we can do this wild," Fox said as he walked her through the spacious living room. "I'm not going to force anything on you. You're very sweet, and God knows you're very sexy, and I really do want to gobble up your sweet little ass. But I'm not going to push anything. I'm just happy that you're here. You, me and no paparazzi. You can't imagine how good it feels to have a secret. You're gold to me, lady."

Nikki remained silent as Fox began unbuttoning his shirt. He stepped closer to her. "Give me your hand, sweetie. I think we're going to be fine."

SEVEN NIGHTS SCATTERED throughout three weeks. Seven insane nights. Marshall Fox was a bad, bad boy, no question about it. Bad, bad, and good, **good.** Fox had a lot of ideas about how to spice things up in the bedroom—or, on one occasion, on the building's rooftop garden. He was a fantastic lover, even without the toys he liked to bring in on the action. It could get rough sometimes before it was all over, sometimes more than Nikki might have preferred. But look who it was. He was famous. And he was choosing to do all this stuff with **her.**

And besides, the sex was—yep—cataclysmic.

He'd asked her that first night not to tell anyone what they were up to. "I need one damn thing to call my own, sweetie. Let's make that you."

THREE WEEKS AFTER their first date, the body of Cynthia Blair turned up dead in Central Park. She had been strangled and her body had been left at the base of Cleopatra's Needle just behind the Metropolitan Museum. Nikki didn't have a phone number where she could call Marshall. Even if she had, she wasn't sure it would have been the right thing to do. But he wasn't responding to her messages on his Lucky Dog e-dress. She felt like she was a million miles away from him.

Nikki watched Fox on television and she cried. He looked so lost. It was absurd to even try to do the show, she thought. Look at him. She wanted to hold him and comfort him. Poor baby, he was in such pain. She thought about just showing up at his building but decided that might be wrong. She'd just have to wait and hope that he still wanted to see her. At his request, she'd gone out after their last date and purchased that plaid wool skirt he'd jabbered on about. He'd wanted it for one of his games. **Call me,** she implored the television set. **I'm here, honey. I'll do anything you need me to do for you. Anything. You're the boss. I'll make you forget everything. I can do it.**

Nine days after Cynthia Blair's murder, he contacted her. E-mail. He wanted to see her. That night.

I need normal. Well, okay, you know me better than that. What I don't need is all the crap that's been going on this week. I need a break. I need a lucky break. You're the one, babe. No one else in the whole damn world.

She wrote back immediately: **Yes!**

Excellent. Danny'll fetch you at ten. And let's go with the schoolgirl look. A little virgin sacrifice is good for the soul.

↜ 21 ↜

FRESHLY BATHED, Nikki headed down the steps at 9:50. Mrs. Campanella on the third floor was taking a bag of kitchen trash downstairs.

"Look at you, all dolled up. It's my bedtime, and here you are going out dancing."

Nikki offered to take the trash from her neighbor and throw it in the can outside the building's front door. The woman waved her off.

"This is my exercise for the entire day, honey. The doctor says I need to keep active. I might still be climbing back up these stairs by the time you get back from your date."

Nikki remembered that she had forgotten a sympathy card that she had bought for Cynthia Blair's family. She wasn't certain if it was right to ask Marshall to deliver it for her. She had signed it with her initials, followed by "Someone Who

Cares," but she wondered if what she was really doing was trying to score points with Fox. Still, she did feel horrible about what had happened to the woman. Nikki climbed the stairs back to her apartment and fetched the card. It was in a pale blue envelope. Mrs. Campanella was nearing the first floor by the time Nikki made it to the bottom.

"Have a good night, honey. You'd better take an umbrella. They're calling for rain."

Danny was leaning up against the Town Car when Nikki emerged from the building. He took her in with an approving look. "Boss man's going to be one happy camper to see you. He's been a real pain in the ass the whole week."

Nikki found Fox in a black mood when she arrived. No surprise. He looked haggard. She handed him the sympathy card. "Maybe it's stupid." Fox didn't say a word about it. He set the card on a small table in the hallway. He seemed distracted, but he tried to pretend that he was fine.

He made them martinis, and they took them out on the balcony. There was a slight rain falling. They remained under the overhang of the balcony above. From up this high—the apartment was on the twenty-sixth floor—the shadowy silhouette of Cleopatra's Needle was just visible. Fox said nothing but stood sipping his martini, looking out across the tops of the trees toward the stone obelisk. Nikki wanted to touch him, to set her fingers on his arm, but she didn't dare. His face was impassive, a granite frown. After nearly a minute, he spoke.

"Believe it or not, it's not Cynthia that's got me all cranked out. It's my wife. It's Rosemary." He drained his martini. Nikki took the empty glass from his hand. Fox's gaze stayed aimed toward the far side of the park. "I spent the afternoon with her before heading off to the studio. It wasn't exactly what you'd call a pretty afternoon. That woman . . . I should give **her** that dog tag of yours. You've got no idea."

Nikki's hand went to her memento. "She'll have to fight me for it. It's mine."

Fox's expression loosened. "Listen. Whatever you do, don't ever challenge Rosemary. I'm serious. You're a sweet kid. Rosemary'd rip you to pieces."

Nikki remained on the balcony while Fox went back in to put together another martini. She couldn't imagine how he must feel. He'd never said anything to her before about his former producer, though she knew from some stuff she'd read somewhere that the professional relationship had ended on a kind of ugly note. That has to hurt, she thought. You work closely with someone, things end badly, and then she's killed. No chance to patch things up. She looked out across the park again, over toward where the body of Cynthia Blair had been discovered nine days before. A shudder went through her as she imagined the woman vainly battling off her attacker. Did she see it coming? Did she have time to call for help, to let out a scream? Jesus, Nikki thought. In the middle of the night, this part of the city can get pretty quiet. She thought of Marshall lying in his bed asleep. Or no—awake. Lying awake and hearing a faint distant scream coming in on the night air. You hear that kind of thing all the time and don't really think anything about it. City noise. You don't think that someone you know is making the last sound they're ever going to make or that—

"Hey."

A splash from her drink ploinked onto her wrist. Fox stepped up behind her. Nikki turned around and looked up at him. Backlit from the living room, Fox's face was in shadow, his eyes black and absent in their deep sockets.

"That's a nice skirt, little girl." There was something absent as well from his voice. His tone was low. Robotic.

Nikki tried a curtsy. "You like it?"

Fox lifted the glass from her hand and finished off the drink, then casually tossed the glass aside. It shattered on impact.

"Little girl like jewelry?"

He pulled something shiny from his pocket and held it up. Light from the apartment glinted off its surface.

Nikki took the handcuffs from him and gave him a coy smile. "Aw. You shouldn't have."

Minutes later, Nikki was lying on the bed, faceup, with both wrists handcuffed to the bars of the antique wire headboard. Her V-neck sweater was bunched on the floor. The dog tag rested just between her perfect breasts. Fox was pulling off his shirt.

"That skirt's got to go, little girl. We've got to get that thing off you."

He picked up something shiny from beside the alarm clock as he climbed onto the bed. A pair of scissors. When he came down on top of her, Nikki imagined the warmth of her own torso melting him. Melting them both. Like hard rubber going soft. She imagined the two of them as warm melting liquid. That was it. Nothing but liquid. Everywhere. Warm liquid all over the damn place. Crazy with liquid.

"Cut it," she murmured into his ear, giving it a sharp bite. "Go ahead. Cut it."

⤬ 22 ⤬

MEGAN STOOD in the drizzle at the base of the Obelisk and read the translation of the inscribed plaques.

> Ramesses, Beloved-of-Amun, who came forth from the womb in order to receive the crowns of Ra, who created him to be sole lord the Lord of the Two Lands. . . .

Okay, she thought. So we're looking for Ramesses, beloved of Amun. This'll be a piece of cake.

The roof of the museum was visible beyond the trees. Megan's dulled mind whirred. The rooftop garden. Mount an infrared camera. Bastard tries for number three, we nail him. She looked over at the sheet-covered body, and the bile rose in her throat. The canopy had been set up to protect the immediate crime scene from any additional rain intrusion. The scene's likeness to a funeral was unavoidable. The body, the canopy, the world's tallest gravestone. Megan's new partner, Ryan Pope—a decent stand-in for the priest—was standing near the edge of the canopy, looking up at the tip of the Needle.

Megan wanted to crawl into a hole and gather the loose dirt in behind her.

A uniformed cop made his way to her. Raindrops beaded like balls of mercury on the protective plastic of his cap. "Found something you'll want to see."

"Show me."

She followed the policeman down the slight slope north of the monument. A copse of cherry trees stood at the base of the slope, some twenty feet from the roadway. Another uniformed cop was crouched in an area where the branches of several trees created a low canopy.

"We found tracks," the cop said.

"Tire tracks?"

"Yes, ma'am."

Megan gave the officer a sharp look. Old women were ma'ams. Old women and southerners. "How old are you?"

"Twenty-five."

"Tell me about your tire tracks."

He pointed toward the roadway. "They come in over the curb. Looks like they stop where my partner is."

Megan nodded. "You mean where your partner is tromping all over the wet ground?"

"No, ma'am. John's the one who spotted the tracks right where he's squatting. He hasn't moved."

She looked at the cop again to make sure he wasn't being a wise guy. "Tell your partner to stay where he is. I'll send down the photographer. Make sure he gets everything."

"If we're lucky, we might get some footprints leading up to the body."

"If we're lucky, I'll buy your partner a cigar."

"John doesn't smoke, ma'am."

Megan started to respond, then changed her mind. She retraced her steps up the slope and directed the crime-scene photographer to go shoot the tracks. Pope asked her, "What've you got?"

"Possibility our package was delivered by car. There's a clump of trees down there just off the road. At night you could pull in there, your car'd be fairly hidden."

"No evidence last time of a car."

"The last time he also didn't have a hammer and nail ready, either. Not to mention the knife to cut open her throat."

"He's refining his method."

Megan shrugged. "Using more hardware. That's not necessarily refining."

The ambulance had arrived to transport the body to the medical examiner's office. Megan asked that the area beneath the canopy be cleared. At a signal from her, Ryan Pope pulled the sheet back from the victim's face, paused, then removed it altogether. He stepped back as Megan came forward for a final look.

The body was splayed on the ground on her back. The woman was petite. Maybe five-one. Long blond hair, clumps of which were saturated with blood. Her slender neck was a mess, the blood in the wound more black than red. Like a mass of insects, Megan thought. The victim appeared to have suffered several blows to the left side of her head, just above her ear. Her right arm was stretched out above her head, a pair of handcuffs attached to the wrist. Her left hand was resting on her chest, held in place by what looked to be a nail, hammered dead center.

"Who'd you piss off, cutie?"

Megan's words were so soft they were barely discernible to Pope. She squatted next to the victim's head and forced herself to gaze at the face. Perfect skin. White as wax. The large brown eyes were open, staring up at the underside of the canopy. Mascara ran from them like dark, blurred tears. A dozen sentiments crowded onto Megan's

tongue, but she forced them all to retreat. The revolving light of the silent ambulance was playing
off the victim's face, lending the illusion that there
was some slight movement there. Megan closed
her eyes and uttered a silent prayer. Not so Pope
could see, her hand dropped and she let her fingers trail lightly along the victim's wrist.

IT WAS LESS than an hour after getting back
from the park that Megan overheard Brian
McKinney starting in on Nicole Rossman. He
was cracking a can of Pepsi at the door of the so-
called lounge.

"I hear we've got someone slashing blow-up
dolls out in the park."

He was talking to Ryan Pope, but his comment was aimed for as large an audience as could
hear him, Megan being the prime target. To say
nothing in response was to hand him a simple
victory. To bother responding was doing the same
thing. Lose, lose. Story of her life these days.

Megan said, "Better go check your locker,
Brian. See if your doll is missing."

McKinney gave a deliberately slow reaction, a
world-class lousy show of surprise. "Why, it **is**
missing, Detective. But I thought you said you
were going to return it last night after you were
finished with it."

Calm, Megan thought. Inhale, exhale. McKinney went on, "I hear you caught yourself a real silicone special over at the Needle. Jackson's promised to share some of the shots he took on the scene. Bodacious. He swears he saw a pair just like them at Hooters the other night."

"Does your mother know you're this cute?"

McKinney leveled a finger at her. "Hey now, Lamby. Don't go bringing my dear mother into this."

"The victim was somebody's daughter, Brian. It might not hurt to keep that in mind."

"Oh, yes, sir. Thank you for reminding me, sir."

Pope shot Megan a sympathetic look. She nodded tersely at the both of them and headed down the corridor toward Gallo's office. As she rounded the corner, she heard McKinney's deliberate stage whisper: "Shake it now, Lamby chops."

Gallo was at his desk, reading the medical examiner's preliminary report. He looked up as Megan entered his office. "I'm looking at a number here, Megan. You want to give me a name?"

Megan dropped into the chair in front of Gallo's desk. "Nicole Vanessa Rossman. Friends called her Nikki. Twenty-four. Single. Employed at the Tigress fragrance counter at Bloomingdale's. Lived in a rental in Tribeca."

"Says here there's evidence of recent sexual activity. Quote, not gentle, unquote. Do we think she was raped?"

"Nothing at the scene takes us in either direction. If it was rape, the panties went back on before the gentleman moved on to his next order of business."

"Cynthia Blair wasn't raped."

"That's correct. However, both women were left at the base of a fairly obvious phallic symbol."

Gallo's eyebrows raised. "I hadn't thought of that. They didn't have cigars in their hands, too, by any chance, did they?"

"Is that supposed to be funny?"

"Sorry. It's just not something I'd have thought of right away."

"Blame it on my therapy."

Gallo ran his hand lightly over his hair. "Okay. First thing's obvious."

"Who was she seeing?"

"Right. Boyfriend. Ex-boyfriend. Wanna-be boyfriend. Next-door neighbor with a peephole drilled into the wall."

"It should be so easy."

"And the other thing," Gallo said. "Probably more important. The connection between Rossman and Blair. Were they friends? Did they frequent the same restaurants or bars or clubs? Maybe the same health club. What was it you said Nikki

Rossman did? Sold perfume at Bloomingdale's? See if Cynthia Blair had any of that perfume at her place. Somebody knew the two of them. That's the triangulation we've got to make. We know we're not talking about a copycat here. We haven't released the information about Cynthia Blair's hand being affixed to her chest."

"And so far, Jimmy Puck doesn't seem to have gotten the word."

Gallo took a beat. "We both knew that Blair's pregnancy was bound to come out sooner or later."

"It would have been nice if it had come from us. I mean officially."

"There's a message for either of us to call Cynthia's mother in Tucson," Gallo said. "If it doesn't make any difference to you, I'm going to make the call."

"McKinney should make the fucking call," Megan said pointedly.

"You wouldn't do that to the Blairs."

"No, I guess you're right. You know, he's already started, Joe. Just now I had to do a little dance with him about Nicole. For Christ's sake, she's practically still warm."

"No one ever accused McKinney of bucking for the Mr. Sensitivity merit badge."

"Let's forget him," Megan said. "I'm sorry I brought him up."

"Look, maybe we'll get lucky. Maybe the word

on Cynthia being pregnant will bring someone forward. Contacting every obstetrician in the city to see if they were seeing Blair hasn't exactly been the lean-and-mean approach. It could prove to be a decent leak."

"Do you want to pin a badge on Jimmy Puck and make it official? This is **our** case. How about **we** control the flow of information? Well, forget it. It's done. Cynthia's going to be background noise anyway, now that there's fresh blood. Nicole Rossman was a pretty little sexpot, to put it bluntly. I'm sure you know there's already a pool on how many days in a row her photo will make front page of the **Post**."

"We need a connection between the two, and quick," Gallo said. "If this is just random women . . . Well, how many random women do we have in Manhattan alone?" Gallo's phone rang. He grabbed it. "Yeah? Okay. Tell them I'll be right out." He hung up the phone and straightened his tie. "Nicole Rossman's parents are here."

Megan groaned. "Take a look through all those papers on your desk, Joe. I know my resignation is in there somewhere."

MEGAN CALLED a Thai restaurant for takeout. When the delivery guy showed up, she had to

walk down the narrow steep stairs of her building to the first floor. One day the buzzer would
work again, she just knew it. Josh had offered to
fix it, but that wasn't what she wanted. She
wanted the landlord to fix it, like he was supposed to do. Of all the battles a person might
choose, Megan knew that this one was among
the most ridiculous. She couldn't explain clearly
why she allowed her slovenly landlord to get
under her skin. She could have opted to avoid
him more often, work around him, call a truce,
go on a charm offensive, ignore her apartment's
problems, any of a dozen options.

That she chose to keep him as an object of her
anger might have been amusing if it weren't so
pathetic. Josh had been the one to suggest that
maybe it was because Helen had always been the
one to square off against the landlord and that, in
her absence, Megan was taking up the battle.
When Josh had floated the theory, it had
sounded too pat to Megan's ear. Typical Josh-
think. But as she reflected on it, she had seen the
logic. She didn't want to see it, but it was there
and hard to deny.

She paid for her pad thai, giving the delivery
guy a good tip. On her way back up the steps, her
toe caught a frayed pocket of the runner and she
stumbled, almost falling to her knees. The blood
rushed into her face. I'll trip and fall down the

steps and I'll paralyze myself and I'll **sue** that fat prick for every fucking cent he's got.

While eating her noodles in the small kitchen, Megan went through the two sets of crime-scene photographs. She laid them out on the tiled floor, Cynthia Blair on the left, Nicole Rossman on the right. The photographs covered nearly the entire floor. Forensics had determined that Cynthia Blair's attack had taken place essentially where the body had been discovered, on the west side of the Obelisk, the side facing away from the park roadway. Apparently, Nikki's attack had taken place elsewhere and she was transported to the site, presumably dead already. Tests were being run on the tire tracks that had been lifted from the wet ground. Megan had sent a team of investigators moving out in widening arcs from the Egyptian monument in search of more evidence of Nikki or her attacker, but by nightfall nothing of consequence had turned up. The teams were going to resume work tomorrow. However, the farther from the Obelisk the teams moved, the less certain Megan was that they would be turning up anything. Still, even notwithstanding the lack of the actual murder site and any evidence that might be gleaned from it, it was significant that whoever had carried out the attack on Nikki had moved the body so that it would be found exactly where Cynthia Blair had been found. Significant of **what**, Megan didn't yet know.

The photographs told her nothing she didn't already know. One a choking with the victim's own scarf, the other a bashed skull and a knife to the throat. Megan sat with her elbows planted on the kitchen table, scissoring the pad thai with the red lacquered chopsticks she had given Helen for some occasion she could no longer recall. Her eyes trolled back and forth along the sets of photographs. As she seared the photographs into her brain, Megan found value in trying to imagine the killer in the moment before he quit the scene. The crime-scene photographer had taken shots from nearly every angle. At least one of these angles had to approximate the view of the killer as he looked down on his handiwork. Megan rose from her chair and stood over the photographs, casting her own shadow on them.

I'm the killer, she thought. I'm taking one last look at what I've done.

She stepped carefully around the photographs of the two slain women, sampling the different angles. Clutching the chopsticks in her right fist, she assumed a sense of being heavier than she was. Taller. With her free hand, she pushed her hair off her face and held it there, clutching it tightly, using the hair to pull her head back, exposing her neck. She looked at a close-up of Nikki's left hand. Two of her sculpted nails were broken off. Megan placed her own short fingernails against her neck and pressed. She imagined a heavy guttural breathing, sharp grunts as the knife worked its way from one side to the other. She lowered herself to her knees and stared at the open eyes of Nikki Rossman. Then it came to her. The utter loathing forthe person who had done this, the person whose actions she was aping in the privacy of her small kitchen. Megan caught her breath. She placed the tips of the chopsticks against her abdomen and pressed them there. Softly at first but then harder. The chopsticks were pressing into her skin. They were hurting. Hurt **him,** she thought. Let **him** feel what it's like. And not a quick slashing cut, either, but something slower and deliberate. Something meaningful. Her hand was beginning to tremble with the effort, and Megan closed her eyes, trying to picture the killer. Faceless. A face in shadow.

Suddenly, as if a fork of lightning had ripped through her imagination, a face did appear. The Swede. Of course. The goddamn Swede. The broad brow. The large dull mouth. **Him.** She pressed the chopsticks even harder as she imagined Albert Stenborg and his large, oafish smile. She wanted to see blood seeping its way out of the Swede's mouth. She wanted to see his heavy blue eyes freeze in sudden bewilderment, followed by the awareness. Hands-on this time. Not from a distance. Not with a handgun. So much more meaningful this way. Megan imagined she could move as close to his face as she wished. Close enough to feel his foul breath. Close enough this time to see her own reflection in his eyes, and to see in them the last thing on earth the murderous bastard was ever going to see.

Her.

The chopsticks snapped. The broken ends fell lightly to the floor, landing on the photograph showing a close-up of Nikki Rossman's hand. The one nailed into her heart. Megan opened her eyes and looked down at her own belly. A tiny pink strip. A quarter-inch cut. In the scheme of things, nothing. On her hands and knees, she gathered up the photographs of the two murder victims, squared off the pile and placed it reverently on the kitchen table. There was enough pad thai in the container for two people. Or for a second meal. Megan finished it off. She took a shower, got into her faded robe and took the photographs into the front room, where she spread them out again on the floor, this time in front of the couch. She poured herself a small glass of bourbon and got onto the couch.

At twelve-thirty, Megan tried getting into bed. She made certain to drink several full glasses of water before she got under the sheets. There was a slight buzzing in her temples. She picked up the remote and turned on the television. Ever since Cynthia Blair's murder, Megan had made it a habit to watch **Midnight with Marshall Fox.** She had never been a particularly huge fan of Fox, which she knew put her in the minority. She found his show oddly uneven. This one was a rerun. Megan realized that this was what she had tuned in tonight to find out. Was Marshall Fox going to stand up and make jokes in front of the entire country on the day when another young woman had been found murdered in nearly identical circumstances as his former producer? Megan was glad to see that the answer was no.

Megan watched the rerun for about twenty minutes, then turned it off. She shut off the light, wondering if this would finally be the night. Praying it might. Immediately, Nikki Rossman and Cynthia Blair climbed into bed with her. Next came Brian McKinney. He was followed by Marshall Fox. Megan flipped the light back on. Not tonight, then, dammit.

She got out of bed and went into the bathroom, where she stared at her reflection for over a minute. After this many months, Megan hoped she'd have started to get accustomed to those eyes. But they were every bit as foreign to her as they were the first time she'd seen them, right after she killed the Swede. But maybe that was actually a good thing, she thought, the fact that she wasn't acclimating to them. She didn't like looking at them, but she felt she had no choice. She had to face them. They were the only real truth she knew these days, even if it was not a particularly pleasant truth. Helen was dead. Truth. Cold, hard truth. So was the Swede. But the one wasn't making up for the other. Not like it was supposed to. The math was off. She had dispatched the Swede, but the pain was still there. If anything, it was still growing, not shrinking away into the past like it was supposed to do. And some nights it hurt so horrifically that Megan didn't know what to do with it. Stay home, she told herself. This was all she knew, her single piece of advice to herself. It was no solution for the pain, but she did know it was the right thing to do. Those several months of crawling into the darkness after taking her leave of absence from the department had not been the solution, not by a long shot. They had hurt. They'd been dangerously harmful. She might have curled up and remained there in the dark places if not for Josh. Thank God for Josh.

Megan shut her eyes and instantly saw Helen's still and battered form, curled at the feet of Albert Stenborg. Megan felt like a knife was slashing at her lungs. At that precise moment, she knew that she should step down from the investigations. Something unhealthy was at play here. Some murky math. Helen's killer was dead and in the ground, but apparently that wasn't enough. It would never be enough. Not one cheap life for one beautiful one. The evil of that bastard was still out there, even if the man himself wasn't. That was the problem. That was what Megan hadn't succeeded in obliterating— the evil. It slipped from person to person. It had slipped up on Cynthia Blair and on Nikki Rossman. Megan had killed the Swede but not the evil. Albert Stenborg was simply evil's discarded skin. Irrelevant. It was still out there, on the hunt, reaching from the shadows and plucking victims whenever it pleased.

Megan went into the living room and fetched the photograph of Helen from the bookshelf. She took it to the coffee table and set it there, facing the couch. She lay down on the couch, pulling the thin blanket off the back of the couch and spreading it over her. Not for the first time—not by a long shot—she told herself that if this kept up, she might as well just sell the stupid goddamn bed, for all the good it was doing her.

— 23 —

NIKKI ROSSMAN HAD LAST BEEN reported
seen by a neighbor in her building. A widow
named Rose Campanella told the police that she
had seen Nikki carrying a shoulder bag, climbing
into a "big fancy car" on the night before her body
was discovered. Mrs. Campanella's various de-
scriptions of the driver essentially neutralized one
another. The driver remained behind the wheel;
he got out and opened the door for Nikki. He
wore a chauffeur's cap and outfit; he was "dressed
regular." The driver's height, weight, hair color—
Megan Lamb calculated that the witness had created a minimum of four completely different
people who purportedly spirited Nikki Rossman
away from her Tribeca apartment some four to
eight hours before her murder.

Megan walked Mrs. Campanella through her

story close to a dozen times. Fact and fiction were so intertwined in the rendering that the detective despaired of culling anything at all useful. Megan conducted the interview in the elderly woman's apartment, two flights down from where Nikki had lived. She could not identify the pungent odor that permeated the apartment; an uneasy blend of peppermint, vinegar and mildew was the best she could come up with. The Lord Our Savior Jesus Christ was heavily represented on the walls, the bookcases, the tchotchke shelves. The furniture was covered in flower-print fabrics. The lamp shades were the color of nicotine and gave off a sepia glow. Midway through the interview, a pillow on the couch where Mrs. Campanella was seated suddenly stood up and stretched. Not vinegar, Megan said to herself. Cat piss. By God, am I a detective or am I a detective?

Megan was ready to toss in the towel when Mrs. Campanella mentioned that Nikki had offered to throw away her trash for her. Megan pounced.

"Trash? You didn't mention anything about trash before."

"I don't think you asked."

"Your building's trash cans are caged out front, aren't they?"

"Yes."

"So what do you mean, **throw** your trash

away? Do you mean she offered to lift the lid so you could toss the trash in?"

"No, no, my legs give me trouble. You see how I walk? It will take me an hour to go where you can go in a minute. I am so slow. The sweet pretty girl. She says she will take my trash downstairs for me and throw it out."

"Take the trash **downstairs**?"

"Yes."

"From where? Where was she when she said this?"

"Outside my apartment. In the hallway."

Megan dug her nails into her palms. To Mrs. Campanella, she continued to show a patient, friendly face. "So then this conversation didn't take place in front of your building. This wasn't right before you saw Ms. Rossman get into the fancy car." To herself, she added: with the tall, short, blond, brunet driver who was and wasn't wearing a chauffeur's outfit.

"Yes. It didn't. This is right here. The girl is coming down the stairs."

"But Mrs. Campanella. If you encountered Ms. Rossman right outside your door, on the third floor, how could you then see her getting into the car in front of your building? I'm assuming Ms. Rossman walked faster than you do."

"A newborn baby walks faster than I do, honey. When I was younger, I could dance, I could stay

262 · RICHARD HAWKE

on my feet all day and night if I wanted. You have no—"

"Mrs. Campanella. If you saw Nikki outside your door and she headed downstairs, how did you also see her downstairs getting into a car? Are there windows in the stairwell?"

"No window."

"Did Nikki accompany you down the stairs?"

"No. That is not what happened. She is dressed to go out and have fun. Not to waste her time with an old woman like me."

Megan silently implored the blue-eyed Jesus on the wall behind the woman. Help me. "So okay. Nikki would have reached the ground floor well before you got there. And there was no window in the stairs. Was the car not yet there and waiting for her? Is that it? Was Ms. Rossman still waiting for it when you got downstairs?"

"No. Not that. She says she is forgetting something. When she sees me on the stairs, she says she is forgetting something, and she goes back up to her apartment."

"She goes back upstairs," Megan said evenly. "You forgot to mention that the other times."

"Did I? Well, I am nervous. This pretty girl in my building, you saw what happened to her. It is horrible. How can I feel safe?"

"Of course. I'm not criticizing you. You're doing fine. Let's just get this straight. Ms. Rossman went back upstairs to her apartment to get something she forgot. Did she mention what it was?"

"No."

"You proceeded downstairs with your trash?"

"Yes."

"And when Ms. Rossman appeared downstairs—"

"She had it."

Megan leaned forward, twining her fingers into a single fist. "It."

"The envelope."

Megan hoped her smile didn't look as weary as she felt. "I don't think I've heard anything about an envelope, Mrs. Campanella."

"A blue envelope. A square blue envelope."

"You mean like a birthday card?"

"Maybe."

"I'm not asking if it necessarily **was** a birthday card, Mrs. Campanella. But that kind of card? The kind of card you buy for someone's birthday?"

"I don't know what kind of card it is. It is an envelope. Blue. Like the sky."

"She didn't happen to mention that she was going to a birthday party or some other sort of celebration?"

"Not to me she doesn't."

"But you think this is what Ms. Rossman went back up to her apartment to fetch? This sky-blue envelope?"

The woman made a clucking noise. "You are the detective, not me."

Megan jotted down in her notebook: **Card. Blue. Occasion?**

"Thank you, Mrs. Campanella. You've been very helpful."

Megan climbed the stairs to Nikki's apartment. Ryan Pope was sitting at the kitchen table, eating an apple. In his other hand was a small circular plastic case.

"Are you on the pill?" Megan asked.

"Somebody was." He offered the case. Megan took it from him and opened it. "Night before last. We can assume she was meaning to come home."

There were footsteps on the stairs, then a knock on the doorjamb. "Dead lady live here?"

It was Rodrigo, one of the department IT guys. Rodrigo came into the apartment carrying a slender metal attaché case, and Megan directed him to a table in the front room. A computer was sitting on the table. The chair in front of it was a miniature armchair. It had one of those beanbag pillows on it, the kind you sometimes see people bringing with them on airplanes. This one was hot pink. The chair looked to Megan like the kind a person would settle into, spend some time in. Megan was curious about the computer.

"I want everything in it," she said to Rodrigo.

"I'll vacuum that puppy."

"No crumbs. Get it all."

"Do you want to dust the keyboard first?"

Megan thought for a moment. "I don't think that'll be necessary."

Rodrigo perched on the edge of the chair, flipped open his attaché case and got to work. Megan stepped into the bedroom. It was fairly neat. A bra on the floor, along with about eight shoes that looked like they'd decided to get up and walk around on their own. The bed was made. Nikki's bedside reading was a stack of **Marie Claire** magazines, **People,** an old **Time.** On the dresser Megan found a merchandise tag from a boutique called Liana: WOOL / PLD SIZE 4. When she was found in the park, Nikki had been wearing a black sweater under a red crepe jacket and a thin black cotton skirt. Nothing plaid. Megan pulled open the dresser drawers and rifled quickly through the clothes. She did the same thing in Nikki's closet. Curious, she went into the bathroom, where she found a light blue duffel filled partway with dirty clothes. Ryan Pope stepped to the door as Megan was dumping the dirty clothes out onto the floor.

"I've seen Kathy do this before," Pope said. "You'll want to sort out the colors from the whites."

"It's not here."

"What's not here?"

Megan was thinking out loud. "It's possible she returned it to the store."

"What store? What're you looking for?"

Megan had a thought and very nearly regretted having it. She pushed past Pope and went back downstairs and rang Mrs. Campanella's buzzer.

"I'm sorry to bother you again, Mrs. Campanella. But I was wondering if you by any chance recall what Ms. Rossman was wearing that night you saw her."

The woman answered immediately. "She had on a puffy jacket. It was red. And a green and black skirt."

"Green and black?"

"Yes. Plaid."

"Plaid? You're sure?"

"I remember thinking that she looked like Christmas. With red and green."

"Green plaid."

"Plaid. Squares on top of other squares. Isn't this plaid?"

Megan thanked her again. As she ascended the stairs, she turned the information over in her head. She leaves her apartment in a new plaid wool skirt, but she's found dead in a black cotton skirt. Means? Obviously, it means she changed somewhere along the line. Changed skirts but not her entire outfit. Why? Megan had no idea. The conundrum popped completely out of her head when she reentered Nikki's apartment. Pope was standing behind Rodrigo, peering over his shoulder at the computer screen.

"Finding anything?" Megan asked.

Rodrigo's eyes remained on the screen. It was Pope who looked up.

"Gold mine."

~ 24 ~

MEGAN LOST IT. She felt the eruption starting and was helpless to lock down the lid.

"Son of a **bitch**!" She grabbed the blow-up doll by the arm, pulled it out of her chair and stormed across the hall. Ryan Pope was seated at a table with two uniformed cops. "Where is he?" she demanded.

She followed the eyes. Brian McKinney was leaning against the soda machine on the far side of the room, nibbling on a partially unwrapped candy bar. "Who's your friend, Detective? She's kinda cute."

Megan crossed the room in a blood fury. Everything blurred except the smug bastard peeling back the candy wrapper as if it were a banana peel. She stopped several feet in front of him. Instantly, she regretted having stormed into the corral like this. She knew how ridiculous she must look, standing there with a beet-red face, clutching the female-figure balloon. McKinney certainly knew how ridiculous she looked. His measured aplomb was a precise contrast.

No going forward, no going back. Lose, lose. Dammit, the man did have his talents. Megan gulped her rage. As much as she could. "Maybe you'd like to explain this." She clenched her teeth in order to keep the waver out of her voice.

"Explain it?"

"Yes."

McKinney glanced past her at his audience. "Really?"

"Yes."

McKinney shrugged and pushed himself off the soda machine. He removed the remainder of the wrapper from the candy bar, and before Megan could react, he prodded the black candy into the ugly puckered mouth opening of the balloon.

"Maybe you can help me out with this. If I understand this correctly, you——"

Megan's slap was dead-on. Her entire hand covered the left side of McKinney's face. "You fucking **bastard**!"

"That's assault," McKinney said calmly.

She wanted to hit him again. There were actual white finger marks on his cheek where she'd slapped him, though they quickly disappeared under the rising pink. The candy bar had fallen to the floor when McKinney took the slap. He reached down and picked it up and held it out to Megan. "I guess a girl like you is a little out of practice for this. Why don't I—"

She went at him. Though she was nearly half his body weight, her shove sent him backward into the soda machine. Her hand came up and slashed at his cheek, cutting a small pink swath. As McKinney attempted to turn his head away from the attack, Megan dug a thumb at the corner of his left eye. McKinney let out a grunt. **"Fuck!"**

His head whipped back against the soda machine, cracking the plastic bubble atop the Pepsi logo. Megan's thumb kept digging, while with her other hand she shoved the blow-up doll at McKinney's face, jamming its puckered ear into his slightly opened mouth and pressing it there with all her strength. The noise coming up from her throat sounded only vaguely human. McKinney took a mouthful of the doll, his head backed up against the soda machine, before he managed to twist his head free. He brought his arm up hard and broke Megan's grip on him. "Bitch!"

Megan heard the skidding of chairs behind her. She reached for her belt. With blurring speed, she unholstered her Glock and brought the muzzle up under the offensive detective's nose, prodding it partway up one nostril.

"**Megan!**"

Joe Gallo moved from the doorway, sweeping past Pope and the two cops. McKinney's fear showed through his nervous laugh.

"Hey there, Lieutenant. I think we—"

"Shut up." Gallo addressed Megan: "Holster it. Now!"

Megan hesitated. She could feel her heartbeat as far out as her elbows.

Gallo repeated, "Now!"

She pulled the gun away from McKinney's face. Her breath dropped away. She realized she was about to cry. Dear God, no. Do **not** cry in front of this ape. Not in front of any of them.

McKinney started again. "Lieutenant, look. Miss—"

"Can it." Gallo looked from Megan to the grotesque doll she was still clutching in her other hand. He held out his hand, snapping his fingers. "Give." Megan handed the thing to him. She felt as meek as a child. It was horrible. "Put your gun away, Detective."

As Megan reholstered her weapon, Gallo plucked a pen from McKinney's shirt pocket and plunged it into the rubber doll. Megan let out an involuntary gasp. Gallo shoved the deflating doll into McKinney's arms. "My office. Five minutes." He turned to Megan: "You. Now."

He spun on his heel and left the room. Megan watched him as if he were disappearing down a tube. She wanted to dematerialize. Behind her, McKinney was scrunching the doll up in his arms.

"You're a sick little twit, you know that?"

Before she could respond, Megan caught Ryan Pope's eye. She could feel the blood surging into her face. Her cheeks felt blister-hot. She eyed the door across the room. It seemed years away.

"IS THERE ANYTHING you'd like to tell me?" Joe Gallo shot his cuffs and landed his wrists gently on his desk.

"He's an ape."

"I don't care if he's an ape, Megan. You pulled your weapon on him. Do you mind telling me what it was you had in mind?"

"I wasn't thinking."

Gallo made a show of rolling his eyes. "You weren't thinking? Let me tell you something. That gun comes out of its holster, I want you to be Albert Einstein, you're thinking so fucking hard. For Christ's sake, do I have to tell **you** how stupid—"

"No, you don't. I know it was stupid. I'm sorry."

"Is that what you would've said if McKinney was lying in there right now with a hole out the back of his head? 'Oh. Sorry, Joe. I was angry'?"

"I **was** angry. He—"

"Then kick a dog! Go into the ladies' room and scream at the top of your lungs. Hold it in until you get home, then wreck your place, I don't care. But I'm telling you right now what I'm **not** having. I'm not having one of my detectives pull her goddamn weapon on another one of my detectives in the goddamn **precinct** house. Or anywhere else. McKinney's an ape, fine. No argument here. They got apes at the Bronx Zoo. You want to go up and take a few shots at them, too?"

"I didn't take—"

Gallo leveled a finger at her. "Are you good? That's what I'm asking."

"Am I—"

"Good. You tell it right here, Megan. I backed you up for reinstatement. You're aware of that. I still think there's plenty cop left in you. In fact, I know there is. You got bucked way the hell off the saddle, that's no secret. It was a hell of a hit you took, but you told me you wanted to come back. And you're back. We talked about McKinney already. We talked about all the other crap that was likely to come up now and then, so nothing's a surprise here. I'm not going to put this delicately. To some people out there, you're a freak. Apes like McKinney are never going to understand people—" He cut himself off.

"People what? People like me?"

"Yes."

"Well, fuck you very much, Lieutenant. At least it's nice to know where you stand."

"You know where I stand, Megan. Don't try to go isolating yourself."

"Not to worry. That's taking care of itself. You're the one who said it, Joe. I'm a freak. To Brian McKinney, I'm the bull dyke who failed to protect my partner." She gave a laugh. "Partner. For Christ's sake, I failed to protect **both** my partners. Though I'm sure McKinney's not too glum about Helen—"

"Stop it!" Gallo slammed his hand down on the desk with such force, it gave Megan a start. "Look, I can't hold your hand on this."

"No one's asking you to."

"Do your job, Megan. To some people here, you're a hero for loading up Albert Stenborg with lead. To some, you're trigger-happy. Those are the facts. Either way, it's on you like a big tattoo right on your forehead. Forget your personal life. I don't give a damn about your personal life. **Professionally,** you're a freak. You're in a small, select club, and not a particularly happy one. You know the speech, it can make you a better cop or it can ruin you. You told me it was going to make you a better cop, and I happen to believe you. But a better cop does not pull the kind of stunt you just pulled in there. The bad guys are out there." He gestured toward his window. "There's one in particular we need to find and find quickly, and if Brian McKinney's schoolboy pranks are going to distract you from your job, now's the time to tell me. That's bush-league distraction, Megan. I won't put up with it. I need you focused. You're back in the saddle. It's up to you. Do you ride or do you slide back off?"

Megan didn't hesitate. "I'm fine."

"You're sure?"

"I'm sure. You're right. McKinney's going to bust my chops no matter what, and I might as well get used to it."

"Good." Gallo leaned back in his chair. "Now. Do you want to file charges?"

Megan's mouth dropped open. **"Charges?"**

"Sexual harassment. You've got three witnesses. Four, including me. If you want to file, I'll understand completely."

"You must be kidding."

"You can burn him if you want to. I'd just like a heads-up if you chose that route."

"Sexual harassment? For Christ's sake, I put a **gun** in the man's face. I'm going to sue **him**?"

276 • RICHARD HAWKE

"Gun?" Gallo made a large point of blinking. "Brian McKinney's a pain in my ass. It wouldn't destroy me to see him transferred out. But the easiest way to do that is to get some leverage."

"Three other men saw me pull my gun."

"Maybe they did, maybe they didn't. I'd have to talk with them."

Megan shook her head. "Joe, that's railroading. Worse, it's perjury."

"It's just a question. I thought I'd get it out there for you to consider."

"If I file sexual harassment charges, I'm finished. You know that. Talk about a tattoo on my forehead."

"That's a little dramatic."

"I'm not filing."

"You should take some time to think about it."

"I've thought about it. I don't want to talk about it anymore. I want to get back to Nikki and Cynthia."

Gallo paused a few seconds. "Good. Let's do it. You've got to give me a few minutes first to read McKinney the riot act."

Megan waved him off. "Forget it. Don't do it on my account. You're not going to change him."

"I could force him to apologize. You two could kiss and make up."

Megan felt a flutter in her chest. It was as if

a feather were fooling around behind her rib cage. Oh Christ, she thought. I'm going to say it.

"Hey, Joe, I don't kiss boys, remember? That's the basic problem here in the first place."

RYAN POPE HAD NOT been exaggerating when he termed the contents of Nikki Rossman's computer a gold mine. The printouts of material pulled from the dead woman's hard drive were beginning to resemble skyscrapers. Sifting through the voluminous correspondences that Nikki had conducted with untold numbers of strangers (the tally was still not complete), Pope had commented, "This kind of throws into question the whole matter of just what **is** a healthy sex life."

Pope and Megan talked to the people Nikki had worked with at Bloomingdale's. They went through her address book. From a friend named Tina, they heard that Nikki had been hitting pretty hard on a bartender who worked at a bar fairly near Nikki's apartment. They checked it out. The bartender's girlfriend was present when Megan and Pope came into the bar to talk with him. The detectives picked up on some tension between the couple concerning the topic of Nikki Rossman, but nothing that suggested either of the two had staved in her skull, strangled her, slit her throat and dumped her body in Central Park. Not to mention that they both presented solid alibis.

At least one question got answered: the connection between Cynthia Blair and Nikki Rossman. Nikki's computer overflowed with correspondence between her and dozens of faux Foxes, or Fox-Trotters. Megan and Pope showed photographs of Cynthia Blair to everyone they interviewed about Nikki, trying to deepen the connection. They also had a team retrace their steps and re-interview everyone who had been contacted previously concerning Cynthia Blair's murder, showing them photographs of Nikki Rossman. Nothing surfaced. Two women from two different worlds.

"Crazed fan," Joe Gallo said to the two detectives as they sat in his office going over what were being dubbed the "prime printouts." "I know you don't like it coming back down to that. I don't, either. That gives us something like six million potential suspects. But that's still the link between these two women. One worked for Marshall Fox, and the other one cyber-flirted with a bunch of his clones. Somebody out there has a screw loose for this guy. Scour the fan sites. Check with the people at the studio. See if anyone can be identified who keeps popping up in the studio audience."

Working with the different Internet providers, Rodrigo and his team had been able to identify the majority of the people Nikki Rossman had corresponded with. Of the Marshall Fox wannabes who had been identified so far, Megan and Pope were finding most of them fairly easy to eliminate. Gallo had given Brian McKinney to the detectives to assist in running down alibis. Megan appreciated the gesture.

There were eighteen Fox-Trotters who had yet to be identified. Gallo was skimming through some of the printouts. "Did this woman ever sleep?"

Pope answered, "Lieutenant, I think we're talking about a woman who had a permanent on switch."

Gallo looked up from one of the printouts. "If that were the case, we wouldn't be sitting here reading her private mail. Someone found the off switch." He leaned forward at the desk and handed one of the printouts to Pope. "This one."

"Some of these people dig themselves in pretty deep," Megan said. "In cyberspace, if you don't want to be found, you won't be."

" 'Won't' don't cut it," Gallo said. "You know

that." He indicated the paper as Pope passed it to Megan. "Unhide this one. This guy had Ms. Rossman spinning on her thumb, if you'll excuse the bluntness. I want him in my office. I want to see if we can make **him** spin a little."

Megan looked down at the printout. "Lucky Dog."

"That one," Gallo said. "Lucky Dog. Fetch."

~ 25 ~

WATERCOOLERS.

Chat rooms.

Talk radio.

Joe Gallo was aware of the talk. How couldn't he be? Hell, his own wife was practically addicted to the topic. Gallo hoped that if he ever had as much free time on his hands as Sylvie, he would find something more productive to do with it than sit around and gossip about people he had never met. For her part, Sylvie Gallo thought her husband was missing the boat.

"My girlfriends think you're a dupe, Joey. Look at him, all smooth and contrite. I'm telling you, he's throwing this thing in your face. My girlfriends can't believe you haven't locked him up yet. You're too cautious, Joey. I'm sorry, sweetheart, but you are."

Marshall Fox.

Even though prevailing sentiment was that an unbalanced fan of the late-night entertainer would eventually be found to be responsible for the twin killings in Central Park, the drumbeat of speculation that Fox was actually the killer was building a steady rhythm across the airwaves, phone lines, cyberspace, backyard fences, all of it. The notion was too delicious not to bandy about. The name of O. J. Simpson was being invoked. "O.J. East," people were saying.

"I don't know," Gallo said to Megan two days after Nicole Rossman's burial. The homicide chief was sitting at his desk, fiddling with a $1.50 wicker tube from Chinatown. Chinese handcuffs. "Are we being stupid? Should we be taking a closer look?"

Megan shook her head. "Based on what? Equal treatment under the law, Joe. Fox doesn't get cut any breaks for being famous, and we also don't send out a premature lynch squad because he's famous. I'm not about to be railroaded by the rumor mill. He'll earn his way onto the suspect list just like everyone else. Reasonable cause. Nothing less."

Gallo eased the tips of his index fingers into the Chinese handcuffs, then gave them the slightest tug. The wicker tightened instantly. "I got a call from Cynthia Blair's mother this morning. She wanted to know what I thought about Fox as a suspect."

"And you told her what?"

Gallo grinned. "I told her he'll have to earn his way onto the suspect list like everyone else."

"And here I thought I was being original."

Gallo slithered one finger farther into the Chinese handcuffs, making a futile attempt to wiggle the other finger free. The toy did not cooperate. "This thing's probably a metaphor," the lieutenant said. "I just haven't sorted it out yet."

"The Chinese handcuffs?"

"Yes."

"The harder you try, the worse it gets."

"Right. But the more you just relax and try to give in, the worse it gets, too."

"There's your metaphor."

"It's a depressing one."

"Welcome to the world."

Gallo's phone rang. He indicated his shanghaied hands. "Do you want to get that for me?"

"What? You get caught in a metaphor and suddenly I'm your secretary?" Megan leaned forward and answered the phone. It was the attorney Zachary Riddick.

"I'm looking for Gallo," he said.

Megan winked at her boss. "I'm sorry, Mr.

Riddick, the lieutenant is tied up for the moment. This is Detective Lamb. Can I help you with something?"

"I'm calling on behalf of Marshall Fox."

"What about Mr. Fox?"

"I want it on record that we contacted you first."

Megan's eyebrows rose. She glanced over at Gallo. "Noted. You contacted us first."

"I need to have a meeting with Gallo right away. Could you please get him on the line?"

"May I ask what specifically is the purpose of this meeting?"

"You may not." If the lawyer was attempting to conceal his impatience, he was failing handily. "I need to speak with Gallo. Where the hell is he?"

"If you would like—"

"Would it help my cause, Ms. Lamb, if I tell you that this is an urgent matter?"

"That's coming through."

Behind his desk, Gallo was managing at last to wiggle a knuckle free of the wicker toy. On the phone, Riddick muttered something under his breath; Megan was unable to catch it.

"I'm writing down the time," the lawyer said. "According to my watch, it is one-thirty-two."

Megan checked her watch. "I've got one-thirty-six, Mr. Riddick."

Riddick muttered again; this time Megan caught it. "It's Lamb, right?"

"That's right."

"May I ask you a favor, dear? If it's all the same to you, can you not fuck with me at this precise moment in time?"

Gallo had freed himself. Megan dropped a dollop of sugar into her voice. "Lieutenant Gallo can speak with you now. Please hold." She clamped her palm over the mouthpiece and held it to her chest.

Gallo asked, "What are you doing?"

"At this precise moment in time, I'm fucking with him."

ZACHARY RIDDICK'S EYES MOVED from Joe Gallo to Detective Lamb, where they lingered a few seconds. Megan entertained an image of whipping her elbow up into his nose. Instead, she maintained a deadpan expression.

Gallo spoke. "Afternoon, Zachary. I don't recall if you've met Detective Lamb? Detective, this is Zachary Riddick."

"You're the girl who killed the Swede, right?"

The question landed in Megan's stomach. "I'm not the **girl** who did anything," she said evenly.

"Right. My apologies. You're the woman who

killed the Swede. I wasn't aware you were back on the force."

Gallo stepped across the threshold. "Are you going to invite us in, Zachary?"

"Of course." Riddick stepped back, pulling the door the rest of the way open. "Straight ahead. They're in the living room."

Megan's eyes remained fixed on her boss's back as she went through the doorway. Riddick enjoyed her profile as she passed. With a low hum, he made sure she knew it.

The detectives followed a short hallway that opened up into a large room dominated by a spectacular view of the thick Central Park plumage. Seated on a tan leather couch was Marshall Fox. He was dressed in jeans and an open-collared blue shirt. His long legs were crossed. He was wearing a pair of mud-red armadillo boots and was picking at the pointy toe of one of the boots, as if trying to scrape away the scales and open up a hole. He looked up as Gallo and Megan Lamb entered the room. My God, Megan thought. He really **is** a handsome devil, isn't he?

Fox smiled wanly. "They're coming to take me away, ha ha, hee hee, ho ho." Megan recognized the obscure novelty song of several decades previous. Rising from a matching leather armchair was Alan Ross, director of programming for KBS Television. He shot a pleading look at Fox. "Marshall."

Fox lowered his boot to the floor. "Yes, dear," he grumbled in a deliberately nasal monotone.

Ross stepped forward, hand extended. He aimed first for the senior detective. "Lieutenant Gallo. Nothing personal, but it would be nice if we could stop meeting like this. Thank you very much for coming."

The two shook hands. Gallo nodded tersely. "This is Detective Lamb. She's lead investigator in the Blair and Rossman killings."

Riddick had stepped into the room. He took up a spot against the entry wall, arms crossed, a slightly bemused look on his face. Ross and Megan shook hands. "You both know Marshall, of course," Ross said.

Fox rose from the couch, addressing Gallo: "No offense, Detective. But you probably could have gotten a lot more out of me the last time we met if you'd brought Miss Lamb along." He crossed to the couple. "Marshall Fox, ma'am."

"How do you do, Mr. Fox?"

"On balance? Does the phrase 'I'd rather be having a voluntary root canal' give you an idea?"

"Marshall." Ross's tone was a bit less pleading this time. The executive addressed the detectives. "Please have a seat. I know you two are busy. We'll keep this as brief as possible."

Riddick remained standing until the others had settled in. Taking an eye cue from Ross, the

298 · RICHARD HAWKE

lawyer crossed to the couch, giving Fox a comradely pat on the knee as he sat down next to him.

The lawyer began. "Marshall has some information he would like to pass along to the authorities." Fox opened his mouth to speak, but Riddick waved him off. "Hold up. Before Mr. Fox shares this information, we would like an assurance that this is a private conversation."

"That's fine," Gallo said. "Except this isn't a private conversation. Detective Lamb and I haven't dropped by for tea. You have something you would like to share with us, Mr. Fox?"

"Whoa, whoa, whoa." Riddick held his hands out as if a herd of cattle were bearing down on him. "Detective, we are making a voluntary statement here. On our own initiative. All we're asking is that we don't open the paper tomorrow and see the details of Mr. Fox's statement splattered across the front page."

"I'm not in the business of doing reporters' work for them," Gallo said.

"I'm not saying you specifically, Lieutenant."

Gallo turned to Megan. She noted the light in his dark eyes. He said, "Are you and Jimmy Puck taking bubble baths together again, Detective Lamb?"

Megan had pulled out her notebook and flipped it open. She produced a ballpoint pen and clicked it. "I'm ready for your statement, Mr. Fox."

Riddick blurted, "Wait. Hold on. We need to be on the same page here." He turned to Ross. "Maybe this wasn't such a good idea, Alan."

Fox muttered, "I could use a drink," and fell back on the couch, bringing his boot back to his knee and recommencing his excavation work.

Alan Ross cleared his throat. Megan had the sense that the executive had agreed to Riddick launching the conversation but was now pulling rank. The sense came as much from Ross as it did from the way in which Riddick let his arms drop to his sides with a poorly veiled petulance. If she needed confirmation, Fox provided it, mimicking Riddick with a pat to **his** knee.

Ross began. "Lieutenant Gallo, you know this from the last time we met. But for Detective Lamb's edification, I am here as Marshall's friend, not as a representative of the network. The network's investment in Marshall as one of our most valuable talents is immaterial to my being here. I want there to be no sense of corporate coercion at play, you understand? I'm here on behalf of my friend. I probably don't even have to be saying this, but just in case, I'd like us to at least be on **that** same page."

He took the opportunity to give Zachary Riddick one of his repertoire's less generous smiles, then continued, "My wife and I are responsible for Marshall having come to New York in the first place. I don't think I'm betraying any confidences in telling you that Marshall has had more than his share of occasions over the past several years to wonder if gracing our city with his presence has been worth it to him in the big picture. Fame might look pretty fabulous from the outside, but Marshall will be the first to tell you that some of the costs can make a person wonder if it's all worth it."

From the couch, Fox cracked, "Alan, you're going to make me cry."

"Hold the tears, bubba." Ross turned back to the detectives. "Lieutenant Gallo, Detective Lamb. I don't mean to be making a speech here. I'll shut up in a second. It's just that you both know full well how huge Marshall is in the public eye. One of the downsides of being so huge is that you make an awfully easy target if someone decides it's worth their while to take a shot at you." He stopped and cleared his throat. "That's what's happened to Marshall."

Gallo cut in. "Are you referring to the rumors, Mr. Ross?"

"The rumors?"

"About Mr. Fox and the Blair and Rossman killings." Gallo turned to Fox. "No offense, but my wife and her cronies are thinking of checking you out for the Lindbergh baby at this point."

Fox held up his hands. "Hey, I never touched the kid. I don't even like kids."

"We're aware of those rumors, yes," Ross said. "They're part of the price of being a celebrity these days. But no. The reason we've asked you here concerns something more substantial. This isn't about the Rossman woman at all, who, by the way, Marshall has no connection with whatsoever. Most ridiculous thing I've ever heard. This concerns Cynthia Blair." He paused, looking at Fox.

"Go on," Fox said. "Air the old dirty laundry. The world insists on knowing."

Ross cleared his throat again. He looked pained. "We have good reason to believe that Marshall is the person responsible for Cynthia's pregnancy."

The room fell silent. Megan's eyes were on her boss, who gave no outward indication of having even heard what Alan Ross had just said. Ross sent a sympathetic look Fox's way. Almost a paternal look, like that of a disappointed but still supportive father.

Gallo spoke. "Is this true, Mr. Fox?"

The entertainer threw a look at Megan that was almost mischievous. He leaned back on the couch and tilted his head, looking up at the ceiling. He remained silent for several seconds, then exhaled loudly.

"Busted."

THE AFFAIR HAD BEGUN some two and a half months before Cynthia Blair's abrupt resignation as producer of **Midnight with Marshall Fox.** Not a soul on the staff had the vaguest clue. The outward behavior of the show's star and its producer had not deviated one iota from its standard combative mode. If anything, on reflection, it might have seemed that the daily antagonistics between the two hardheaded personalities was spiking more than usual.

It had started, appropriately enough, with a fight. Fox, at his acerbic best, had tied his producer into ever more infuriating knots until, finally, she had exploded with clenched fists raining down on his head. This had been followed by a burst of angry tears. The simple ugly truth was that Cynthia Blair adored Marshall Fox—her dirty little secret. Herculean efforts notwithstanding, Cynthia had failed to convince herself that she was ever likely to meet another man with the same infuriatingly wonderful qualities as her colleague and erstwhile combatant. At the same time, he offended her in more ways than she could count. Talented, charming, smart, sexy and about as self-centered, arrogant and old-fashioned sexist as anyone she had ever laid eyes on. What Cynthia had hated the most was that from the moment she met him, he had been, for all his evident faults, consistently the single most vibrant person she had ever encountered. Marshall Fox made all the other men she dated bland and pale by comparison, even some of the otherwise considerably dynamic ones. It wasn't fair. For Cynthia, the son of a bitch had become the gold standard. Damn it all to hell, no one else need apply.

And, of course, he was still married.

Not to mention a royal shit.

Their argument had taken place at Fox's borrowed apartment early on Friday evening. Fox had invited Cynthia to continue the spirited postmortem of the week's shows that had kicked up in his office after the taping of the Friday program. Somewhere along the line, the argument had gone terribly awry, and the two had ended up in a sweaty clutch on the tan leather couch. She had remained the entire weekend. If anyone at work on Monday morning noticed that Cynthia was wearing the same outfit she had been wearing on Friday, they didn't say anything. For her part, Cynthia had felt as if she were going through her workday stark naked, with a big SCREWED BY MARSHALL FOX stenciled diagonally across her front and her back. By the end of the workday, she had determined that the orgiastic weekend with her boss had been an exquisite fluke and that both she and Fox were already back on their standard argumentative footings. But later that evening, Cynthia's cries echoed in her own ears as her fingers clutched at her boss's back. This time she managed to get herself home, where she crawled into her bed, curled into a fetal position around her feather pillow and laughed herself to sleep. An open, free, lung-cleansing laughter she could not recall experiencing since she was a child.

For two and a half months, Marshall Fox had driven her into a delirious oblivion. Ten times a day, Cynthia declared silently that she was disgusted with herself and that she could see right through Fox and his king-of-the-mountain game. I'm smarter than this, she told herself. I know better.

And then it ended. She had known it would. In the months since leaving his wife, Marshall Fox had already run through nearly a dozen minor relationships that Cynthia knew of, the most recent being that striking Quaker girl he'd picked up at the Rosses' annual Long Island orgy. Naturally, it would end. That was the Fox way. Even so, Cynthia had pretended that with her, it would somehow be different. But really, the only difference between her and the others was that she worked with the goddamn man. **That** was how stupid she had been.

And then the other difference. Or maybe she was being extraordinarily naïve and it wasn't a difference at all. Maybe Fox had been forced to finesse this development before. She was pregnant. Careful here, careful there, it had still happened. On learning the news, Cynthia had realized instantly that she had no intention of aborting the child. Absolutely not. Being a mother had always been somewhere in her plans (or, if not plans, then intentions), and Cynthia was under no illusions. She was seeing more and more women throwing in the towel early, as far as hoping to land one of the world's rapidly vanishing species—the worthwhile single man—and when she discovered that she was pregnant, she knew this was her moment. She sobered up concerning Fox himself. There could be no illusions that he would respond to the news with any intent to be a real part of the child's life. And she was ready for all that. She could see her future. Finally. And she accepted it.

What she had not expected was Marshall Fox's adamant insistence that she "lose the kid."

"**My** fucking **seed**? **My** kid? Oh, I don't think so, Miss Cindy. That's not the plan, girl. Word will get out, I know it will. You'll tell. One of your friends will tell. Or the little bastard will **look** like me. Uh-uh. No, ma'am. I've got some plans of my own, you know. I'm waking up and smelling the coffee, honey, and it still smells like the lovely Rosemary. We're in negotiations as we speak, so don't even think you can go pulling a stunt like this. It goes. If I have to rip the damn thing out myself. This isn't going to happen. Have you got that? Not in the script, Cindy. **Not in the script.**"

Back in her office, Cindy broke the glass on her display case in her fury to get at the Emmy Award she had received for her work on the show. She pounded the base of the award against the wall separating her office from Fox's. My God, she thought as she pummeled at the drywall, I've gone insane. **Well, fuck him!** She had succeeded only in creating a large hole in the wall. She wondered what in the hell she was thinking. Was she going to climb right through the wall back into Fox's office and sink her heavy statuette into his skull? The hole in the wall, about the size of a bowling ball, broke through to an open space. Cynthia shoved the award into the open space, and it disappeared. Five minutes later she was in the elevator, wishing Marshall Fox were in it with her, wishing that the cable would snap and send the two of them (rubbing her stomach, the **three** of them) plunging to their stupid, stupid, stupid, deserved deaths.

· · ·

MEGAN ASKED if she could be directed to the bathroom.

Fox flicked his head. "Down the hall, on the right."

As Megan left the room, Gallo addressed Marshall Fox. "I'm sure you know my first question."

"Why didn't I tell you before? Why do you think? It was something private between Cindy and me. It has no significance to what happened to her."

Gallo was already shaking his head. "Not good enough."

"It's going to have to be."

Ross began, "Someone like Marshall—"

Gallo cut him off. "Please. I really do need to hear this from Mr. Fox."

"It's okay, Alan." Fox turned to Gallo. "Look. It's pretty simple. Doing what I do, the first thing that goes is a private life, okay? The entire population of the state I come from could probably fill up the buildings between here and the Hudson River. I could go entire days without seeing a single soul. So, yeah, I tossed that out the window. My choice, I'm not whining. Or fine, maybe I am. But ever since the separation from my wife,

I've **really** lost anything like a personal life. You've just got no idea. I'm trying to patch things back up with my wife, Mr. Gallo. I miss her. Hell. I **need** her, is what it is. And it's touch and go, believe me. I screwed up pretty big over this last year. Now, you're a smart man. Maybe you can figure out which way she's going to lean if she finds out that I slept with my producer and got the damn girl pregnant. Do you want to do the math for me on that one?"

Gallo understood. Fox was human. The homicide lieutenant wasn't certain what he himself might have done under similar circumstances.

"Okay," Gallo said. "I hear you. So why are you coming forward now?"

Megan was returning to the room. It seemed to Gallo that his junior detective was giving Fox a peculiar look. But when she glanced Gallo's way, she seemed to be giving it to him as well.

Alan Ross spoke up. "I'd like to answer your question, Lieutenant, if you don't mind."

"Go ahead."

"Marshall?"

"Run with it, Bunky."

Ross's cell phone went off. He checked to see who it was but didn't answer it. "Both Marshall and Zachary received a call recently," he said. "They've decided that it is in the best interest of this whole event not to reveal who it was who called them."

"You can just refer to her as 'little bitch,' " Fox muttered. "That's what I'm doing."

"So you knew the identity of this caller," Gallo said.

"Oh yeah, I knew her. She knew me. The whole thing. Zack hasn't had the pleasure, but I'm sure he'll live."

"And the call? What was it about?"

"She knew about me and Cynthia. That we'd been naughty little boys and girls."

Megan asked, "And she knew about Ms. Blair being pregnant?"

Fox tapped his finger to the tip of his nose. "That's it, lady. And that one's my own fault. Trusting people I now know I shouldn't have trusted. One of the occupational hazards of being on top of the world."

"And this person contacted both of you?" Gallo asked.

Riddick answered, "That's right. Short and sweet. 'I've got Marshall by the balls, now what are you going to do about it?' "

Megan addressed Fox. "So you decided to tell us the news before this friend of yours did?"

"I never called her a friend."

"But that's what you decided?"

"That's right. If you're going to hear this anyway, I want it to be from me. Mouthpiece here wasn't so sure it was a good idea. My word against hers and all that. But I'm not a fool. How would I look if I held back on this and you found out from some other source?"

"You did hold back," Megan reminded him.

"Well, I'm laying it out now, aren't I?"

Gallo said, "It would help if you'd be willing to tell us the identity of this person."

Fox shared a glance with Riddick, then with Alan Ross. "We've all sort of decided there's no point in that, Lieutenant. If she's looking for publicity, we're damn well not going to give it to her."

"I'm correct, though, that this is someone close to you?"

Alan Ross answered, "A person in Marshall's position attracts a lot of people. They're like barnacles. This was one of his barnacles."

"I understand."

"The point is," Fox said, "all those calls you're probably getting, this one would have credibility. So I decided to preempt it. I thought I'd go ahead and take me a chance with the truth." He smiled at Megan. "Hell of a concept, isn't it?"

AN ELDERLY COUPLE WAS on the elevator when it arrived. Megan and Gallo rode in silence.

Once they reached the street, Gallo asked, "What did you make of all that?"

"He killed her, Joe. He killed them both." Megan craned her neck, looking up at the apartment building. "Bastard."

Gallo unlocked the driver's-side door. "He got the woman pregnant. It's a far leap from that to murder."

"When I went to look for the bathroom, I made a wrong turn and found myself in Fox's bedroom."

Gallo's eyes narrowed. "Very clumsy of you."

"Yes, it was. Since I was there, I went ahead and conducted a quick unlawful search. The unflappable Mr. Fox likes to play with handcuffs, Joe. I found a pair in his bedside table. Top drawer."

"Lots of people have handcuffs, Megan. **You** have handcuffs."

"But do lots of people have this?" She pulled something flat and pale blue from her pocket.

"What's that?"

"It's a sympathy card for Cynthia Blair's family. It never got delivered. It was in the top drawer, too."

"A sympathy card."

"A blue one."

"And you're making a point with this card?"

Holding the envelope by the edges, Megan worked the card out and handed it to her boss.

Gallo handled it gingerly. The fuzzy photograph on the front was of a disembodied hand holding a large bouquet of flowers.

IN SYMPATHY FOR YOUR LOSS

"When Nikki left her apartment the night she was killed, she had a square blue envelope with her. Open it."

"Anything we learn from this is completely inadmissible. This is stolen property."

"I'll return it when we're arresting Fox."

"You mean plant it?"

"I mean return it."

"I don't like this, Megan."

"Sorry, but I don't want him destroying it. He's been a fool to keep it as it is."

"Taking something from a suspect's residence is just as foolish."

"Fine. He's a fool and I'm a fool. But he's a fool who killed two women in cold blood. The way I score it, this makes me the one with some latitude. Why don't you just look at the card and we can talk about it later."

Gallo opened the card and read the printed inscription. It was a six-line verse, a message of sympathy as disembodied as the fuzzy hand on the front. But it wasn't the inscription that was holding the detective's focus. It was the personalized scrawl beneath it. Gallo gazed at the inscription for nearly ten seconds while Megan dropped onto the hood of the car. "Well?"

Joe Gallo turned his gaze to the apartment building. Specifically, up to the twenty-sixth floor. His whistle was low and strong.

"Well, holy shit."

~ 26 ~

"WE HAVE JUST LEARNED that Marshall Fox has surrendered to authorities in the matter of the brutal slayings of Cynthia Blair and Nicole Rossman. The popular late-night entertainer, accompanied by his wife and his lawyer, was taken into custody at approximately ten-thirty this morning at the couple's Upper East Side apartment and brought here to police headquarters at the Twentieth Precinct. Sources tell me that at this moment, Mr. Fox has not yet been formally charged, but we do expect within the hour to hear that the host of **Midnight with Marshall Fox** will in fact be charged in the slayings of Ms. Blair and Ms. Rossman. It's all quite something. Just several days after Ms. Blair's murder, not yet a month ago, Mr. Fox vowed tearfully on his television show that he would do anything in his power to bring his former colleague's killer to justice. It's too early to say with anything approaching certainty, but it may well be that with his arrest this morning, Mr. Fox has begun to make good on his promise. This is Kelly Cole, reporting live from the Upper West Side. Back to you in the studio."

ROSEMARY FOX EYED the scrum of reporters and cameramen gathered on the sidewalk outside her building, and she instructed her driver to keep driving.

"Anywhere. Just get away from here."

"Yes, ma'am."

Rosemary lit a cigarette and cracked the tinted window half an inch. She stared dully at the passing buildings. Marshall was sitting in a jail cell this very minute. Unbelievable. Totally fucking unbelievable. At least Zachary had promised that Marshall would be issued his own cell. Fine. But he had also promised a discreet and orderly arrangement for Marshall to turn himself in that morning, and instead, that blond cookie had slapped handcuffs on Marshall and dragged him through the front lobby of the building like a common criminal. Infuriating. The poor boy. Rosemary had never seen such a look of helplessness on her husband's face. All his cocksure silliness and charm had drained away at the sight of the handcuffs coming off that girl cop's belt. She'd said something to him in a low voice, but Rosemary had missed it. In the insanity of the next several hours, she'd forgotten to ask Marshall what it was the little girl Kojak had said to him.

The phone mounted on the door chirped. Rosemary eyed the caller ID. Gloria Ross. Rosemary wasn't sure she wanted to talk with Gloria right now. It was one thing if either of them had to be out on the coast the day Marshall was being arrested. That was the job. New York and L.A. But Alan was out there, too. He'd flown out suddenly two days before. How convenient, an entire country separating the Rosses from their soiled prodigy.

Maybe I'm just being harsh, Rosemary thought. I mean, really. What could Alan have done if he'd been in the East? Hold Marshall's hand? He could make Marshall famous, he'd proved that, but he couldn't make him invulnerable. Marshall had been an idiot. He'd knocked up his producer, and then he'd let himself get involved with that flat-backed, round-heeled, half-pint Barbie-doll tramp on the Internet. You plays your games, you takes your chances. Big. Stupid. Cowboy.

Rosemary lifted the phone.

Gloria sounded flustered. "Rose. I'm so glad I got you. Where are you, honey?"

"Hello, Gloria. I'm holed up in the backseat of the Town Car. I'm getting a tour of Manhattan. How's the coast?"

Gloria Ross answered, "Dry, sunny, stale and full of phonies. Listen, honey, Alan is going to be back in the city tomorrow afternoon. He's tied up in meetings all day. He's over in Century City as we speak. He told me to tell you he's thinking of you. How's Marshall doing?"

The car was drifting slowly past the Metropolitan Museum of Art. Rosemary shifted in her seat. She wasn't in the mood to maybe catch a glimpse of the top of Cleopatra's Needle.

"Marshall is scared shitless," Rosemary said. "He's convinced they're going to ship him out to Rikers and offer him up as a sacrifice to men with tattoos on their teeth."

"I thought they only sacrificed virgins."

Rosemary took a beat. "Not funny, Gloria."

The line crackled. "I'm sorry, honey. Of course it isn't. This whole damn thing is just so surreal."

"Tell me."

"He's going to be fine, Rose. It's a huge cosmic mistake. Marshall has been targeted. We know that. Alan said just this morning it wouldn't surprise him to find out it was all a plot by one of the rival networks."

"Your husband has a paranoid mind."

"My husband is in tears over what's happening to **your** husband. Seriously, Rose. Alan broke down this morning at breakfast. You know we're going to fight this thing with everything we've got."

"I know, I know."

"How are **you** holding up?"

Rosemary took a final drag on her cigarette and prodded the butt out the window. The smoke eased past her lips like dry ice. "I have thick skin. With all the crap Marshall's pulled this past year? It's probably alligator tough by now."

"There's a lot of sympathy for you out there. You stood by your man. You're a beautiful victim of Marshall's silly irresponsibility. That plays well."

Plays well. Is everything a goddamn angle for these people? Get real, Rosemary thought. She laughed out loud. Gloria Ross wouldn't know real if it hit her in the face. Alan, either. Their careers depended on fiction and fantasy, the mere appearance of truth.

Gloria asked, "What's so funny?"

"Nothing."

"We're going to get you out to the house when we're back east," Gloria said. "You're free to go out to the Island anytime. You know that, right? I don't think you'll want to stay in the city the next several days."

"I'm staying. This is where my **man** is, remember?" Rosemary flicked another cigarette from her pack. "I've got to stand by him."

"You sound bitter, dear."

Rosemary sighed. "I'm fine." She squinted out the window at the Plaza. The Plaza was where she and Marshall had first made love. She smiled despite herself. Son of a bitch kept his boots on the entire time. His big ear-to-ear grin, too. **Miss Boggs. Miss Boggs** . . .

"I'm fine," Rosemary said again. "Thanks for calling, Gloria. If I talk to Marshall, I'll tell him you were asking after him."

"Do. Please do that. And Alan, too. He'll be back tomorrow."

"I'll talk to you later."

"So long, dear."

Rosemary thumbed the off button. She instructed her driver to take her home. The press wasn't going to fold their tents and leave. Her building was going to be under siege for the duration of the mess. She'd have to think of something, but for now she wanted to be home.

She pulled out a compact and touched up quickly. She knew her role. And she knew the power of her best assets.

· · ·

ROSEMARY WOULD WATCH the footage on television later in the evening. CNN was running the clip over and over. The Town Car pulling to a stop. The driver getting out and opening the back door. Rosemary stepping out, holding her coat collar tight at the neck and calmly facing the onslaught of cameras and microphones. As always, she looked beyond exquisite, her sea-green eyes registering a deep sadness as well as a deep resolve.

"I want to say that the people we should all be thinking about at this moment are the families of the victims. These are the people whose pain can only be increasing the longer this goes on and the murderer of these two women remains at large. My husband is innocent. The pain that Marshall and I are suffering is temporary. It will pass. We're not the story here. We're the distraction from the story."

Rosemary aimed the remote and fired. The image vanished with a light **sizzle.** She was sitting up in her bed. The sleeping pills she had taken a half hour earlier had not yet kicked in. She took a sip of her warm Scotch. As she was setting the glass back down, the door buzzer went off.

Two short, one long.

Rosemary got out of bed and pulled on her white robe. Her Zsa Zsa, as Marshall always called it. She glanced at her mirror as the buzzer rang a second time. Same pattern. She pushed at her hair and gave her cheeks a quick slap, then went to the front door, peered through the peephole and pulled the door open.

Her visitor was leaning against the doorjamb. The smile was too large, the eyes in partial dilation. "You in bed already?"

"It's been a tiring day," Rosemary said. "Perhaps you've heard, my husband is spending the night in jail."

"I caught that."

"I assume you came up through the garage?"

"Do I look stupid?"

"What you look is stoned." Rosemary stepped back from the door and let her visitor in. She asked, "Don't you think you're being a bit ballsy?"

"I thought you might be lonely."

"I took some sleeping pills." Rosemary closed the door. "I plan to be zonked out in ten minutes, tops."

"I can show myself out after."

"This **is** ballsy."

Her visitor followed her as she retraced her steps to the bedroom. Rosemary stopped a few feet before the foot of the bed. Now that she had gotten out of bed and moved around, she was aware that the sleeping pills had kicked in. Her brain felt cloudy. In a nice-feeling way, though her feet weren't feeling the floor.

She unknotted the sash and shrugged the robe off her shoulders. It fell to the carpet with a satin whisper. God, Rosemary thought vaguely, how cheap a move is that? She stepped away from the bunched robe, climbed onto the bed and crawled to the pillows. I'm a jungle cat, she thought. As she settled in, closing her eyes, she heard a laugh. It took her a fuzzy moment to realize it had come from her.

Her visitor was standing at the foot of the bed, working at the buttons of his shirt. "What's so funny?"

Rosemary decided her eyes were too heavy to open. She felt as if her head were still sinking into the pillows. Deeper and deeper. Everything's funny, she thought. All of it. It's all one big cosmic joke. She felt the mattress shift and sensed a darkness moving down on top of her. An unshaved jaw scraped along her cheek.

Big joke. Great big joke.

ROBIN BURRELL SAT FROZEN in front of her television set. The only movement she had made the last hour and a half was with her arm, pointing the remote at the television and punching the button to change the channel. There was nothing new. Every clip she had seen now more than a dozen times. Marshall then; Marshall this morning; Cleopatra's Needle and a white sheet covering a dead body; Marshall pacing aimlessly on the set of his show, aching over his former producer's murder; a fuzzy snapshot of a petite buxom blonde in a bikini; Cleopatra's Needle again. All of it. Ad nauseam. Over and over.

Robin didn't blink.

She wasn't answering her phone. Eighteen messages had racked up on the machine. Michelle. Edward Anger. Denise from work. Reporters. She had nothing to say. For three months, she had felt like she was on a delicious drug. What normally mattered had no longer mattered. What people thought had been of no real concern. Robin had slipped more easily into fantasyland than she ever would have imagined possible and had remained there until things turned ugly and Fox snapped his fingers and the fantasy ended.

Near midnight, Robin set down the remote. She rose from the couch and shuffled to the bathroom, barely lifting her feet. She turned on the shower and got out of her clothes. Stepping into the spray, she paused and looked at herself in the full-length mirror on the wall opposite the showerhead. For just an instant, a form superimposed itself on her reflection, which, in the steam coming up from the hot water, was already beginning to grow blurry.

She spun around. There was no one there. Not this time. Robin crossed her arms across her chest and stepped into the stream of water. She closed her eyes and tilted her head back. And cried.

PART 3

~ 27 ~

A VOICE.

"I think I see something."

I thought I did, too. To be more specific, a voidlike awareness thought so, too. There was no I. The void was comprised of black splinters in a black space. Fission lines. Cracks in blackness. But not inert. They were in frantic motion, ripping trails across the blackness like the crescent tails of dying stars. Reverberating at the edges of the void was the suggestion of things familiar. Familiar and also vital. But out there. Inside out. Awareness sizzled faintly off along the horizons, far from where it belonged.

"I thought his eyes were opening. I guess it was just a flicker."

More cracks were appearing in the void, multiplying in a blur. Cracks within cracks. The voice fell away, like a receding surf, and then a faint signal sounded. A primitive beacon, orderly and welcome. A dull red pulse.

Beep . . . beep . . . beep . . . beep . . .

WHITE FLUORESCENCE OVERCAME me. It came on like the first intake of air after you've held your breath longer than you thought possible. I thought it would drown me. I was saturated with strobing light as I blinked my way through the adjustment.

I was horizontal. For a brief moment I thought I was floating. I felt dangerously buoyant. Then my eyes narrowed and forms dissolved into place.

Margo.

She was seated in a chair by a window off the foot of a bed—my bed—reading an issue of **Vanity Fair.** There was a look of intense concentration on her face; she was essentially scowling at the page. In my mind's eye, a gilded frame dropped around her, the peripheral details all going fuzzy, and she was a portrait leaning up against a wall. I simply wanted to look. I had a craving to savor. But a moment later, she licked a finger, turned a page, looked up.

"Jesus Christ!" Already dropping the magazine, she rushed out of the frame. Her pale face filled my vision. "You shit. You big old goddamn son-of-a-bitch **shit**!"

There were tears on her cheeks. Her hand fumbled for something near my ear. I turned my head to see. A plastic button. Margo's thumb was bloodless white on the button. A woman entered the room, a cartoon moving swiftly. A nurse. Breasts like soft mountains.

"What is it?"

"He's awake."

The nurse surged forward. I thought she was going to fall on top of me. "Hello, Mr. Malone." She gave me a piano-keys smile to focus on as Margo bobbed on her horizon. The nurse held up an object in front of her nose. "What am I holding?"

I felt my eyes crossing as I focused on the object. It was a pen. Blue. Ballpoint. Paper Mate. Behind the nurse, Margo was scrutinizing me with her scowl.

"An elephant," I said. My voice sounded harsh and unfamiliar.

The nurse blinked with confusion. "I'm holding an elephant?" She looked over at Margo, who was no longer scowling.

"He's fine."

~ 28 ~

I'D GONE UNDER the ice. Witnesses saw me hit (the one who called 911 said I hit headfirst, the other thought I landed on the small of my back), and for a short period of time, I had remained on its surface, motionless. When I finally did move, it wasn't to prop myself up on my elbows and shake it off. Quite the opposite. Both witnesses agreed that it was my feet that went first. They slid down into the crack that my body had made when I'd landed. The widening crack. My feet lolled into the water, then, as if a voracious aquatic creature were reeling me in, I slid cleanly off the splintering ice and disappeared into the black water without a splash. Only a thin smear of blood on the ice gave any suggestion that I had been there at all.

The wound that Ratface and his kitchen knife

had given my side required seven stitches. Fortunately, nothing vital had been pierced. Another set of stitches had been required to close up the nasty gash on the back of my head, where I'd hit the ice. This was where the doctors were placing concern. My head. They were worried about brain swelling, a concern that had prompted Margo to blurt, "God, that's all we need."

Perversely, the several minutes I had spent partially under the ice were to thank for my head injury not being quite as threatening as it otherwise might have been. The East River had performed first aid on me, the bracing water freezing the swelling in its tracks. However, it had also taken the opportunity to fill my lungs with a gallon or so of its chilly swill. But that was the least of my problems. Mainly, it was the concussion that preoccupied the doctors. I was given a list of symptoms I needed to be on the lookout for. Trouble remembering things, disorientation, difficulty making decisions, headaches, irritability.

My doctor insisted that I remain in the hospital through the day and overnight for observation. I wanted to wrestle him on the matter, but he refused. My memory seemed to have holes in it. My mother and my half sister, Elizabeth, came by to see me, but I have no recollection of what we spoke about. Joe Gallo's face appeared at my bedside, but when it vanished, so, too, did my memory of our conversation. I got calls from Peter Elliott and Michelle Poole and Megan Lamb, but General Margo refused to let me take them. Kelly Cole put in a call as well. Margo jotted her number on the back of one of my business cards and stuck it in my wallet for me.

"I don't think you're up for that kind of syntax right now."

I felt remarkably better the next morning and was dressed and ready to go by the time the doctor came to check on me. He aimed a penlight in my eyes and had me follow his finger as he waved it like a symphony conductor; then he told me I was to rest, not drive a car, keep off alcohol for at least a week and also to refrain from sex. Margo was seated on the large windowsill, posing with her hands on her knees. "Thanks, Doc. You're a pal."

I lost the argument with Margo about staying at my place while I convalesced. Truth was, I put no real heart into my end of the argument. Neither Margo nor I had touched on the subject of our recent sword crossings. My injuries had forced a truce, and I was just as happy to keep the issue unspoken. Margo took me from the hospital to a tiny country-food-themed restaurant near Gramercy Park, where I ate a double helping of eggs and sausage and home fries. After breakfast, we went to Margo's, where I picked up the phone, set it back down, then crawled onto the couch and slept until eight that night. Margo shoveled some pesto pasta into me. I showered, got into bed, made a lame pass at Margo when she joined me, then went out with the light.

I can't say I felt like a million bucks in the morning. More like enough for a down payment on a small dump somewhere unpopular. But that would do. Margo dutifully retrieved a three-day-old copy of the **Post** that she'd been holding on to for me. "If your head was a hundred percent, you'd have asked for this already."

She flipped the paper open to page five. There was a short article about my unscheduled trip into the East River. Accompanying the article was a police sketch of my alleged attacker. If he looked like anyone, he looked like Thurman Munson, the beloved Yankees catcher who was killed midseason in a plane crash a quarter century ago.

"This looks like Thurman Munson," I said to Margo. "The guy who attacked me didn't look like this. **You** look more like him than this does."

"Thank you, sweetheart. You're doing a fine job of patching things up."

Margo had a meeting at ten o'clock. She made herself pretty, then climbed into a thick winter coat and a mighty fur hat. I told her, "You look good enough to tackle."

334 · RICHARD HAWKE

"You'll be careful," she said, not even pretending to make a question of it. "I don't do hospital visits twice in one week."

"I'll be careful."

"Lies," she said, grabbing her keys. "All lies."

After Margo left, I called my answering service. Among a dozen dumpable calls were ones from Kelly Cole ("I know a suffocated story when I hear one. I want to know what was going on. Call me.") and Alan Ross. I dug Kelly's number out of my wallet and tried it, but I hung up when I was delivered into Ms. Cole's voice mail. I had better luck with Alan Ross.

"I read about your adventure in the paper," the executive said after his secretary put me through. "How are you holding up?"

I gave him a brief status report. "The doctors are giving me another forty years minimum, so long as I play my cards right."

Ross said that he would like to meet with me. "I have a business proposition to discuss."

"When would you like to meet?"

"Today, if that's possible. How does noon sound?"

Noon sounded fine. He gave me the midtown address of his office, and we hung up. I showered, careful to keep my various sets of stitches dry. Not exactly your fun-loving singing-in-the-rain kind of shower. On the checklist I'd gotten of possible concussion symptoms, I was feeling low-grade most of them. Especially the headache. Despite the siren song of the couch, I pulled on a thick Irish sweater, double-wrapped a scarf under my chin, shrugged into my bomber jacket and gingerly tugged a watch cap over my battered skull. A bastard wind hit me full force in the face as I exited Margo's building. Across the street, Robin Burrell's Christmas tree was gone from the bay window. The final witness shunted off.

MEGAN LAMB CAME OUT to the front desk to meet me. She looked as if she'd gone a few rounds in the ring with a determined kangaroo. If there weren't exactly bags under her eyes, it was close. She saw me noticing. "Crappy night."

"I didn't say anything."

"I don't sleep much. But hey, you're not looking so bad, considering. Word was you were half dead."

"Half alive. It's all a matter of viewpoint."

"I understand you took a knife."

I gave my kidney a light pat. "Came in through the side door. I was stupid, he was lucky. Won't happen again. Trust me."

I followed her down a corridor to a roomful of desks. Megan's was in a corner. She dropped into the chair behind her desk and motioned for me to sit. Her phone rang and she took the call. The desk was a mess of papers and folders. The way they were spread clear across the large desk, it looked as if Megan had slept here overnight. There was a framed photograph of an attractive brunette posing next to a table piled high with summer produce. I angled it for a better look. I recognized the spot. The farmer's market at Union Square. I also recognized the woman.

Megan ended her call. She followed my gaze. "That's Helen."

"I know."

She picked up the photo and looked at it. "Her acupuncturist used to prescribe a visit to the farmer's market every weekend. He had a whole energy theory going. The harvest. Locally grown foods. He said that just walking through the market was therapeutic. I could never quite catch it all. Kidney energy. I kept hearing about Helen's kidney energy, whatever the hell that was." She set the picture back down. "She swore by him. If he'd wanted to put his damn needles in her eyes, she'd have let him. He had her on this thing for a while where she stuck these fuses to the bottom of her feet and then I lit them for her. Some kind of heat acupuncture. Don't tell me it sounds crazy, I already know. But guess what? Helen was the healthiest person you'd ever want to know, so what can I say? Every Saturday, religiously, off to Union Square to talk with her tomatoes."

She picked up a pen and tapped it thoughtfully against the picture frame, then tossed the pen on the desk. "You make sense of it. Helen taught sixth-graders how to read and write while I run around for a living with a gun on my hip. But which one of us is still here to tell the story? When I think of how that woman used to worry herself sick over me. That's a real laugh, isn't it?"

"It's not a laugh. It's normal," I said. "Margo would be quite happy if I sold paper clips for a living."

"Well, look at you, fished out of the East River. She might be right. I don't know, sometimes I think people who do what we do for a living don't have any business getting ourselves involved with civilians. Helen was all about cute and stupid things the kids did at school that day, while I'm sitting there sucking in exit wounds and bloated floaters. 'How was your day, honey?' 'Oh, fine, you know, just another romp through mankind's butcheries.'"

"My old man used to describe his job as toxic."

"Your old man was right. That's exactly how I feel sometimes—like I'm slowly being poisoned. And it's not only the victims but the nut monkeys out there, the ones who are doing this shit. You get to thinking the human race in general is toxic. You've got your crazy butchers, you've got your perfectly normal-seeming butchers. Kids shooting other kids. **Parents** killing their own kids, for Christ's sake. Helen wanted us to adopt a baby. She loved the idea of raising a child. Jesus. In **this** world? I break out in a cold sweat just thinking about it."

"Hell of a responsibility."

"Forget it. I used to think how unfair it'd be to Helen, we adopt a kid then I get killed on the job and leave her to raise the kid on her own. Look what happened instead." She laughed. It wasn't a particularly joyful laugh. "If some poor kid had to count on me these days, God help her. Or him. They'd go back to the agency and demand a new placement."

"Maybe you're being too hard on yourself."

Megan looked at me a moment without speaking. "That's exactly what my shrink says. I'll tell you what I tell her: sure, I'm hard on myself, but there's no way in hell I'm **too** hard on myself. I deserve all the crap I throw at myself."

"I'll bet your shrink doesn't agree with that."

"That's an easy bet to win. Anyway." She flipped open one of the folders on her desk. It contained the police sketch of my attacker.

"That's not him," I said. "I don't know where you got it, but it's no good."

"Michelle Poole worked with our sketcher on this."

"It's no good."

"I had a feeling. The girl didn't seem very sure of herself." Megan picked up the sketch and studied it.

"Thurman Munson," I said.

"Thurman what?"

"Former Yankees catcher."

"That's who threw you into the river?"

"That's who the sketch looks like. But like I said, the sketch is no good. The guy this sketch doesn't look like was stalking Michelle Poole. I guess she told you that. I saw him that day. At the Quaker meeting."

"Could be he was first stalking Robin."

"I was hoping to get a chance to ask him that question, but he decided to show me how fast he could run."

"I guess he didn't run fast enough."

"What do you mean?"

"You caught up to him."

"Right. Lucky me."

"So, are you up to a session with a sketcher?" She picked up the phone and put in a call. She covered the mouthpiece. "Twenty minutes. Can you wait?"

"I'm in no hurry."

She told the person on the phone that twenty

minutes was fine, then she hung up. I asked her for some of that fine NYPD coffee, and she fetched me a cup. I discarded a couple of easy jabs about the burnt mud. Megan told me that she had spoken with Edward Anger from the Quaker meeting and that he was in the clear. Out-of-town alibi for the evening Robin was murdered. She also told me that Allison Jennings had given Gallo the same two names I'd gotten her to cough up. They'd both cleared as well.

"I wasn't real keen on those two anyway," I said. "Though it wouldn't have been the first time that a long shot came in. But Anger. I guess I was holding out some hope for him. Sometimes the excessively gentle ones—well, you know."

"A name like that was too good. But the alibi's fine. Anger's out."

"So what do you think, Megan? I mean about Riddick and Robin. Are they copycat jobs, or is it possible that Fox was innocent all along?"

She was shaking her head before I'd even finished the question. "It's him. The case is too strong. We got the fibers from Nikki's plaid skirt off of Fox's scissors. That was huge."

"You never recovered the skirt itself."

"Doesn't matter. We had the receipt. We got the positive ID from the clerk at Liana who sold it to her. Nikki's neighbor saw her leaving the building wearing it, a green-and-black plaid skirt.

Fragments of the same skirt end up in Fox's bed-side scissors? Plus the blood on the scissors?"

"But the defense leaked the story that it was all just sex play. A game of dress-up. They said Nikki got nicked by the scissors when Fox was hacking her out of the skirt."

"Of course they leaked the story. We got the DNA match on blood that was on the scissors as well as the semen the M.E. recovered from Nikki's body. No question she had sex with Fox just before she was killed. Or possibly it was even **while** they were having sex. A man who likes to pretend he's in bed with a schoolgirl and he's attacking her with a pair of scissors? I wouldn't put anything past him. If the defense was so confident about their version of things, they could have put Fox on the stand and had him tell the tale. Uh-uh. He's our man, Fritz. And ladle in the case for Cynthia Blair. Fox was desperate to keep a lid on that affair. And I mean **desperate.** When she told him she was going ahead with the pregnancy, that was pretty much her death warrant. You heard the testimony. Fox's attitude toward fathering children was lethal."

The sketch artist showed up, and we got to work. The good ones employ a relaxing technique of mild hypnosis. This was a good one. We moved into Joe Gallo's office so we could have some privacy. Megan took the sketcher out into the corridor, where she briefed him on what we were looking for. The two came back in, and Megan pulled the blinds. I was instructed to close my eyes and think about the ocean. It took me a moment to clear the beach and to locate the big open expanse the sketcher was looking for, but I eventually got it. The sketcher moved me into a trancelike place. He had a voice like one of those classical DJs. I expected him to introduce Rachmaninoff any minute. I heard my disembodied voice talking with him, and I heard myself describing the man who had thrown me into the East River. An image of his face floated in my head crystal-clear, and I calmly ran down his features. When the blinds were opened and I opened my eyes, I was handed a sketch that looked 70 percent like Ratface. I worked with the sketcher until we got to about 85 percent, then I had to beg off. My head was really doing a number. I didn't want pieces of my skull breaking off and littering Joe Gallo's desk. The sketcher told me I was a good subject and took off. Megan told me to drink a cup of water—it had appeared miraculously on her desk—and she left the room and came back a minute later with a large brown envelope. Several copies of the sketch were in the envelope.

"I'm not giving these to you."

"No, ma'am."

She handed me the envelope. "You're not to distribute these."

"No, ma'am."

"I don't generally find 'ma'am' to my liking."

"Yes, ma'am."

Megan walked me to the front door and followed me outside. Megan wasn't dressed for outside, and she hugged herself tightly. She looked like a woman in a straitjacket.

"That conversation we had. About the job. The part about it being toxic."

"What about it?"

"I'd like that not to go anywhere."

"I wasn't planning on hopping on the phone."

"You know what I mean. I've been back to work since the fall, but I've still got a lot of eyes on me. There are some people who think I lost it with Albert Stenborg, that I got spooked and that I'm still spooked."

"I don't see anything wrong with admitting you're spooked. It's human."

"Being spooked and admitting you're spooked are two different things."

"You don't seem to have a problem admitting it to me."

"You're not a cop. I don't work with you. Besides, I don't know. I remember that time you pretended to run into me at Mumbles."

"That was the name of it. I'd forgotten."

"What the hell was a guy like you doing in a place like that?"

"A guy like me what?"

"A guy."

"I do recall I seemed to be in the minority."

"The point is, it was a nice gesture."

"That's not how you reacted at the time. As I recall, you told me to mind my own goddamn business."

"So original."

I shrugged. "I'd heard you weren't treating yourself so good. It's not unexpected, given all you were in the middle of. I've had some pretty sour points in my time. Sometimes you welcome a person nosing in, and sometimes you tell them to mind their own goddamn business."

Megan released her grip on herself and blew into her hands. Her lips were going blue. "Let me ask you something. Something that's none of my own goddamn business."

"Shoot."

"You've killed someone," she said. "That's not a question. I happen to know it."

"Okay."

"You can tell me to shut up if you want."

"Go ahead."

"I hate this word, it's gotten so self-helpy, but did you get closure on it?"

"It?"

She could read my tone of voice. "Jesus. You've killed more than one person? I'm sorry. I didn't know."

"That's okay. All part of the résumé. As for your question, I can't answer it. Or if I can, I think the answer is no. Closure isn't a concept that makes sense to me. Not in this context. That kind of closure is too cold for my tastes. Plus, I don't really buy it. I think it's denial, to use another self-helpy word."

"Then you understand what I'm talking about." She indicated the precinct house behind us. "There's no one in there I can talk to about any of this. Joe, I guess. But only so much. Pope is too green. I don't want to spook him. But what you just said, that's the problem. There's this idea that I'm supposed to shake off what I did. But what I did was I failed to save my girlfriend and I failed to save my partner. Both of them went down on my account. That's not something a person just shakes off. And believe me, killing Stenborg didn't do it for me. Not by a long shot. The time to kill him was before he did his damage. I could unload pistols into that bastard all day long and it wouldn't make any difference. That's what I'm carrying around. It's this feeling that I owe Helen. I owe Chris Madden, too, but if I'm brutally honest, that's not where the trouble is. It's Helen. I feel like I still owe her. And the thing is, I owe her what I can't give her."

"Thinking like that is only going to drive you nuts."

"You rest my case."

"You said you're not getting much sleep. Is that it?"

"Let's just say I find it's a lot easier the less I close my eyes."

I headed for the subway. The station was like a deep freeze. People stood on the platform stomping their feet and beating their arms up and down. Deep freeze or a nuthouse. The 1 train came in, rocking slightly as it hurtled forward. I caught a glimpse of a rat scurrying to get out of its path. I'd moved closer to the edge of the platform than I'd realized; I could practically smell the train. The sight of the scurrying rat brought to mind a memory I wasn't particularly fond of.

Yeah. I knew what she meant.

~ 29 ~

ALAN ROSS CAME OUT from behind his desk
and clamped a solid two-hander on me. "It's good
of you to come, Mr. Malone. What can Linda get
you? Coffee? Sparkling water? Tea?"

The office was just shy of an airplane hangar,
a festival of teak and glass and polished metal.
The walls were choked with photographs of Ross
in the company of celebrities. Through the large
window behind his desk, sunlight danced off the
stainless-steel spire of the Chrysler Building. Visible in the distance, beyond the steel and con-
crete, was a thin ribbon of my old friend the East
River.

I let Linda off the hook. "I'm fine," I said. The
secretary flashed an unnecessarily large smile. I
was made a midget by the large plushy leather

chair Ross directed me into as he returned to the ergonomic throne behind the desk.

I asked, "How many people say 'nice place' when they come in here the first time?"

Ross laughed, giving the huge room an approving glance. "Nearly all. It's an absurd amount of space for just one person, no question. But you have to remember, I deal with some pretty colossal egos. You'd be surprised how quickly this room fills up."

It was a canned response, but for that, not so bad a one. Ross poured himself a glass of water from a moist pewter pitcher on his desk, then set the glass down without taking a sip. He fixed me with a direct gaze. "Marshall Fox is an innocent man."

I thought he was going to elaborate, but he didn't. I squirmed in the leather valley, working my way forward. "Okay. Fox is an innocent man."

He frowned. "You don't sound convinced."

"I didn't try to sound convinced. I have no idea if he's innocent or not."

"I'm telling you, he is. Marshall is many things, and unfortunately, not a few of them are far from attractive. But being a vainglorious egotist is not the same as being a murderer."

"I'm sure the dictionary would back you up on that. But what does any of this have to do with me?"

Ross paused before answering. On the wall just off his right shoulder, Bette Midler eyed me mischievously as she landed a big wet kiss on Alan Ross's cheek.

"I don't believe the police are doing all they can to find out who murdered Zack Riddick and the Burrell woman."

He paused for me to respond. I didn't give him much. A slow nod. "Okay."

He went on, "Frankly, I think they've got major egg on their face and they don't dare admit it. They took a high-stakes risk when they arrested Marshall for those murders. You've seen the circus. Marshall's career is tanked, regardless of the trial's outcome. A lot of ugly testimony flashed coast to coast. The whole thing has been a complete abysmal mess. You had better believe the police are invested in making those charges stick. Can you imagine the fallout if Marshall were to walk?"

I glanced off to my left. Alan Ross and Sylvester Stallone were arm wrestling. Rocky was losing, if you can believe it. Ross followed my gaze, his expression relaxing.

"Sly. He's a good man. Beautiful Act One. No Act Two. A real waste."

"I thought he was good in **Cop Land**."

"Too little too late."

Ross brought his fingers together and touched

them to his lips. "Mr. Malone, perhaps you're not aware how invested I am in all this. Zack Riddick was a friend of mine. Admittedly, not super close, but even so, I liked the man. Zack had his obnoxious side, I'm not pretending he didn't. But at heart he was a decent person. He definitely didn't deserve to have his throat slashed."

"Few do."

"And Cynthia. To a degree, she was a protégée of mine. I personally chose her to work with Marshall when I brought him in from the sticks. She was as sharp as they come. Very driven. Her entire life in front of her, poor girl." He paused for a sip of water. "I'm going to tell you something I try not to think about. I feel responsible for these people, for what happened to them. Less so the Burrell and Rossman women, although that's only because I didn't know them personally. But Cynthia most of all. I delivered her to Marshall like a gift."

"But you're saying Fox didn't have anything to do with her murder."

"Directly, no. That's right. He didn't. You're missing the point. Whoever killed these people did it **because** of Marshall. I can't explain the killer's motivation, but it's clearly something to do with these people's association with Marshall. That's obvious. So do you understand what I'm saying? **I'm** the one who brought Marshall into the public eye. My wife and I. We're the ones who took a nobody and made him famous beyond belief. You see how it works? If I don't make a superstar of Marshall Fox, four people aren't murdered in cold blood. Two of them friends of mine. That's what I'm trying to say. Whoever did this did it because of Marshall, and I created Marshall. He's my Frankenstein. I don't know if you can understand what I'm saying, but it is a horrible, horrible burden. For the sake of providing what I'm quite willing to admit is essentially silly entertainment five nights a week, four people are dead. It doesn't make me happy, Mr. Malone."

As he sat back in his chair and folded his fingers into a ball, a thought occurred to me. Possibly it was the same thought that had led Ross to call me up to his sanctum.

"You," I said.

"Me? What about me?"

"Your safety. If Fox really is innocent, and the same person who killed Cynthia Blair and Nikki Rossman is at it again—"

Ross was waving his hands. "No, no. This isn't about me."

"But it could be. If someone really has a problem with Marshall Fox and they're taking it out on all these people who are associated with him, what about the actual person who created him?"

Ross shook his head. "That's not why I asked

you here. Though, believe me, I've been looking over my shoulder ever since last Friday night. But I'm not looking for protection. What I want is someone who isn't invested in this whole thing the way the police are. I'm not saying they're sitting on their hands; they're trying to find out who killed Zack and Robin Burrell. But I happen to know that they prefer the copycat theory. The fact that the killer might be the same person who performed the murders they've already arrested Marshall for? They don't want that."

"No offense, but how is it you know what the police are thinking?"

"I'm putting myself in their shoes. I'm reading between the lines."

"You're guessing."

He let out a sigh. "Yes. I'm guessing."

"And what do you want from me?"

"You're a private investigator. Let me emphasize. **Private** investigator. I thought of you the day after Robin Burrell was killed. Running into you in the courtroom. And then I saw reports the other day about your, um, incident. You're looking for the killer as well, aren't you?"

I tried to keep a neutral expression. "And if I am?"

"You are. Your sweetheart lives directly across the street from where Robin Burrell lived. I'm a stickler for research. I find things out."

"You know, people don't like other people nosing about in their business."

Ross erupted into laughter. "Oh well, **that's** choice. A private snoop lamenting someone else doing a little snooping? I like that. Maybe you'd let me set up a screen test for you, Mr. Malone. I could see a series developing out of that." He made a square with his hands and held it up in front of him. "**The Selfish Detective.** Have you ever considered the slippery slope of show business?"

"My slope is plenty slippery, thanks anyway."

The tension that had been growing in the room evaporated. Ross was only kidding about the TV-show idea, of course, but even so, slipping back into his element seemed to relax him somewhat. The color came up in his face.

"Here's the story," Ross said pleasantly. "I would like to make it official. I'd like to hire you. You've already heard my angle. There's plenty self-serving on my part, I'm the first to admit it. But so what? I feel guilty about my man Marshall being the springboard for some pathetic sicko out there killing people. I want Marshall found innocent, and I want these killings to stop. I want to clear my conscience and Marshall's name all at once. Nice tidy package."

"The police are doing everything they can."

"Then why are you running around looking for Robin Burrell's killer?"

"Remember, that's your theory, Mr. Ross."

"Fine. The point is, I'd like to hire you. Like I say, I've done my research. It turns out you're not so bad at what you do."

"It's been an okay Act One," I said.

"So it's settled. You've seen my absurd office, I don't like to quibble over money. Whatever's your normal fee, I'll double it. I'm sorry, Mr. Malone, but I'm in the business of buying people. I want to be your top-priority client. And I want to hear from you every day. Progress reports. I'm not trying to bully you. I just have a certain way of operating."

A pigeon floated gracefully past the window behind Ross's head, angling down for a sharp descent. I shoved myself to the edge of the annoying chair.

"I have a certain way of operating as well," I said. "It starts with my not having the client tell me how to go about doing my job."

"You have connections. I know about your father. You've got friends on the force. At one point you were even planning to become a cop yourself."

I stood up. "Hats off to your researchers, Mr. Ross. It looks to me like you have all the snoops you need."

"Wait. I'm sorry. I'm not handling this too well." He pulled open a drawer and removed an envelope. "I make no demands. That's just how I'm used to operating. I want this nightmare ended." He tossed the envelope onto the desk. "That's five thousand dollars. If nothing else, it's for coming in to see me."

I picked up the envelope. It was thick and crunchy. I slapped it against my palm. Five thousand dollars makes a sweet slap. "If word gets out, you'll have every gumshoe in the city bugging Linda for an appointment."

Ross smiled wanly. "I feel helpless, Mr. Malone. It's not a mode I'm accustomed to, believe me. It's just that I'd like to feel I'm doing something to undo what's happened."

"Dead's dead, Mr. Ross."

"I know that. You decide if you'd like to accept my offer. I hope you do. Either way, keep the money. Or give it to your favorite charity, I don't really care what you do with it. I just want to help in some way. If you decide it won't kill you to keep me posted, either on your progress or the progress of the police, wonderful. I'll pay you for my own peace of mind. Maybe that sounds pathetic to you, but don't forget, I operate in a superficial world. Maybe if I hired a good writer, I could script a more meaningful gesture."

I slapped the envelope against my hand a second time. "How about I get back to you?"

He stood. "Sure. That would be fine. I appreciate your taking the time to talk to me." He clasped his hands behind his back and gave me a professional smile. It felt like an anti-handshake.

Linda's smile was also way below wattage as she fetched my coat from the closet. I've yet to know a secretary who didn't know everything that was taking place in her boss's office, if not his mind. I looked to see if her ear was red from pressing against the door.

"He's in pain," she said softly as she handed over my coat.

I had an almost irresistible urge to chuck her on the chin. I fought the urge with all my might, then made my way out to the elevator for the long ride back to Planet Earth.

30

THE DOORMAN REMEMBERED ME.

"Hey, you're the guy they fished out of the river the other day. Somebody up there must like you, brother. That'd been me, I'd be dead." He bounced his hands off his substantial gut. "Sink like a rock. You're one lucky guy."

A lucky guy wouldn't have ended up stabbed and tossed into the icy East River from a substantial height, but hey, context is everything. I pulled out one of the sketches that Megan Lamb had photocopied for me and handed it to the doorman. He studied it as if it were a logarithm.

"Nasty character," he opined.

"Have you seen him before?"

"Him? No. Not me."

It had occurred to me that when I'd been in pursuit of my attacker, his zigzags had led him directly to the Waterside Plaza complex as if maybe he knew exactly where he was headed. And after managing to flip me over the wall, he had disappeared instantly. No one had reported seeing a person fleeing from the scene. I'd wondered. Through the glass doors and up the elevator? With a nod and a wave to the friendly doorman? Given the lousy sketch that had made the earlier rounds, it was conceivable that the doorman had seen it and made no connection whatsoever with the man himself.

I asked, "There's no one living in any of these buildings who looks like this?"

"Here? This guy? I don't think so."

"How about the super? Or a maintenance man?"

The doorman pursed his lips and tilted the sketch. Why people do that, I'll never understand. What? You tilt the thing and suddenly recognize it's your uncle Billy?

"Sorry, brother." He tried to give me back the sketch.

"Keep it." I handed him my card. "The police will probably be by sometime and run you through this whole routine again."

He looked at the card. "Private investigation, huh? Hey, I've never met a private investigator before. So are you like those detectives on TV? Get hit on by all the ladies? Beautiful widows coming out of your ears? I lose a few pounds, I'd like to try that out. You must deal with a lot of cheating husbands. You carry a piece?"

I tapped the sketch in his hand. "I'd like to locate this guy. You help me out, maybe I'll try to dig up a beautiful widow for you."

He smiled. Big and toothy. "Don't get me dreaming, brother."

I left him to his dreams. Crossing back over First Avenue, I worked the shops and bars. There were plenty of both to keep me busy. At first no one recognized the face in the sketch, though more than a few sneered at it when they looked at it. "What'd he do? Kill his own mother?" But at a Laundromat on Twenty-seventh, I got a hit. An elderly Asian woman about the size of an eight-year-old told me that she recognized the face.

"He come here. He smoke. I tell him no. Clean clothes, clean clothes! No smoke!"

I asked if she knew anything about him. A name. Where he lived. She didn't. I've been taking my laundry to the same place in Little Italy for ten years, and if someone told them my name was John Jacob Astor, they wouldn't have any reason to say it wasn't, except to wonder why someone so stinking rich couldn't send his laundry in with the butler. I asked the woman if I could post the sketch on her bulletin board, next to the flyers for dog walking, yoga lessons, teaching guitar and all the rest. She didn't like that idea but agreed to take the sketch and show it to customers, and if they knew anything, they could give me a call. At least I think that was the arrangement. My pidgin English isn't all that good.

I concentrated on all the business establishments within a five-block radius of the Laundromat. I got a maybe at a food market on Twenty-first.

"Did he have kind of a beard before?"

"Could be," I said.

"I couldn't swear to it. You see a lot of faces in this city. This one might've come in here a few times. He does look sort of familiar."

After several hours of footwork, my fuel cells were pretty drained. I tried to give them a charge with a pastrami sandwich from a reputable joint, but the results were mixed. I made a phone call. "Paddy Reilly's in an hour. Can do?" The answer was in the affirmative. "Good."

I worked the sketch for another sluggish hour, but I got no more hits. Still, I found myself imagining that along one of these streets I was going up and down, Ratface was there, maybe even sitting up in his goddamn Ratface apartment looking out the window at me. It was a powerful feeling and a little unnerving—as if his eyes were boring laser holes into the back of my head—and it was all I could do to keep from scanning the building windows as I moved about.

The stitches in my side weren't real happy with all the activity, but they didn't get much of a say in the matter. The sun was still off on vacation somewhere—the South, I suppose—and what with the raw cold and the colorless sky and the dingy heaps of snow, the life seemed sucked out of the city. Or maybe it was just sucked out of me. It took me a while before I realized that this was one of the things the doctors had cautioned me about. I was irritable, flirting with something along the lines of fury. I was impatient. A blast of cold air whipping around Twenty-fifth Street worked me over and I wanted to hit something. There was a dull throbbing just behind my eyes. I pulled off my watch cap and touched the stitches on the back of my head. They felt hard and grisly, like the whiskers of some savanna beast. I looked at the sketches of Ratface that were clutched in my other hand, and a ball of rage rose up in my chest. It snagged my breath, precisely as if the rage itself were a scramble of barbed wire lodged in my sternum. I brought my fingers away from the wound. They were splotched with blood. It was going to ooze, the doctors had warned me. I ran my fingers along one of the sketches, bloodying the man's cheeks.

The bartender at Paddy Reilly's was a giant with a shaved head, a neck tattoo and a tuft of carrot-red hair below his lower lip. We were nodding acquaintances. He wrote poetry, the kind with a notable paucity of flower imagery. I'd heard him read a few times at some poetry slams in Alphabet City. He was reading one of his poems to Jigs Dugan off a scrap of paper as I came over to the bar.

> Got a hustler's laugh and crowbar arms
> And a Puerto Rican kid like a shadow
> Won't let him be, thinks he's a god
> And he finds a Coney Island mermaid
> The one of his dreams
> Rolls her in popcorn
> In a room, with a view, of the sea
> Streams of paper whipping off the wire
>   fan
> Cool breeze, cool breeze, cool breeze.

He folded the paper and stuck it in his T-shirt pocket. Jigs was playing with an unlit cigarette, looking thoughtful. He tapped the filter against the bar. "Yeah, I guess that's good. So. He's balling the mermaid. Am I hearing that right?"

I set one of the sketches on the bar. "Ever seen this most happy fella?"

The bartender did the doorman thing. Tilted

the sketch and pursed his lips. "Can't say it rings a bell."

Jigs had a tumbler in front of him. It was either iced tea or whiskey, and who wants to pick? I asked the bartender for a cup of coffee. Jigs asked, "You want he should Irish that up for you?" I waved off the offer, and the bartender moved down the bar to slap the coffee machine around.

Jigs picked up his glass. "I hear you took a spill, friend."

"You hear correctly."

"Darkened my day to hear it."

"I stuck around the hospital an extra day in case you were sending me flowers."

"I don't do hospitals well," Jigs said.

"I'd have thought you might come fishing for a pretty nurse."

"I went with a nurse once. A Janice. Or Janet. I can't remember. She gave me a lovely sitz bath. This was when I had that little knee situation."

Little knee situation. A lead pipe swung like a Ty Cobb bat at Jigs's knees. He was off his feet for half a year.

The bartender returned with my coffee. The mischief came into Jigs's eyes. "I've been thinking about this mermaid of yours, Kevin. It seems—"

The bartender cut him off. "It's a metaphor."

Jigs made a sound like he was loosening a hairball in his throat. "Ack. Metaphors. Perfectly lovely mermaid, and you want to shunt her off as a metaphor. You poets need to start facing reality on more of a regular basis."

The bartender didn't seem to care what Jigs thought. He found a far corner of the bar that needed polishing.

"I'm after the bastard who's been slitting throats," I said.

Jigs cocked an eyebrow at me. "Is that so? Town's kind of jumpy on that topic."

"So am I."

He indicated the sketch. "Would this be him?"

"I don't know. It's possible. This is who packed me into the East River. It'd be nice if he was also the killer."

"Here's what I don't understand," Jigs said, eyeballing the sketch. "I watched some of that trial on the tube. Ugliest show in America. Impossible not to watch. I saw the pretty girl getting the once-over from the dead lawyer. He wasn't dead yet, and neither was she. But now they are. The both of them. How does that play out, Fritz? There was surely no love lost between the two of them. They were adversaries. Who would hold a grudge against one of them and then go on to be-grudge the other to the same result?"

"You mean why would someone target Robin Burrell and then go after Riddick?"

"To put it less poetically."

"That's the question. Were they targets in their own right, or was it more a case of somebody targeting Marshall Fox? Or people associated with Fox?"

"That's where I go," Jigs said. "You find someone who's too furious about what Mr. Fox did to those two girls last year. An avenging angel, tit for tat."

"But why now? Fox is in the fight for his life."

"Not in this state, honey. Here he gets packed off for ten to twenty and he comes back out somewhere in the middle."

"Still, why shake things up so close to the verdict?"

Jigs consulted his whiskey. "Maybe an acquittal would play in to our good fellow's hand. It does put Mr. Fox back out on the street, after all."

"So you mean kill two people to even the score, then if Fox is set free, wham, bam, thank you, ma'am."

"Now, **that's** poetical."

I considered what Jigs was saying. It made as much sense as anything else being bandied about. I figured the police were already looking closely at family and close associates of Cynthia Blair and Nicole Rossman. They'd surely be working that angle.

I squared the drawing of Ratface on the bar. Had **he** known either of those two women? My gut was saying no.

I realized my gut was also saying it didn't matter.

"I want this guy." The voice didn't even sound like mine. It was a profound baritone. Just an octave or two up from a growl. I tapped a finger heavily against the sketch. "I don't know his angle, and to be honest, I don't care. This bastard lives nearby. In the neighborhood somewhere. I've gotten a couple of positive IDs."

Jigs set his glass down. "And you want him."

I looked past the row of bottles behind the bar and confirmed it with the cranky fellow in the watch cap. From my pocket, I took Alan Ross's envelope and laid a large stack of twenties down on the flyer. "That's right."

Jigs nodded sagely. "Yeah, brother. I can see that."

~ 31 ~

MEGAN WAS LOOKING DOWN at her fingers when the woman approached. "Hey. Remember me?"

Megan looked up. Large. The ubiquitous big-boned. Cute face under a Louise Brooks cut. She was wearing orange jeans and a black T-shirt with a William Wegman dog on it. A Weimaraner. This one wasn't dressed up in a costume like they usually were. It was sitting on a white box looking terribly cute and perplexed. Megan wondered if that was how she was looking. Cute, she couldn't say. Perplexed, definitely.

"I'm sorry. Uh. I'm waiting for someone."

The woman showed her a classic ear-to-ear. "I notice you've been waiting for a long time. Maybe you're being stood up. Do you mind if I join you?" She didn't wait for an answer but pulled back the chair opposite Megan and made herself at home. "What are we drinking?"

Megan had been staring at a Scotch and soda for forty minutes.

"You want me to freshen that? What is it?"

"It's Scotch, but—"

The woman called out. "Two Scotches!" She turned back to Megan. "You really don't recognize me, do you? That's okay. I'm not offended."

Megan didn't know where to put her eyes. This was ridiculous. She had no business coming back to this place. Why not? a voice in her head demanded. What the hell's wrong with getting on with your life? It's just a place.

"Ruth," the woman said.

Megan looked up from the table. "I'm Megan."

Ruth skidded her chair back from the table. She lifted her shirt slightly while tugging down on her jeans. Megan leaned forward. Part of a tattoo showed just below the woman's belly button. A dragon of some sort. Most of it remained below the belt.

"You don't remember?"

Megan shook her head. She did, vaguely. Like in an uncomfortable dream. "Maybe it wasn't me."

Ruth grinned. "Oh, it was you, sugar. I don't forget a face like yours."

The drinks arrived. Megan could feel her first sip travel to the tip of each limb. It felt good.

Ruth touched her lightly on the wrist, then pulled back sharply, as if she'd received a shock. "You need to smile, little girl. Nothing can be **that** bad."

Two hours later, Megan switched on the overhead light and stepped aside. The keys slipped from her hand and fell to the floor. She didn't dare lean over to fetch them. Instead, she kicked at them with her foot. It didn't even feel like her foot.

Ruth followed her into the apartment with a slight stumble. She laughed, holding her arms out from her sides like a high-wire artist. She turned around as Megan closed the door. "I'd kill for a place in the Village."

Megan kicked the keys across the floor. "You want it? It's yours."

"Yeah, I should be so lucky."

"Serious. I don't give—" Megan had to grab hold of a chair.

Ruth started forward. "Are you okay, sweetheart?"

"Fine."

"Look. Do you want to get high?"

As Ruth reached into her pants pocket, Megan grabbed hold of her arm. "Don't." It was a fleshy arm. Megan closed her eyes tightly. She was afraid she was going to be sick.

"I'm just thinking of a little nightcap." Ruth

began singing: " 'Nothing could be finer than a little mariwhiner in the eeeeeeevening.' "

Megan squeezed the woman's arm. "Don't."

Ruth shrugged. "Hey. Okay. That's how you want it. I'm just trying to be a good guest." She grinned, reaching down and hooking her fingers into Megan's belt loops. With a jerk, she brought their pelvises together. Megan's hit Ruth's below the hips. She stumbled. Ruth cooed, "Don't worry, I've got you, sweetheart."

Megan couldn't remember putting away such quantities of alcohol since forever. She could taste the bile in her throat. Ruth was holding her close. She cupped her hand on Megan's ass. "I think we can loosen you up."

Megan's head lolled forward onto the woman. She felt as if she were being drawn into a cave. A cave with a dragon hidden in the darkness. This was wrong, all of it. Megan told herself this was not what Helen would have wanted her to be doing. Soft, silly Helen. Where was **she**? Dammit, why wasn't she **here**? Why wasn't she coming in the front door right now and telling this Ruth woman to kindly get her big bones out of here? Ruth was kneading Megan's ass with her fingers. Megan couldn't breathe. Where the **fuck** is Helen!

Ruth nuzzled forward and tried to kiss her. Megan jerked her head away.

"Hey!" Ruth tightened her grip on Megan's ass and pulled her closer. "Let's just start relaxing already, okay? Come on, now. I remember you were a real sweet kisser. Let's be friends here."

Megan worked her arms up between the two of them and pushed with all her strength, twisting her torso as she tried to squirm free. The women's feet tangled. Ruth stepped on her own foot and with a cry fell backward onto the floor. Megan managed to shake free and remain standing.

"Jesus Christ!" Ruth crawled onto all fours. "Honey, you've got a very fucked-up . . ." She stopped. Megan saw her eyes grow wide. "What the . . . fuck is **that**?"

She was staring at Megan's bookshelf. Displayed one next to the other were three black-and-white framed photographs. Eight-by-ten. The first one showed a woman with a scarf of some sort knotted at her neck. Clearly dead. The woman in the second photograph—a blonde, Ruth recognized her from the newspapers—had had her slender throat cut open. The woman's eyes were open and staring off into space.

"Oh my God."

The third photograph was the most horrible. It didn't appear that there even **was** a neck. The cheeks looked like they'd been raked by a wild animal. Ruth scrambled to her feet. Megan had not moved but stood shaking in the middle of the floor, pale as a sheet.

"What the hell are you into, little girl? Where the hell'd you get these?"

"Go." Megan's voice sounded hoarse.

"Oh, don't worry. I'm changing my plans right now." Ruth brushed past Megan, pausing at the door. "That's not good form, honey. You want some advice, you put those pictures away, or you're going to stay awfully lonely."

Ruth left. Megan's feet walked her to the door, and her hands locked it. Turning from the door, she confronted the three photographs across the room. They were swimming. Megan made it halfway across the room before she got sick.

FOR NANCY SPICER, foreperson on the Marshall Fox jury, life had been reduced to a tiny hotel room, the pine-paneled jury room, the van that shuttled her from one to the other, and to those eleven other hateful people whom Nancy didn't especially like and who definitely did not like her. She was either too white, or too indecisive, or too religious, or too scared. Too something. Too anything. Too **nothing**.

Nancy Spicer decided to see what would happen if she swallowed twenty-seven barbiturates in the space of something like fifteen minutes.

Over the past several months, Nancy had come to fear that the eleven other jurors were right. The world is a brutal place. It takes courage and strength and conviction in order to maneuver, in order to survive. Nancy had none of these. There might have been a time—she could recall having a thin grasp on conviction once, though this seemed a lifetime ago—but in the large scheme, not really. Never enough. Bruce was the provider. The rock. Bruce had always filled in where Nancy came up lacking. He had the conviction and the strength and the courage. Bruce knew his place in the world, and he surely knew his purpose. He knew right from wrong, black from white, and he knew sin when it made its inevitable appearance. Nancy's husband was clear on all matters, a man of unshakable resolve. If **he** were foreman of this jury, there would have been none of this contentiousness. There wouldn't be the sniping and the hostility and the disgust. Bruce could have pulled everyone together; he was a leader of men. He saw things with a razor-sharp clarity, and he knew how to put people in their place.

Nancy was a lesser person, and she knew it. Bruce was kind, so **kind** to put up with her, to have admitted a cripple into his home. His rage soon after their marriage at the discovery that Nancy was barren and would be unable to deliver his children into the world had been understandable. The disappointment was mighty. If Nancy had known, she would not have married him. She never could have been that knowingly selfish. Bruce's anger was acceptable. It was the devil who poisoned the wombs of the unworthy; it was the devil Bruce raged against. Nancy had accepted all that. She'd welcomed it. A husband who will cleanse his wife's impurities is a treasure to cherish. Bruce was so good to her. He was magnificent in his disappointment. He was full where she was empty. The world had no idea what a precious messenger of Truth it had in Bruce Spicer. God bless him, Nancy thought as she cupped her first handful of pills. Take care of him. I have failed in every aspect of my life. I am too weak. I can't face those other people anymore. Their eyes. Their disgust. I am too confused now. How can I sit in judgment? The devil has put me here, and he is enjoying my misery. He is enjoying the mess I am making of things. Bruce has told me so. But . . . but I will **not** be his agent. I will crush his enjoyment. Bruce will understand. He will not be angry, but he'll rejoice in this one selfless act that I have managed to perform in my entire life. My entire crippled, useless life.

The lights of Times Square outside Nancy Spicer's window had never looked so remarkable, like an array of colored stars in a close-up universe. They blurred and merged. Angels, Nancy thought woozily. Angels forming my bed. Her arms were covered with tears. She wondered if she had ever been so happy. Bruce will be proud. He'll be so proud. The bed of lights was swimming. Swinging. Like a hammock. Nancy made a sound that was intended to be a laugh. It came out as a sob. Followed by another. Then came the pain. The devil clamped his red fists onto her abdomen, and his barbed fingers dug into her useless womb. An agony like none she had ever experienced or could have ever imagined rose up in her belly, and she was struck with unspeakable fear. She fell back from the window and began beating her fists against her belly, trying to make the pain stop. She began to convulse. Her last conscious thought was the horror of seeing, right there in her belly, the devil's gnarled hand digging and twisting and probing. On his vile hand was the wedding ring. Shiny and gold. One she knew very, very well.

❧ 32 ❧

PETER ELLIOTT PHONED ME with the news in the morning.

"My foreperson is in a coma," he said. "Life doth suck."

I met Peter out in front of Saint Vincent's. The media was well represented. So was the NYPD. Vehicles parked every which way. I spotted Kelly Cole standing on the corner of Twelfth and Seventh, speaking into her cell phone. When she saw me, she raised a manicured finger, mouthing for me to hang tight.

A dark car had just pulled up to a fire hydrant. "Are you sure it's not the pope they've got in there?" I said to Peter. Lewis Gottlieb was climbing out of the back.

"Lewis and I have to get inside," Peter said.

"Bruce Spicer is in there threatening to explode. This whole thing is headed for the toilet."

"I'll catch up to you."

Kelly Cole flipped her phone closed and stepped over to me. The coat itself must have cost a few thousand bucks. It was long and tan and cut like something for a Russian czarina.

"Did you get the flowers I sent to you in the hospital?" she asked.

I told her I hadn't.

"That's because I didn't send any." She laughed. "I did try to call you, though."

"I got that. I called you back, but you weren't in. I didn't feel like leaving a message."

"So tell me, who dumped you into the river?"

"You know what? The gentleman never stopped to give me his name."

"But he's a suspect in Zachary's murder, isn't he?"

"Come on, Kelly. I chase bad guys for lunch."

"The short way to say that is 'No comment.'"

" 'No comment' is shorthand for 'yes.' "

"So **is** he a suspect?"

"Nice coat, Kelly. Is that wool or synthetic?"

"Come on. Give a girl a break, will you? At least tell me whether you're investigating the murders. That's not a state secret, is it?"

"No comment. Yes. No."

"Hey, I'm just trying to make a living, for Christ's sake. The police are completely constipated on the whole thing. I'm only trying to assure my audience that **someone** is making some progress. Can't you just tell me, off the record, who it was that got the jump on a tough guy like you?"

"I like that. Take a compliment and split it in two. I told you, I honestly don't know the man's name. All I know is that it appears he's been stalking a friend of Robin Burrell's. I wanted to talk to him about Robin, but he got all shy on me."

"What's this I'm hearing about another phone threat? Do you know anything about that?"

I looked past Kelly and spotted Megan Lamb crossing at the corner. "There's your chief investigator. Why don't you go collect some no-comments from her?"

Kelly followed my gaze. "The Lambinator. I can't figure that one out. She's gay, you know."

"Well, hey, you figured that part out." As Megan angled in our direction, I whispered, "Say something nice about her hair."

"As **if**."

Megan came over to us. "Any word?"

"Something about the jury foreperson in a coma," I said. "Apparent suicide attempt. I just got here."

"I got the call as I was leaving my apartment.

I live just over on Hudson." She acknowledged the reporter. "Morning, Ms. Cole. Any scoops you'd like to share with us?"

"You took the question right out of my mouth."

"Has the juror's name leaked yet?"

Kelly shook her head. "No. Would you care to leak it for me, Detective?"

"Don't worry. Hospitals are sieves. It'll come out. When it does, I suppose you're ready to contribute to the shutting down of this trial."

"I do my job, Detective. You do your job. Mine is reporting the facts."

"Sometimes your job makes my job ten times harder."

"I pass information on to the citizens. That's how a free society works."

Megan turned to me. "Little early for a civics lesson, don't you think? Come on." She started for the emergency room doors.

"Uck foo you too, sister," Kelly murmured as I turned and followed.

"You all right?" I asked Megan as we entered the hospital.

"Not relevant," she snapped.

Bruce Spicer was a man surrounded. Seated against the far wall in a visiting area down the hall from the ICU, he was nearly drowning in members of Marshall Fox's defense team. Peter Elliott and Lewis Gottlieb stood nearby. A dozen cops, a doctor and several other people I couldn't identify were part of the cluster. Spicer was talking as Megan and I added to the crowd. Actually, he wasn't talking. He was railing.

"Why in the world should I **not** speak my mind? My wife has been kept in virtual incarceration for nearly **three months,** forced to undergo torture and abuse at the hands of state-appointed imbeciles who don't seem to know which hole their heads are supposed to pop out of. Let me tell you something right now, I am **tired.** I am sick and tired and disgusted at the bend-over-backward efforts to so-called protect the so-called rights of a rapist and fornicator and murderer! Who's nuts here? Is it me? Have I landed on a backward planet? The man is a despicable **sinner.** He is **guilty** of all the charges. Not to mention a whole lot more that the state has been too lily-livered to even bother to **bring.** I'm sick of it. I'm disgusted. I'm fed up. My wife is on death's doorstep, thanks to **you people**!"

He sent an accusing finger around the room, punctuating the air as he aimed it at every single person present. Even Megan and I got stabbed.

"You are **all** guilty of sending my wife to the grave, if that's where this ends up. So are those eleven ninnies you saw fit to put into the jury box with her. I'm telling you this: you lawyers—you want some work? It's coming. **I'm** coming. Are you ready? I'm coming strong. I'll get you a whole big pile of work to do." He counted off on his fingers. "I am suing the **city.** I am suing the **state.** I am suing the **ninnies.** And you can damn well be certain I am suing KBS Television and the company that owns it and Mr. Marshall Fox **and** that prostitute wife of his!"

I looked over at Megan and mouthed, "Prostitute?"

Megan answered in a low voice, "You might want to tell that reporter friend of yours. I think that's a scoop."

Spicer looked out over his small crowd. "Where are the reporters? I'm sick of talking to you people. I need to speak to the God-fearing Christians out there. Some people with common sense. They need to hear what I'm saying. Those women who were killed last year were whores! Marshall Fox is an indiscriminate fornicator. Let the swine go down with the swine. Why should taxpayer dollars be spent on any of this? Why should my wife be sent to her **death** on account of a pack of godless sinners? Where's the press? We need to get the word out. Have you got them locked out? I guess they're in on the conspiracy with the rest of you heathens. I'm sick of it. I'm sick of it all. Ye shall know my strength and ye shall fear my wrath, you sniveling pack of whores!"

Lewis Gottlieb stepped forward. His demeanor was impeccably calm and civil. "Mr. Spicer, I hear all that you're saying. I honestly do. This is a terribly delicate situation. I feel horrible about what has happened to your wife. Matters should not have been allowed to reach such a point, and on behalf of the court and the state of New York, I want to apologize personally to you and your family. But please, we need to contain the damage here, we don't—"

Spicer interrupted. "Gottlieb, is that right?"

The attorney inclined his head. "That's correct."

"I'll be suing you, too! Personally!"

The attorney demurred. "What you need right now is to be alone with your wife. This is not the time to be raising a holy fuss. Your wife's health should be your only concern right now. If there is—"

"My wife's health had better be **your** concern. All of yours. Is anybody listening to me? I want to talk to the press, and I want to do it right now! What's going on here? Am I under some sort of house arrest?"

Peter spoke up. "Mr. Spicer, we really do not want this trial to fall apart. The wise thing is to wait until we've heard from Judge Deveraux—"

"Him?" You'd have thought Spicer had just stepped on a land mine. "Sweet Jesus and Mary, the man in the black robes. I wouldn't cross the street to spit on him."

Lewis Gottlieb had had enough. "You are a contentious low-life little **shit** is what you are."

As the attorney started forward, Spicer leaped to his feet. "I don't think any killer of the Lord Our Christ is going to judge **me** one iota." He grabbed the chair he'd just been sitting in. Before he could lift it, Peter Elliott lunged forward and grabbed hold of it. Spicer tried to yank it free, but Peter had a good grip. With his free hand, he tried to move Gottlieb back, but the elderly gentleman tripped on his own feet and went tumbling to the floor. Spicer cried out.

"Baby killer! Heathen pig!"

Peter sunk his fist hard into Spicer's stomach. The man doubled over and the police leaped into action, two of them taking hold of Spicer while another one pulled Peter away from him. Spicer continued bellowing, "Heathens! Blasphemers!"

Peter snarled at him, "Just shut the hell up, would you?" as the policeman guided him over to the far wall. Lewis Gottlieb was helped to his feet. He slid into a chair. Spicer was still thrashing to free himself of the police grip, and he attempted to kick the elder attorney, but the police jerked him out of range. Gottlieb waved a freckled hand in the air, like a wizard concluding a spell.

"Please take that man away from here. I'd

like to consider assault charges. Please detain him somewhere until this has been sorted out."

Spit was flying from Spicer's mouth. "I demand to see my lawyer!"

Gottlieb dusted off the arms of his jacket and addressed the man. "Luckily for you, Mr. Spicer, there are plenty of lawyers who **would** cross the street to spit on you."

He waved his hand again at the policemen. "For goodness' sake, take him away."

33

LEWIS GOTTLIEB WAS CHIDING his protégé.

"You've got to let a man like that put his own
fool head in the noose. He'll do it. He did it. I
sacrificed my can, and then you come along and
actually assault the damn fool. What in the world
were you thinking?"

"I'm sorry, Lewis. It was the slur."

"Oh, the **slur**. Screw the slur. You think I
haven't lived my entire life on the edge of a slur? I
could care less at this point. Especially from a
psycho like our Mr. Spicer. The point is that now
he can charge **you** with assault."

"The list of charges Bruce Spicer wants to
bring is so long it'll take him a year to get around
to that one."

"Let's hope."

Megan and I were sitting with the two lawyers in the hospital cafeteria. Gottlieb, it turned out, had smacked his elbow fairly hard on the floor when he'd gone down and had injured it some-what. The attorney's jacket was hung carefully on the back of his chair, and the left sleeve of his shirt was rolled up to his biceps so he could hold an ice pack to the injury. Peter was look-ing glum. He knew he'd screwed up in attack-ing Spicer. Gottlieb's demeanor was surprisingly wily.

"The trial's sunk, that's obvious," the elder attorney declared. "Bruce Spicer's big mouth is not going to be denied. And a forewoman with a husband like that? If Fred Willis doesn't demand that Sam declare a mistrial, I will. This is the most hackneyed affair I have ever been involved with."

Peter groaned. "New trial. I think I'll just shoot myself now. How are we going to pull that off? The entire country's been handicapping this one up close and personal. What rock are we going to look under to get an untainted jury at this point?"

"I'm afraid that's going to be your problem, young squirrel," Gottlieb said. "I've got eighteen holes calling my name, and this time they will not be denied. It would have been nice to add Mr. Fox's pelt to my collection, the self-righteous son of a bitch. But don't worry, Peter. The groundwork's been laid. The country knows what kind of sicko Fox really is. You'll be fine. Detective Lamb here and Joe Gallo did a superb job of boxing that little prick into the corner, and the evidence isn't going anywhere. We'll take some public relations hits, no doubt about that. You'll get your usual clamor that mistrial means the man must be innocent. Just ignore all that. Don't get caught up in the sideshows. That's all an idiot like Bruce Spicer is, a sideshow. And there's your irony. Spicer hates Marshall Fox's guts, but all he and his wife have succeeded in doing is giving the man a whole new day in court. Spicer's got his agenda over here and his brains out in West China somewhere." He turned to me. "Now that you've seen him in action, is my idea so crazy?"

Megan asked, "What idea is that?"

Peter explained, "Lewis believes we should be considering whether Spicer had something to do with Zachary's and Robin Burrell's killings."

Gottlieb interjected, "Not 'something to do with.' Stop pussyfooting around, Peter. My contention, Ms. Lamb, is that Bruce Spicer's our killer."

Megan turned to me. "You were looking into this?"

"Lewis mentioned his theory to me the day I got dunked in the East River. I haven't really had a chance to pursue it."

Gottlieb lowered the ice pack. "We've got nothing to contain at this point—not after Nancy Spicer's gesture. I suggest very strongly that you and your boss look into this. The man's a fanatical anti-abortionist, and Ms. Burrell admitted on the stand to those two abortions. Not just one but two."

"What about Riddick?"

"Lifestyle, Ms. Lamb. Our Mr. Spicer is fond of words like 'heathen' and 'fornicator.' Our dear departed Zachary surely falls into these categories."

I turned to Megan. "What do you think?"

She steepled her fingers and rested her chin on them. Her gaze bored through the table to the floor below. "Something Spicer said just now. Upstairs . . ." She let the sentence drift off, unfinished.

"What?"

"Oh my God!" She looked up sharply. "Did you hear it? When he was going on about suing everyone? 'I'm coming.' I knew there was something that's been nagging me."

Peter's mouth dropped slowly open. "My God. You're joking."

"I'm not. It's what he said. 'I'm coming.' The same voice. 'Can you taste the blood?'" Megan's eyes traveled from face to face as the meaning sank in.

Four chairs screeched abruptly away from the table.

HE WAS GONE.

After his rant, Spicer had been escorted from the visiting area to the room that was being read-ied for his wife. Nancy Spicer had emerged from her coma nearly simultaneously to her husband's histrionic display in the visiting area, and accord-ing to the aides who wheeled her up from the ICU, Bruce Spicer had whispered something in her ear, given her a squeeze on the shoulder and exited the room. A quick search of the floor told us that he was no longer on it.

"I'm going downstairs," Megan said. "I'll put in a call from one of the cruisers. He can't have gotten far."

Peter wasn't so confident. "He could be on a subway. He could be headed anywhere."

"We'll flood the Port Authority," I said. "We'll alert the airports. Airport security will pluck him out in a heartbeat. Don't worry. He's stuck in the boroughs. Plus, you saw him. The man's like a mad chicken. He won't be able to hide."

I joined Megan. We took the stairs two at a time. As we approached the hospital's front door, I had a thought, and I pulled up short. "Allison Jennings."

"What about her?"

"Spicer called her. He threatened her. We still don't know why." I pulled out my cell phone. "I'm going to see if I can get ahold of her. See if the name means anything to her."

"I'll be outside."

I had to track around in the lobby before I could get a decent signal. I leaned up against a wall engraved with the names of financial Samaritans and pulled Allison Jenning's card from my wallet. Something felt peculiar as I punched in the numbers. Just before the final one—a four— I realized why it felt peculiar. I shifted my thumb over one number and hit the five instead. It picked up on the second ring.

"Kelly Cole."

Son of a bitch. That was it.

"Kelly, It's Fritz. Where are you?"

"I'm still outside the hospital, why?"

"I want you to put your hand lovingly on your pretty throat."

"My . . . what are you talking about?"

"And then I want you to say a prayer to whatever God you believe in."

"I don't believe in any of them."

I switched ears, huddling in to the wall to fix the reception. "You might want to reconsider that stance, sweetheart. Just a heads-up."

～ 34 ～

THE DIN WAS LIKE the amplified chewing of an army of ants, but it was only Brasserie on a Saturday night. Above the long sleek bar ran a bank of brushed chrome video monitors, ten in all, displaying in black-and-white stop-action the comings and goings of patrons, captured by a small video camera mounted just inside the glass entrance. The trip from the first monitor to the tenth and final one took about twenty seconds. It was a novelty that never failed to crane necks. Caught on hidden camera. ("There you are! That's you!") From Patty "Tania" Hearst to Princess Di at the Paris Ritz, no one can get enough of it.

Sometime shortly after eight-thirty, the image of Rosemary Fox pushing through the glass door began its stuttering trip along the monitors. She was accompanied by Alan and Gloria Ross. No one at the bar seemed to recognize Marshall Fox's wife on the screen. However, diners seated at their tables turned their heads and watched as Rosemary and the Rosses were ushered to a table in the far corner of the large loud room. The Rosses took a seat on either side of Rosemary, who looked pale and angry, even behind her blue-tinted sunglasses. She also looked lovely in her $10,000 Versace "smock," her thick hair falling nearly to her elbows. The hostess had given the invisible signal, and by the time the three were settling in, a basket of cracked poppy-seed bread was being slid onto the table, a deep blue bottle of sparkling water was landing on the linen, and a frog-faced man in a deliberately oversize silk blouse was folding his hands together and silently kissing the air in front of him as he crooned, "How might I please you with cocktails this evening?"

Rosemary answered that one. "Double vodka martini. Three olives. Tell your man he's never built one so dry. Tell him also to wait approximately seven minutes and then build another one. No olives in that one."

The frog-faced man practically snapped his heels. "The lady knows what she wants."

"Yes." Rosemary sighed. "The lady does, at that."

Samuel Deveraux was going to declare a mistrial. This wasn't officially official, but it was what Fred Willis had all but guaranteed when he'd phoned Rosemary earlier in the day. Something about the jury foreperson wigging out. A suicide attempt? Rosemary hadn't paid much attention to the details. Apparently, the husband was a nut. That much was abundantly clear. There was even a rumor making the rounds that he was wanted for questioning in the murders of Zachary and the Quaker girl. As of early evening, the man was not yet in custody. Rosemary had also received a phone call from that woman detective, the one who had put Marshall under arrest in May. Real balls on that little gal, Rosemary thought, making that call herself. The detective had wanted to tell Rosemary about the juror's husband, equivocating on whether she thought the man was really the murderer everyone was looking for, but she did feel confident that he was the one who had left the crude message on Rosemary's phone machine. "A friendly warning, Mrs. Fox. You might want to be extra-cautious until we bring him in."

Alan and Gloria Ross sat silently, waiting for their cue from Rosemary. Rosemary was only slightly difficult to read behind the blue sunglasses. Her left index finger was tapping rapidly on her folded napkin, and her perfect chin was dipped slightly. Ross couldn't help but steal a glance at her breasts, pale and full, nudging the silver fabric of the dress. Familiarity with Rosemary Fox had bred no lack of astonishment on Ross's part at how beautiful and sensual the woman was, even wound tight as a clock, as she clearly was this evening.

Gloria was giving her husband a signal: a head bob in Rosemary's direction. Ross reached over and placed his hand over Rosemary's fingers, snuffing out her nervous tapping.

"I know a new trial seems like just about the worst thing on earth, honey," he said in as soothing a tone as he could muster in the noisy restaurant. "It pushes the time line way back for getting your life back to normal, I know that. But that jury was getting more and more freaked by the minute, Rose. They could have easily come in with a guilty verdict, you have to remember that. Marshall could be in the stew this very minute, but he's not. We all live to fight another day."

He glanced at his wife, who nodded nearly imperceptibly. Ross continued, "That's how you have to look at it, Rose. And there'll be no surprises the next time. We've all seen what they've got. Fred can work with that." He patted her hand again. "You'll see. Fred says there's a decent argument for getting Marshall out on bail now. It ain't gonna be cheap, honey. But think of it. Marshall free. That would be huge."

Rosemary's martini arrived, along with a pair of gin and tonics for the Rosses. The frog-faced man started to make nice with his customers, but Gloria caught his eye and waved him off with barely a movement.

Rosemary took up her drink. The Rosses followed suit.

"To Marshall," Gloria said.

As they toasted—somewhat lacklusterly— Rosemary spotted two men sitting several tables away, staring at her. Good-looking men. Rosemary lowered her glass and picked out one of the olives, making just a bit more out of sucking it into her mouth than was called for.

God, she thought. I am such a cunt.

Gloria was talking now. Rosemary wasn't tuning in fully. More about Marshall this, Marshall that, future this, future that. Rosemary trained her eyes in the direction of Gloria's face, just to look as if she were listening. Who was this woman kidding? Future? **Future?** Okay, Rosemary had a future. She had a lot of future, for that matter, as well as a lot of ideas about how she would like to spend it. She had no intention of bungling any more of her time than she already had. Rosemary was kind of surprised to hear Gloria talking that way. Gloria was in the business, she knew how a future could be cut short like **that.** She had to know full well that there would **be** no Marshall Fox after all this, whatever the outcome and whenever this endless tedious soap opera of a trial finally ran its course. Rosemary didn't mean to be cold about it, only realistic. Marshall Fox was dead.

Rosemary finished off her drink. The frog-faced man appeared as if by magic, bringing her second martini on a tray.

"You tell your man he is making me happy," Rosemary said.

The frog-faced man made a flourish. A laugh traveled about the table. The beautiful woman shared a smile with her dinner guests, both of whom responded eagerly. The good-looking men at the other table were still looking at her. Rosemary picked up her drink, tipping it ever so slightly in their direction, and allowed them the tiniest of smiles. Men. She thought about what was waiting for her back at the apartment. Her best-kept secret. She had to laugh. The lucky bastard would never have it so good again, that was for sure. He was probably not the future for too much longer, though that wasn't important right now. Right now he was still there—that was the point—willing to cater to her whims. The power of a woman can be almost frightening. Rosemary never tired of marveling at it. She knew she'd have to start putting distance between the two of them. She'd waited way too long already. But for Christ's sake, her husband was behind **bars.** What was she supposed to do, shave her head and find a convent? Rosemary anticipated some trouble when the time came for her to lay down the law. There'd be a scene; he'd already surprised her with his ability to make scenes. She realized she'd better start devising her plan of action now, just to be on the safe side.

The menus arrived. Yet another waiter. Rosemary held the single sheet down near her cutlery and looked over the options. The waiter was reeling off a list of specials, each one more elaborate and yummy-sounding than the next. There was an appetizer special of oysters. Rosemary envisioned the ugly little things. Floating in their own milky swill. Presented in those gnarly misshapen shells. The things people chose to consider special. The emperor's new oysters. She thought they tasted disgusting. Squishy slime. Like swallowing someone's mucus.

"I'll have those," Rosemary said. "The oysters." A giddy thought came to her mind. No. Yes. Must be the martini. She reached out both arms, graceful and swanlike, and placed her fingers on Alan's and Gloria's hands, eliciting a smile from each of them. She looked back up at the waiter.

"And please. Offer a serving to every table here, could you? I'd like to do that for everybody."

～ 35 ～

I NOTED THAT the faint scar running along Jigs Dugan's jaw was picking up the blue from the neon Canadian beer sign in the window behind him. The man who had given Jigs that scar some fifteen years back had lived just long enough to regret it. Jigs shocked not a few people by attending the man's viewing, at Campbell's funeral home on the Upper East Side. His face half hidden in a sloppy bandage, Jigs had pulled out his knife while bowing his head at the casket and quietly run the blade along the polished mahogany. Gave it a three-inch cut. Just like his scar. Tit for tat, if you don't take into account what Jigs had already done to the man.

Jigs was wearing a gray Irish sweater under a herringbone jacket. His cheeks were clean-shaven, and a comb seemed to have found a way into his hair. Argyle socks and black shoes that picked up the light. He handed me a slip of paper with an address jotted down on it.

"Our boy's name is John Michael Pratt. He's a painter, though not of the Rembrandt school. Mainly houses and apartments. That is, when he's not enjoying the largesse of the state."

"Largesse of the state. This would mean prison time?"

Jigs smiled across the table at me. "Maybe one day I'll marry you, you're such a smart fellow. Exactly. Our John Michael likes to steal things that don't belong to him. Sometimes people try to stop him and he knocks them down. The last time he did this, he used an iron pipe. Two darling girls have a halfwit daddy as a result of that little maneuver."

The address was on Nineteenth Street, near the FDR Drive. Jigs and I were at a bar on Twenty-first.

"I took a quick look," Jigs said. "Door's got a bit of a rattle. I wouldn't want to be stashing the Hope Diamond or anything in there, if you see what I mean."

I folded the piece of paper and put it in my shirt pocket. "You were fast on this."

"I was. I gave you the full-court press. Belated Christmas gift."

"I thank you."

392 • RICHARD HAWKE

Jigs gave a two-fingered salute. "As the lady said to Bogie, if there's anything else, just whistle."

"I'll do that."

"Be sure you do. You're not up to your hundred percent, that's clear."

"You're looking sporty," I said.

"It's Saturday night, lad. Maybe you can't remember anymore, it's still the night for peacocks."

"So what are your plans for the evening?"

Jigs ran a finger along his chin. "It's the city that never sleeps. I suppose I'll stay up and keep it company. Don't you worry on my account. I can always put together a dance card."

GETTING INTO Pratt's building was a simple matter of leaning against the vestibule door and giving it a sharp shove. A sour smell greeted me in the hallway. A buzzing fluorescent tube sent a harsh white light down from the flaky ceiling. I took the stairs in front of me to the top floor. The sour smell was less pungent here than it was downstairs. The hallway was dimly lit by a half-dozen sad wall sconces that gave off a dull buttery glow.

I pulled my gun.

Pratt's apartment was at the end of the hallway: 5C. A television was on in one of the apartments across the way. Chatter. Laughter. More chatter. More laughter. A nontelevised male voice called out something, and a woman's voice answered, but I couldn't make out what was being said.

I had a plastic bag with me. I set it down and put my ear to Pratt's door. I heard nothing. I kept my ear there a full minute, picking up vibrations from the building, a few hums, a sound like distant ice breaking. Nothing else.

I tried the doorknob. It turned partway, but the door didn't open. After another minute, I knocked on the door and called out, "John!"

No answer. I tried the doorknob again and pumped the door. It rattled. Just like Jigs had said. "John!"

I put away my gun and picked up the bag and took from it a hard rubber mallet Jigs had been kind enough to bring along when we met at the bar. Taking aim at the dead-bolt keyhole, I swung the mallet, using all the single-pointed focus I could muster, which proved sufficient. The doorjamb splintered, and the lock went askew under the mallet. When I turned the doorknob this time, the door swung easily open.

The man's perversity was in his bedroom. Photographs and clippings—hundreds of them, all over the walls. Asian girls and women. Hardly a bare square inch to be found. Many of the pictures had been ripped from skin magazines and featured naked and semi-naked women rising up on their knees, bent over spread-eagle, cavorting on a bed wearing high heels, arching their backs on lounge chairs, peering dead-eyed from a hammock, on and on. Just as many had been pulled from regular magazines. Fashion models. Movie actresses. Asian teens dressed in retro American schoolgirl outfits. The pictures were taped onto all four walls of the small room. Many of them had been outlined in thick red Magic Marker. On some of them, the marker had been held on the picture to bleed splotches on the breasts or the crotches of the women. There were also Magic Marker phalluses drawn all over the place, disembodied torpedoes prodding at the images.

Moving farther into the room, I felt the eyes of the hundreds of girls and women on me, tracking me as I stepped over to the bed. Stacks of ravaged magazines and Asian-language newspapers were piled next to the bed. What interested me was a cluster of pictures taped together on the closet door just to the left of the bed. They were all the same picture. I counted seventeen of them. It was a color photograph that had been cut from the pages of a glossy magazine, maybe **People** or **Us**, from the look of it. One of those types. The photograph featured two women. One of them was wearing a pair of sunglasses and walking down a sidewalk with her head lowered, in evident distress. She was clearly trying to avoid having her picture taken. Next to her was a young Asian woman in calf-high leather boots and a short pink winter coat, her hair pulled back and tied with a bright yellow scarf. I noticed a scarf identical to the one in the picture knotted around Pratt's closet doorknob. The Asian woman's arm was around the other woman, and she was consoling her. In all seventeen of the pictures, the Asian woman had been outlined in thick red Magic Marker. The phalluses appeared on a few of the pictures.

The woman in the sunglasses was Robin Burrell.

The other woman was Michelle Poole.

I went back into the front room and closed the apartment door. I pulled a roll of duct tape from the bag and did what I could to tape the dead bolt on and the splintered door back into place. No one was going to be fooled; I just wanted to get things so that I could engage the lock again, even though a simple push would open the door. A very iffy alarm system.

I flipped over one of the cushions of the ratty couch and sat down to wait for him. Rats always return to their holes. I could practically feel the presence of all those hundreds of girls and women crowded onto the walls. They say everyone should have a hobby, but I was somewhat less than impressed by Pratt's. No wonder Michelle Poole had felt creeped out. People don't necessarily have to **see** someone to know that they're being watched. The hair on the back of the neck. The unexplained fear that wants to become a panic. Lord only knows how many other women besides Michelle had sensed a pair of unwelcome eyes consuming them as they moved about the city. I thought of Pratt's face. Ratface. Scurrying around the city like a one-man infestation, then coming home and going into his tiny room to encourage his infection. My hand tightened around the rubber mallet in my lap. My pistol sat right next to it. The pulsing in my temples wasn't too bad, considering. Didn't really matter, in fact. I welcomed it.

I WAS ASLEEP when he came in.

I had dozed off. It was only my so-called alarm that alerted me. The sound of the door rattling woke me.

"What the—?"

The door swung open as I struggled to get up from the low couch. My gun fell to the floor. Pratt stepped into the room. I stood there with the rubber mallet in my grip. I was the intruder, but I had the mallet. Pratt took a step forward, then I saw his eyes noticing the gun at my feet.

He turned and took off, racing back out of the apartment. I heard his feet pounding down the hallway, then I heard a grunt and the sound of something hitting the floor. This was followed by a low murmuring. Then silence.

I bent down and retrieved my gun. I checked my watch: 2:10 in the morning. I'd slept like a baby. No dreams that I could remember. I checked to see that nothing had fallen out of my pockets and slipped behind the cushions. All clear. I stood a moment, waiting for my heartbeat to come back to normal, then I left the apartment and made my way up to the roof.

He was on the ground. Jigs had him by the shoulders and was dragging him along the gravelly surface as I emerged from the stairwell.

"Nice of you to join us, sweetheart. You want to lend a hand, or are you just here to watch?"

Pratt's hands were tied behind his back. The pervert's face was a mess. Jigs is a kicker. Pratt's nose and mouth were nearly indistinguishable. A single splotch of red and gristle. He was moaning very softly.

"He can breathe, can't he? I don't want him choking on his own teeth."

"Your kindness always touches me, Fritzy," Jigs said. He followed this with a hard kick to Pratt's throat. He leaned down. "Are we breathing, John Michael? Anything we can do to clear your passages?" He grabbed Pratt by the shoulders again. "Help me here."

I stepped over and grabbed the man's rubbery legs, and together Jigs and I carried him to the edge of the roof. Jigs positioned Pratt so that his bloodied head was dangling over the side of the roof, five flights above the sidewalk. He kicked the man's legs apart and settled himself between them, grabbing hold of Pratt's belt.

"Row row row your boat." Jigs inched his way forward on his tail, letting gravity assist as Pratt's torso began making its way over the edge of the roof. Jigs continued wiggling forward until Pratt was halfway over the roof. Jigs had his heels dug in hard, keeping a good grip on the belt, leaning back as far as he could as a counterweight.

"Tickle me, Fritz. Go ahead."

From below the roofline, Pratt let out a holler. He sounded something like a moose in labor. Even in the pale moonlight, I could see Jigs's face gone red with the effort of holding on.

"I'd like to see if he'll bounce, Fritz. Just give me the word."

I stepped to the edge of the roof and looked down. There was no one on the sidewalk below us. No one was watching. The mallet was still in my hand. I closed my eyes and saw seventeen pictures of Robin and Michelle taped on a closet door. Jigs was speaking in his low, seductive voice.

"He stabbed you, isn't that so? This man tried to kill you. He put you in the river. The Good Lord only knows what else he did. I don't think we need a man like this on this good earth, I really don't."

I opened my eyes. Jigs was tilted so far back his head was nearly touching the graveled roof. His eyes were wide and white in the moonlight.

"Well?"

I shook my head. "Reel him in." I dropped the mallet and grabbed hold of Pratt's belt and jerked him back onto the roof. He was blubbering, snot and blood in equal measure. I got hold of the lapels of his coat and jerked him onto his knees. I got right into his face, disgusting as it was.

"What do you want to tell me about Robin Burrell?" I jerked on his lapels. "What do you want to tell me, Pratt? You can either tell me or you can tell my friend here. Are you clear on this? It's your choice."

There was a stench of beer mixed in with the smell of blood. I had to turn my head to get a hit of fresh air. Jigs was on his feet, wiping gravel off the back of his pants. Pratt made a sound.

"What was that? I missed that."

"Never. Touched her."

"Never touched **who**? Never touched Robin? Or are you talking about Michelle now?"

"Nobody. Never touched nobody."

"And I'm supposed to believe you? Is that it? Just take your word for it?" I rattled him again. He moved in my hands as if he were boneless. "You don't have a healthy take on women, John. You're aware of that, aren't you? Did Robin Burrell excite you? Did she piss you off? What was it? Were you jealous because she was friends with Michelle? Did **you** want to be friends with Michelle? Was that it? Was Robin standing in your way?"

His eyes found a semblance of focus on my face, one eye more than the other. "You're out of your mind."

I jerked my hands and brought his head down hard on the roof. It bounced once, then fell back to the gravel. I stood up and went back down to Pratt's apartment and fetched the roll of duct tape I'd used to rig up the dead bolt. I noticed a skylight in the kitchen. I went back into the bedroom and got a half-dozen T-shirts from the dresser. Back on the roof, I knotted the T-shirts together. I located the skylight over Pratt's kitchen and kicked in some of the glass. Along with the duct tape and the knotted T-shirts, Jigs and I secured the man to the metal framing of the skylight. Jigs wanted to snap his knees and tape his legs up in a funny way, but I persuaded him to back off.

Before we left the roof, I taped one of the police sketches to Pratt's back. I scribbled a note on it: SPECIAL DELIVERY. JOSEPH P. GALLO. Jigs and I made our way downstairs and called the police from an all-night diner on Twenty-third Street. We told the woman on the other end of the phone that there was a package for Joe Gallo and where to find it. I was famished and asked Jigs if he wanted something to eat. I planned on something with lots of carbs and lots of protein and lots of fat. Jigs demurred.

"I've got to see a man about a dog," he said, producing a comb and moving it over his wavy black hair.

"What man?"

"Well, it's not really a man," he said. He gave me the smile so many mothers fear. "Not really a dog, either."

～ 36 ～

THE ACTRESS Greer Garson was balanced on
the branch of an apple tree, laughing that little-
bells laugh of hers and jogging the branch in
order to send a cascade of apples falling to the
ground. That's where I was, standing below her.
Scores of war planes darkened the sky overhead,
but the lovely Miss Garson was oblivious. **Look
out belooow,** she sang as the apples plummeted
earthward. I'd just caught one of them and was
about to bite into it when the ringing telephone
fought its way into my consciousness. Greer Garson and her apples dissolved.

I dragged the phone onto the bed, hoping in
my guilty haze that it wasn't Margo. It wasn't. It
was Joe Gallo.

"Did I wake you?"

"You ask that with a smile in your voice."

"I wanted to thank you for the package."

"The . . . ? Right. Anytime."

"I'm not going to ask you how you were able to track down our friend so quickly."

"I have elves."

"I'll bet you do."

I threw the blankets off and brought my feet to the floor. I don't use the word "rarified" too often, but that was how the light in my room felt. I cranked my eyes open. Snow was falling steadily outside the window.

"Your special delivery arrived pretty banged up," Gallo said. "I guess he offered some resistance."

I took the phone to the window. It was a beautiful snowfall. "Joe, it was so long ago."

"So do you want to ask me the sixty-four-dollar question, or should I just tell you?"

I knew the answer already. "Pratt didn't do it."

"Is that a guess, or do you actually know something?"

"It's a guess," I said. "What I do know is that it's probably a good one. This guy had a hard-on for Asian women. Robin Burrell was zilch to him. Not to mention Riddick."

"He's got an alibi for Robin. His parole officer."

I shouldered the phone to crack the window. White sparks of snow leaped in under my fingers, along with a welcome blast of cold air. "That's a good alibi. One of the best."

"We're filing attempted murder charges against Mr. Pratt. I hope that makes you happy."

"My heart frolics on sylvan clouds."

"What does that mean?"

"Nothing, I'm just being not so clever. So tell me, any word on Bruce Spicer? Have you hauled him in?"

"Not yet." Gallo paused. "Not that I'm on silver clouds about that."

"Sylvan."

"Whatever. We'll get him. He's been making calls to the media. He's talked three different times that we know of to Jimmy Puck. If you want to call it 'talk.' More of the raving-lunatic garbage Megan told me about yesterday."

"How's Nancy Spicer doing? What's her condition?"

"It looks like she'll be fine. We're having Saint Vincent's hang on to her until we've tucked her husband away."

"Let's hope that's soon."

"Sooner than soon," Gallo said.

"Right."

I hung up the phone and stood another minute

or so watching the snowfall. It really couldn't have been prettier. A part of me wanted to stand there all day watching it coming down. That's the part that the other part of me always disappoints.

~ 37 ~

ROSEMARY FOX LEFT the man lying in
bed. He didn't stir as she slid out from under
the deadweight of his arm. She crossed to the
closet and put on the green satin robe. As she
knotted the sash, she saw that one of her nails
had broken.

"Shit."

She looked over at the bed. He hadn't moved.
He was lying on his front, diagonally across the
bed. Hog, Rosemary thought. One of his feet jut-
ted out over the edge of the mattress. Size thir-
teen, as he was always so fond of remarking. The
foot had patches of dark hair along the top, as well
as wiry tufts sprouting below the toe knuckles.
I'm fucking an ape, Rosemary said to herself. I
moved from a cowboy to an ape. Where do I go
from here? She laughed inwardly as she thought

about the Turkish race-car driver she'd met recently. *Maybe I can get him to run over my dear little ape.* She thought of the Turk's hands and the strength it must take to keep control of a machine tearing around a track at those insane speeds. She imagined the strong hands gripping her shoulders and how much she'd have to struggle to free herself from them. That had been one of the disappointments with Marshall; he'd been nowhere near as physical as she'd anticipated. She thought they grew 'em tougher out there on the ranch. Marshall had never lacked for invention, she'd grant him that—a hell of a lot more sexual creativity than the sleeping ape—but in the end, ideas are only as good as their execution. At least the ape had delivered. You couldn't take that away from him.

Rosemary moved into the front room, where she saw that it was snowing. She crossed the checked tiles, grabbing up matches and a pack of cigarettes from the glass table as she swept by, and stopped at the sliding glass doors that led out to the patio. *I should be in fucking Vail,* Rosemary thought. She scooted a cigarette from the pack, imagining the mountaintop crawling with people in their garish skiers' garb. The parties. All that laughter. She lit her cigarette and blew the drag out to the side. *This is like being under house arrest,* she thought. *Marshall's in a* jail cell, and I'm in my penthouse prison. Standing by my man. This is how it's done. She knew the tedious script, and she hated it.

She yanked at the handle and stepped out onto the patio. The air felt arctic. The overhang allowed for an area up against the building where no snow could gather. Rosemary felt her legs turn to ice. Her bare feet were either burning hot or biting cold, it was the same thing. She stepped to the edge of the snow line, taking a long drag on her cigarette, letting the smoke spill out of her mouth of its own accord.

Marshall would piss in his pants if he had even a clue what Rosemary had been up to since the very first day of their estrangement. Poor boy. Such an old-fashioned view of the world. Boys will stray but girls will remain faithful. Marshall knew this wasn't technically the case, but it was how he operated. It had infuriated Rosemary, how arrogant Marshall had been about his adventures, as if he really were the great gifted god that the hype machine had conjured up and sold so well to the willing public. Hubris. The brilliant god hadn't even known the damn word when Rosemary had accused him of it. And who **were** some of these women, anyway? That was where Marshall really put it in Rosemary's face. Easy-lay actresses were one thing. But these working girls. Women with their one-room apartments and their garish friends and no sense of how to really fucking **live**. Especially that little one with the fake breasts and the tiny doll body. How low can you go?

Rosemary tossed her cigarette aside and stepped forward onto the dusting of snow on the edge of the patio. It crunched beneath her feet like pulverized glass. No one could see her. The snow was a dense white curtain. Unknotting her sash, she pulled her robe open, holding it out to her sides like a pair of green satin wings. The snow fell on her bare skin, melting on contact. It felt good, like a soft shower of whispers, or thousands of tiny attendants kissing, kissing, kissing . . .

MEGAN LOADED HER CLIP and slapped it into place. She adjusted her goggles and her protective ear covers. She felt as if she were still very much in her morning dream, operating in a haze. The muffled sounds from the half dozen other shooters were oddly pacifying.

It was a private shooting range, located in the basement of a midsize building on West Twentieth Street. A place to blow off steam and lead in equal measure. Megan assumed the shooting stance, clamped her left arm onto her right forearm, and sighted along the barrel. Like a lot of cops, she was fond of the old-fashioned target, the black-and-white drawing of the beefy antago- nist hunched over his snubby. Gus. At least that's the name she'd picked up for the target along the way. Sweat was pouring down Megan's face. Her goggles had fogged somewhat, but she didn't care. She didn't need to see the target clearly. In fact, all the better if Gus remained cloudy. She could apply any face to the target she chose. Even her own.

Megan logged a half hour at the range. She slaughtered Gus over and over and over. He kept coming back for more. Fresh and crouched and ready. Megan's entire body was drenched in sweat by the time she left. She caught the subway back down to the Village and showered and dressed for work. Before she left, she threw a plate at the kitchen wall. By the time she headed uptown, she was sweating all over again.

THE SNOW EDGED around Rosemary's pink toes. Her eyes were still closed. She was making some decisions.

She thought again of Vail. She thought of Santorini. She thought of Tuscany, where the Turk had told her he had a place on a small hill surrounded by olive groves. She imagined a patio,

not frosty like this one, but baked warm by the
Tuscan sun. The sea of soft green rows. The
burnt-sienna horizon.

What the hell was she still doing **here**?

Rosemary reknotted the sash on her robe. She
felt remarkably new. Cleansed. Fresh. Most
amazing, really. Now she just had to get rid of her
ape. Wrap up that business. Pray he wouldn't
make a scene. The story of Rosemary's life, it
seemed. They always made a scene. Big, strap-
ping men, and in the end they acted just like ba-
bies. She wondered if she should even bother
with the Turk. She was just so damn tired of
scenes.

Rosemary went back into the apartment. More
than anything, she wanted to be alone. Right now.
She wanted to plan out her next moves, and she
didn't want a large hairy presence moving about
the apartment as she did so. He'd been getting
more possessive these past few weeks, she'd noticed. Insisting more often on remaining the entire
night. Hanging around as if he owned the joint. As
if he owned **her,** which was a great big ha!

Do it quickly, she told herself as she entered
the bedroom. He doesn't know from nuance anyway, so just spell it out and be done with it. It's
been a good run, it's been a crazy run, it's been a
dangerous run. The smart thing is to end it. Stick

it in the memory books, lover, and be glad we got away with as much as we did.

He was awake, frowning as she approached, almost as if he knew what she was about to do. Good, she thought. That will make it all the easier.

She didn't even sit down on the edge of the bed but remained standing, her arms crossed tightly, signaling him that the goods were off-limits now.

"I want you out of here. This has gone on too long, and we both know it. Let's not make a big deal out of it, okay?"

He argued. Rosemary had figured he would. He didn't have much to argue about, and she tried to tell him so. The next thing she knew, she was on the floor. She'd barely seen him lurch up from the bed. Rosemary slashed at him with her fingernails, but she knew full well the extent of his strength. Ants against elephants. She tried to wriggle backward away from him, but he got her by the hair and jerked her head back with all his strength. She couldn't find the breath to cry out. His fingers tore at her robe, and she realized what he was intent on. She found her breath.

"No!"

Rosemary wasn't accustomed to hearing fear coming from her own mouth. Her cry was followed by a fist to her mouth. She thought her lip had exploded. She felt the blood spilling onto her chin. She attempted to get at his eyes, but he reared back and she thrashed at empty space. Her legs were being shoved apart. **No way!** She knew where she had to hit him, but before she could manage, the ape rattled her head so hard against the floor she thought her skull was going to crack. She felt all her strength waver, and then it was too late. He had the nerve to try to kiss her as he did it, but she was able to twist her head sideways. Small victory.

It ended. He rolled off her, getting up first onto all fours, looking more than ever like the brute creature he was, then rising up slowly to his feet. She remained on the ground. The taste of her own blood was disgusting. Rich and gooey, where just minutes before, light sparkles of snow had melted there so effortlessly. Her body was beginning to shake, which for Rosemary was the largest embarrassment of all. She didn't want him to see her quiver.

He ran an arm across his mouth, as if he required the enormity of the entire limb in order to wipe clear whatever was there. From where Rosemary lay on the floor, he looked a thousand feet tall. He wiped a second time, then looked down at her with sullen eyes. "Has anyone ever told you how ugly you are?"

⌐ 38 ⌐

MEGAN LAMB POKED her head in to Joe
Gallo's office. The homicide lieutenant was seated
at his desk, scissoring the blinds to look out at the
snow.

"Rosemary Fox," Megan said. "She's at the
Cornell Medical Center with a sprained neck, facial abrasions and signs of possible rape."

Gallo released the blinds. "Then what are you
doing here?"

"I'LL GET YOU a platter," the doctor said to
Megan. "You'll want something to put your head
on when she hands it to you."

"You didn't tell her you phoned the police, I
hope."

"The patient did not make the request. So, technically speaking, no. But given the circumstances—"

"Don't worry," Megan said. "How about we say I just happened to be in the neighborhood on other business and spotted Mrs. Fox being taken out of the ambulance?"

"Taxi," the doctor corrected. "Apparently, she got a cab at her building and went right into shock. The cabbie brought her here."

"Was she carried or walking under her own power?"

"The cabbie helped her. So did an orderly."

"Right. I remember now. Cabbie and an orderly. So what's the damage?"

"I've seen worse. Facial lacerations. Severe neck trauma. There's definite vaginal tearing. It looks ugly to me, but she's swearing she had consensual sex. I know this can be a rough town, but I think she's lying."

"Covering up for someone?"

"I'll leave it for you to draw the conclusions." As Megan started for the door, the doctor added, "You might want to consider a chair and a whip."

"Thanks. I'll take my chances."

Rosemary had been outfitted with a neck brace. As Megan entered the room, Rosemary's eyes moved first, then her head. The eyes darkened. Her lower lip was twice its normal considerable size, and it sported a pair of nasty stitches. A large circle on Rosemary's cheek looked as if she had gone seriously overboard with her rouge. A white rectangular bandage was in place just above her left eyebrow.

"What are **you** doing here? I didn't ask for the police."

"I saw you being brought in," Megan said.

"Is that so? Why don't I believe you?"

"What happened, Mrs. Fox?"

Rosemary tried to sneer, but her cuts and stitched lips rendered the attempt pathetic. "Nothing happened. I fell down a flight of stairs."

"The doctor says there are no other injuries indicating a fall. Are we to assume you bounced all the way down on your head?"

"Assume what you wish."

Megan turned a rolling chair backward and dropped into it. "And the sexual assault. That occurred where? Midway down the stairs?"

Rosemary's natural imperiousness was made a parody by her neck brace. Megan noticed that Rosemary had arranged her long thick hair to conceal the restrictive device as best as possible. "Sexual assault, as you put it, is the fantasy of that lecherous doctor."

"You're saying you weren't sexually assaulted?"

"If anyone will listen, yes."

"But you have had sex recently. This morning sometime. The lecherous doctor isn't wrong about that, is he?"

Rosemary felt the shaking coming on again, and by a force of will, she stilled it. She'd be damned if she was going to allow this incident to turn into a horror show. It was already surreal enough, all of it.

"I don't discuss my personal life with strangers."

Megan asked, "Does your husband know that you're seeing someone while he's in prison?"

"Who says I'm 'seeing' anyone?"

"It's just a hunch. You're protecting somebody. I'm guessing it's someone who is more than just a one-night stand."

"Oh, please. Stop it already."

"You've managed the loyal-wife thing wonderfully, Mrs. Fox," Megan said. "You had most of us fooled."

Rosemary remained cool. "Marshall needs my support. You might have noticed that his reputation is a bit tainted. I hardly think I gain anything by running off on him or ganging up on him."

"Let's get back to your assault."

"I told you, that is my business."

"From the look of things, somebody was pretty angry with you."

Rosemary snapped, "Well, I'm pretty fucking angry with him, too."

Good, Megan thought. Bonding. "Just a word of advice, Mrs. Fox. You're going to need a better story than I-fell-down-a-flight-of-steps."

"Who says I'm going to need a story at all?"

"You're a public commodity. People are going to insist on hearing what happened to your beautiful face."

"Since you ask, I've been thinking of taking my beautiful face away somewhere for a while. It's a big world, Detective. I know how to hide in it when I have to."

"I thought you just said you gained nothing in running away from your husband."

"Who says I'm running away? My lawyer tells me that the judge is about to declare a mistrial. Marshall might be released on bail soon. I wouldn't be running away. Perhaps I'd be preparing a place where my husband could get some long-needed privacy."

"I'm afraid that even if your husband is allowed out on bail, he's going to be required to keep very much in plain sight. I can assure you, he is not going to be given a leash so long that he can fly off and join you somewhere halfway around the world. It just doesn't work that way. Perhaps it would be wiser if you were to stay close to home as well."

Rosemary's eyes narrowed. "I can go anywhere I damn well please."

Megan backed off. Her mind was racing. She needed to get it in control. She needed to layer her thoughts calmly, one atop the other. "I suppose your personal life is none of my business, Mrs. Fox," she said, rolling back in her chair away from the woman. "If you want an assault and rape to go unreported, I guess that's your affair. We can't force a wife to testify in court against her husband, and I guess we can't force a woman to prosecute her abusive lover."

"Former lover, Detective, if that makes you feel any better."

"Former? So what am I looking at? Was this your boyfriend's idea of a swan song?"

"It's my fault for letting it drag on so long," Rosemary said. "Lesson learned."

Drag on so long. Megan was dying to know just how long it had dragged on. Months? A year? Just how long after her husband was put behind bars had Rosemary taken her mystery lover? For that matter, had Rosemary perhaps been cheating on Fox even prior to the murders?

"Would you like me to drive you back to your home?" Even before Rosemary could begin to answer, a second thought came to Megan. "Wait. That's not such a good idea, is it? I'm sure there are photographers hanging around your building. One look at you in this condition . . . Is there someone you can call who'd come get you and take you somewhere more private? At least for the day? I'm sure you don't need the aggravation."

Rosemary gave the idea some thought. She liked it. In fact, she knew exactly where she'd like to go. The Hamptons. In the dead of winter it was like a morgue out there. She could give Gloria a call and have a car sent. In a matter of hours, Rosemary could be sitting in front of a fire in that big ugly empty house, glass of wine in hand, looking out the glass doors at the misty ocean. Nobody around to take pieces of her. It sounded nice. She could do her thinking there, start to get her exit strategy sorted out. No way was she going to abide sitting around through a whole new trial. She knew that much. Sorry, Marshall, but the time had come. She could begin to plan the next phase of her life in earnest. Getting banged around might have been the best thing that could have happened to her.

Rosemary looked over at the detective and gave her what, on any other day, would have been her killer smile. "Lady, I like the way you think."

MEGAN MOVED right past her car. She waited until she was a block away from the hospital before she pulled out her phone. It wasn't as if she was afraid that Rosemary Fox could hear through walls; what Megan needed was the trudge up York through the snow to think things through. Before she could punch in the number, her phone went off. It was Joe Gallo.

"Got him!"

"Who? Got who?"

"Who do you think? Spicer. You'll never guess where we grabbed him. Saint Patrick's Cathedral. He managed to spend the night there, then went off into the wrong restroom this morning. A nun came into the women's room, and there he was in one of the stalls, screaming fire and brimstone over his phone to Jimmy Puck. The nun fetched a pair of cops from out in front of the church. We just got him in the box a few minutes ago. He says he doesn't want a lawyer. I'm putting him on a low boil until you can get back here. What's up on your end, anyway? Do we know who beat up Mrs. Fox?"

"She didn't give a name."

"Didn't give a name? What does that mean? She has a name but she wouldn't give it?"

Megan chose her words carefully. "She's in shock, Joe. And she's very bullheaded. When a woman like that wants to clam up, she clams up."

"Okay. You can fill me in later. I need you back up here. Spicer's already blowing off like Vesuvius. If he killed Burrell and Riddick, I don't think we're going to have any trouble coaxing it out of him. This is a man who is proud to be angry."

Megan clicked off the call and pocketed the phone. Bruce Spicer was in police custody. A man with a motive—several of them, in fact, however perverse they seemed. Megan knew she should be hightailing it back to the car and hitting the cherry lights and getting back uptown as quickly as possible. This was the moment of the kill.

Except it wasn't. Megan closed her eyes and tilted her head back to face the falling snow. Her lips parted slightly as she took the flakes with her tongue.

It's not him. It's not Bruce Spicer.

She knew it in her heart. In her gut. Yes, the man had made the threatening phone calls. Unquestionably, the very existence of Robin Burrell and the other women he had phoned—or attempted to phone—had inflamed him to no end. And he had desperately wanted his wife off the jury. The man was eminently capable of causing havoc, no question about it. But it wasn't him. And Megan knew she was right. The person who had gone on a killing rampage was the man Rosemary Fox was protecting. What was worse—much worse, Megan realized—was that a horrible mistake had been made. And she had made it.

Marshall Fox wasn't guilty, either. It was this

man. Rosemary Fox's lover. It was **Rosemary** herself.

"Oh my God."

Megan's hands shook as she pulled out her phone and punched in a number. It answered after two rings.

"Malone."

Megan almost hung up. There was the right way to do this. By the book. Megan knew better. This was hardly the time to go cowboy.

Screw it.

"Fritz, it's Megan Lamb. Listen. I've got a question for you. I don't have much time here."

"Okay. Shoot."

A yellow snowplow was moving north along York, the diagonal snow flashing in the truck's amber beam. The blade rutted roughly along the pavement with an angry animal sound. Seeing the cascade of salt stones coming her way, Megan turned her back to the street and huddled in to the phone.

"Any chance I can convince you to break the law a little?"

39

"THIS IS MRS. FOX," Margo snapped into the phone. "Who is this?"

"This is Luis, Mrs. Fox. Are you okay?"

Margo threw me a wink. "Luis, listen to me. The police are going to be coming by sometime in the next hour. I want you to let them into the apartment, do you understand?"

"Are you all right, Mrs. Fox? Is—"

"Luis. Just do what I ask. Please."

"Well, yes, ma'am. But I—"

"Thank you, Luis." Margo hung up the phone. "So, do I make a grade-A bitch or what?"

I stepped over to the couch, knotting my tie. "Amazing." Margo adjusted it for me. I shrugged into my coat and slid my thumb along the brim of my hat. "Well?"

"Are you honestly going with the fedora, too? This isn't 1930."

"It's snowing. People wear hats in the snow."

"Good thing you're prettier than Humphrey Bogart. That's all I think of when I see a fedora. Sorry, but I think it's overkill."

"Do I look cop enough for you?"

"A uniform would clinch it."

"A uniform would clinch me jail time."

She shrugged. "This'll do fine."

I TOOK A CAB across the park. The cabbie had his opinions about the snow, but I tuned them out, and by the time we were passing the Boathouse, he'd stopped sharing them with me. I had other matters to mull.

Megan Lamb had laid out her case quickly but succinctly. She'd emphasized that it was only a theory, but the pitch of her argument betrayed the conservative note. What if Rosemary Fox already had a lover of her own at the time her estranged husband was shagging everyone who came down the pike? What if the two of them had cooked up a scheme that not only generated some pretty audacious revenge on Rosemary's part—the elimination of two of Fox's lovers—but also succeeded in focusing the police investigation on Fox himself?

426 · RICHARD HAWKE

Megan hadn't had time to embellish her theory or to poke and prod it to see where all the weak spots were. But she'd sounded convinced.

"Robin Burrell. There's lover number three. I don't know where Riddick fits in. Maybe he was becoming suspicious of Rosemary. Or maybe he was coming on to her and she set her goon on him. The point is, I need to find out the identity of Rosemary's lover. This guy did a real number on her this morning, and for whatever reason, she's willing to give him a pass. As my mother used to say, that don't stink good."

The cab came out of the park, and I directed the driver to drop me a block from Rosemary's building. No need to let the doorman see "Captain Nicholas Finn" of the NYPD getting out of a taxicab instead of a department vehicle. Nick Finn had been a friend of mine in the days when I was attending John Jay College with an eye toward following my old man's footsteps into the police force. Nick's death had coincided with my abandoning those plans, and not a few people think it's somewhat perverse that he lives on in a drawer full of falsified documents that I keep in my desk at the office.

The doorman barely glanced at my shiny badge when I presented it to him.

"I wanted to call the police when I see Mrs. Fox like that. But I don't dare. She said she is fine, but she looks like she was hit by a bus. I got her a taxi, like she asks, but she—"

I interrupted him. "Luis, I need you to let me into Mrs. Fox's apartment. If you'd like to call the station and speak with her first—"

The man shook his head rapidly. "No, no. It's okay. I spoke with her already. I'll let you in."

Nicholas Finn slipped his badge into the pocket of his trench coat. Heeding Margo's advice, he'd passed on the fedora.

I SAW THE BLOODSTAINS on the carpet the moment I entered the bedroom. A greenish robe was bunched nearby. I crossed to the robe and knelt down to examine it. In front of me was an accordion wall made completely of mirrors. A clothes closet. Its reflection included me and the door to the bathroom, which was open behind me. As I picked up the robe, there was a shifting of the light, and in the reflection I saw a figure— a man—stepping into the bathroom doorway. The reflection froze and so did I, but only for a split second.

"Who the—?"

He didn't finish his own question but instead took two speedy steps into the room and shoved me with all his strength just as I was twisting around to face him. I tumbled up against the mirrored wall. The man was out the bedroom door by the time I had scrambled to my feet. As I raced into the front room, he was snatching a down jacket off the couch. He turned. He charged me. I'd been reaching for my gun but yanked my hand free to ward off the attack. The guy barreled into me and sent me reeling backward. I slammed into a small table, toppling a brass lamp and an ashtray. The man veered toward the front door. I grabbed the table and whipped it sideways at him. It hit him behind the knees, and he stumbled to the floor.

"Fuck!"

I grabbed hold of the lamp as if it were a baseball bat and gave it a sharp tug. The plug came out of the wall, the wire arcing in the air like an animal's tail. As the man started to his feet, I charged forward and took my swing, aiming for the fences. Unfortunately, he saw the swing coming and lurched to the side so that the lamp took him on the shoulders and not the head. He wheeled around, and his fist caught me just below my ear. There was muscle behind the hit. As he came at me for another blow, I brought the lamp up and smacked it against **his** ear, then released it and got off a double set of hard jabs. I felt his nose collapse under the second one. As he staggered backward, I came after him, landing a pair of punches to his throat. He made a hollow swing that I easily avoided, and before he could get off another, I raised my foot as high as I could and slammed it down on his left knee. He howled. I whipped my gun from my holster, and as the man collapsed to the floor, I staggered backward, safely out of his reach.

"Stay down!"

My arms were aching, and the last thing they wanted to do was be held straight out. But I wanted him to see the gun, and I wanted him to see that it was aimed right at his bloody face. "Stay down," I said again as he made a half-hearted move to get up. He stopped. Blood from his damaged nose fell to the tiled floor.

"I can't . . . breathe," he said in a choked voice, then began coughing.

"You can breathe." I lowered my arms halfway, still keeping my aim. "Lie down on the floor."

He didn't move, so I stepped over and swept my leg under one of his arms, taking out his support. He landed on his chin and then complied, lying out flat on the ground. I moved around behind him and pressed the barrel of the gun against the back of his head. "Give me your hands."

He obeyed, bringing around his large paws to rest at his lower back. Using the cord from the table lamp, I bound his wrists, yanking the knots as tight as I could. I requisitioned a second lamp and used its cord to secure his ankles. It was crude but sufficient. I dragged an upholstered chair over and upended it on top of him, not unlike a turtle shell. Then I went into the kitchen and splashed my face with water, gulping several mouthfuls in the process. I ran a glassful of water and fetched a tea towel from a magnetic hook on the refrigerator door and went back into the front room. The man hadn't budged. I wet a corner of the tea towel and knelt down and dabbed at the blood on the man's nose. He stared at me sullenly, saying nothing. He was wheezing a bit—his mouth was dropped open like a gulping fish—but he was breathing.

I returned to the kitchen, fetched a fresh glass, and filled it, this time for me. I went back out and pulled the chair off him and slipped his wallet out of his pants pocket, then helped him squirm up to a seated position on the floor, leaning against the wall. There was a driver's license in the wallet. It told me that his name was Danny Lyles and that he lived in Long Island City, not far from Charlie Burke's neighborhood. I told him not to get any ideas as I went through his other pockets. I found an electronic pass card and two key rings. In the down coat that Lyles had taken his detour into the front room to grab, I found a vial of pills and a baggie of pot. Thick. No stems, no seeds.

"Are you familiar with the Rockefeller drug laws, Danny? A stash like this can ruin your day."

He wasn't impressed. From the looks of things—especially his nose—his day was already ruined. I kicked an ottoman over to where the man sat wheezing on the floor, and took a seat. I took a long, satisfying sip of the water.

"Okay. I'm ready."

～ 40 ～

DANNY LYLES WAS Marshall Fox's former driver. Also his bodyguard. Not a towering sort but plenty of muscle. A free-weights guy. He'd held the position for a little over a year, a year he described to me as one of the wildest of his life. In addition to being Fox's driver and protector, Lyles had also been his occasional night-crawling buddy. Lyles described himself as "a party hound" but admitted that he held a backseat to Marshall Fox in that department.

"Marshall was dangerous hungry, man. You've got no idea."

Roughly a month before Cynthia Blair's murder, Lyles had taken on additional duties, though in a completely unofficial and secret capacity. He became Rosemary Fox's lover. Lyles told me that he'd had no illusions the evening when Rosemary first came on to him. He knew what she was all about. After a separation of eight months, Fox had recently started making overtures to his wife; he wanted Rosemary to take him back, to give the marriage another go. Rosemary had Marshall on the hook and she knew it. Lyles said that he'd gotten a phone call from Rosemary asking that he come by the apartment. He did, and she sat him down on the living room couch and demanded that Lyles fill her in on all of her husband's escapades over the months of their separation. Lyles balked at first. He played the loyalty card. But Rosemary trumped it easily. She possessed her own set of cards, and she knew exactly how to lay them out to her own best advantage.

"Right behind you, man. Right there on the couch. She's one superior pain in the ass, no question about it. But I'm telling you, you've never met anyone's got the goods like that, I swear."

Lyles admitted to me that he had known all about Fox's affair with Cynthia Blair. He was pretty certain he'd been the only one who did know.

"I drove the guy everywhere. I knew everything he did. I'll tell you, when he found out she was pregnant, he got more drunk off his ass than I'd ever seen. The man was out of his gourd, he was so pissed off. It was all pretty trippy for me. Even though I'm shagging his old lady on the side, we're still partying together. I mean, he was clueless. I was also seeing this other chick at the time. Tracy Jacobs. You've seen her. She's all hot shit now on that show. **Century City**? She plays the clueless wife of that older guy? Perfect casting, man. Girl couldn't act her way out of a paper bag, then she lands a plum role in a show like that. Anyway, one night right after Marshall'd found out about Cynthia and how she was planning to have the kid, he tagged along with me and Tracy. He ended up going way over the top. He was drinking like no tomorrow, popping uppers. The guy was a mess. This is all before Tracy'd gotten her show, by the way. She was nobody at this point to Marshall. Just another bad actress all googoo to be hanging out with Marshall Fox."

As Lyles described it, somewhere along the way, Marshall had started getting nasty with Tracy. At first he argued with everything that came out of her mouth, but soon he was trying to put the moves on her.

"He'd do that sometimes, man. Show his mean side, then start trying to get in their pants. It kind of freaked Tracy out. Marshall got a real bug up his tail about Tracy, and I had to pull him off her before he hurt her. He's got this ugly streak, man. You don't want to see it. It all sort of cooled down, but the evening was pretty much tanked. Then when I was dropping her off at her place, Marshall suddenly got out of the car and went after her again. I'm telling you, though, it was the whole damn Cynthia thing. He just needed someone to take it out on. Anyway, I had to pull him off of her and shove him back in the car and all that crap. Tracy cut things off with me after that. That's how it goes, I guess. Thing is, though, she ended up getting **me** fired. How's that for fucking irony?"

I went back into the kitchen and fetched more water. I tried Megan's number but got no answer. Lyles was tugging against the lamp cord when I came back out.

"How about you loosen this up, man. My circulation's cut off."

"Go on with your story. If I like it, we'll talk then."

He grumbled a bit but went on. Lyles said that several days after Cynthia Blair's body had been discovered at the base of Cleopatra's Needle, he got a call from Tracy Jacobs. She was extremely upset and talking about contacting the police to tell them about Marshall Fox's violence.

"The thing is, like I said, she didn't know a thing about Marshall getting that girl pregnant. All she knew was that he'd scared the hell out of her that night we all went out. I got her to hold off on calling the cops. I lied and told her that Marshall had an alibi for the night Cynthia got killed. Thing was, he didn't. Cynthia had actually been up to his place the night she was killed, but I sure as hell wasn't going to tell that to Tracy. She said it was her duty to contact the police and all that shit, but I got her to agree to hold off for a day. I didn't know what to do. Crazy as he was, Marshall didn't kill that girl."

"How can you be sure?"

"Some things you just know, and I know that. But all the crap he was going through, the last thing he needed was Tracy getting the cops all excited about him. So I called Mr. Ross."

"Alan Ross?"

"Yeah. I guess you can say he's Marshall's boss."

"Why would you call him?"

"Ross is the guy Marshall always goes to when he's in any kind of a fix. He's connected, he's smart. He's one of those take-charge guys. I just thought it made sense."

"And what did Ross say?"

"He said he'd take care of things. Just like I knew he would. Cool as a cucumber, that guy. He got Tracy's phone number from me and told me not to sweat it."

"And that was it?"

"Hell no, that wasn't it. The next thing I know, Marshall's all over my ass. He's ready to kill **me**. He's saying Tracy called up him and his lawyer and threatened to tell the police not just about him and Cynthia but about her being pregnant with his kid. I swear to you, I never breathed a fucking word to anyone about any of that. Especially Tracy. Not even that the two were screwing each other. No way she got it from me. But Marshall was ready to take my head off. He fired me on the spot and said if he ever saw me again, he **would** kill me. Meanwhile, Tracy flies off to Los Angeles, and the next thing you know, she's on **Century** god-damn **City**. It's totally nuts. This whole fucking show business is nuts."

I took a minute with Lyles's story. Then I took another one. There was a piece of his story I didn't like. I could tell he was giving me the truth, but something wasn't fitting. It was the same thing that hadn't fit for Danny Lyles.

I asked, "You're absolutely positive you didn't tell Tracy Jacobs about Fox and Cynthia Blair? Or maybe she overheard you two talking about it."

"No way. Totally positive, man. Marshall was completely nuts on that subject. The whole kids thing freaked him in general. You've never seen a guy who was so paranoid about ever being a father. Plus, he was already working on trying to get Rosemary to take him back. The last thing he needed was for the thing with Cynthia to come out."

I got up and wandered over to the sliding doors leading out to the patio and stood looking at the falling snow. A pack of cigarettes sat on a cast-iron table, half covered in snow. A minute or so later, I returned to Lyles.

"Tracy Jacobs. Where is she now? Is she in Los Angeles?"

Lyles scooted up farther against the wall. "Yeah, that's where she's been. Except I ran into her here about a week ago. She was in town for a visit. The show's not shooting right now. Can't say she really wanted to talk to me."

"She's in the city? Do you have any idea where she was staying? Or how I could get ahold of her? A phone number?"

He grunted. "Hey. It's fuck-you time, man. You want to talk to Tracy? Sure. I can tell you where she was staying. I don't know if she's still there. But you're going to fucking untie me first, man. Time's up. I'm not handing out any more freebies."

I went into the kitchen and fetched a steak knife. May I say that the man looked just a tad uneasy as I approached him?

• • •

A FALSIFIED POLICE CAPTAIN'S BADGE isn't the kind of thing you want to get into the habit of flashing if you can help it. I went with my slightly less impressive PI license, held up to the door that had opened only as far as the chain would allow. "I'm looking for Tracy Jacobs."

The woman who peered at me had green eyes, burgundy hair and a tiny gem planted in the side of her nose. "Tracy's not here."

"But she's still in New York," I said. A statement, not a question.

The green eyes narrowed. They were quite pretty, in an almond-shaped heavy-lidded sort of way. They suggested the sort of person who always looks sleepy. Or slightly stoned. "I didn't say that."

"If she wasn't in New York, you'd have said she's not in town, or not in town anymore. You said she's not here."

The eyes took a moment to study my face. "You think you're pretty clever, don't you?"

"I am pretty clever. But it's just from years of talking to people through cracks like this. Anyone can learn to do it."

That coaxed a smile. "Let me see that license thingy again." I held it up next to my face. "Okay.

It doesn't say you're a serial rapist or anything. Hold on."

The door closed. I heard the chain being removed. The door opened again, this time in the complete welcoming position. A woman in her early thirties stood there. She was wearing a navy blue leotard and a man's white oxford shirt with the top several buttons open, though no man had ever likely done for the shirt what she was doing.

"I'm Jane."

"Fritz Malone."

"I know. I read that on your thingy."

～ 41 ～

JANE SETTLED ONTO the large plush armchair, hiding her feet under her fanny. I took a wooden rocker. The apartment was clean and pleasantly furnished, much like its occupant. I spotted several framed theater production posters on the walls, as well as a large framed photograph of a bewigged Jane landing with overstated exuberance on the overstated lap of what could only be a Falstaff. A familiar stone parapet against a dusk-blue sky was visible in the photo's background.

"Delacorte?" I asked, indicating the photograph.

"Last summer. That's Tim Robbins. He was a fantastic Falstaff. Who'd have thought?"

"Sorry I missed it. So if you're doing Shakespeare in the Park, you're doing okay. You're the envy of a million waiters out there."

"My, my. You've got a whole cute thing happening, don't you? Have you ever acted?"

I thought, **Like an idiot a few times.** "Look, Jane, I really need to speak with Tracy."

She gave an actorly pout. "Shakespeare's not good enough, huh? Everybody wants the television star. So what do you want to see Tracy about? Is she in some kind of trouble?"

"I understand you and Tracy were roommates when she was living in the city."

"That's right, sir. Tracy and I were struggling actresses together."

"Shakespeare in the Park isn't exactly struggling."

"Fine. **She** was struggling. Would you like me to be blunt about it?"

"I think I'd enjoy that."

She had already warmed to the subject. "The only way Tracy saw the inside of a legit theater was with a ticket. I'm not being snippy, I'm just telling you. Tracy and I shared this place for a couple of years. I brought home an OBIE nomination, and she brought home a case of herpes."

"Okay, **that** might qualify as too much information."

"Sorry. I'm just a bitter old washed-up thirty-two-year-old. Any of a dozen regional theater directors would vouch for my talent, but look who ends up the TV star. Tracy's the laughingstock of that stupid TV show she's on, but do you think she even knows it? The whole thing is like a big cosmic joke. Tracy Jacobs, an **Argosy** client? I'm sorry, but that's Alice-through-the-looking-glass time."

"What's Argosy?"

"Only the top boutique agency in the biz. They take only the cream of the cream."

"And what you're saying is that Tracy Jacobs is not cream."

"As an actress? Low-fat skim. Curdled."

"You **are** bitter."

"I'm just a jealous bitch. This town is full of us."

Jane offered me a cup of tea. Lapsang souchong, which is a tea that tastes like smoke. I passed. "I really need to speak with Tracy."

"Tracy has been in Paris. They're still on holiday hiatus with their show. She came here for about a week and then she went over to Paris. She'd never been. Check this out. She actually told me that her character on the show has been to Paris and that she thought it'd be a good idea if she went so she could be more convincing about it." She rolled her eyes. "I've never been a barmaid in Elizabethan England, but you know what?"

I said, "It's called acting."

"Don't get me started."

"When is Tracy due back from Paris?"

Jane consulted her watch. "You've got impressive timing, I'll give you that much. If the snow doesn't slow things down, she's due to land about an hour from now."

I asked, "What do you know about her relationship with Danny Lyles?"

She made a face, and she made it well. "You know him?"

"We met this morning."

"If you'd like to take a shower, I'll understand."

"How long were Tracy and Lyles seeing each other?"

She shrugged. "I don't know. No more than a couple of months is my guess. They met at some club in the meatpacking district. Tracy had a thing for trolling the hot venues. Though if all she's going to come up with is a charmer like Danny Lyles, I say stay home and watch water boil. I'm sure Tracy thought that by hooking up with Danny Lyles, she was getting herself in tight with the Marshall Fox club."

"According to Lyles, Tracy did meet Fox."

"Oh, sure, she met him. Big deal, meeting a celeb. Though it's totally screwy. I mean, Tracy thought that by sleeping with Marshall Fox's driver, she was making a real career move. And it turned out she was right."

"What do you mean?"

"I mean Argosy. The TV show. Miss Hotshot flies to Paris. The whole thing. If not for the fluke of her meeting Alan Ross, none of that ever even becomes a pipe dream. If you—"

"Slow down a minute. Where does Alan Ross fit into this? Lyles told me that he gave Tracy's number to Ross."

"Oh yeah. You said a mouthful. Somebody got somebody's number, all right. Sure. Ross called her up. He had her come into his office to meet with him. And the next thing I know, she's going back the next day for an audition, so she says. By the time I come home, she's sitting on that couch over there with a bottle of champagne and she's landed a plum role on **Century City** and she's moving to Los Angeles immediately. **And** Ross has told her he'll get his wife to sign her up with freaking Argosy. People slit wrists to get a meeting with Gloria Ross." Jane leaned so far forward I thought she was going to fall right out of the chair. "You have to understand something. Our friend Tracy? Didn't. Even. Have. An agent."

She fell back in the chair, disgusted. "I put it right to her. I asked her if she slept with Ross. She thought I was kidding at first, but I was serious. It's the only thing that makes any sense. Tracy swore up and down that it was nothing like that. She said Ross told her he had this role in one of his shows that he thought she might be perfect for. I don't know, maybe the guy's a genius. Essentially, the character's a trophy wife. And not the brightest bulb in the pack, or whatever that stupid phrase is. So maybe you can say typecasting, right? But still, there are plenty of actresses out there who'd have killed for that role. I mean name actresses, not this total unknown."

"What's your take? Do you think she slept with Ross?"

"It's too screwy. A guy like that doesn't need Tracy Jacobs. Or let's put it this way—he doesn't need to promise her the moon if he wants to get her in the sack. Tracy told me that Ross had her back to the network the next day for what sounds to me like the world's lamest audition. It was just him in his office running the camera and audio. She read a monologue. Cheesiest dialogue in the world. She showed it to me. You can't believe they pay people good money to write this dreck. Not that **Century City** is exactly David Mamet, but please. On the basis of **this**, she lands a gig like **that**?" Jane wrapped her arms around her knees and gave herself a good hug. "Oh well. Fuck it. I'll always have Tim Robbins, right?"

Before I left, I asked Jane what airport Tracy was scheduled to fly into. Kennedy. Air France. At the door, Jane told me she would be appearing in a show in February in Chelsea.

"I play a Mormon lesbian who's running an orphanage in Kabul. There's some music in it, too. It could be good or it could stink. If you're interested, I could probably get you some comps."

I told her I'd keep it in mind.

"No, you won't," she said flatly. "You've already written me off as a theater flake. That's okay. It was nice snooping with you."

On the street, I hailed a cab. As we made our way slowly up Sixth Avenue, I dialed Margo's number.

"I'm going to throw a name at you," I said when she answered. "Tell me what comes to mind. Free association."

"Sure," she said. "Fire away."

"Tracy Jacobs."

"Tracy Jacobs. Easy. Actress. TV show. Looks like a hundred other actresses."

"Have I ever seen her show?"

"**Century City**? I think it came on the tube once, and you said something like 'Life's too short.' It's not so bad, as those things go. It can take in a sucker like me. But Tracy Jacobs is definitely the weak link. She's pretty, but no big deal. Why do you ask?"

I gave her a quick rundown of what I'd picked up from Jane and from Danny Lyles concerning the meteoric rise of Tracy Jacobs. Margo listened without interruption. As the cab crossed Twenty-

448 · RICHARD HAWKE

third Street, a florist delivery van in front of us went into a slow-motion skid. My driver whipped the wheel left then right and tapped the brakes, and we slid deftly by the van at a slight angle. The driver muttered a creative curse.

"Somebody's lying," Margo said. "If Tracy Jacobs called the police and told them about Marshall Fox and Cynthia Blair, then clearly she knew. Maybe she overheard Fox saying something to his driver."

"No. Lyles swears that didn't happen. He says she was threatening to call the cops, but only to give them a heads-up about Marshall Fox's penchant for violence. That's when Alan Ross contacted her and ended up offering her the role in his TV show. According to Lyles, Tracy supposedly called both Fox and Zachary Riddick sometime later and said she knew that Cynthia Blair was pregnant with Fox's kid and that if Fox didn't come clean to the police, she'd tell them."

"Was she trying to get money? Was it an extortion thing?"

"Lyles didn't say it was. But maybe. He was out of the loop by then."

"So what do you do next? Take your taxi up to Seventy-first Street and mull it all over with your one and only while the gorgeous snowfall continues?"

"Can I take a rain check?"

She laughed. "In this weather?"

"I'm here to see Alan Ross."

The woman at the security desk picked up her phone and slid a ledger toward me. "Sign here. Your name, please, and— Oh. There he is." She pointed in the direction of the front doors. "See the man standing there?"

Through the revolving doors was a figure in a gray coat, wearing a hat.

"Thanks." As I turned for the doors, a silver car pulled up. The driver got out and Ross climbed in behind the wheel. I was spinning through the doors as he pulled away from the curb. The cab I'd just taken was still idling at the curb. The driver was busy jotting down something in a notebook. I yanked open the rear door and hopped back in.

"See that silver car? I want you to stay with it."

The driver turned around in the seat. "Hey. It's you."

"Silver car."

"You're kidding, right?"

"Go!"

Ross followed Sixty-sixth across the park. At Lexington, he cut over to Fifty-ninth then went east toward the river. At Second Avenue, he took a right. I didn't need to instruct the driver to hang too far back. Who in New York City sees a yellow taxicab in their mirror and thinks they're being tailed? We were as ubiquitous as the snow.

"Looks like he's heading for the tunnel," my driver said. I'd just had the same thought—the Queens Midtown Tunnel. And just like that, I knew where Alan Ross was headed. Before we went into the tunnel, I tried Megan's number. As the signal began to break up, I got her voice mail.

"Rosemary Fox's rough boy is a guy named Danny Lyles. Lyles was Fox's driver. It's a cozy bunch, these people. But forget about Lyles. Alan Ross. You want to start shaking every tree with Alan Ross's name on it and see what starts falling." I added, "And answer your goddamn phone, would you?"

The mouth of the tunnel loomed. I've got a thing about tunnels, particularly the ones that go underwater. Not a good thing. Dark, closed-in places. I took a deep breath as we plunged into the hole.

～ 42 ～

ROSS PULLED INTO short-term parking. I had the cabbie pull over at the parking gate. The lot wasn't terribly full, and I was able to keep an eye on Ross's car. I paid off the cabbie and tracked Ross at a parallel, several hundred feet from him. As soon as he entered the terminal, I raced over to the door he'd used and followed him.

I found him standing at a bank of monitors. I moved off to a nearby electronic check-in kiosk and mimed the securing of a boarding pass. Ross remained staring at the monitors a long while, then broke away and turned in my direction. I leaned in to the kiosk screen. The image of a woman in her crisp flight attendant's uniform came up. **What can I do for you today?** Ross passed me. I took a ten-count then went over to the monitors. Air France Flight 8830 from Paris.

Like most of the others on the screen, the Air France flight was delayed. It wasn't due to land for another forty minutes. Gate C3. Even as I looked at the monitor, several more flights were being shifted to delayed. Low groans sounded from the people around me.

Because Tracy's flight was coming from overseas, all the passengers would be funneled through customs, which I knew was on the level below. Ross apparently knew this, too. I took the escalator down and spotted him taking up position in front of the retractable barriers where all the passengers would be emerging. He had removed his overcoat and folded it over his arm. He stood there a few minutes, consulted his watch, crossed his coat to his other arm, went over to a row of black chairs and took a seat.

I had a decision to make. My impulse was to lay back and wait for the Air France passengers to begin streaming out from customs and baggage claim. I was more than a little curious to witness the reunion of Ross and Tracy Jacobs. A lot can be drawn from whether two people greet each other with a handshake or a pat on the shoulders, or whether they bury their tongues halfway down each other's throats. My curiosity was far from cursory. If the lovely Jane was to be believed—and who would doubt the lovely

Jane?—the crossing of Alan Ross's and Tracy Jacobs's stars suggested something less than a natural and readily explained trajectory. A no-talent nobody lands a continuing role in a popular television series mere days after threatening to blow the whistle on one of the network's top talents. From where I sit, a plum TV role and an invitation to join the roster of a prestigious talent agency sound like pretty enticing hush money. I knew about Ross and his money. Had giving Tracy Jacobs the **Century City** role been Alan Ross's way of taking extreme measures to protect his boy Marshall, or did Ross know more about the murders of Cynthia Blair and Nicole Rossman than he'd been willing to share with the authorities? When I'd met him in his office, Ross claimed he'd wanted me to go out there and dig up information for him. It seemed the network executive had a few interesting items in his pocket already. I considered briefly the old trick of waiting until the passengers were emerging, then having Alan Ross paged to a different part of the terminal so I could be the one to greet Tracy Jacobs and see if I could pull a few answers out of her. But I realized that I didn't even know what she looked like. That's what I get for not watching more television.

My phone went off. It was Megan. I stepped

behind a rack of paperbacks, where I could still keep an eye on Ross.

"I thought maybe you'd decided to take the rest of the day off," I said.

"I got caught up in some stuff. The Spicer investigation was a bust. The top brass has been reading us the riot act. I'm sorry. Where are you now?"

"I'm at Kennedy. Alan Ross is waiting for Tracy Jacobs."

"I got your message. What's the story with Alan Ross?"

"That's what I'm trying to find out. You know who Tracy Jacobs is, don't you?"

"Tracy Jacobs the actress? What does she have to do with anything?"

"She's the person who called Fox and Riddick and put the squeeze on for Fox to fess up to his affair with Cynthia. She was sleeping with Fox's driver. Except the thing is, he swears the information about Cynthia didn't come from him. I believe him."

"Why is Alan Ross meeting Tracy Jacobs at the airport?"

"I don't know. Would you like me to go over and ask him?"

"No. Where's she coming from?"

"Paris. She's been catching up on her culture."

"What do you think's going on?"

"I don't know. Except that Alan Ross called me into his office two days ago and gave me an envelope full of money. He wanted me to look into the Burrell and Riddick murders. In fact, he wanted me to tell him how **you** were faring on them."

"Me?"

"The police. He wanted progress reports."

The line was silent for a few seconds. "Listen. When she shows up, I want you to keep a tail on them. Call me as they're heading back to the city."

"What if they don't go back to the city? There are plenty of no-tell motels between here and there."

"You think they're lovers?"

"It was suggested to me that this might be the case. I don't know what they are. Except that Mr. Ross seems to have set Ms. Jacobs up pretty nicely. He's the one who got her the **Century City** gig. I think we'd like to find out why he did that."

"Shit. Okay. Wherever they go, stay with them. Let me know what's going on."

I broke the connection. Ross was still seated in the plastic chair. I checked my watch. Plenty of time. Going back outside, I waited a few

minutes in the taxi line and caught a cab. When
I told him I only wanted to go over to the car-
rental lot, he tried to dump me. I pulled
enough bills from my wallet to convince him
not to. There was a longer line than I'd anticipated at the rental desk, and by the time I got
my car and was driving into the short-term lot,
Tracy Jacobs's flight was—unless things had
changed—on the ground. I located Alan Ross's
car and pulled into a nearby slot. The wait was
shorter than I'd expected, maybe fifteen minutes. Ross appeared, rolling a small suitcase
behind him. Next to him was a woman who
was not dressed for a snowstorm. She was holding a magazine over her head. They reached
Ross's car, and he opened the passenger door.
The woman got in. Ross moved around to the
trunk and put the suitcase in. Before closing the
trunk, he removed his overcoat. Reaching into
the trunk, he pulled out something that I
couldn't see. It went into the folds of his coat.
Before he yanked open the driver's door, he
paused and looked around. His eyes moved
right past where I was parked. I was too far
away to get a true read of his expression. He got
into the car, started it and backed up. This
brought the car closer to mine. Just as the car
shuddered into forward, the trunk rose slowly

and the brake lights came on. Ross got back out and came around to shut the trunk, this time making certain it was secure. He looked around again. This time I could see the look on his face. Let's just say this: I was glad I would be on the man's tail.

❧ 43 ❧

THE CONDITIONS ON the Long Island Expressway degenerated the farther east Alan Ross traveled. By the time he was approaching Melville, they were near whiteout. Tractor trailers were pulled over and parked along the sides of the highway, as were dozens of passenger cars and SUVs. Every few miles, a vehicle had run off into the median strip and remained there, the taillights blinking an anemic pink. From the swirling white haze in Ross's rearview mirror, the occasional snowplow materialized. Pellets of salt rattled against the side of his car as the plows overtook and passed him.

Ross was perspiring like a man in the desert. His head was aching from the strain of squinting into the white wall in front of him. What he wanted was silence, some time to think. But this wasn't likely, not with the hyperactive actress seated next to him. You'd have thought the woman had invented Paris. She wouldn't shut up about it. Ross couldn't count how many times he had been to Paris. Dozens? By the time this ride was finished, Tracy Jacobs might well have managed to ruin the city for him forever.

Ross was maintaining an achingly slow speed. He was not going to run the risk of either being pulled over by the police or sliding off the road like the half-dozen or so cars he had already passed. If there was one thing to be said for doing all this in a snowstorm, it was that the snow rendered Ross's car virtually invisible. That part's good, he thought. In a way, you really couldn't ask for better. Not only here on the damnable LIE, but later, once they'd arrived at their destination, invisibility would be a wonderful advantage. Ross smiled to himself. It spoke to his sense of perfection. All he wanted at this point, his single goal, was to make all his problems and headaches disappear. Like a polar bear in a snowstorm. It's there and it's not there all at the same time. Now you see it, now you don't.

He glanced over at Tracy Jacobs. She was in the middle of telling him everything he didn't need to hear about the Musée d'Orsay, but noticing him looking at her, she came up for air. Would wonders never cease?

"You look happy all of a sudden. What are you smiling about?"

"I love hearing your stories," Ross said suavely. "It's nice to see a girl who can get all excited like that. It's so nice you're not jaded."

Tracy flashed her huge smile. "Do you know what I thought when I was looking at the **Mona Lisa**? I mean **the Mona Lisa**."

"Tell me."

"I was thinking, and I'm serious about this, I said to myself, 'Alan Ross is the man responsible for this.'"

Ross demurred. "Don't you mean Leonardo da Vinci?"

Tracy laughed. God, that laugh. Try as they might, the vocal coaches for **Century City** hadn't made a whole lot of progress on that horrific laugh.

"Alan, you know what I mean. Not just Paris. The whole thing. Everything. It's true. I owe you my entire life."

Alan Ross turned his attention back to the slick roadway. Yes, you do, dear, he thought. That's exactly right.

~ 44 ~

MEGAN GOT THE CALL from Fritz as she was clearing the snow off her windshield.

"They're heading out onto the Island. I remember Robin telling me that Ross and his wife have a place out in the Hamptons somewhere. That's my guess."

"The **Hamptons**? In this weather?"

Megan looked up and saw Brian McKinney coming out of the precinct house. She turned her back on him. The interrogation of Bruce Spicer had been a fiasco. If Spicer bellowed "Whore!" at Megan once, he'd bellowed it a dozen times. McKinney and a few of the others had found the whole Bruce Spicer show vastly amusing, crowding around the one-way window outside the box to watch Spicer heap his verbal abuses on Megan. The interrogation had gone nowhere, except round and round. Megan knew she might have handled Spicer better, but her mind had been elsewhere.

Malone was asking her a question, but the connection was breaking up.

"Say it again, Fritz. I couldn't hear you."

". . . get the address . . . Hamptons. That way . . . follow him."

"What?"

"Ross's address."

"You want me to get Ross's address? The Hamptons?" Malone's answer was unintelligible. "What do you think he's doing out there?"

The connection crackled again. Megan repeated her question. Malone's voice came on abruptly. Loudly.

". . . **DEFINITELY NO GOOD.**"

Megan jerked open the driver's-side door and tossed the snow scraper onto the seat, then slid in behind the wheel. In the side-view mirror, she saw McKinney getting into his car. "I'm coming out," she barked into the phone. "I'll get back to you with the address. Just stay with him. Corner the bastard. Shove him all the way out to Montauk if you have to. I'm coming out there."

"The roads are a mess. You don't need to—"

She threw the phone onto the seat and fired up the engine. McKinney had pulled up next to her. He signaled for Megan to roll down her window. She hit the gas and jerked the wheel, fish-tailing sluggishly from the curb.

TOO MANY QUESTIONS. Ross was getting sick of stringing stupid lies together. He'd told Tracy when he met her at the airport that he was taking her to a surprise birthday party for Gloria out at the Hamptons place. Anyone else would have asked the obvious question right up front ("In a **blizzard**?"), but in tossing out a bogus list of who was allegedly coming to the nonexistent party, Ross had ignited Tracy's expectations and she'd spent nearly the first forty minutes of the drive gushing over the fanciful gathering. Only as they crawled past the Central Islip exit did Tracy begin asking why the party wasn't being held at Ross's place in Westchester. And wasn't Gloria's birthday in March?

Where was jet lag when you needed it? Ross wished she would just clam up. His temples were pounding, and he fantasized about snatching hold of the gabby woman's neck with his right hand while still piloting carefully with his left, pressing his thumb into her windpipe as hard as he could. His heart quickened with the thought. He just wanted everything **over**. Enough was enough was enough.

He glanced over at Tracy. She was sitting upright in a sexy something she'd told him she got on the Champs-Élysées. Okay, Ross conceded, a little fame and a lot of money hadn't hurt the girl in the least, he'd give her that. Compared to the shrill, awkward young woman who had sat in his office the previous spring, going on and on about how violent and dangerous she thought Marshall Fox was, this Tracy was a vast improvement. The new hairstyle, the fix-up on the nose. Some eyebrow work. It wasn't a face with much of a repertoire of expressions—especially for a so-called actress—but it was sunny and fresh and eager, and sure, he'd have considered getting into this one's pants if he'd had anything remotely close to the urge, which he didn't. How easy. Slide the car over to the side of the road. Work a quick number on her. Remind her who the hell got her where she was today and who had the power to take it all away. Easy. Ross was 90 percent loyal to his wife. Hell, in their industry, that practically made him a prince. And since the whole debacle with Cynthia, Ross hadn't strayed at all. Not once.

But that wasn't the plan. Maybe by the time they got out to the house, he'd consider it. Who knows? Maybe in a perverse way, it would make what he had in mind easier. She's already gotten further in life than she had any right to. I've already given her that, Ross thought. Maybe one final dizzy moment before it all ends.

He'd think about it.

Tracy ran her palms across the flat plane her skirt made of her lap. "Would it be all right if I talk to you about the show?"

"The show?"

"Well, my character, actually."

"You know what, Trace? It's tricky concentrating on the road. If it's all the same to you, can it just wait until we get to the house?"

"Sure. It can wait. It's just about expanding Jennifer a little. I really don't think her potential is being realized."

Ross gave her a paternal smile. "But it can wait."

"Sure. It can wait."

Ross stared into the swirling snow. He thought of Gloria. She was in L.A. Hopefully, she wouldn't try to reach him. Ross's cell phone was turned off. Doubtless it would be collecting messages, lots of them. Ross spent half his day talking on the phone. If things got screwed up somehow, that could be a problem. His dropping out of sight for all that time. If it came to that, he'd have to sort through it. There'd be a way; he'd figure it out. He'd gotten quite good at that sort of thing. Alan Ross was nothing if not methodical. It was how he had made his way. Organization. Knowing exactly how to play people. Moving them around like chess pieces. It was an art. Ross truly felt that. It was something he had shared only with Gloria, the fact that he considered what he did art, that he considered himself something of an artist. Like Picasso. Beethoven. Grinning to himself, he ran his fingers along his row of CDs in the well between the two front seats and picked out Beethoven's Seventh and slid it into the CD player. The music swarmed richly from the speakers like intoxicating smoke.

"That's nice," Tracy said. "What is it?"

"It's Richard Strauss." **Ree-shard Strauz.**

"Yeah. It's nice."

Ross stole a glance at Tracy Jacobs's legs. If he wanted, when they got where they were going, he could tie them up like a pretzel. Who would stop him? Her?

"Oh God, Alan. I am **so** glad you picked me up at the airport. I can't wait till we get there. This is too much fun. Really. I love you. I really mean it."

Ross leaned over and patted her on the leg. "I love you, too, honey. You're something special."

He let his hand linger on her leg a few seconds. The thought of Cynthia's firm legs came to him, the brief moment he had taken to stroke them as he'd choked back his tears. It was **her** fault. This whole stupid endless maze of hell was that infuriating, sweet dead woman's fault.

Tracy smiled over at him, and he gave her leg a squeeze. Good Christ, it felt nice. The kid was a real specimen. No taking that away from her. He'd have to consider exactly how he wanted this whole thing to play out.

～ 45 ～

A HUNDRED THOUSAND DOLLARS had gone into the master bathroom alone. The fixtures were all Bagni. Eight thousand alone just for the showerhead. Nine-inch diameter. Solid chrome. Gloria had pointed out to Rosemary the different rings, each one responsible for a unique spray. But it was the chrome pipes on opposite walls of the shower, she'd said, that made the real difference. Prickling jets of water from the shoulders to the knees. Or, if one preferred, a strong hissing mist. Just adjust the control. The marble was Italian, cream with pinkish veins. Overhead, a chimney-like flue ran up about twenty feet to a skylight, operable by remote control right from the shower.

The ride out to the Island had been a blur. Three cheers for the Demerol that she'd been given at the hospital. Rosemary had made the driver stop at Paragon, instructing him to go inside and buy several pairs of sweatpants, both lightweight and heavy, a few sweatshirts, some T-shirts and several pairs of warm wool socks. Gloria had plenty of other clothes in the closets and dressers if necessary. Rosemary had found a flannel robe that she liked; she'd be fine.

Rosemary adjusted the temperature and stepped into the shower. Her body ached from Lyles's brutish attack. What was his problem, anyway? Rosemary wondered. Was he **offended** that I told him to pack it up and get out? What is it with men? Maybe that lesbian detective knows what she's doing after all. Maybe there's something to be said for sticking with the more intelligent sex. Rosemary increased the pressure of the water. God . . . it felt so good. She hadn't yet activated the two chrome pipes.

Okay. Men are useful, let's not get silly about it. They're fun. Get the right one and they're more than just fun. Lord, Rosemary thought, tilting her head cautiously to look past the eight-thousand-dollar streams of water at the few flakes of snow drifting through the distant skylight, I am **so** ready to burst out of the stable. Where in the world has my life been, anyway? The entire past year was feeling as hazy as the past three hours. Even though she was in a fog, she felt as if she were finally making her way out of one.

Rosemary had to be careful with her wrenched neck. No sudden movements. And it would be several days at least before the bruising on her face went away. Not that she planned on seeing anyone. This was major downtime. Rosemary. A big empty house. An ocean. It was fine with her if it snowed ten feet. Twenty feet. Bring on the next Ice Age, she didn't care.

Looking down, she noticed a bruise on her right thigh. Bastard, she thought dreamily. She took the oval bar of translucent soap and began rubbing it along the bruise, as if somehow she'd be able to lather it away. She rubbed counterclockwise, then clockwise, then again, both directions. At last she released the soap, letting it drop next to her feet. It looked like a very fat toe. I need to get to sleep, she thought. Or maybe she'd spoken aloud. She wasn't sure. The jets of water were beginning to sting. It felt like her skin was burning where the water hit.

Okay . . . let's try the big blast, and then it's mattress time.

Rosemary reached for the nozzle that activated the chrome pipes and gave it a turn. The water blasted from the pipes with unexpected force. Too hard. And **way** too hot. Scalding. Rosemary spun. Her neck torqued. The pain shot through her entire body, and a shriek erupted from her lungs. It echoed through the upstairs rooms of the empty house and down the empty staircase. It also traveled out the skylight far above her head, traveled outside into the soft white silent world, where its sound barely registered.

A faint noise.

Brief. Unintelligible.

Then nothing.

～ 46 ～

AFTER SHE CAME OUT of the Midtown Tunnel, Megan phoned Ryan Pope. She explained what it was she needed from him, and when he questioned why she needed it, she requested that he simply do her the damn favor and not ask questions.

"This has to do with Fox, doesn't it?"

Megan sighed. "Ryan, everything I do these days has to do with Fox. My pancakes in the morning have to do with Fox. Please just get that address and call me back."

Megan hung up and pulled around a slow-moving Mini Cooper and settled in for a stressful drive. Pope phoned her back fifteen minutes later.

"It's in East Hampton." He gave her the address. He started to ask another question, but Megan cut the connection and phoned Malone.

"Got it. East Hampton. Seventeen Skyler Drive."

Malone thanked her. "Now I can finally pass this guy. Ross is driving worse than an old lady."

"What are you going to do?"

"I'm going to drive up ahead. I'd like to be in place when Ross and his gal get there. I'll ditch the car a couple blocks away from the house."

"Try not to do anything until I get there."

"I'm not planning to do anything. We don't even know what the score is here. I just want to keep an eye on things."

They hung up. Megan brought her flashing light up onto the dashboard. She didn't want to attract the attention of any police out on the highway. But a few flashes every now and then would be good to get slower traffic out of her way.

This was it. She felt certain that this was it. She flexed her fingers, stretching them wide, and dropped her hand on the seat. An old habit. A signal to Helen.

"Hand, please," she muttered. She took a beat, then wrapped her fingers closed and squeezed as tightly as she could.

This was it.

~ 47 ~

THE BLACK SUBURBAN WAS going too fast. I swore under my breath as it passed. Just because they're sitting high and mighty, people think they're in some sort of damn protection bubble. The Suburban cut abruptly back into my lane, forcing me to hit my brakes. The rental started into a slide, but I righted it.

"Jerk."

There was a tractor trailer in front of the Suburban, maintaining a safe speed. The Suburban pulled out to pass the truck, but it remained too close. As it began to overtake the truck, it skidded to the right, bouncing off the rear wheels of the trailer.

"Shit!"

I pumped my brakes to avoid the skid. The two vehicles moved away from me, and as I watched, the cab of the truck angled to the left, directly into the path of the Suburban. The trailer, which continued moving straight, began to shudder. It rocked sideways several times then seemed to lie down almost gently on its side. The instant it hit the highway, it sent up a cloud of snow and bounced in the air. As it did, the Suburban went into a skid, spinning nearly 180 degrees. When the trailer bounced back down on the road, it landed squarely on top of the Suburban.

The jackknifing continued as the Suburban rolled out from under the trailer, which then seemed to fold itself into an embrace around the vehicle. Sparks leaped from both the vehicles as their metal gouged into the pavement. It was almost beautiful, except that it was horrible.

I managed to come to a stop some fifty feet from the two vehicles. Immediately, I looked in my rearview mirror, where I saw the VW behind me swerving to avoid rear-ending my car. I saw a flash of headlights as someone **did** rear-end the VW. Horns were going off. More headlights. A car slid sideways off the highway. A **crunch**. A **bang**. A **thud**. I remained with my grip tight on the steering wheel, holding my breath. No one hit me. I twisted around in the seat for a look.

Cars at all angles. It looked like a parking lot of drunken sailors.

～ 48 ～

ROSS SAW THE LIGHTS up ahead, the glow of pulsing red and yellow lights filling the air. He gently pumped the brakes.

"What is it?" Tracy craned forward as if the few extra inches would bring any additional vision.

"Accident." Ross shifted to the right lane and continued to slow down. Up ahead were at least a dozen vehicles, maybe more. All stopped. A tractor trailer had jackknifed and was on its side. It looked in the whirling snow like a large beached whale. A partially crushed vehicle was tucked up against the truck. Baby whale. Ross checked his rearview mirror. Traffic was coming in slowly behind him. In another minute, he'd be trapped.

"Hold on." Ross put the car in reverse and flung his arm over the back of the seat to look behind him.

Tracy was alarmed. "What are you doing? Are you backing up?"

No, I'm doing the fucking Charleston.

That's it, Ross thought as he maneuvered partway onto the shoulder in order to squeeze past a pickup truck, I'm having nothing more to do with this simpleton. She's been nothing but trouble ever since I first heard her goddamn name. His eyes went to the backseat, where he'd laid his overcoat. The edge of the crowbar that he'd fetched from the trunk when they were in the airport parking lot was showing. Ross stretched back farther and flipped an arm of the overcoat over the metal bar. The car swerved dangerously close to the far shoulder of the road, but he pulled the wheel in time to avoid the ditch.

Tracy asked, "Are you going to try another road?"

Ross kept his voice level. "That's right. The exit's about half a mile back. It's bound to be slower. But if we sit here, we're dead in the water."

He stole a glance at the woman. She was sitting straight up, eyes wide, jerking her head to look in all directions at once. Poor, stupid, silly thing. She didn't know it yet, but she was already dead in the water.

COLD DAY IN HELL

49

THE SKY WAS dark gray and growing murkier by the minute when Ross finally pulled into the driveway. He had a moment of panic, fearing that the car might not make it through the unplowed snow. The last thing he needed was for his car to be hanging out for anyone passing by to notice. There'd been another accident, this one on Route 27A. Nowhere near as large as the tangle on the LIE. This one had involved only three cars, but it had still brought traffic to a standstill for nearly forty minutes. Ross had not enjoyed a single one of them.

The automatic door rumbled as it opened, and Ross pulled the car in to the garage, next to his prized cream '68 Caddy. Ross turned off the car and lowered his hands to his thighs.

Stillness.

Tracy let her head fall back onto the headrest. "Gosh, it seems like we've been driving for days. You did great."

Ross remained silent. He sat stone-still, gazing through the darkened windshield at the images flashing in his brain:

Cynthia Blair bumping into him as she emerged from Marshall's building.

The Rossman girl, so fatally gullible, getting into his car.

That unfortunate young woman's huge Christmas tree.

"Alan?" Tracy twisted to look out the back window at the darkening day. "Um, where is everyone? When's the party supposed to start?"

Now.

Ross leaned his shoulder into the driver's-side door. "They'll be here. We've got to set things up. The caterer should be here any minute. Come on. There's something I want to show you. It's going to be the big surprise."

He got out of the car and pulled open the back door, fetching his coat as well as the crowbar hidden in its folds. As Tracy got out, Ross put on the coat and dug his left hand into the pocket, slipping the crowbar under the coat so that he could hold it in place under his arm.

Tracy met him at the back of the car. She was shrugging into her stylish blazer. "What's the surprise?"

"It's out in the boathouse."

Tracy hugged herself and performed a parody of shivering. "Maybe we should go inside first and get me a sweater or something."

Ross brought his right arm around her shoulder and hugged her to him. She responded with a small giggle. "Ah, you're a tough kid," Ross said. "I'll keep you warm. Come on. It won't take long."

The two left the garage, Ross activating the automatic door to close it behind them. They started around the side of the huge house. What with the snow and the fast fading of the day's remaining light, the water was only vaguely visible. The boathouse, newly painted the summer before, was the sole piece of color visible as the two made their way across the large backyard.

"Alan, my shoes are already completely soaked. They're going to get ruined. Let's just go inside. I'm sure Gloria's got some boots or something I can use."

It wasn't an unreasonable request. Quick detour into the house and then head straight back out. But Ross was tired. Now that he was no longer behind the wheel, the full weight of his fatigue was coming down on him. He wanted to sleep. He wanted a peaceful sleep. It didn't matter if it was only a five-minute detour, enough was enough already. He scoffed at the notion that he'd even considered enjoying himself with this girl before wrapping things up.

"Alan?" Tracy lowered her shoulder and attempted to squirm out from under his arm, but Ross was quicker, and he held on to her. "Alan. Let go! Stop it."

She tried again, this time shoving her hand against his chest. She managed to roll away from his arm, but Ross reached out and caught her arm before she could get away.

"What are you doing? Let go, Alan! It isn't funny."

From a distance it might have looked like a dance. Astaire and Rogers. The man in the long coat leaning back slightly to hold the weight of the woman at the end of his arm, the two of them arching backward like a pair of wings opening up. But there was nothing graceful in the sudden appearance of the black iron rod. Or in the way that it came down on the woman's head over and over and over.

Nothing graceful at all.

~ 50 ~

MEGAN WAS UNABLE to get a signal. The last she'd spoken with Malone, he was still stuck in the snarl of vehicles around the accident. Megan had taken Route 27A to avoid the mess. Even there, she had passed several tow trucks on either side of the road, securing a pair of cars on their beds.

She pulled to a stop in front of Alan Ross's driveway. She could make out tire tracks in the snow leading up to the garage. The garage door was closed. Megan decided to keep her car where it was and approach the house by foot. The wind was gusting hard, and when Megan opened the car door, a blast of whipping snow stung her in the face.

There were no lights on in the house that Megan could see. She knelt down to inspect the tire tracks. They seemed fairly fresh, the tread marks still quite distinct, not covered with any appreciable snowfall. The car that had made them could not have been here for long.

Approaching the garage, Megan made out two sets of footprints leading around the side of the house. She followed them through a wooden gate, where they led into the spacious backyard. As Megan moved forward, crouching somewhat so she could follow alongside the two pairs of footprints, she was unable to clear from her mind the evening—just over a year before—when she had located the Swede on his houseboat at the marina in Sheepshead Bay. Walking stealthily down the pier in the dark, placing her feet with the silence of a cat, her heart thumping hard in her chest, just like it was doing now. She tried to will the memory to recede, but it refused to budge.

Through the blowing snow, Megan could make out a small dark structure. The footsteps appeared to head in that direction. A boathouse. As she moved forward, a light appeared briefly in one of the windows. A brief, buttery flash and then it was gone. Then it happened again. A flashlight. Someone was waving a flashlight around.

Some hundred feet from the boathouse, Megan froze. The footprints in the snow stopped being parallel pairs and the snow became a scramble, like a cluster of failed snow angels. Several feet beyond, there was something dark on the snow. Megan knelt down and scooped up a handful of the dark snow. She touched the fingers of her other hand to the snow, and they came away darkened.

Megan wiped the bloody snow off against her coat and blew into her cupped hands, then reached to her hip holster and unfastened the safety strap. Her pistol felt heavy. She felt like she was palming a lead brick. Megan's heart was no longer simply slamming in her chest; it seemed to have expanded to fill her entire torso. No need to step softly, as the snow would muffle her footsteps. She plunged forward. The darkness on the snow ran in smears, alongside a wide track, the imprint of a body being dragged. Megan ran her arm across her eyes to clear the blowing snow. She heard a voice letting out a fearful whisper. It could only be her own.

Helen.

ROSS WAS GOING to take the Boston Whaler. He'd have preferred the Chaparral, especially in this sort of weather, but the sleek runabout wasn't wise for his purposes. Though not without effort, he'd be able to paddle the Whaler out into the ocean some distance before turning over the engine. That was one consideration. The other, frankly, was cleanup. What he had to do was going to be messy. The Chaparral had white leather seats, cream-colored cushioning, the padded dashboard. Much easier to mop down the Whaler.

Ross couldn't wait until this whole stupid episode was over. All he wanted was to get the mess over with and go inside and crawl into his bed. Grabbing the prone body of Tracy Jacobs by the arm and dragging her along the dock beside the Whaler, Ross glanced up through one of the boathouse's windows, where he could see the rear of his house, see his bedroom window. He was shocked to see that a light was on. For an instant, panic flooded his system. Slow, he told himself. It's probably just a timer. Focus. One thing at a time, you know how this has to be done.

He thought of Cynthia. That one hadn't been planned. There'd been no time for the sort of organization that he prided himself on. After it was concluded, yes, sure. A quick minute to think things through. The bit with the hand over the heart. A smart move. The others had been more to his liking. Problem. Plan. Execution. In Ross's view, a smart person could accomplish anything he set out to accomplish. Anything. You just had to be the one in control of the situation. Plan. Execute. And make sure your ass was covered. Life was so simple, really, it was laughable.

Ross didn't know whether the young woman was alive or dead. It didn't matter. She was out cold, that was the important thing. It was her own fault, those several extra hits with the crowbar. She'd just been so fucking **irritating**. And not just now but in general. All he'd done for her. He'd given her a **life**, for Christ's sake. If only she'd remained on her side of the country.

Ross paused and looked at the battered head at his feet. He thought he might throw up. He hadn't needed to hit her **that** hard. It was Fox, dammit. He was the person to blame for all this. Marshall and his insatiable ego. And Cynthia, of course. The both of them. What Ross still marveled at was how in the world those two had managed to pull off their affair without Ross knowing. The secrecy, and especially the betrayal, that's what was so infuriating. How many times had Ross made a complete ass of himself in front of Cynthia Blair, begging her, **begging** her to take his feelings for her seriously? She had no idea how urgently she had mesmerized him. No idea at all. She never listened properly. She never **heard**. Cynthia had said she was "flattered." Who the hell cared about flattery? Alan Ross flattered people every day of the week; he could flatter a cement wall if he had to. Cynthia didn't understand. He **had** to have her. This wasn't a negotiation, it was a requirement. It was a **need.** Ross had groomed Cynthia at the network. He'd watched her grow and develop. He'd helped train her, helped her to sharpen her skills, to put the bite into her work. And hadn't it paid off when he brought Marshall onto the scene? His two creations? **His** creations. Cynthia owed him. Big-time. Ross treasured the dynamic he and Gloria had established in the industry. They'd become a true power team. But that was Act One. Ross wanted the intoxication again, this time with Cynthia. He needed it. He needed to do it all over again, with fresh supple blood. If Cynthia played her cards right, she was definitely going places. Ross planned on going there with her, as simple as that. And if patience was what it required, he was prepared to remain patient. Power comes from action; it can also come from patience.

What Ross hadn't been prepared for was running into Cynthia leaving Marshall's building in tears one night the previous April. He had not been prepared for their walk through Central Park and her confession of her affair with Marshall. She'd allowed Ross to hold her, to keep his arm around her as she told him the squalid details. The words had moved about in

Ross's head at precarious angles, crashing into one another. **Marshall. Lovers. Affair.** Cynthia had allowed Ross a closeness like never before. She had told him she trusted him more than anybody else in her life, that his coming along at that precise moment was a miracle. The two had traveled arm in arm along the southern portion of the park, past the boat pond, pausing at the Alice in Wonderland statue, so creepy in the moonlight. Especially the Mad Hatter, with his large bony nose and his bad teeth. They'd moved on, traveling north, pausing at the base of Cleopatra's Needle, where Cynthia had said she had something else she needed to tell Alan. Something more important to her than anything else in the world and that he had to promise not to breathe a word to anyone. This was something she would be handling in her own way. She had already made her decision, she said, and she was ready to live with the consequences. In fact, she was overjoyed with her decision. Taking hold of Ross's hands, Cynthia had placed them on her stomach and held them there. Her touch sent an electrical current jolting through Ross's system. He dared to massage her belly, ever so lightly. His fingertips kneading her pliant flesh. Then she smiled at him. Ross had never seen Cynthia smile like this before. Angelic.

COLD DAY IN HELL • 489

"It's so perfect, Alan. I mean, that you're the first to know. It couldn't be better. Because really, if you think about it, without you, none of this could have happened. Seriously. This is all because of you."

She squeezed one of his hands, helping it to massage her belly a little harder as she told him her wonderful news.

TRACY JACOBS LET OUT a groan. Small and gurgling. Ross nudged her with the toe of his shoe. Oops, he thought. DNA all over my Lazzeris. So she was alive. Barely, he was sure. It didn't matter. Maybe some duct tape on her ankles and wrists, to be safe. Certainly on her mouth. Ross aimed his flashlight beam at the wall, where several tools were hanging. There was the duct tape, just where he knew it would be. He wrapped the woman's ankles together, then her wrists. He scraped the bloody hair back from her mouth and allowed her to complete her next groan before securing a large piece of tape on her mouth. He decided that the kind thing was to stick some duct tape over her eyes as well. She really didn't need to see what was coming next.

Ross straightened. God, his knees ached. Isn't aging a bitch. He shone his flashlight down at the black water lapping against the sides of the

Whaler—paper-thin sheets of ice had formed—then trained the light back on the wall, stepped over to it and lifted the hacksaw from its nail. He returned to Tracy and eyeballed the distance between the edge of the dock and the gunwale of the boat. If he attempted to roll her into the boat, he could well miss and she would go toppling instead into the water. Not good. Not here. And not all in one piece.

He'd have to lift her at least partway. This would be the awkward part. He set the flashlight down on the wood so that its beam was trained on Tracy. He set the hacksaw down next to it. Taking a deep breath, he knelt and wrapped his arms around the woman's shoulders and hugged her torso to him, then rose to a squat. For a cute young thing, she was surprisingly heavy. Ross adjusted his grip and pulled her closer. Her head flopped onto his shoulder.

It was then that he heard a noise and looked up to see the boathouse door opening.

⤙ 51 ⤚

THE CONE OF LIGHT from a flashlight was illuminating a body lying prone on the wooden dock. A long slender boat bobbed between Megan and the body. It took Megan several seconds to realize that the body—it was a woman—was bound at the ankles and wrists and that something was terribly wrong with her face. Then she saw, directly behind the woman, a pair of legs, a shadowy figure. It was holding something metallic, something that caught a portion of the flashlight ray.

"Drop it!"

Megan fell to one knee, her Glock aimed at the area just above the illuminated legs. A silent shriek was whistling in her ears. **If he has a gun, I'm dead.** She shouted again. "Drop it! Police! Show me your hands!"

It was duct tape on the woman's eyes and

mouth. Her forehead was smeared with blood. The figure standing over her was not moving. Megan registered that what the figure was holding was a handsaw. Panic raced through her system. The Swede! Her gun wavered.

"Drop it! **Now!**"

Her words echoed in the hollow structure, almost as if a second Megan were straddling the narrow roof beams up above, calling out from up there. The figure standing over the bound woman knelt down slowly and set the saw on her hips. A man. He was wearing a fedora-style hat that partially covered his face. As he set down the saw, Megan heard a small scraping sound. Of course it wasn't Albert Stenborg. The Swede was very dead. Even so, Megan strained to make out Albert Stenborg's nearly invisible blond mustache. He'd stood straddling Helen just like this, his clumsy six-five frame rocking gently with the movement of his fetid-smelling houseboat, obsessively stroking his imperceptible mustache.

"Get down!" Megan ordered. "Lie down right next to her! On your front. **Do it!**"

"I'd just as soon not, thank you." His voice was every bit as calm as Megan's was aflame.

Megan could make out his outline better now. Her eyes were adjusting. Directly in front of her, the narrow boat wobbled in the water. The faint lapping of water sounded like tiny slaps.

Megan's finger tightened cautiously on the trigger. He killed them. He killed them all. This is him. This is the one. She could taste salt on her lips. Her face was blazing hot.

"Lie down on your front. Let's just do this calmly. Hands out in front."

"You're trespassing," the man said. "You shouldn't be here. This has nothing to do with you."

Megan rose slowly from her crouch, tracking her aim as she did, keeping it trained on the area of the man's chest. "Do what I say."

Ross scoffed, "And if I don't? What then? What exactly are you going to do, Detective? Are you going to **shoot** me? Is that it? In cold blood?"

Megan took a sharp breath, held it and squeezed the trigger. The Glock bucked in her hand and the barrel flashed. In the confined space, the noise was a thunderous roar. The shot sailed well to Ross's right. As intended. He ducked seconds late.

"Are you fucking crazy?"

She'd gotten his attention.

"I'm fine," Megan replied. "Now let's just end this thing quietly. And for your sake, I hope that woman is still alive."

Megan's vision was sufficiently adjusted that she could now make out the contours of the boathouse. There were two boat slips, the one between her and Ross with the Boston Whaler in it, and a second one behind Ross, where a larger boat rocked gently in the black water. Ross was essentially trapped. The only escapes were the door behind Megan or the water at the end of the dock. Assuming Ross wasn't foolish enough to take the icy leap, he'd have to go through her first if he wanted to get out.

"There's no point in this," Megan said, beginning to edge to her right. "You're a smart man, Ross. I don't know why you did all this, but it's finished. Okay? Just do what I'm saying and let's get on with it. If that woman's still alive, we've got to get her to a hospital."

Megan edged farther, keeping the pistol trained on the man. She didn't want to glance down at the bloodied body at Ross's feet, but she couldn't help herself. It had to be Tracy Jacobs, though there was no way she could identify the pulpy face of the woman lying on the dock. It dawned on Megan that there was no way Ross could have delivered such damage with his bare hands. Not the handsaw. It wasn't nearly heavy enough.

The bastard has a weapon.

"I want your hands, Ross! Right now!"

"I don't think—"

She jerked the gun and fired again, this time toward the larger boat. Its triangular windshield

COLD DAY IN HELL · 495

exploded. The gun muzzle swung immediately back to Ross. "**Now!**"

Ross brought both of his hands up slowly in front of him. Something long and skinny and black was in his right hand. A crowbar. Megan took another step. *I can shoot him. The bastard has a weapon. He came at me with it. I had no choice. Rule number one: defend yourself at all costs. I can blow this bastard into the water.*

But Megan didn't want to fire from here. She wanted her pistol barrel jammed up right against the bastard's tonsils.

"Drop the crowbar, Mr. Ross."

He did. With a flick of his wrist, the crowbar dropped into the water, next to the boat. In the same movement, Ross snatched up the flashlight and flicked the beam directly into Megan's eyes. She could see nothing but white spears.

Shoot! Now! He's going to come at you. Shoot!

Ross flicked the light away from Megan's face and trained it on Tracy Jacobs. Megan was still somewhat blinded. The prone body shimmered blue and out of focus. Ross lifted a foot and placed it on the woman's back. He nudged slightly, rocking the prone body. She let out a soft groan.

"You hear that? She's still alive."

"Step away!"

Ross trained the light on Megan for a few seconds, then again on the body lying at his feet. "She's alive, Detective. I'm sure she'd be very grateful to you if you'd help her out."

He reset his foot on the woman's back and grunted as he shoved. The body rotated easily. Three quarters of a turn and she dropped cleanly off the dock, landing with minimal splash in the black water. Ross trained the flashlight on her. The bound legs swung down and out of sight. Her hair fanned out on the surface. In the flashlight glare, the top of her head resembled a softball. It followed swiftly after the legs.

Ross flicked off the flashlight. "Your call, lady."

52

MEGAN'S CLOTHES TOOK her down. Even without her coat and her shoes, which she had frantically pulled off, her saturated clothes took her down like an anchor. She hadn't expected it. She groped for the sinking body but found nothing. She didn't even know if her eyes were open. There was nothing to see. Total blackness. Megan thrashed at the water.

She was flying.

She was floating.

She was swimming.

She was sinking.

Dark as the grave, Megan thought, sweeping her arms in front of her. Dark as the womb. She was already lost. Up. Down. Her lungs were holding, but the shock of the water's temperature—

delayed at first—arrived. It attacked her like cold knives slashing at her skin.

Her limbs were already losing feeling. Was she flexing her fingers? She thought maybe. All the switches were being flipped off. Megan could not have imagined anything this cold.

She kicked her feet. She groped. She gathered the blackness into her chest. Her lungs were beginning to ache. And she knew what was happening.

Josh.

Her brother's face appeared to Megan as if it were right there in front of her, as if it were inside an illuminated bubble. For weeks and weeks he had pulled her out of herself, dragged her back into the light and sat there with her, coaxing her back. Patient. Loving. Loyal. Oh, Lord. Josh. Please don't look at me now. All your efforts. Your sweet efforts.

She felt ashamed.

Failure is cold and black.

Megan's arms crossed back and forth over each other. There was no seeing them at all. There would be no more seeing. She was kicking her freezing feet. Going where? Out to sea? And for what? She imagined herself grabbing an armful of slick weeds at the bottom and holding tight, curling up to them.

Her lungs were hurting badly now, as if a

corkscrew were working its way into her chest. This was a fool's end. She scissored her legs one last time, kicking with all her remaining strength. Arms outstretched, fingers splayed, Megan kicked and opened her mouth as wide as it would go.

～ 53 ～

ALAN ROSS DASHED across the snow. The poor woman. She had looked pathetic, struggling to strip off her overcoat, as if the sleeves were suddenly three times too long. She was so small, he doubted she'd have the strength to pull Tracy out of the water even if she got the chance.

Ross went around to the front of the house and let himself in the front door. His fingers went automatically to the house alarm, but halfway through the code, he realized that the alarm was not activated. He frowned. He couldn't remember if it was he or Gloria who had been the last one out the door on their most recent trip. It wasn't like either of them to forget the alarm.

Ross was dying of thirst. He started for the kitchen then veered into the dining room, where he fetched a bottle of Dewar's from the liquor cabinet. He took the bottle into the kitchen and dropped a few ice cubes into a tumbler and poured the glass three quarters full. Swiftly he took it down to a quarter in one gulp.

There were a million questions but no time to find answers. If the police detective didn't freeze to death or drown, she'd be back on the scene any second. With or without Tracy. Frankly, he hoped it was with. He couldn't afford to have Tracy Jacobs's body washing ashore somewhere. He had to return to the original plan. If need be, he would deal with the detective in the same manner. It was getting so **complicated**. Ross stared hard into his glass. The one piece of information he'd like to know was whether the detective was the only person who had pieced the murders together, or if there were others. The good news was that she had apparently come out here alone. This suggested she was on a cowboy mission, rushing out by herself, like a fool. Ross prayed he could be so lucky. If Lamb was the only one wise to him, it was still possible he could manage events to keep himself safe. If not . . . He wasn't ready to think about it. He'd have to disappear. How the hell he was going to do that, he didn't know. If it came to it, he'd figure it out. Problem. Plan. Execute. It's what he was all about.

Ross finished off his drink and slammed the glass down hard on the counter. Fuck you, Marshall! He downed another half glass then went into his study and, using a key from the top drawer of his desk, unlocked the narrow closet on the east wall where he kept what Gloria snidely referred to as his "coon gun." An old Winchester pump-action .22, less for raccoons than for squirrels and groundhogs, which seemed more plentiful in these parts. Ross wasn't anything near a full-fledged hunter. Sometimes he liked sitting out on the patio with the rifle propped up on the banister. Point and shoot. Squeeze and kill. It was so easy. Anyway, there were more squirrels and groundhogs on the planet than necessary. Ross enjoyed the pump action. What normal, healthy guy doesn't like the pump action?

Ross glanced out the window at the boathouse. No movement that he could see. He had to get back out there. If the detective did make it out of the water, he needed to be there waiting for her. Squeeze and kill. Ross went out into the front hall. What he saw there made him stop cold.

Rosemary Fox was descending the staircase. She was in a neck brace and was wearing one of Ross's own bathrobes, the belt tied loosely. Her semi-wet hair fell down over her half-exposed breasts. Her face was horribly bruised. The expression on it was dreamy, serene. The corners of her mouth turned up in a smile. The eyes didn't join in.

"Alan?"

Abruptly, the front door opened. A man was standing there holding a pistol in his hand. Ross swung about, his rifle hip-high, and fired.

~ 54 ~

THE BRASS MALLARD NEXT to my face tore off the door. The wood splintered, and I took a few shards on the face. I leaped to my left into the house, performing a complete—if clumsy—roll, then a second one. Anything so long as I was a moving target. I came to a stop on my elbows.

Alan Ross was standing at the foot of the stairs, pumping his rifle. Behind him on the stairs stood Rosemary Fox. She wore a green bathrobe, and the fingertips of her right hand rested lightly on the banister. A huge bruise dominated her face.

I brought my gun up. Ross fired before I could, but his shot sailed over my head. I sighted on him. Rosemary Fox screamed. **"Alan!"**

I held my shot. Ross darted to his left, disappearing into the next room. As I scrambled to my feet, Rosemary Fox took a poor step. Her feet came out from under her and she landed sideways on the stairs, bumping down to the bottom step. I dashed past her.

Ross was slamming through a swinging door at the far end of the room. The kitchen. I crossed quickly and caught the door as it was swinging closed. Ross knew the house. I didn't. He wouldn't knowingly trap himself. The kitchen led elsewhere. My guess? Outside.

Or the garage.

I retraced my steps at a dead run. Rosemary Fox was still on her fanny at the bottom of the staircase. Her robe had fallen open. She looked like a serious lush.

I ran out the front door and around to the driveway. As I did, I heard the sound of a car engine revving inside the garage. I knelt down on the snow at the edge of the driveway and readied myself. The garage door slid open, and for a moment, nothing. Then a cream Cadillac leaped forward. Holding my breath, I tracked and got off the shot, hitting the front right tire. The Caddy swerved toward me and straightened as it passed. I pivoted, locking my arms in place, and fired twice, the second shot hitting the right rear tire.

The car skidded on the snow, sliding sideways into a standing lawn lamp.

I was up and running. Ross was gunning the engine, but the rear of the car slid slushily back and forth in the snowy driveway. I grabbed hold of the driver's door handle and tugged, but the door was locked. I could see Ross through the smoked glass. It took two hits with the butt of my pistol to shatter the glass. Ross was reaching for his rifle, which was on the seat next to him. My pistol barrel went snugly against his left temple, as if the two pieces were made to fit.

"Let it go."

He hesitated.

I didn't.

I reared back and landed the gun butt sharply just above his left eye. His head lolled forward. I groped for the door lock on the driver's armrest and pushed it, then I pulled back out of the window, yanked open the door and dragged Ross by the collar out onto the snow.

"Where's Lamb?" When he didn't answer, I gave him another taste of my gun butt. "Where is she?"

Blood was running into his eyes. He blinked it away and looked at me as if I were some sort of curious artifact. I dropped the gun and took a double grip on his coat.

"**Where the hell is she?**" My throat would hurt later from the strain.

He ran a tongue across his lips. "Dead in the water. How should I know?"

FOR A BRIEF INSTANT, I wasn't sure what I was seeing. Two dark slick bodies, one of them stretched out flat on its back, the second one hunched over the other, looking for all the world like it was feeding on it. It was dark, but then I pieced it together. I was in the boathouse. In front of me were Megan and Tracy Jacobs. Megan was frantically performing mouth-to-mouth on the actress. Blowing into her mouth, pumping her hands on the woman's chest. Blowing, pumping . . . She looked up at me. Her face was a shock mask. Her teeth were chattering so loudly I could hear them.

"Help." Her voice was a plaintive croak. I pulled off my coat and wrapped it around her. She shook her head violently. "Her."

Megan turned her head and vomited water onto the dock. I knelt down next to Tracy Jacobs. Even in the dark boathouse, the paleness of her face showed like a dull moon. I took over the mouth-to-mouth, spitting brackish salt water from my mouth every other breath. I pressed my hands to her sternum and pushed.

508 · RICHARD HAWKE

"She's alive," Megan said weakly behind me. "There's a heartbeat."

I kept at it, and after what was probably only a very long minute, the body under me spasmed. Her back arched involuntarily, and a rush of black water gushed out of her mouth. Her coughs were otherworldly. They were followed by a groan that built slowly but steadily, tightening until it reached a piercing siren shriek.

MEGAN COULD WALK. She followed me as I carried Tracy Jacobs across the large yard into the house. Tracy's face and head were horribly beaten. I didn't see the extent of it until I set her down on Ross's living room couch. Rosemary Fox was seated in an armchair, looking dreamily amused.

Megan instructed her to go into the kitchen and boil some water. When the woman hesitated, Megan barked, "Now!"

Rosemary Fox rose from the chair and floated out of the room.

I asked, "Boil water?"

Megan was lightly touching one of Tracy Jacobs's head wounds. She shrugged. "I just wanted her out of the fucking room."

I had called 911 from my cell phone at the boathouse. Megan's lips were blue, and her breathing was beginning to speed up. I took her cheeks between my hands and rubbed vigorously. Then I took her hands—they were ice—and rubbed them as well.

"Hold on," I said. I ran up the stairs and found the master bedroom. There was a down quilt on the bed. In a second bedroom, I snared a blanket, then returned to the living room and wrapped the quilt around Megan. I placed the blanket over Tracy Jacobs. The actress's eyes opened briefly. She blinked and looked right through me; then her eyes closed again.

Rosemary Fox came in from the kitchen. "The water's boiling."

"Make some coffee, Mrs. Fox," I said.

She asked, "Who are you?"

"I'm the person asking you politely to please make some coffee. Very strong."

"I would like to know what is going on here. Where's Alan? Who are you? Who's that girl?"

I stepped over to her. As I approached, she took a step backward. She also managed a haughty look, even with that nasty bruise. She crossed her arms defensively on her chest.

"My name is Malone," I said. "That young woman on the couch is Tracy Jacobs. Your friend Alan tried to kill her. What I want from you is some help, in the form of a pot of hot coffee. Can you handle that, Mrs. Fox?"

"You're a bit of a shit, aren't you."

"On a good day, sure. By the way, I met your friend Danny. Bit of a shit himself, isn't he?"

Her eyes narrowed. "Do you want milk?"

Back in the living room, Megan was shivering within her quilt. She had pulled a chair up to the couch and was sitting in it, stroking Tracy Jacobs's cheek. She looked up as I entered the room.

"Where is Ross, by the way?"

"I've got him locked away."

"Locked away? Where?"

"He's in the trunk of his car."

"Outside?"

"Yes, ma'am."

"Kind of cold out there, isn't it?"

I nodded. "Yes, ma'am."

Megan laughed. Too hard, it turned out. Her shoulders began to shake, and her breath got away from her. The transition to tears was seamless. Her smile curdled, and she pulled the quilt tight around her neck. Her eyes grew large and frightened as the tears flooded down her cheeks. I took a step toward her, but she shook her head. "No."

She doubled over in the chair and began sobbing. I came forward anyway and touched her lightly on the top of her head. You'd have thought I pushed a button. She came forward out of the chair, out of the quilt, and wrapped her thin arms around me, pressing her face into my chest, crying unashamedly. Hanging on for dear life.

~ 55 ~

AFTER STRANGLING Cynthia Blair and leaving her body at the base of Cleopatra's Needle, and at the last minute hitting upon the inspiration of driving a pen into her chest so as to secure her hand over her heart, Alan Ross had assumed that the authorities would immediately turn their attentions to Marshall Fox. Naturally, Fox had been questioned, but the police had been interested primarily in obtaining background information concerning Cynthia. Not once had their questions suggested any suspicion of Fox.

Although Marshall Fox had trusted Ross possibly more than anyone else he knew, his affair with Cynthia was one aspect of his personal life that he had chosen not to share with his trusted friend. Ross was privy to most of Fox's numerous dalliances, more so than he cared to be. Marshall liked to brag. Ross had known about Nicole Rossman, although not by name. Fox had been unable to keep from boasting about some of the outrageous things he had been doing with the malleable doll-woman he had met online. In the days following Cynthia's murder, as it became clear to Ross that the police were not including Fox on their list of top suspects, the television executive had formulated a plan. Under the guise of concern for Marshall Fox's mental state, Ross arranged with Fox's driver to be kept informed on the entertainer's doings and his whereabouts. And so it was that when Nicole Rossman emerged from Fox's building at three in the morning ten days after Cynthia Blair's murder, she was met by none other than Alan Ross of KBS Television.

Gloria was off in Los Angeles, so Ross had no tracks to cover on that front. Getting Nikki Rossman into his car proved even easier than he'd guessed. He'd merely had to give her his credentials and tell her that he needed desperately to talk with her about Marshall. The attack took place just north of Central Park. Ross pulled to a stop near the Duke Ellington statue on 110th Street and produced a hammer. Three swift blows and Nikki Rossman was crumpled against the passenger door. Ross drove into the park, pulling off the road into a cove of trees just north of Cleopatra's Needle. The forty seconds required to transfer Nikki's body from the car to the base of the monument was the riskiest part of the endeavor, but Ross took the gamble and won. Using a hunting knife he would later discard, he opened up the young woman's throat. Then he nailed her hand to her chest. Four-inch nail. Driven all the way to its head.

When Fox wasn't arrested the very next day, Ross went ballistic.

TRACY JACOBS UNDERWENT emergency surgery at Eastern Long Island Hospital and was then transferred to Manhattan's Hospital for Special Surgery. My small concussion was nothing compared with the damage Alan Ross had inflicted on the actress. It was deemed highly unlikely that the doctors' facial reconstruction efforts would eliminate all evidence of the severe beating. Word emerged almost immediately from the entertainment industry that a replacement actress for Tracy Jacobs's role in **Century City** was being actively pursued.

Investigators going over Ross's cavernous office at the network turned up what Joe Gallo referred to jokingly as "a little Nixony thing." Ross's office was wired to record all conversations that took place there. There were wireless microphones located at key spots throughout the office. A sound technician at the network confirmed that Ross had been a fanatic about recording every single encounter that took place in his office. This included his phone calls. All the recordings were downloaded onto Ross's computer. Rodrigo and his IT team went to work. My chat with Ross surfaced, but Gallo wasn't overly interested in that. He was interested in retrieving Alan Ross's interview with Tracy Jacobs when she allegedly threatened to go to the police with her allegations of Marshall Fox's abusive and violent tendencies. He was even more curious to hear the recordings of Tracy's audition for **Century City** and Ross subsequently offering the role to her. It was no real surprise that neither of these recordings appeared to exist.

Gallo called Gloria Ross in several times and roughed her up in his gentlemanly way. She was generally cooperative. She admitted to having heeded her husband's "urgent request" that she sign Tracy Jacobs to an Argosy contract, only half believing his story that the actress was a recent lover of Fox's who was threatening to raise a very public stink in the media about the entertainer. To the extent that she bought her husband's willingness to cave in to such a craven extortion scheme, Gloria had chalked it up to the pressures that Ross was under concerning Fox's growing difficulties. During an extended period of questioning, Gallo managed to extract from Mrs. Ross her suspicions that her husband had harbored "excessively proprietary feelings" toward Marshall Fox's producer, Cynthia Blair. When Gallo pressed her concerning any thoughts she might have had on her husband's possible role in Cynthia's murder, Gloria had demurred, if only slightly: "I didn't go there. That's all I'm going to say."

A WEEK AFTER the final surgery, Tracy Jacobs was moved to a rehabilitation center located in Briarcliff, under five miles from Alan and Gloria Ross's Westchester home. Gallo took the short trip north out of the city to speak to the woman. Despite the doctors' warnings that Tracy's memory could be compromised, the actress's recollection of the events "that changed my life" proved intact. She told Gallo that she had indeed met with Alan Ross in his office and voiced her concerns about Marshall Fox. She told Gallo that

Ross had treated her with exceptional respect and, after hearing her concerns, had pleaded gently but firmly with her not to go to the police. "As a personal favor to me" was the phrase he had used, she said, over and over again. Eventually, he had steered the conversation away from the topic and over to her career—such as it was—and had floated the offer of the audition as well as the possibility of having Tracy talk with his wife about representation. Tracy told Gallo that she'd found it peculiar that her audition the following day took place in Ross's office and with no one else present except Ross himself. He'd set up a video camera on a tripod and given her a short script to read. He made her read the script nearly two dozen times, each time asking that she read every word with a different emphasis than she had used in the previous run-through. At one point, she said, Ross seemed to become frustrated and demanded that she read the script one word at a time. No sentences, simply word after word, as a means, he said, of getting her to loosen up.

She thought she'd blown the audition. The following evening she was on her way to Los Angeles.

Tracy had kept her copy of the audition script, and she was able to tell Gallo where it could be found in her apartment in West Hollywood. Gallo immediately contacted the LAPD, and within hours, the single page was faxed to New York. Joe showed it to me in his office.

I want you to listen to me and I don't want any interruptions. Kevin Daly can't be trusted. He was having an affair with Missy Welch and I know that he is the one who got her pregnant. If he knows what's good for himself, he'll go to the police and tell them about Missy. If he doesn't, I'll do it. And I mean it. Don't think I won't.

"Scintillating," I said.

Gallo asked, "Do you see what I see?"

I nodded. "Ross already had the tape of Tracy's visit from the day before. She'd have been throwing Fox's name around, accusing him of being the violent punk he really is. Ross sends her off with the promise of a so-called audition, then he cooks up this piece of crap and has her come back in and read it a dozen different ways. All sorts of inflections."

"Exactly. Do a nifty splice job with bits from the day before, and he's got her on tape saying whatever he wants."

I looked down at the fax again. " 'Marshall Fox

was having an affair with Cynthia Blair. He's the one who got her pregnant. If he doesn't tell the police, I'll tell them myself, blah, blah, blah.' "

Joe nodded. "When Megan and I went up to Fox's apartment, he and Ross and Riddick all said they wanted to get Fox's affair with Cynthia on record themselves rather than have us hear it from this other source. This source that Fox thought was credible."

"Except Tracy never knew."

"That's right."

I held up the fax. "So which is it? Is our man Ross brilliant or pathetic?"

"We got Fox's and Riddick's phone records and checked all the calls that came in the week Tracy's threat showed up. We found a pair of calls made to both of them within several minutes of each other, from the same public telephone five blocks from Alan Ross's office. Tracy Jacobs wasn't in New York at the time of the calls, so we checked all calls that came in to Fox and Riddick from the Los Angeles area as well. They've all been signed off as legit calls from known associates. Nothing from Tracy."

"Thorough bastard, aren't you? I'd sure hate to work for you."

"I'll remember that if you ever come crawling."

"If I'm crawling, Joe, you won't want me."

· · ·

NOT FORTY MINUTES BEFORE talking his way into Robin Burrell's apartment and killing her, Alan Ross had been making nice with me in Samuel Deveraux's courtroom. It took some work for the thought not to depress me. Cool, calm bastard. DNA evidence placed Alan Ross inside Robin's apartment. Besides the hair samples from Ross located in Robin's apartment, skin tissue samples removed from beneath her fingernails provided a match with Ross, as did a spot of blood lifted from the large mirror shard that Robin's killer had thrust into her neck. The small sample of blood was located on the portion of the shard that the killer would have gripped while working the glass into place. Since there were no unaccounted-for fingerprints taken from Robin's apartment, the assumption was that Ross had worn gloves but that either a finger or a thumb had gotten torn on the glass and the thumb or finger beneath had been nicked. A claw hammer retrieved from Ross's garage also yielded blood samples that were traced not only to Robin Burrell but to Nicole Rossman as well.

The case against Alan Ross strapped on rockets.

• • •

MEGAN AND I TOOK the Metro North train up to see Tracy Jacobs. A golf-ball-sized lump remained under her left eye, which itself sagged somewhat and wasn't opening completely. Her jaw was wired in place, and a temporary latex piece had been affixed to her lower gums in lieu of the teeth that were no longer there. She was having problems with the right side of her body; the leg in particular wanted to behave more like a noodle than a leg.

Megan did most of the talking. For the most part, she steered the conversation in neutral directions. Tracy's family. Her recent trip to Paris. What it felt like to kiss Matt Damon during his recent guest appearance on **Century City**. I silently awarded Megan a daytime Emmy for her performance during that line of questioning. She actually behaved as if she really gave a damn.

We spoke with Tracy in the facility's solarium, overlooking a sloping ten-acre lawn at the edge of which sat a half-frozen pond populated by black ducks. Tracy cried a few times during the visit. Thankfully, she had no memory of the beating she had taken at the hands of Alan Ross. Her final memory of the afternoon was of Ross's car pulling into his garage. For her own peace of mind, she had not been informed of Ross dumping her bound body into the water. She had no clue of Megan's role in her rescue. In the hour and a half we spent with her, Tracy thanked me half a dozen times for saving her life. A strong look from Megan the first time Tracy gushed this way had warned me off from setting the record straight. I didn't like it, but it wasn't my call.

Before we left, we picked up a key piece of information. Three days before leaving New York for Paris, Tracy had bumped into Zachary Riddick at a DreamWorks party in midtown. She told us she had been unprepared for the re-action she'd received. Riddick lit in to her for the calls he said she'd placed both to him and to Marshall Fox, allegedly threatening to go to the police with her story about Fox's relationship with Cynthia Blair. Of course, Tracy had never made those calls, and she went to great pains to convince Riddick that she had no idea what he was talking about. She swore that Danny Lyles had never breathed a word to her about Fox and Cynthia Blair. Tracy told us that Riddick had seemed baffled, then troubled, by her insistence that she in no way had placed the calls. She did tell him that she had raised her concerns about Fox with Lyles and that the driver had contacted Alan Ross. She related her meetings with Alan Ross, going on at some length about what a wonderful man Ross had been to take her under his wing the way he had.

"I thought Alan was a god," Tracy said to us, gazing off toward the pond. "He was a god, and I was one of his very favorite angels." She turned her broken face to us. The tears in her left eye seemed unable to fall. "How could he despise me so? What did I do?"

As we were leaving, Tracy's mother and brother appeared, and I had to go through the whole hero thing again. Megan drifted off and looked out the window as I collected the praise.

"You know your humble act gets old fast," I said to her on the ride back to the train station.

She fixed me with a look I hadn't been ready for. "I've had the spotlight. I detest it."

On the train back to the city, Megan and I put the scenario together. Riddick must have smelled a rat. In buying Tracy Jacobs's story that she had not placed threatening phone calls to him and to Fox, the lawyer must have begun to suspect who was actually pulling the strings. He must have contacted Ross and aired his suspicions. Or if not, he must at least have put some hard questions to Ross.

"Ross couldn't afford to have Riddick poking into this," Megan said as the train raced past Valhalla. "Riddick was Fox's lawyer. His job was to get his client cleared of these charges."

I agreed. Zachary Riddick spelled trouble for Ross. "But why Robin?" I asked. The words were no sooner out of my mouth than I knew the answer. Megan did, too.

"Misdirection."

"Precisely."

"Ross targets yet another of Fox's former lovers and arranges her killing to look just like Cynthia's and Nikki's. And who should know better than Ross how to do that? The result? Uproar and confusion. Big headlines. Is Fox innocent after all, or is there a copycatter coming out of the woodwork?"

"And the next day Riddick gets it. Ross must have arranged to meet him at the Boathouse Café and then somehow lured him into the Ramble."

"But no nail in the heart," Megan said.

"No time. That one was a risky kill. But it was still in Central Park, and it included the throat slashing. And Riddick was closely associated with Fox, so Ross could bet that the killing would be lumped in with Robin's murder. Any questions of a relatively sane motive—like covering his own ass—weren't likely to be raised. Which they weren't."

"Why did Ross try to hire you?" Megan asked. "Do you really think it was his way of keeping tabs on how **we** were doing?"

"He's an admitted control freak. And manipulator. This is a guy who likes to have all the angles covered."

Megan turned to watch the cemetery at Hawthorne racing by. A small crowd was gathered near the top of the hill. Two seconds, then gone.

She turned from the window. Her skin was ghastly pale. "So Robin Burrell's murder was a control freak's ploy to camouflage his motive for killing Riddick."

"Essentially, yes."

She leaned her head against the glass and muttered something under her breath. I missed it.

"What?"

"I said I should have killed him." She continued staring out the window. "I mean that, Fritz. With all my heart. I should have blown him into the water."

WHEN WE REACHED Grand Central, Megan and I went for a drink at the Oyster Bar. She fiddled with a white wine. I took two fingers of Maker's and then two more. I might have been happy with a whole fistful. The Oyster Bar is a good place for this kind of drinking. You feel like you're at the bottom of a deep cavern, sealed off from the outside world. For all you know, the outside world might be gone. Up in smoke. Vaporized in a single white flash. The only woes and problems left in the entire world might be the silly ones you're nursing in the underground bar along with your silly drink. If you think about it, there ought to be a sense of hope embedded in a notion like that. I suppose on some days there is.

Megan switched to water after her glass of wine. We didn't talk much. We watched a couple at the bar having an argument. Corporate types, boxed neatly into their suits. He seemed to be taunting her, and she seemed to be taking the bait. I was tempted to go over and tell them both to quit it, which was when I realized it was time to let the rest of the ice in my drink melt away.

"You should go see your girl," Megan finally said. "If I had a girl, that's what I'd do." She looked up toward the ceiling. "I don't know about you, but my head's swimming with questions I know full well I'm not going to find any good answers to."

"What kind of questions?"

"Big ones. Stupid ones. The mankind kind."

I skidded my glass on the table. "I'm afraid I can't help you."

"I'm not asking you to. Come on. Let's get out of here."

I tossed some bills on the table. The corporate couple had stopped arguing and were playing kissy-face as we passed them on our way out. There's mankind for you.

Out on the street, the light was fading fast, nearly gone. Forty-second Street was slipping into its black-and-white mode. Collections of silhouettes swam both ways across the street. Taxis, taxis, taxis . . . nothing but taxis. God knows which twenty of them were honking.

I said goodbye to Megan at Fifth Avenue. Actually, I didn't say goodbye. She squeezed my hand, and in half a minute, she was passing the library lions. I considered angling across Bryant Park to my office but then congratulated myself for not being a complete fool. Megan was right. I should go see my girl. I needed to do some work on that front.

I peered down Fifth for a last glimpse of the small detective, but the dusk had swallowed her up. I hoped she wasn't still carrying around her big stupid questions. A woman like that worries me.

THIS JUST IN
James Puck

He's back! Loose lips are telling this reporter that Marshall Fox and KBS Television have mended fences and are ready to put pen to paper for a three-year renewal of Fox's popular late-night show, **Mid-**

night with Marshall Fox. With Fox's ex-boss, former KBS director of programming Alan Ross, behind bars and awaiting the first of what promises to be a string of trials running longer than some of the shows Ross himself heralded at KBS, the popular entertainer released a statement declaring his "satisfaction that the disinfectant they're using over there at KBS seems to be working." Since the dropping of all criminal charges against him five months ago, Fox has been splitting his time between his ranch outside of Jackson Hole and his beachfront estate in Maui, working on a book about his recent roller-coaster ride through the public zeitgeist. Responding to a call from this reporter concerning the increasingly erratic behavior of Fox's estranged wife, Rosemary Boggs Fox (and who hasn't seen the photographs at this point?), Fox replied, and I quote: "What can I say, Jimmy? Fruitcake. It's not just for Christmas anymore." Unquote. My, my. Don't the beautiful people say the most beautiful things?

Meanwhile, in related dirt . . .

About the Author

Richard Hawke lives in New York City. He is the author of **Speak of the Devil,** and under the name Tim Cockey is the author of the award-winning "hearse" novels. Visit his website, www.RHawke.com.

LIKE WHAT YOU'VE SEEN?

If you enjoyed this large print edition of
Cold Day in Hell, look for Richard Hawke's
Speak of the Devil, also available from
Random House Large Print.

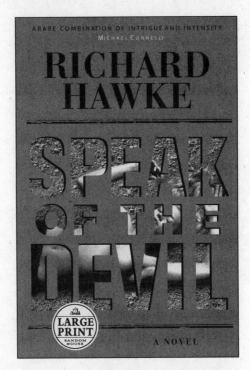

SPEAK OF THE DEVIL
(hardcover)
978-0-7393-2582-7 • $23.95/$33.95C

Large print books are available wherever books
are sold and at many local libraries.

All prices are subject to change. Check with your
local retailer for current pricing and availability.
For more information on this and other large print titles,
visit www.randomhouse.com/largeprint.